"There is poetry and hardship to spare in Mills's 1
on the human capacity for repair, for regeneration.

> —Junot Díaz, author of *The Brief Wondrous Life of Oscar Wao*, which won the 2008
> Pulitzer Prize and the National Book Critics Circle Award

"Susan Mills' *On the Wings of a Hummingbird* is an eminently readable novel about Guatemala and the resilience of its people. It illustrates how the power of love and community can triumph over the most dire economic and social conditions. I am certain that *On the Wings of a Hummingbird* will find a wide and devoted readership."

> — Pablo Medina, author of *The Cuban Comedy*

"On The Wings of a Hummingbird is an essential read for anyone who wants to understand more deeply the reasons people leave their ancestral homes in Central America, in this case Guatemala, and make the dangerous journey north. The main character, Petra, is a smart, thoughtful teen living with her caring indigenous grandparents in a small town in rural Guatemala where brutal gangs have been terrorizing residents, especially young women. It becomes clear over time that her refusal to give in to gang demands is endangering her grandparents, so she needs to flee to join her mother in the United States. The process of eluding the gangs and making a new life is a challenge, but Petra's insights into her experience will stay with the reader for a long time."

> — Nancy Braus, Everyone's Books, Brattleboro, VT

"When gang violence threatens fifteen-year-old Petra in her village in Guatemala and follows her to the streets of Providence, she draws on the strength of her family, village elders, and Mayan culture as she tries to find a way to make her dreams a reality. In this provocative debut, Susan Mills illuminates the human reasons for and costs of immigration. Lyrical, thrilling and thought-provoking, Petra's journey is irresistible."

> — Barbara Morrison, poet and writer, Author of *Innocent: Confessions of a Welfare Mother* and *Terrarium*

"By weaving together the trauma of gender-based violence, the inescapable clutches of Guatemalan gang violence, and the resilience of the human spirit, Susan Mills has proven herself to be an incredibly impactful storyteller. This is one of the most realistic renderings of the struggle to address trauma and abuse on an individual level that I have seen in my 35+ years of work to end domestic and sexual violence."

> — Deborah DeBare, Senior Deputy Director, National Network to End Domestic Violence, Washington, D.C and formerly Executive Director of RI Coalition Against Domestice Violence for 22 years

"I have represented immigrants seeking asylum from Central America for over 30 years. I have never seen a more eloquent distillation of their story. Anyone who cares to understand the crisis at the border must read this book."

> — Stephen Born, Lead attorney at Boston-area immigration law firm

"A story about growing up through violence and loss, and a fable about how faith and intentionality help an adolescent girl make sense of a world filled with chaos. The reader will learn about Guatemalan folklore and mythology, gang rituals, and the vagaries of the US immigration system. A tale about coming to America and making a new life. It's a page-turner with a sympathetic main character who is practical and resourceful but who is also in touch with magical dreams filled with Mayan gods."

— Erica Walch, Former Director of Moore Free Library and Italian-English translator of Le Strade by Ada Negri, Newfane, VT

"This novel is an engrossing glimpse into the impossible life or death choices that daily face children and adolescents in Mexico and Central America--victims of cartels, corrupt governments, and organized crime. As a clinical counselor, I have researched and provided personal therapy around acculturation issues and psychological crises of Mexican and Mexican-American kids. The rampant violence perpetrated against children in the form of sexual and physical abuse (all over the world), particularly against girls and young women, ignores borders, and is always as close as family and friends. This story is a hard look at the question of forgiveness. Petra's journey as a survivor is inextricably woven together with re-claiming, or re-defining, one's own story, rather than being defined solely as a victim. Ultimately, her indomitable spirit and faith in the future made me want the story to continue even beyond the novel's end."

— Carla Zubiría, Clinical counselor, Researcher on Mexican-American acculturation issues, San Diego

"Susan Mills's novel is fresh, imaginative, and grounded in a very real sense of girlhood as it intersects with family and culture, poverty, sexism, and the development of sexual identity. As a university dean, I am well aware of how these issues play out among emerging adults of all cultures and classes. I was moved by how real the character of Petra is, and how much we identify with her without regard to the reader's background. By providing us with such a three-dimensional protagonist and a storyline that weaves easily between everyday life, memory, and imagination - and, finally, spirituality—Susan Mills has given us a window into a very vibrant thread of the immigrant experience."

— Carol Cohen, Academic Dean, Brown University

"A fascinating voyage into the inner and outer life of Petra, a heroic young girl growing up motherless in an impoverished, gang-torn Guatemalan village. As she struggles to find her own place in the world, she must reconcile the contradictions and conflicts of an environment that has become all too distant from its Mayan roots. The book contains depictions of terrible violence – but also poetically evokes the glorious beauty of the Guatemalan landscape with its Mayan culture and mythology. Immigration, recovery from trauma, forgiveness, reconciling modern culture with ancient traditions, and much more—a marvelous story full of complex and timely issues. As a retired psychotherapist and someone who has lived for many years in third world countries, I find the story wonderfully authentic."

— Margot Born, Retired psychotherapist, author of Seven Ways to Look at a Dream, long-time resident of Haiti, India, Australia, France, Turkey, Bangladesh

ON THE WINGS
OF A HUMMINGBIRD

Laura y Marce,
   Convertimos lo imposible
en posible !

ON THE WINGS
OF A HUMMINGBIRD

Susan Mills

Apprentice
House Press
Loyola University Maryland

First Edition

Casebound ISBN: 978-1-62720-372-2
Paperback ISBN: 978-1-62720-373-9
Ebook ISBN: 978-1-62720-374-6

Printed in the United States of America

Design by Lark Thompson
Edited by Lara Pagendarm-Winter
Promotion plan by Claire Marino

Published by Apprentice House Press

Apprentice House Press
Loyola University Maryland
4501 N. Charles Street
Baltimore, MD 21210
410.617.5265
www.ApprenticeHouse.com
info@ApprenticeHouse.com

Dedicated to the Central American youth
still struggling to find a peaceful home.

Author's Note

The discussions about writing across difference, or cultural appropriation, will continue to flourish for some time. Indeed, we must argue in order to move forward on these issues. I wish to acknowledge up front that many may view this book within the framework of these controversies. For I am a white woman, born in the U.S., writing in the voice of a Guatemalan adolescent girl with a Mayan background. For most of my adult life, I have lived, loved, and worked among Central Americans. I have been immersed in the language, the culture, the history, politics, and literature of Latin Americans, all of which gives me a unique perspective to write this story. It does not, of course, change my identity. I am well aware that I am not Central American, and that this story would likely be different if I were. I hope it will be read, appreciated, and understood in that light. I sincerely hope that contributions to this dialogue—including this book—will ultimately play some role in leading us toward a world where racism, sexism, and the othering of immigrants recedes, and where we can all acknowledge the simple humanity of immigrants.

Tu puedes volar aaa...
Extiende ya tus alas.
Y atrévete soñar.
Convierte lo imposible en posible, pero hay que luchar.

No dejes que mala muerte te despierte.
La larga noche si termina tienes suerte.
Cierra los ojos y disfruta lo que tienes, que el corazón te
guíe hasta el infinito celeste.
Siente la sangre que te fluye en las venas y sin pena baila,
canta, grita, haz lo que tu quieras.
No tenemos nada por eso queremos darlo todo, dar tus alas,
sacude el lodo.

Tu puedes volar aaa...
Extiende ya tus alas.
Y atrévete soñar.
Convierte lo imposible en posible, pero hay que luchar.

Rebeca Lane, Volar

•

You can fly tooo ...
Spread your wings now.
And dare to dream.
It turns the impossible into the possible, but you have to struggle.

Don't let wicked death wake you.
If the long night ends you are lucky.
Close your eyes and enjoy what you have, that your heart
leads to celestial infinity.
Feel the blood that flows in your veins and dance without shame,
sing, shout, do what you want.
We have nothing so we want to give everything, give your wings,
shake off the mud.

You can fly tooo ...
Spread your wings now.
And dare to dream.
Turn the impossible into the possible, but you have to struggle.

Part I

CHAPTER ONE

A hamlet outside the village of Las Leches, Guatemala
March 2017

Dust kicked up from the dirt road hung in the air, clinging to her sweaty torso, finally settling on the forest in a gray veneer. Grit flew against her calves from behind.

"Quit it," Petra snarled at her older brother Carlos.

"Sorry." He spoke like someone whose mind was already on something else. He put two fingers to his forehead to let her know he had important thoughts to attend to. Most likely he was trying to figure out how to pay for the beer he wanted to drink with his friends at the midday break.

The mango tree spread gloriously just below them, where the steep path down from their house turned onto the road that took her to school. Briefly, the air shimmered around her, until a rumbling sound encroached. A cloud of dust surrounded the profusion of colors of the *burra*, the local workhorse bus, and it trundled down the road past them.

As they turned up the road toward school, the stream below churned and gurgled. "*Aguas!*" Petra muttered to herself. So exactly right. In Guatemala, the word for water also meant "watch out." The stream paid no attention, continuing its sinuous journey toward the ocean.

The stream froze the sweat on Petra's neck. A hush fell on its banks, and Justina's screams reverberated against the tangle of woods. As much as she tried to push the memories away, they echoed through her mind even while the song of the pink warbler lingered delicately in the background. Guilt and innocence beat their wings against each other. The beautiful and the poisonous coexisted in every corner of the alluring forest around Las Leches.

It had happened just there, by that sweet acacia tree at the stream—of course it would be the tree with the thorns at the base of each leaf—where the thugs, and her old friend Emilio, had carried Justina off into the trees just nine months ago. She and Justina were only fourteen years old when it happened. Only a few years before, Petra, Emilio and Justina ·had been the closest of friends.

Somehow, she would escape from this trap. The trap gave her so few choices, none of them good. She could marry young, as soon as next year, when she turned sixteen—like her grandmother Nonna wanted, like her mother had done. Just look how it turned out for her mother. Married at sixteen years old, gave birth to two children, then abandoned them when she fled to the United States to escape her husband's abuse. Or she could join the gangs. Heck, she could accomplish both those paths at the same time by marrying Emilio. That's what he wanted, why he alternated between stalking her and courting her through Nonna.

A few days before, Emilio had come by the house again. He was dressed up in a starched white shirt and church pants, his hair slicked back and combed neatly. Petra ran out to intercept him, but he raised a hand and said he needed to talk to her grandmother. He clutched a bunch of wildflowers behind his back. It was way too easy to win her Nonna over with a bit of false chivalry.

While Nonna oohed and aahed, so happy to have an attractive young man visit with her, Petra sat on the porch strumming her fingers on the bench. Nonna's usually proud demeanor melted before the possibility of youthful romance. She poured him a coffee and they talked at the family table. Petra cringed at Emilio's easy access to her home. Usually, she stalked away as soon as she saw him coming up over the hill.

"Your granddaughter, um... Petra," Emilio started. He really was an idiot. "We were friends as kids, you know." A tight laugh. "She's... um... well, I want to say —"

Nonna chuckled. "*Cálmate*, Emilio."

"I mean, now that we're older, I'd like to get to know her better. Again, that is." Petra wished she could see the expression on his face. Surely he wasn't serious.

"Oh?" Nonna responded.

"I just need a chance to show her my good side."

"You've grown into a handsome fellow, Emilio. I'd give you a chance if it was me."

"She might not altogether trust me, I think. But I have good intentions. I can prove it to her."

"I'd suggest you walk her to school in the morning." Petra's eyebrows shot up. "It's too dangerous for a pretty girl like Petrita to walk alone, and Carlos… well, he doesn't really want to be a bodyguard. But… she won't hear of it."

A pause. Maybe he was hanging his head in shame. That's what he ought to be doing.

Emilio said, "Yeah. It's an idea." A full minute passed in silence. "She won't listen to me. She won't talk to me."

"I know, *muchacho*. She's very independent-minded. I will talk to her again."

"*Señora, muchas gracias.*"

Emilio's efforts at courting her nauseated her. So instead of listening in, she had squatted down to clean up a pile of chicken droppings at the edge of the porch. His bumbling attempts with Nonna might impress her, but Petra would brave the road to school alone every day before she let Emilio get that close to her.

Carlos kicked another rock, this time away from her, watching it disappear into the forest. A straw hat, made brittle by the scorching sun, perched on his head, obscuring his eyes in shadow.

Lanky eighteen-year-old boys didn't make great bodyguards, especially against the gangs, but he was the only one available.

She could never forgive herself for not paying attention that day when Emilio and the others took Justina, for not hearing the men's footfalls in the leaves. She clutched at her ears, trying to shake the memory away. The more she tried not to think about it, the more it took her over. As her thoughts started to spin, she became dizzy. If she could just focus on walking, one step at a time, she would make it to school.

Her chest tightened, and the screams harangued her, reflecting off the riverbank below. Petra felt faint. By sheer force of will, she clamped down on her body, and tried to push the imaginary screams away. *Ay Dios.*

She wasn't afraid. She *wouldn't* be afraid. She was the one who took care of everyone. She could make out just fine without a mother. She especially watched over her Nonna and Nonno. Before Emilio went and joined the gangs, she had even protected him, to his little-boy macho consternation. That was the problem: She hadn't taken care of Justina. That's why her head spun. But she just wasn't the kind of person to be afraid.

Carlos trudged beside her, oblivious.

Every day, this fight with her mind. The best way to master the memories was to picture something else: the other alternative for the future, the one she clung to, desperately—futilely. She imagined herself as a doctor with her own office in Las Leches. She would work tirelessly to build a relationship with one of those organizations that gave free medicines to poor people. A line of people at the clinic would keep her late into the night so she could see all of them. With her help, they would slowly get their lives back. She would treat her *tío* Oscar, who didn't have money to buy insulin for his diabetes. She would know what was wrong with her friend from church, and she could cure the pain in her grandmother's stomach. She could save girls who bled after they were abducted by gangs, so they wouldn't die, like Justina did.

Petra tried to reach across the wall between her and Carlos. "Do you ever think about what you want to do with your life?"

"Sure. I'd like to kick this grouchy stone here all the way to the top of Sibalq'aq." The volcano loomed over their lives, an ominous but compelling constant.

She reached over and flipped up the back rim of his straw hat. The sarcasm made her crazy. He scowled and set it back onto his head.

At the next bend, the road passed beneath a two-story house with fine features—glass windows, red ceramic tile roof, and a porch. Clearly, Don Fabio's son in the U.S. was sending good money home. The structure was brand new and in a luxury location—the man no longer had to climb a steep path to get home.

Petra tried again to connect. "Don Fabio's house is nice, don't you think?"

"Yeah, it's okay." Carlos had gotten monosyllabic and impenetrable like this since he'd begun having to walk her to school.

"It'd be nice to have a house like that for our family someday. To have a stove so Nonna doesn't have to breathe all that smoke from the fire. An inside toilet and plumbing. Can you imagine?"

"Darn, Petra, what do you want me to say? Of course it would be nice." He turned to her with a scornful look. "I'm working as hard as I can!"

Disconcerted by the bitterness, she said, "I didn't mean—" She stopped herself. It wasn't worth it. Ever since their father had thrown an iron in their mother's direction ten years ago, Carlos had changed. Shortly after their mother had disappeared to the United States, their father left to chase another woman. Carlos quit school. The way he saw it, it was up to him to get food on the table. To keep everyone safe. But what Petra saw was her beloved brother becoming quick to lash out, like their father.

She didn't want to argue with her brother. Instead, she playfully punched his shoulder. *Caramba*, he did have some serious muscle under his thin frame. "You're getting strong from mashing all that sugar cane." It got a small grin out of him, and the reward swept over her. Sometimes she surprised herself when she realized how badly she wanted Carlos's affection.

Caught up in her brother's moodiness, Petra didn't see the bicycle skewing a tight arc around her to avoid a pothole. Her muscles tensed as she vaguely registered the sound of panting. When the boy's handlebar brushed against her arm, she jumped back in fright.

Carlos said, "It's just a bike. *Tranquila*." She squelched a snide retort in favor of putting up a good face. *A mal tiempo, buena cara.*

Enough of his short temper. "Go home, Carlos," Petra said. "Go back to work. I can take care of myself."

Carlos shifted his feet and stumbled over a root. "Maybe you think Emilio should walk with you to school instead of me," Carlos scoffed. "Nonna wants to give him permission."

Petra glared at him. "Are you serious, Carlos? You, too?"

He shrugged. "No, not really. I'm just afraid you might give in. Like Nonna says, you're fifteen now. Time to start cozying up to a *muchacho*."

"If you don't want to walk with me, *bien*. I'm going alone." With small steps, she inched along the road. Carlos stood there, contemplating his feet.

A gust of wind cracked a small branch that floated down and glanced off her arm before landing on the road. She looked in the direction of her school, reluctant to go on by herself. Emilio would never win her over. Not after what he'd done.

Her feet remained rooted to the road. Should she smooth things over with Carlos or go on alone? Eerie cries shuddered through the dense undergrowth next to her. Leaves hissed in the breeze.

Don Fabio leaned out from one of those nice glass windows and waved.

"*Buenos días*," Petra shouted cheerfully.

But Don Fabio was looking up the road with a wrinkled brow. Her neck craned upward to the grand old ceiba tree that grew beyond the house.

The unreliable dirt road was rife with holes that shifted in the shadows, as likely to flip over a motorcycle traveling at otherwise normal speeds as deliver the driver safely into the village of Las Leches. In their hot and dry corner of the coastal plains of southwestern Guatemala, people were eagerly anticipating that the onset of the rainy season any day or any week now would settle the earth in their crowded but lonely *aldea* and the nearby village. This morning, the volcano cast long shadows, offering endless varieties of speculation about where they were headed.

Petra was determined to know where she was heading. She was going to make a mark on her world.

Whatever Don Fabio was looking at troubled him, and he disappeared into his house.

Ahead of her, silhouetted, a man sat on the lowest branch of the ceiba tree. When he saw her approaching, he slid awkwardly to the ground, tripping over his feet. He stood up, waiting.

A bird that glittered green and yellow called out sternly from above. Petra raised an arm to shield her eyes from the morning sunlight and so failed to notice right away that the figure who'd jumped down from the limb was Emilio. When she recognized him, she recoiled with such fright that Carlos hurried up to her. He said, "It's just Emilio. Calm down."

When they were kids, this might have been a normal scene—Emilio scrambling up this or that tree thinking he'd impress his friends, then Justina laughing when he panicked and Petra helping him back down.

But now, his voice came at her in a terrible singsong, pushing at her, pricking at her consciousness. "Tita, Tita, Petita!" The brash voice rattled her like a rising tempest. She forced it back down and remained in the refuge of her thoughts.

"Tita, Tita, I need you…" The voice became insistent and intoned her name again.

Carlos stuck out an arm to slow Emilio's approach, but Emilio was suddenly all motion. His leg swung around and hooked Petra's ankle, swiping her feet off the ground. Stones on the ground scraped her bare shoulder.

In the back of Petra's head, Justina screamed again.

"Get away from me!" Petra said. "I dont want anything to do with you, never again."

"What do you think you're doing? Get away from us," Carlos said.

Emilio stepped on the crook of her arm, pinning her down to the dirt, and threw his shoulders back.

"Easy, Carlitos. Just some old friends playing an old game. I've been looking for you, Petita. Come with me, Tita, I want to do so many things with you." Sweetness and edgy bravado contorted his meaning.

Carlos sidled over and shoved Emilio away, just enough to free Petra. "Emilio, leave her alone. She already told you." He stood ramrod straight and put his hands on his hips.

"Carlitos, you're looking skinnier every day. Got your puppy here with you today, Petita?"

"Shut up, Emilio." Petra tried to keep walking.

Emilio closed in on Petra, blocking her way. He grabbed hold of the machete that hung from his belt, hand on its hilt. There was no doubting the threat.

"I came by your house this morning," he said, "but your Nonna told me it was a school day."

Recently, Emilio may have been pestering her and flirting with her, but he hadn't been this aggressive against her. Confused, Petra froze, but the fear quickly turned to anger. The agony of standing next to this boy who had killed their best friend!

"Find something else to do, Emilio." She tried to push past him again.

He let the machete drop down by his side again but put his face so close she could see the little hairs in his flaring nose. He leaned over her. "I want you to be my girlfriend. Come with me. Leave behind this little brother of yours."

Carlos cringed with the "little brother" insult. Petra could smell his fear. He said, "She told you no, jerk. Now get out of here."

Emilio's lips curled up into a sneer. His temples shone with beaded sweat.

And his fist came out of nowhere. With a smack, Carlos's head snapped back. Petra reached for him, then pulled back when she saw his nose bleeding. Emilio kept punching. Carlos dropped to the ground, waving his arms feebly. Petra grabbed a rock on the ground and hurled it toward Emilio. As it glanced by his ear, Emilio stopped and stared at Petra in surprise. She'd actually thrown a rock at him. For a terrifying moment, she wondered if he was about to turn his fists on her. But instead, Emilio kicked at Carlos once more, then grabbed Petra around the small of her back.

Carlos rolled into a ball in the middle of the road. The straw hat lay next to him covered in dust, its brim frayed.

Emilio was stiff and tense, breathing in weird gasps. His mouth twisted into a crooked smile, and his eyes darted about. He raised his index finger and pointed it in her face. "Just one more thing, Petita. I have an important message for you." He panted hard into her face and gripped her elbow tightly. "The powers that be in our neighborhood have let drop an important tidbit. It seems your grandfather knows about a very valuable secret place not too far from here." His tone turned snide. "Perhaps you and I could go on a visit there one day. Your Nonno can show us the way."

"You're making stuff up now, Emilio. I have no idea what you're talking about. But get my grandfather out of your moldy mind. He's got nothing to do with you anymore. Not since you've rotted away into this miserable life."

"Ah, but you can't wish this one away, my sweet. You understand, this is straight from the boss of my little group. And a few others. I'll give you a couple of days to bring back some information, but if you don't, your grandfather might find himself with some visitors from the X-14."

"What could my grandfather possibly know? He's just an old *campesino*."

"Old men have pasts, *chiquita*. How much do you know about his?"

Even if she had known what Emilio was talking about, Petra was done with this conversation. She felt sick, done with his command over her body. As if she was just some object he could grab and use however he wanted. Offended, furious, Petra wriggled away from his grip and ran. She was pretty certain Carlos could fend for himself.

How did her former friend's soul become twisted into the delinquent he was today? Now, safely out of Emilio's grasp, she stopped and took a deep breath. She turned her head back toward Emilio and saw a boy, confused and defeated, grasping his head between his hands.

Her anger softened a bit. For a moment, she was nine years old again. She yelled, "I'm sorry, Emilio! I didn't mean to!" His head cocked to the side, flustered.

Her eyebrows twisted in confusion. Why did she say that? She pivoted and considered the road ahead, then ran and ran, not looking back, until she got to the village and plunged into the school building.

CHAPTER TWO

When the family came together again that evening, Carlos wouldn't meet her eyes. His body sagged as he sat on the porch bench—his elbows perched on his knees and his back hunched over. His head drooped, and he held a rag full of ice to his forehead. The sun hung suspended between puffy clouds and the horizon. The disturbances of the day had settled a bit.

Petra had almost gone back to check on Carlos. But her brother had experienced worse. He had undoubtedly gotten banged up a bit, but she didn't worry too much about him. She had been more afraid that Emilio's cohorts would show up and carry her off into the woods like they'd done to Justina. That the dark forest would swallow her whole. Not to mention her mind had seized up, stuck in the foggy notion that she had wronged Emilio somehow. But whenever she searched for the reason, she couldn't pull the memory out from her childhood.

Emilio was full of himself, but he wouldn't really hurt her or her family. Whatever he'd become since his mother died, he wouldn't forget the friendship he'd had with Petra. Would he?

She resolved to stick with that conclusion for now.

Gingerly, Petra sat down near Carlos on the bench. The aged bench sagged, too. To avoid the tendency to slide inward, Petra and Carlos separated themselves on either end. But what could she say to reach him? Nothing came to her. Nonno meandered about the front yard, stacking wood for the next day's cooking, glancing discreetly in their direction.

Abruptly, Petra stood, tired of making futile efforts to reach out to Carlos. She began to traipse back and forth along the length of the porch. Carlos's head twitched, and he peered up at her for a moment, then his head dropped down again. Minutes passed in this cat and mouse game of silent scrutiny.

Without warning, a five-hundred-pound pig barreled past Petra, down the length of the porch, oblivious to the murky atmosphere. Its companion followed, snorting repeatedly as the two clambered over a pile of corn husks, the pile now spread thin off the corner of the house. Petra giggled. The pigs had perfect timing.

Nonno appeared from behind the pigs like an *alux*, a Mayan sprite. With a faint smile, he leaned up against a porch post, its wood fraying into splinters. His chin leaned on his fingers, the index finger pushing his nose upward. The breeze swept his sparse but electric gray hair into a billowy mass around his head.

"Carlos, you have grown too old for my stories, and yet there is one I wish to tell. This is a simple Mayan tale my parents told me as a child. You are both ready to listen?"

Petra nodded eagerly. Carlos's shoulders heaved in an exaggerated sigh.

Nonno began. "A coyote came to visit the hen. The coyote said he had good news. The hen did not trust him. He said the news was about the two of them. There had been a peace treaty on the other side of the mountain, and coyotes and hens were going to be friends. He asked the hen to come down from the tree so they could hug each other and celebrate the peace.

"The hen did not trust him. The hen accused him of lying, but he swore it was true.

"The hen thought about how to respond to the coyote. She told him that a dog was running toward them to join the fiesta because coyotes and dogs were also going to make peace. Coyotes are afraid of dogs; the coyote believed her and ran away. The hen realized that he was telling her lies, and if she had come down in front of the coyote, he would have eaten her."

Still looking at the ground, Carlos muttered, "This time the dog was afraid of the coyote."

"Carlos…" Petra began.

Nonno intervened. "It's okay to be scared, Carlos." How Petra cherished the love in Nonno's eyes, no matter that it wasn't directed at her. Carlos looked away, his eyes scanning the horizon like he was searching for the answer out there. Nonno added, "The coyote today had a weapon, an unfair advantage. Emilio is a particularly depraved coyote."

Carlos closed his eyes briefly, and his head nodded so slightly that Petra may have been the only one to see it.

Upon hearing Emilio's name, Nonna appeared at the doorway. "*Oíganme.* That young man deserves a chance. I see potential in him."

"*Mujer*, enough of your romantic ideas about Emilio," Nonno said. "He's become a menace to the community. Even young men we knew as cute children can be corrupted in the local gang. It is no good to deny what we can plainly see."

Nonna pursed her lips. "Some young men can be grumpy and reticent with their words." Her lips jutted out toward Carlos. "Others lash out with violence and anger. Generally, they grow into more high-minded ways." She thrust her chin up sharply, and the ridges of her forehead deepened.

Petra's pacing came to a stop next to Nonno. She said, "Emilio is rotten, Nonna."

"Maybe not so rotten as you think."

Her insides roiled, but—she had to stay calm and respect her Nonna. "How can you say that? He killed Justina!"

"He was with the group that killed her, yes, I know."

"What's the difference?" Petra's cheeks had turned bright red.

"You don't really know what he did that day, do you? Or what might have led him to stand with those boys who took her?"

Petra began to pace about the porch. "He was there! He's as guilty as the others!"

"Are you sure, Petra?" asked Nonna. She sucked air in through the gap in her front teeth.

Sure enough that calmness eluded her now. Her chest muscles tensed against her heart, and she wrapped her arms around herself. How she wished it was her mother's arms wrapped around her. Surely her mother would understand. Her mother, who had run away from her children instead of finding another way to protect herself and her kids from their father's abuse.

"Carlos," Petra said, "at least you and I are not running away from our problems like our mother did. Emilio isn't—"

Carlos blew up. "Mamá didn't run away!"

Chastened, Petra turned to Carlos. "You remember her, don't you?" Petra only remembered missing her.

"She's safe now. That's all that matters." Then Carlos was gone, his eyes staring off beyond the fields.

Alocinia stirred in her heart. Alocinia was the name of the clay hummingbird that lived in the cherished corner next to her bed, ever since her mother gave it to her just before she left. Alocinia was a part of her now, with or without the physical figure, threaded into the fibers of her imagination. But the reassuring presence of the spirit of the hummingbird never lasted long. As usual, she floated in, surrounded Petra with love, then drifted away, leaving her with a hole, albeit a warmer hole.

The edge off slightly, she said, "Nonna, I can't forgive Emilio. I don't want anything to do with him. That I know. Although—" There was that moment before she turned and ran when he seemed almost human again. Vulnerable even. "There was something in him when we were friends years ago. Maybe someday—"

Carlos interrupted. "You apologized to him! After he had me at his feet!"

The heel of her hand knocked against her temple, then pressed against the thick black line of her brow. Of course. She hadn't realized. "Carlos, I'm sorry. I looked at him and saw a wounded animal. He looked scared and helpless." There was more, but she couldn't say it out loud. Something gnawed at the back of her mind. The reason she kept thinking she owed Emilio an apology. She had done something, she didn't know what, that pushed Emilio toward the vicious life he led. Whenever this feeling came over her, dread weighed down her lungs and panic pounded in her heart. Then it promptly slipped away.

"*He* looked helpless? While you decided to run off and leave me on the ground?"

Confused, Petra's mind scrambled for words.

Nonno said, "Enough, everyone! It was a moment. A charged

moment. We will all stir the events in our minds until some greater wisdom arises. That is all we can do."

The last of the light flickered off the tips of Nonno's ears. Deep furrows lined his forehead. The creases around his mouth, grown up around years of struggle between worry and good humor, quivered. Petra leaned her head against his shoulder. Her heart stopped racing.

Quietly, Nonna said, "Petra, let us meet after school tomorrow and go to church together."

"*Sí*, Nonna. I would like that." Yes, church would quiet the upheaval inside her.

The hen had gathered up her experience and turned it into useful wisdom. Petra would never believe the coyote's lies. Her grandmother might think Emilio just wanted to court her, but Petra knew better. No one could claim innocence after creating such terror.

The pain of losing Justina throbbed against her skull. Her death had stung so deeply, there had been no room left to explore the details of what had happened. But Nonna had a point. There was more to understand. Why did the gang kill Justina?

CHAPTER THREE

Petra didn't want to leave the school building. But when the little bell that signaled the end of the junior high classes jangled at noon, most of the kids were soon out the door, anxious to get home for lunch and start on their afternoon work—except for Petra. Anything could happen in the outside world. Local delinquents loved to recruit outside her school. She couldn't face them today, not again.

She would never drop out of school in fear, like so many other kids had. It could be said that Petra was a bit cocky about her ability to fend off the dangers that came her way.

Except—there was just that bit of anxiety that gnawed at her. There were those times when sweat drenched her body for no apparent reason, or her head suddenly swooned until she almost fainted. An occasional nightmare came over her at night, and, well, sometimes the terror that she had to cope with it all by herself took hold of her and she couldn't stop trembling. Her mother had left her alone and abandoned, and her grandparents—well, they tried, but they weren't parents.

She'd managed these difficulties for years, though, and she kept it all at bay and went on with her life. It was the only way she knew of to eventually cross over to the life she dreamed of.

If she applied herself more than anyone, she could overcome the limitations of her small village school. But it wasn't easy. The teachers only had a few more years of schooling than she did. The books and resources were woefully inadequate. School was only in session for four hours a day, and sometimes it closed altogether for weeks at a time.

She could put off leaving the shelter of the building awhile longer. Nonna wasn't due to meet her at the church for a few more minutes. She would have liked to spend some time setting down her thoughts in writing, but she didn't want to use another page of her only notebook, so instead she sat and read over all her notes and homework assignments. When she picked up the class's science book, which covered only the natural world of Central America, it fell open to the section on spider monkeys.

The textbook failed to tell the most essential story of the spider monkey. The monkey figured in one of the Mayan creation stories that her grandfather told her.

The gods created the earth and the sky, then the animals and living creatures. They kept trying to create the kind of humans they preferred, who would walk and talk and worship them. On their first try, when they fashioned people out of earth and mud, the humans disintegrated. For their next effort, they added wood, and this time the humans were sturdier, but they had no minds, no memory, and nothing in their hearts, so the gods were still not satisfied. They destroyed all of humanity in a great flood and began again.

The only survivors of those first efforts to create people became spider monkeys. Spider monkeys behaved like demonic clowns during the creation of humanity. Petra pictured a monkey with a wicked laugh, up in the trees outside her school.

When she peered closely at the monkey, its face had Emilio's plump, sultry lips and big coffee-colored eyes. The monkey watched its cousin the howler monkey in the next tree over, who cried and moaned vociferously but pursued its work with seriousness, while Emilio the spider monkey laughed, danced, pulled relentless pranks, and made the gods laugh. He'd fled up into the tree out of humiliation at the gods' laughter. Forevermore, he would be suspended between the earth and the heavens, not quite belonging anywhere.

Her mother had told Petra in one of their monthly phone calls what ninth graders in the U.S. studied: genetics, fungi and bacteria, DNA, single-celled organisms, mitosis, and photosynthesis. All those words had stuck in her brain but had only whetted her appetite for more information. The subjects must be interesting if she didn't even understand what they were.

In her school here in Las Leches, the ninth graders still shared books with the two younger grades, and there was only the one general science book for all three grades. Petra had a start on becoming an expert on the animals and plants of Guatemala since she absorbed all the information she could wring out of her class.

Her mother could learn more about science from her housemate's son than Petra could as a regular student.

Shortly after her mother went off to the United States, Petra started primary school. She kept thinking her mother would send for her to join her in the U.S. any day, so she didn't care too much when the school closed down for two months for a teacher's strike in her second year. In her fourth year, Petra felt reassured that she would make up the education time when she went to the U.S. with her mother. That's when the bus drivers went on strike for six weeks, and the teachers who mostly commuted from San Luis Hunahpu couldn't get to school. She did sometimes cry in her bed at night, though, despairing over when her mother would come and get her.

By her sixth school year, Petra started to worry that it would be hard to catch up to her grade in the U.S. Teachers kept repeating the material because kids came and went, going to school for a week, then staying home for two weeks. The pace of learning was slow, and many of the students never did learn to read and write. By the end of primary school, two-thirds of the girls had dropped out, and half the boys.

When she graduated into junior high school, and she moved from the little school in her *aldea* to the bigger one in Las Leches, Petra no longer dismissed the worries. Instead, she lost faith that her mother would ever bring her to the U.S. She sought ways to learn more than anyone else at her school. She started to resent that her mother had more access to Petra's school subjects than she did.

Her aunt Dolores had a little store in Las Leches with a television. Sometimes she kept Dolores company and got immersed in an afternoon program on the ecology of Central America.

The school did have a dictionary, though its cover had disintegrated from years of use, so she looked up DNA. It wasn't there. She thought DNA probably stood for something, but she didn't know what. Photosynthesis was listed, but she didn't really understand the definition. There were no other resources.

Gang members were mostly the only ones with access to the internet. She'd seen Emilio staring and typing into his phone, but she certainly wasn't going to ask him to show her how to use it. Her family couldn't afford one.

Worse, to continue on to high school she'd have to commute to San Luis Hunahpu. That meant more money, perilous bus rides every day, and time away from her tasks at home. It depended on how much her mother could help. Sometimes the money she sent would be enough, then for long periods, she didn't send anything. But, honestly, even if her mom could help, bus rides were dangerous, especially for teenage girls.

Petra's teacher raised her head, and her lips began to form words. But she said nothing. She just watched Petra.

Teachers in the U.S. probably had much more stimulating, dynamic teaching styles. She would never say it out loud, but her teacher here could use for somebody to light a fire under her.

Petra had better get going if she was going to meet Nonna at the church. She got up and helped straighten up the chairs and put away the handful of books they used in class. She nodded her head toward her teacher, wished her a pleasant day, and went on her way.

The babble of male voices just outside the doorway stopped her. Gangs did much of their recruiting just outside the school, so she always checked before stepping out. She tucked herself just inside the school entrance and listened.

A gravelly voice said, "He should be ready to pay up now. Gorto, stop by the pharmacy tomorrow and talk to him again."

"But I just went yesterday. He gave me everything he had."

Gorto's voice sounded like a squeaky wheel. Gorto—a nickname nobody would want. He must be short and fat, a misfit trying to look tough by joining up with the delinquents.

"Go again, man, I'm telling you."

"What if he says no? Then I'll just look stupid." Gorto was whining.

"Sometimes, my man, they just need to be persuaded. You might find him more willing this time."

The laughter of several men rumbled.

"How'd you do it, Chofo? How does the pharmacist find more money so fast?"

Chofo guffawed loudly. "Gorto, sometimes I forget you still need refining. You were there! You didn't know?"

"You mean last night? Ah, *sí*, there were lots of pretty girls at the dance. I *almost* got one to go home with me at midnight. She was *this* close to going with me, but her cousin came up and started squawking. Then she slapped me."

"Shut up, Gorto. Not them, *estúpido*, the one with the lips."

"Oh. You mean the stupid *puta* slut hanging on the arms of that boy I knocked over. She *did* have big lips, all painted purple. After I looked at that guy cross-eyed in the woods up there, he gave me some change, and I set him loose."

This was what men thought about girls who went to a dance and hooked up with guys. They were all whores.

Chofo said, "You know who the girl was? Why we told you to get rid of him for a while?"

"I didn't think about it, *compadre*. I figured we were just fleecing him for the extra cash. Who was it?"

"That, my man, was Señor Menendez's daughter. The *jefe* ordered us to punish her to loosen up his pockets. Scare him into raising some more money for us."

A third man spoke up. "We had to work on her awhile before she shut up, Chofo. She didn't go down easy. *Pero sí*, she finally did go down." Fake coughing, feet scuffing.

Petra shivered in the doorway. Inside her head, Alocinia pounded away, trying to get her attention. She mumbled, "Get away from those men!"

Without warning, a little piece of the concrete that Petra was gripping broke off and bounced on the pavement. She gasped, and without checking to see if the hoodlums had heard her, she fled back down the hall of the school, turning to look over her shoulder every two steps. She slammed into the back door, jammed in its frame, but it opened when she stopped and lifted it slightly. Thank God she knew the building's quirks. She rushed out onto the stone-lined street.

Her eyes darted down the street, searching for a friendly open door. She peeked through the darkness into the home of her grandmother's friend but didn't see anyone there. The long block of sun-drenched cement walls was full of doors propped open to catch the scarce breeze.

At the end of the block, another group of young men was hanging out by the corner, some leaning on the wall, some with folded arms, one gesturing loudly. Her heart beat wildly. The two groups knew each other, Petra was sure. It was too far away to see clearly, but it looked like one of the men was holding a cell phone to his ear. If Gorto and Chofo's group had heard her, they might be calling them right now, and they'd be looking out for her. As she stood contemplating them, two of the men broke off from the group and started walking toward her. They weren't looking directly at her, but she wasn't taking any chances.

Petra quickly ducked into the household goods store. Dolores put aside the rag she was using to wipe the dust off sets of plastic bowls lining several shelves, and peeled her eyes away from a *telenovela*. Breathing hard, Petra stared up at the television. Any one of those Mexican soap operas featured more wealthy blond Hispanic women than Petra had ever seen in her life.

"Petrita, come in. Come in and visit with me!"

"*Buenas tardes*, Dolores. *Tía*, can we close the door? I just overheard an awful conversation between some gang members. I'm afraid they saw me."

"Of course, *niña*." Dolores threw the wooden bolt across the door and nodded to the stool. Petra sat and tried to calm down.

"Have you seen Señor Menendez today? Is he okay?" asked Petra.

"No, I've only been here about an hour. What's the matter, Petra?"

"They're saying they attacked his daughter last night to force him to hand them over more money." Petra wiped the sweat off her brow with the back of her wrist. She grabbed the stool seat with both her hands to try and steady herself.

"*Ay mi Dios*, Petra. They'll be here next, demanding their 'taxes.' The only thing saving me is that we have so few customers. As long as I'm poor, we're relatively safe."

"Are things that bad in the store?"

"Well, you see what I'm doing. Television chases away the silence."

"Dolores, can I go through the store to the back way out? I don't want to run into those guys outside." With the door closed, the only light in the store trickled in through a small window covered in wire mesh. Her aunt was too nice to complain, but Petra had to leave her to her business.

"*Claro que sí*, Petra. It gets worse all the time, especially for a pretty girl like you. Did you hear what happened to Julinita last week?"

"*Tía, no me digas.* Tell me nothing bad has happened to her!"

"She was holding a few quetzals in her hand from a customer. A young guy she'd never seen before barged through the door like he'd just been waiting for her to leave. He grabbed hold of Julina's arm and shook loose the quetzals. And he walked right out the door." Dolores's forehead wrinkled as she paused. Her lips tightened.

"Oh no. I'm sorry, Dolores. Is Julina all right?" Petra's favorite niece had just celebrated her tenth birthday the week before.

Girls learned a lot about local gangs starting around their tenth year. Sometimes, that learning was more intriguing than what they learned in school. Julina was too smart, though—she hoped—to let a handsome young man persuade her with shiny jewelry and tantalizing promises. An impulsive decision could muddy a girl's future faster than a raincloud could burst its water.

"She was shaken up, but she'll be okay. They didn't hurt her. Just be careful, Petita."

"Where is Julina? She's not working with you this afternoon?"

"I told her to go home today. There's a project she's working on at home, and things are quiet here, so I told her go ahead. Maybe you'll see her when you go home. If you do, check on her, make sure she's okay, Petita. Will you do that?"

"Of course, *tía*." Petra hated to sneak around, but she went out the back door, and followed the quieter alley to the church plaza. Glancing around behind her, she saw Dolores at the doorway watching over her progress.

As she emerged from the alley, the church rose up before her. No one would hurt her so close to the church. Even the gangs didn't violate the sanctity of its presence, the heart of the village. At the head of the plaza, it was the oldest and most impressive building around. In the plaza, life became grander. Petra blocked out the gang's loathsome conversation and looked for Nonna.

On Sundays, she would sit next to Nonna in the church. Sometimes Nonna sang a bit too enthusiastically and out of tune along with the hymns that were played on guitars by the *conjunto* of parishioners assembled at the priest's side. As Petra walked toward the adobe-stucco church building, she hummed a refrain to herself. The soothing song of the guitars eased her mind, even as they plucked her imagination. If she could, she would go to church every day. Any opportunity to sort through the confounding mysteries of her life. A sermon opened her mind to a new way to pry open a problem; a prayer whisked her off to heaven for a fleeting moment.

"*Hola, qué tal,* Mina!" She waved to her classmate who had just left school and was already sweeping out her family's food store. The dirt rose in a small cloud out the back-alley door. In another world, Petra could have been friends with Mina. She was nice enough, and a good student. But Petra didn't want friends anymore. Bad things always seemed to happen to friends. Mina smiled at her but turned away to pick up the hose and began to wash off the alley by their entrance.

Petra glared at the bar across the plaza. Two older men stood before the altar to Maximón on the corner wall of the bar, the smoke from their cigarettes obscuring the mustachioed figure in a black jacket, brightly colored Mayan scarves and *sombrero*. Somebody had propped an empty beer can in Maximón's hand. Petra sided with the Catholics who called him San Simón and dismissed him as the saint for corrupt souls.

The bar must have been built even before the church, when the Spanish Pedro de Alvarado and his men first moved into the Mayan land in the 1500's. That they would build the bar first seemed appropriate because drinking, in her estimation, was more the foundation of the local culture than church life. Most likely, Alvarado and his conquistadors had raped her own ancestral grandmother. They had certainly spread their seed around to make a bunch of mestizo descendants.

As she made her way across the plaza to the church, the usual raucous male voices spilled out the door of the bar. She quickened her pace.

Her mother once sent her to that bar to locate her father when she was just a little girl. Her big eyes goggled at the alien environment, and the men whistled at her as soon as she entered. For them, it was all fun.

For her, it was terrifying and maddening. She concentrated on finding her father amongst the brash clutter of men. Spilled alcohol on the floor clutched at her bare feet. The back of a chair stuck to her small hand. The air was thick with the stink of smoky, cheap beer.

Music played through scratchy speakers, and a woman on the tiny stage up front drew Petra's eyes. Her mouth gaped open as her tongue explored the space where she had recently lost a front tooth. She took in the half-naked woman slinking along the floor while men dropped coins into her open blouse. A man patted his lap, and the woman sat down on him, threw her head back and pursed her bright red lips while he stuck a hand into her bra. Within half a minute, she sprang up and began to swing herself around a wooden pillar.

Distracted, Petra didn't notice the man behind her who pulled on her ponytail and slapped her on the butt. The tolerance she had endured on a thread snapped, and she yelped and ran out of the bar.

Fortunately, her father had spotted her, and he followed her out. She wondered how long he'd been watching her.

As she dislodged herself from the troubling memory, the church's facade grabbed her attention. It never failed to inspire her. It stood tall, sculpted with ornate designs of plaster, a frieze of Mary and baby Jesus hanging above the huge doors, beside a large wooden cross. Despite their treacherous world, the church doors were always open.

"Petra!" She turned her head abruptly at the sound of her name. Nonna was hurrying toward her. "I've called you three times! Where is your head, *muchacha*?"

"I'm sorry, Nonna. In the clouds, apparently." She kissed her grandmother's cheek.

Then her name again, now from a deeper, familiar voice: "Petra!"

Por Dios! Emilio, again.

Nonna turned. "Emilio, come! Petita, Emilio and I have been sitting on the fountain talking. He offered to walk with me on the road." She smiled up at Emilio.

Emilio shifted self-consciously and observed Petra through narrowed eyes. Petra moved to her grandmother's side, taking her hand in her own. Emilio crept over to Nonna's other side and whispered in her ear, causing Nonna to laugh.

"What's up, Emilio?" Petra would make an effort to be civil in front of Nonna.

"I guess I owe you an apology for the other day."

"An apology? Do you really think that covers it?"

Emilio swung his head back and forth, as if it was hanging loose from a pair of old hinges. He tried on his most charming smile.

Petra said, "Nonna, let's go into the church. I have nothing to say to this boy." Just a small jab. Emilio would take offense at being called a boy.

Emilio arched an eyebrow and rolled his eyes flirtatiously instead.

Nonna pulled on her hand. "Please, Petra. He's trying to be nice."

"I'm sorry Carlos's head got in the way of my fist. I lost my temper a little. I just... Petra! Hear me out!"

Petra had dropped Nonna's hand and was climbing the church steps. Sharply, Nonna said, "Petra! Don't be rude!"

So she stopped. She settled on a step just above Nonna, using her as a shield against Emilio. "Emilio. Is your memory so bad? You threatened me with a knife."

Nonna gasped. "Emilio? Really?"

Emilio spluttered. "No, no, no. You misunderstood. This machete," he lifted a hip to show them it was still there, "it keeps pulling my pants down." He grimaced uncomfortably. "I have to hike it up all the time. I didn't take it out or point it at you or anything, did I?"

"Seriously, Emilio? And you didn't threaten to come with your gang buddies to our house to force Nonno to—" She searched her memory. "To do *some*thing. I have no idea what you were talking about."

"Look, I didn't want to get into all that now. That's... *pues*, I don't want to talk about business. This is about me and you. I just wanted to share a few kind words with an old friend." Emilio's eyes begged Nonna for help.

Nonna looked back and forth between the two of them, squinting her eyes at each of them in turn.

Emilio spoke quickly, before Nonna could come to an unwanted conclusion. "Petra, come." He held out a hand. Such a pretense of gallantry in front of Nonna. "I promise I won't bite."

He wasn't even original. Nonna, however, looked at her, her eyes hopeful. "Nonna, I'm sorry, I can't." Petra turned and headed up the stairs. "I'll meet you inside. *Adios*, Emilio."

Before she reached the door, Emilio rushed up the stairs behind her. Arm outstretched, leaning forward just slightly, he proffered a handful of purple petals. These were the very petals from the jacaranda tree in front of the house where he had lived with his mother! Until— Her eyes misted over, and she used the back of her hand to clear her vision. Gently, without meeting Emilio's gaze, she touched the petals in Emilio's hand. Then, leaving them there, she pivoted and walked through the church door.

CHAPTER FOUR

How could Nonna be so gullible! So naive about Emilio's hollow attempts at pursuing her! But that jacaranda tree—how beautifully it used to frame their games in Emilio's yard, hide the little lizards and slithering things in speckled shadows, protect the confidences they shared. Until it didn't ever again. Until the petals fell and were covered with dust.

Just inside the church doors, she let the cool breadth of the church sweep over her, calming her nerves. She fixed her eyes on the flame of the candle she placed under the Virgin Mary. Next to Mary stood another altar, gayly adorned with flowers and colorful tassels, the town's patron saint, clothed in white cotton breeches, secured beneath the knees with woven cords, with a red sash around his waist and a straw hat. She lowered her head before San Vicente, the saint of reconciliation.

Her chest heaved with a sigh. Where to find reconciliation amidst the killings and threats? As much as it sounded good in theory, the events to reconcile kept coming so fast it didn't leave time to process, let alone accommodate in some useful way. The weight shifted between her shoulders as she took in the imposing entry, the cold stone floors, the spacious hall so full of grace.

Quietly, she passed along rows of wooden benches, peering at the sacristy. Above, Christ hung from his cross there, dark red paint dripping from Jesus's hands and feet in a bloody confirmation of the violence done to him. It put her own suffering in perspective.

On a bench near the back, she prayed quietly for Nonna, refusing the intrusive thoughts about Emilio. A few minutes went by before Nonna slipped in beside her. Nonna leaned forward onto her knees.

Prayers flowed easily for the people in her life until she came to her mother, far away in the United States living a life she couldn't imagine in a place she couldn't envision. Surely her mother would understand better than Nonna what Emilio had truly become. That she could no longer trust him. A tear formed in the corner of her eye. She hadn't seen her mother for ten years. Not all the time, but sometimes, she needed a mother. It was possible she loved her mother, but she wasn't too sure. Mostly she felt torn up inside.

Nonna told her that her mother was sacrificing herself for her family. She should be thankful for that, and the money her mother sent sometimes, but in a place she didn't tell people about, she was angry. Promises to take Petra to join her had turned up empty.

Then the guilt seized her. Her stomach clenched, and the muscles around her forehead squeezed together. It hadn't been easy for her mother. She often wept when Petra spoke to her on the phone. Petra hated that— it made her want to hang up right away. But her mother suffered, she knew. There were so many families where the mother stoically carried on despite years of beatings by a drunken or womanizing father. Petra knew the ever-suffering woman. True, a fate like that for her mother would have been worse. At least she and Carlos had Nonno and Nonna. Petra tried to hold on to gratitude, for her life and for her mother. She could find her way without her mother right here in Guatemala.

She wanted so badly to picture her mother. Her Nonna kept a photograph of her mother by her bed, but it was taken before Petra was even born. Nonna kept the photo close and kissed it before going to sleep every night. But Petra didn't know her mother from the photo. That was Nonna's daughter, not Petra's mother. She shook off her mother and finished the prayer for Nonna.

Thoughts of Emilio buzzed around Petra's head like an annoying fly. What part did he play in the attack on Señor Menendez's daughter? It was true she missed the boy from her childhood. As much as she wished the spirit of that boy could still be found in the grown version, the gangs had ripped it out of him.

It all started at the foot of that jacaranda tree. In a different version of her world, she could have helped Emilio's mother so she would have lived, and Emilio wouldn't have gotten lost in the gang world. Right after that day, she began to dream of becoming a doctor.

When Petra was nine and Emilio ten, her uncle Jacinto brought a couple of bicycles home with him from the United States. Having glimpsed but never touched with her own hands a bicycle before, she didn't know how to ride it. But she was fascinated. The bikes were rusty, their formerly shiny colors faded, but all she saw were two wheels that could carry her far and wide. Her hands gravitated toward the neon streamers hanging from the handlebars.

Emilio grabbed the red one, wrapping a hand around the handlebar and twisting his thumb to ring the bell. The two of them straddled the bikes in the dusty courtyard in front of her house and pondered how to conquer the things.

"Emilio, how do you make this thing stay up?"

"I'll show you. Just put one foot on the pedal and push with the other." The bike promptly fell over, dumping Emilio on the ground.

"Nah, I think it's like this," Petra said. Holding tight to the rubber grips at the end of each handlebar, she ran next to the bike then tried to swing herself up. But she swung herself over to the other side and landed on her butt.

Emilio laughed at her. "You better not laugh too hard, *señor*, or you'll break an arm."

They lost their breath in laughter. Emilio had a way of curling his lower lip under and looking just a little nervous when he lost himself in laughter like that. It made Petra want to protect him.

Round and round the little yard, dust kicking up around them until their skin became a shade darker. They kept climbing on, pushing forward, falling off.

Petra figured it out first. Her body felt it, the balance that just seemed to happen. "OK, here's the thing. You have to stop thinking. Get on and imagine yourself balanced on a cloud, way above this dust—and you'll just go!"

Of course, he didn't just go. He fell over so many times his skin was red and scraped from running into the ground. Petra skinned an elbow and scraped both knees. They looked like dusty twins swerving and bobbling, crashing into this palm tree and that woodpile.

Emilio cocked a brow and pursed his lips tightly. His eyes traced a resolute path across the yard. And so found his balance. The triumphant warriors whooped in anticipation of future travels.

"Like Chac!" Petra shouted in her glee.

"Say what?" No one told Emilio Mayan stories like her Nonno did for her.

"You don't know Chac? His nose was long and curly, like this handle-bar. A conquering warrior, like us! And he made rain and threw bolts of lightning—especially when kids flew down hills on their bikes, to show how amazing it felt!"

Emilio's voice sang out, louder than usual. "Petra, let's ride down to my house, so I can show my mom!" In the joy of the moment, he neglected his usual awkwardness.

Off they went, gazing delightedly at each other. Walking their bikes down the scrubby hill from her house to the mango tree, turning right on the dirt road. Wavering on their bikes at first, then overtaking the hens who sneaked under the barbed wire fence and clucked about while they did their best to interfere with travelers. Shouting out to Vicenta at the store, and to an aging neighbor who leaned over the corn stand-ing in her small garden, jolted by spinning wheels rapidly crossing her line of vision. Spraying dirt toward the mud houses, the shacks with tin roofs, the occasional wood-framed house. All the while bantering back and forth, swept up by the wind sailing through their hair as they sped along by bike.

They turned left at the jacaranda tree, at the corner of another dirt path that led down the hill to Emilio's house. In full bloom, the flowers of the jacaranda radiated purple amidst its fine, glorious spread of fern-like leaves, reaching across and above the road, shining beauty and hope on everything in its expanse.

Petra loved going to Emilio's house just so she could feel enveloped by those purple flowers. She picked up a couple of fallen blooms from the ground and wound the stems around the springs under Emilio's seat, so the flowers waved along beside him.

And then they both stopped and quickly dismounted the bikes, dropping them and the flowers that hadn't yet tumbled off. All trace of joyousness evaporated into terror at the spot where Emilio's mother lay, her body spread thin on the ground in front of his house, a gash in the side of her head. Ragged bits of a bottle stuck to her matted hair, blood pooling and parting into channels around slivers of glass.

Emilio screamed, "Mamá, what's going on? What's happened?" Petra had never seen him like this. His face turned pale; his brows drew together. His hands fluttered, as if trying to land on the thing he needed to do next. His eyes bulged with fright and darted between his mother and the house. Petra followed his glance to the house, expecting, hoping someone else would emerge.

Señora Aquejado's voice cracked feebly, "*M' hijito*, run and get help. Your father has run off, and I can't get up." Indeed, she seemed barely able to form words.

Already crying hysterically, Emilio said, "Petra, I have to stay with my mamá. Run as fast as you can and get help!"

"But where? Where should I go?" The seams of the world were tearing apart. The adult world was pulling on them both, and it hurt.

"Go, Petra, just go!" So banished, she turned and ran, leaving the bikes in a pile at the entrance to his house.

She tore back up the path toward the road, toward help, desperately thinking what to do. As she approached the road, she peeked through the foliage. What luck, there was a car parked in the ditch, its windows darkly tinted. She put her face to the window, looking for the driver to beg a ride.

Seeing no one, she turned to sprint up the road. Instead, she almost slammed into a middle-aged man emerging out of the woods by the car. She skidded to a halt, gaping at the sight before her. Tattoos completely covered his shaved head. Petra had seen tattoos before, but not so many on one body.

The man held up a hand to stop her. He circled her, his face dimmed by a dry, pasty smile. "Need a ride to town?" He opened the car door for her, and she clambered in, desperate to get home quickly.

He sloughed off an outer shirt, baring sculpted shoulders and swollen muscles, all outlined in twirling tattoos. Gripping the steering wheel with one hand, his elbow stretched out, inches from her face. She stared at the words emblazoned in bright red on his forearm—"*Rosita, mi vida*." It was carved in extravagant lettering, the writing encircling a baby's head.

"Rosita, my mother," the man said.

"*Qué bonito*," Petra said. She squirmed uncomfortably. The cracked leather seat rubbed against her thigh, and a gold-colored chain hanging from the mirror threatened to swing into the side of her head.

"You'd think. But really, not. My mother ran off with another man when I was just a *patojo*. About your size." Wrinkles shot out of the corners of his eyes as they narrowed to slits.

Petra fiddled with the broken seat belt. "Please, sir, could you go fast? You can drop me at Vicenta's store."

"I got the tattoo when she came back a couple years later. She promised me the world, and I swore my undying love to her." He laughed cynically. "A few days later, *púf*, I never saw her again. The tattoo makes a fool out of me." The big vein in his neck was throbbing.

"It's just around the next bend."

But instead, he pulled the car off into a narrow path, tight enough that twigs and branches scraped along the sides of the car, tugging at the outside mirrors. A hundred feet in, he pulled to a stop and killed the motor.

She tried to pull the handle and squeeze out the door, but her hands felt like jelly. The muscles wouldn't do what her brain commanded. The man came around to her side and hauled her out. The dust turned to mud and pulled her to the earth. She struggled to move forward, away, but she was lost in a dream. Tattoos twisted around her. Weights clung to her feet. The man's hands were cold on her body.

She dragged herself up, shuddered in the cool air, and scrambled forward, crawling on her hands and feet. Tattoos bobbed through the trees as the man staggered away, his hands hovering about the waist of his pants. Once she regained her legs, she tore up the road. Something tacky rubbed against her thighs, and a white pastiness stuck to her hands when she tried to smooth her dress. Spasms of pain shot through her. A blank space grew in her mind.

Vicenta glanced out from her perch at the store with concern as she charged by, arms flailing, concentrated only on her destination. The only real clinic with a real doctor was in San Luis Hunahpu. In Las Leches, there was just the pharmacist, just Señor Menendez. Best to ask her grandparents.

Thankfully, Nonna was home when she got there, sweeping off the porch like it was just any ordinary day.

"Nonna! Nonna! What should I do?" Petra said through grasping breaths. She blinked to make her eyes focus. "I'm so late, I'm so sorry!" The guilt began to weigh on her.

"Quiet, child, what's wrong? What's happened?" Nonna batted at Petra's dress, which was stained as if she had rolled on the forest floor of green brush and sap.

"It's Emilio's mom. She's hurt, she needs help!"

Nonna sighed deeply, her jaw clenched. "Petra, catch your breath, and help me put a few things together. Then run to the village and get Señor Menendez. I'll meet you at Emilio's house."

They gathered up a couple of clean rags, a bucket of clean water, and a can of beer from the six-pack that Nonno had hidden behind the house. Petra wondered if Nonno knew she had discovered his hiding place.

In about half an hour, Petra breathlessly arrived with Señor Menendez, and found Nonna dribbling a few drops of beer into Señora Aquejado's mouth. The glass shards had been thrown aside, and Nonna was stroking Señora Aquejado's hair behind the gash. Petra backed off to let the adults do their work and stood next to Emilio. Her body suddenly felt heavy. She collapsed onto the ground, sitting cross-legged, her eyes fading into dark cesspools. But no, she couldn't give in to exhaustion. Her friend needed her help. She would be strong for him.

She rose again and said, "She'll be okay, Emilio. Just wait, everything will be all right." She touched his hand to comfort him.

Emilio abruptly flung her hand away. She stumbled backward, looking at him in surprise. His wide eyes burned like a shaft of lightning at the scene in front of him, but their gleam faded as he struggled to bear the sight. His face was streaked with tears mixed up with the dirt of their bike rides. His whole body had stiffened, rigid—with fear, or with she couldn't tell what.

Petra reacted as she picked herself up. She ignored the aching in her legs as she stood. "Emilio! *Jesucristo!*" Then, trying to help again, "Who can we get to help?"

"Girl, get out of my face. You can't help here. You have no idea what's going on."

Thoroughly rebuffed, Petra felt the legs of their bond cut out from under her. A distance opened up between Petra and Emilio, where she had never known distance before.

Was Emilio angry with her? Anger and pain lashed like whips in the air, becoming grievously intertwined. She felt wretched that she had taken so long to get help. If only—she had tried to run, but her legs had been so heavy. Why hadn't she gone faster?

But she hadn't had a chance to consider what had happened to his mother. Was it possible that she was completely ignorant about an essential part of Emilio's life? She thought they had shared everything. But she certainly couldn't ask now. Later. Later she would ask Emilio what he meant, and what had happened to his mother.

In the meantime, the situation wasn't improving, from what she could see. Nonna tried to clean the wound on his mom's head with water and alcohol, but Señora Aquejado was shaking and sweating. The blood slid down the side of her head in ugly streaks, running off to turn the dirt rusty brown. Señor Menendez kept pulling little bottles out of his bag, mixing liquids together and soaking bandages, then tying them around her head. Surely these two adults would take care of everything. That's what adults did.

Nonna spoke gently to Emilio's mom. "Liana, it is a beautiful day. Remember those beautiful days when you and my daughter Sorelly climbed the hills to try to reach the sky? You gave each other so much love, it was an example to me. Look at the blue sky, and the small, innocent clouds floating by. We are all like these innocent clouds, passing through this life, doing our best to make a contribution."

Why was Nonna talking to Señora Aquejado about the clouds? Now of all times. Emilio's mother and her mother had been friends? That was new information. Nonna continued: "The Bible says, 'Blessed be God, even the Father of our Lord Jesus Christ, the Father of mercies, and the God of all comfort; Who comforteth us in all our tribulation, that we may be able to comfort them which are in any trouble, by the comfort wherewith we ourselves are comforted of God.'" Prayer meant you should bow your head and feel great respect, so that's what Petra did.

Her voice barely audible, Señora Aquejado said, "May God protect you and your family."

Nonna raised her arms as if trying to touch the clouds. Suddenly a low moan escaped from her and enveloped the four of them. "She is gone," she said.

Shock descended from those clouds and engulfed all of them in a haze. Nonna sat down with Petra, and they wrapped their arms around each other. After a moment, Nonna grasped her hands before her and recited.

> "God is our refuge and strength, a very present help in trouble.
> Therefore will not we fear, though the earth be removed, and though the mountains be carried into the midst of the sea;
> Though the waters thereof roar and be troubled, though the mountains shake with the swelling thereof."

Emilio let out a sharp gasp, as if he were forcing his tears back inside. Abruptly rising, he picked up the flowers which had fallen from his bike and hurled them at the body of his mother. He grabbed hold of the bike and threw it into the woods next to the yard. And he fled. Hurtled into the woods, his legs kicking out his anger and confusion.

Señor Menendez bowed his head a moment and paid his respects to Señora Aquejado, to Nonna and to Petra and, quietly, he left. Petra stood and turned her face to Nonna, a bewildering sense of shock paralyzing her. Nonna held her without words, gently and silently.

Nonna abruptly stepped back as they became aware of heavy foot-steps hastening toward them from beyond the house. Petra recognized Emilio's father, Fernando, and the man with the tattoos. As soon as she registered the tattoos, she collapsed. Her legs shook uncontrollably. Her eyes refused to look at the tattooed man.

At her side, Petra's grandmother took her hand and pulled her up. Nonna almost fell back, too, as she looked up and took in the sight. Nonna whispered to Petra, "Go carefully, *mi amor*."

 Fernando's voice was harsh. "Where is that bitch woman? I told her to wait for me." Nonna looked down toward the spot where Señora Aquejado's body now rested. "What the hell! What is she lying there for?" Rust-colored stains marred his t-shirt, on the front of which Petra made out the words "Yale University, Lux et Veritas."

How could her friend Emilio have a father who was so blindly insensitive? And why was he wearing such a dirty shirt? Thankfully, in a moment, he realized the situation that lay before him. He flinched, but quickly controlled himself. This was not what he had expected, but he barreled forward.

"Gusano," he turned to his companion, "it seems we have a situation here. This woman has succumbed to her weakness." Why did he call this man "Worm"? Succumbed to her weakness? "I saw her just this morning—you know I was here, right? I told her to lay off the cocaine. She was begging me for more, and I told her she'd had enough. She was always garbage. She couldn't even please the father of her child enough to make me a nice breakfast when I came by this morning. Worthless woman. Well, now, she seems to have found her fate. May God Salva her!" His laugh made the most unpleasant sound Petra had ever heard. "Salvatrucha her!" Laughter mixed with hiccuping chortles. In the back of her mind, Petra echoed "Mara Salvatrucha." She tried to place the name. "Right, Gusano?"

Gusano had been wandering around, looking bored. Swords and boxes, letters and arrows, random lines, like someone had taken a pen to Gusano's head, first shaving the hair, then drawing all over his skull, face, down his neck to the line of his tight shirt. Like tattered ivy that had grown up his torso and he couldn't control, infecting his head. "Rosita" blared out from his arm—a sweet name for a mother. And his sneakers! Black and gray, with swoops of black on the side, and red soles lapping up the sides. She'd never seen shoes so fancy.

Gusano said, "*Vaya compadre*, let's blow out of here. What are you looking at, little girl?" Accusingly.

Petra quickly looked away. She couldn't seem to control her body, which was desperately quivering.

"Right, Gusano, give me just one minute though." Fernando turned to face Petra and Nonna. He grabbed little Petra by the shoulder, pushing her into the earth, making her knees buckle. Nonna glared a warning at him. "Don't worry, old woman, I'm not going to hurt anybody. Not yet. You all take care of this little situation here, right? And keep your mouths shut, if you know what's good for you. And Petrita, have you seen my son? Where is he?"

She couldn't answer, but she couldn't not answer. Petra didn't understand anything. This was Emilio's father. She hadn't seen much of him all the time she'd known Emilio. When she visited with Emilio at his house, he usually wasn't home. Emilio always said he was out working, so she figured that was normal.

What was wrong with him? But it was clear he expected an answer. Was Emilio going to be in trouble? Could she expect this man to act like a father should?

She blurted out, "He ran off. I think he was upset. That way," pointing to the woods. She fought to get her composure back. Had she said the right thing?

The cute curl to Emilio's lower lip was apparently a family trait, but in his father it became a menacing snarl. "You did good, *muchachita*. Don't worry about anything. I'll take care of him."

Petra shivered with the cold that had come upon her as they marched off into the woods the way Emilio had gone. Suddenly, she couldn't contain the cold enveloping her. Nonna held her shoulders and whispered to her, but the cold penetrated.

Her feet suddenly dragged like frozen blocks, so heavy she couldn't lift them. Purple flower petals floated to the ground as she trembled. The sky filled with menace. Ash fell from the clouds, covering everything in gray. Red ribbons blew by. Dust and ashes shrouded the sky.

Petra cast about for support, searching the trees, the vast sky, her vague memories of her mother. The cold lifted, and she found herself embraced by Alocinia.

- I am here, Petra.
- I can see your shape, but not your color.
- There is no need of color. Keep your head high. Your friend is within you.
- He is gone, Alocinia. He ran away, and everyone hurts.
- Dust and ashes weigh little. They blow away in the breeze.
- Yes, and they resettle in new places. The more I sweep them off our porch, the more they settle in our yard. When I return to the kitchen, they follow me there. See how they cover the flowers?

- Nothing is complete, Petra. We have to keep sweeping.
- Will you stay with me?
- Yes, if you look, I am here.
- Why can't I see your color?
- You have the color, Petra.
- My color has faded. It is my fault. My legs hurt, and I couldn't make them run.
- Something got in your way.
- Do you see the flowers drifting by, Alocinia?
- Of course. You can catch them if you like. But better to let them go.
- Twisting tattoos, on the trees, plastered on the ground.
- The earth is innocent. So are you, Petra.
- I don't want the flowers. I don't feel cold anymore, so I will follow my grandmother. She's gotten ahead.

Petra tried to shake off the grime and ache. When she caught up, she reached out her hand to grasp Nonna's.

The emotions of that little girl overwhelmed Petra as she sat on the church bench. She wiped a tear from the corner of her eye. For a moment, she wanted to clasp Emilio's hand, the jacaranda petals held tightly between their palms.

A month or two after Emilio's mother died, Petra and Nonna paused at the San Luis Hunahpu market between two vendors, a mound of onions on one side, a pile of coconuts on the other. Early morning haze hung over the cacophony of farmers, almost all of whom had trudged miles from their farms in the humble corners of the surrounding hills, their wares wrapped and bound in tarps and carried on their backs and heads. The Mayan Quiché world that only vaguely surrounded her daily life moved front and center at the market, where the bustle and festivity nourished her distant roots in that world, but also repelled her in its stark poverty.

The occasional shawl and *huipil* she spotted in Las Leches multiplied at the market into a delightful array of sights and smells as she wove in and out, content to greet faces she saw only a dozen times a year. A store in Las Leches might have a few peaches, half a dozen oranges, and a couple of old tomatoes, another store a different batch of ordinary items. But here, in one swoop, she could indulge her senses with the rich patchwork of commodities. The smells mingled in a sensual feast.

The tableau of the plaza was an uproar of brilliant colors. It was as if droves of hummingbirds and quetzals had flown down to the market, dancing, prancing, dropping their resplendent feathers and mixing their aspirations. A palette of rainbows in the traditional woven clothing and tapestries covered the women's bodies. Floors and tables were laden with merchandise that shimmered and hung from every hook and rod of the stalls. Gaudy orange and red tomatoes twinkled in the misty light, piled in pyramids as tall as the soiled children counting up the sales. Makeshift ground covers and tables were littered with earthy green avocados, aromatic pineapples, and tiny speckled bananas which defied gravity in their delicate curves, and calabazas bursting out of their thick skins.

Petra sorted through tomatoes under the watchful gaze of an elderly, strikingly elegant Mayan woman. She was about to comment on the woman's brilliant blue headwrap, which so gracefully set off her dress, vivid as a scarlet macaw, when she glimpsed Emilio out of the corner of her eye. Emilio, whom she hadn't been able to talk to since the day of his mother's death.

Several rows away, his father was gesturing roughly at him, and he was nodding, edging away from his father. And suddenly a slab of meat from the butcher's table was in Emilio's hands, then tossed into a bag slung over his shoulder. In the same instant that Petra registered shock, the butcher looked up startled and began to formulate an objection, but Emilio had already bolted off beyond the confines of the market stalls, until Petra lost sight of him amid the ever-shifting throng.

What was Emilio doing? He never stole things.

She abandoned the tomatoes and took off in pursuit of Emilio, vendors grumbling as she shoved by them. Her desperation to finally talk to him propelled her legs. In the field beyond the market, she caught up with him. She always had been faster than him.

Black and bluish-green streaks radiated from his eye and coursed across the soft skin of his cheek. His eyes flickered back and forth, as if he couldn't still his mind to stand and talk to her. She'd better not mention the eye, though.

The surrounding area contrasted with the market in its drab humility. Wind picked up litter discarded at the market and blew it about the field. A few hardy blades of grass poked out of the open field of dirt, tumbleweed trudged slowly across, and random pieces of concrete lay about, as if blown there, but more likely were jettisoned by a neighbor building a new home. The stench of dried mud complete with garbage and the urine of men who had relieved themselves after imbibing beer the night before hovered thickly around them.

"Emilio! Where are you? I miss you. Justina misses you, too."

"Petra, I can't talk to you anymore. My papá—my papá—you can't come around anymore. You have to leave me alone!" One leg lifted with the resolve to run off, but his flashing eyes clung to her and bound his feet to the ground.

Petra's heart tore a little. "But... I just want us to be friends."

Emilio began to speak faster and faster, piling words on top of each other. "My papá is teaching me things. Important things. To survive, because he says the world is a cruel place, and we have to learn to come out on top. There's all these bad people, and we have to fight to survive, it doesn't matter if it hurts, we just have to prove we're the strongest, then we'll be okay. But we won't be okay, so I have to learn what to do, even before my father tells me, and it's too important to waste time in school, we have to make money and be fierce."

"Emilio, what are you talking about?" It seemed that being with Emilio now was an exercise in sorting through confusion. The colored petals she couldn't reach, the cold that made no sense. The pain of loss, the ache of legs unable to progress.

He gulped his breath. "Anyway, we can't be friends anymore. My papá—my papá—he wants me to stay with him. I don't want him to get mad at me." He kept repeating papá like it wouldn't stick to him, like he had to remember.

The thought slammed into Petra's mind that this was her fault. She had delayed too long in getting help to his mother, so long she had bled to death. If she'd only been faster. If she were Emilio, she probably wouldn't want to be friends with her either. She didn't know why she hadn't run faster for help. The tattooed man had given her a ride, but then there was a delay. It had felt like her feet were stuck in the mud.

At least that's what had happened in her dreams since that day. A terrifying feeling held her to one place, mud like white glue clasping at her legs, and she couldn't run, couldn't get help.

She could apologize to Emilio, but that would be such a trivial response compared to the life-altering consequences for him.

Successive gusts of wind gave rise to a cloud of dust around them which sucked the moisture out of her mouth. Rolls of tumbleweed came flying toward them and momentarily became tangled up in her legs. Once she cleared away the gritty murkiness, she said to Emilio, "What's wrong with you? And why are you stealing? You aren't like that!"

"Things change, Petra. You don't understand. Stay out of it, okay?" He was pleading with her. But whether to stay away from him, or to help him, she wasn't sure. Emilio looked at her directly for the first time, squinting like his eyes had to adjust to her presence.

Petra could barely discern their bond in his eyes, but his words told her to leave him alone. She'd gone down to his house at least three times since Emilio hadn't reappeared at school. He had stomped around his yard, punched at trees, and told her to go away. At least she had his attention this time.

He used his free hand to cover his eyes from the glare of the sun, just rising above the market stands, and his feet kicked at the dirt. "It's another world you don't want to know about." He gave a full-throated sigh, the kind she wouldn't expect to hear from a kid her own age. "My father says if we make that butcher suffer a little now, then he'll respect my father and me. Now he knows we're serious when we tell him to make contributions to us. And Gusano, my papá's friend, will believe he can trust me, that I'm old enough. And my papá —" Emilio swallowed hard; his eyes screwed up tight.

"Old enough for what, Emilio? You're only ten!"

"Old enough to... to... so they don't have to force me to do things." Without thinking, Emilio touched the bruise around his eye, and a glimmer of what was happening came through to Petra. Emilio was holding back. His face was red with the effort. This was a whole new world to her, and she was quickly losing her friend to it. Emilio turned away—in shame? wanting to go? to avoid showing her his tears?

Petra desperately wanted to hang on to this moment. There must be some way to help him break through the wall that was quickly being built around him—by whom?—but maybe he didn't know how to let her in. She had to find a way to reach him, somehow.

He began to walk on, and Petra started to leave. If she had a tail, anyone would have seen it then, hanging defeated between her legs.

Petra turned toward Emilio. Her voice slowly rose in despair. "Emilio. What if—Can we just—Why can't you...?" The right words were so close, if she could just find them. "I miss you, Emilio. You. Not this person your father wants you to be. You. I miss you!" And with that, she hurried back to the market and rejoined Nonna.

And on that church bench, Petra cried for the loss of her friendship with Emilio. The boy she had known disappeared into the world of his father, never to be found again. The new Emilio reappeared to harass and threaten her. And he reappeared when he took Justina from her. But thinking about Emilio and Justina at the same time hurt like a festering infection. She thrust the thought to the ground and smashed it into the cement floor.

Petra reached a hand out toward Nonna, but it landed on an empty bench. Nonna had gotten up and was talking to Deacon Eduardo over near the confessionals.

Emilio had turned into another person, a mean and destructive person, lost to her forever. She didn't care about him anymore. She hated him, for the awful gang he was part of and the terrible things he was involved with now, had been involved with for years now.

Petra lowered herself to her knees in prayer and struggled to shift to more compassionate thoughts. She quieted herself for several minutes. Sniffling and wiping her cheeks, she tried to get Nonna's attention. She crossed herself as she stood.

The Deacon motioned for her to stay a moment. Surprised, she pushed her way along the pews toward them. Nonna told Petra she would wait for her outside and left them alone.

Eduardo was not from the neighborhood, and she did not know him well. Like the priest, Padre Correa, he had come from Bolivia only a few months ago. Eduardo was a young man, in his early thirties, though his mostly balding head made him look older. Despite his serious, studious appearance with his wire-framed glasses and thick brows, he had a warm presence. He had a good rapport with many of the Catholic youth like Petra, and he took a more familiar tone with them than other respected adults did.

"Petra, I am happy to see you here today. You will play soccer at the match this weekend, yes?" He, too, played soccer on the local field, like many of the young men of the area, but unlike those men, he also supported the girls' team, frequently going to Petra's games. "It's a big game, with San Luis Hunahpu, no?"

"Yes, Deacon Eduardo, I believe we will beat them."

"Oh, well, I expect so. Take care to keep humility about you, however." He smiled.

"Sorry, Reverend Deacon. I am carried away in my excitement. I have been anticipating this game for many weeks."

"I do understand. Petra, could you call me Eduardo, please? It's so much easier."

"Yes, sir, I will try."

"Can you sit with me for a few minutes? We have not had a chance to chat." He pointed to the front pew. Petra took a seat on the pew behind Eduardo. He turned to face her.

"Petra, you are a fine young woman. I see you here at the church many times a week. Your grandmother is concerned that you may be troubled. I have seen you now several times, sitting somberly on that bench in the back. I wonder if you would allow me to help."

Why would Nonna have talked to Eduardo about her? She felt self-conscious under his kind gaze, his prominent eyebrows arched in anticipation. "Thank you, Eduardo, your words are kind. I try my best. It is true, though, that my head is always full of questions."

Eduardo removed his glasses and said, "What can I help with? I know these are difficult times for young people."

He gazed at her with unassuming patience. So many things worried her. Where to start? It was easier to remain silent. Silence was slippery, sliding over her like a perfectly fitted sock, or sidling up next to her like a poisonous snake. Speaking seemed more of a risk. Still, how could she do all the things she wanted to accomplish in her life if she didn't speak up?

"Well, Deacon." She spoke slowly, choosing her words with care. "I cannot deny that I have ambitions. I am afraid I do not have the humility a woman needs to be content here. I want to study. I will complete my ninth year of school this year, and I am afraid I will not be able to continue to high school in San Luis Hunahpu."

"You speak well for yourself, Petra. Please don't worry that you do not show sufficient humility. Humility before God is not the same as accepting a life you do not want. What is your ambition then?"

Petra had shared her true ambitions only with her grandfather, and no one else, out of a sense that her goals were presumptuous, and completely unrealistic. She looked toward her feet. "You will not scoff if I tell you?"

"Absolutely not."

The cock of his head and softness in his eyes communicated his sincerity. Tentatively, she opened the door, willing to see what might happen. "I want to help people. To make a difference. But with real skill and knowledge, so I can really help them. People like my uncle with his diabetes. I want to stop the bleeding. I want to be a doctor, Deacon." If only she could become a doctor, she could give others in the community reason to hope.

"I am glad we are sitting! You are quite serious?"

The stethoscope would swing from her neck. The cool blue jacket over a clean white shirt. If she could just figure out how to take small steps toward her dream, then she would walk tall and know it wasn't just a pipe dream.

Petra hesitated, but nodded her head. "I know very little, Eduardo. I know that. I go to a small village school, and I have never walked even as far as that volcano." The majestic Sibalq'aq volcano with its hovering, small white clouds loomed in the distance beyond the church spire. There it had overshadowed Petra her whole life. She often dreamed of climbing it, imagining what she might find beyond it.

"Have you done anything to explore the world of medicine, Petra?"

"I have seen only the pharmacy here and a small clinic in San Luis

Hunahpu. I read what I can, but there are few books in our *aldea* or in Las Leches. It is an unrealistic goal, I know. Just a dream. I do not mean to burden you with my silly ideas."

"Do not diminish your dreams, Petra. They are the most important things we have, and the most important seeds from which we grow into the world. Even better, dreams are an indication of faith."

Petra blushed. She always carried faith in her mind's eye. Alocinia glowed with encouragement. "Eduardo, may I share something else with you? It is harder to talk about."

"Please, it would be a privilege to hear your thoughts."

"I am afraid. I try not to think about it, but I am afraid. There is so much violence, Deacon. I do not want to become resigned to 'fate,' and I don't want to accept that bad things will always happen."

Eduardo sighed. There was only so much he could offer. "Do you know who St. Augustine was?"

"I know very little, Deacon."

"Forgive me if I give you a mini-sermon to mull over in the upcoming days. New thoughts can give us a new approach to our fears."

"I feel honored. Please."

"Augustine was an important Christian philosopher. He lived during the early fifth century when the Roman Empire was beginning to disintegrate, so it is easy to imagine the chaos and violence that surrounded his life. It is unfortunately enlightening to consider Rome in light of the circumstances here in Guatemala.

"He believed that the grace of Christ is indispensable to human freedom. God is most apparent when we feel that we are mortally insufficient to the world, and the world is mortally insufficient to us. Augustine said that God loves each of us as an only child. I know that, here in Guatemala, in times like this, this is hard to believe.

"In Revelations 21 it says God shall wipe away all the tears from people's eyes; there shall be no more death, neither sorrow, nor crying, neither shall there be any more pain: for the former things are passed away."

"But Deacon... How can this be true? People have always suffered. When is this time when there will be no more death or sorrow?"

"Biblical passages can be difficult to understand, Petra. Augustine was a gentle soul who believed that human nature is flawed. He taught that we must have compassionate tolerance for those who sin in their weakness. True freedom, he said, could only be achieved through a long process by which his or her will is healed by the grace of God. Lasting joy and wealth of soul can only be found ultimately in God's kingdom.

"Petra, there is a reason that people continue to find hope in the most unlikely places. Jews found hope in their Exodus from Egypt, and we will find hope here because God is within us and shows us the way. We must listen. It is not meant to be easy."

"Do you think Augustine would have compassion for the gangs who attack young girls and steal from people?" She said it almost under her breath.

"Yes, Petra, even for them."

Petra stared at the ceiling, trying to prevent the Deacon from seeing her moist eyes. Had Nonna talked with him about her desire that Petra forgive Emilio? Suddenly, the confines of the church were smothering her. She needed to go outside, right away. "I must go now, Deacon, but I will think about your words."

Eduardo lifted his last words to reach her as she made for the exit. "One more word, Petra. About becoming a doctor, all is possible. The world is not insufficient to us when we have faith. I will look into what I might do to help, and you must make your own inquiries and take your own steps to realize your dreams."

The door swung shut. The wooden cross out in front hung over her as she went on her way. She would do her best to show God that she was mortally sufficient to the world. She ignored the young men drinking and arguing on the wall of the waterless fountain in the plaza.

CHAPTER FIVE

Nonna turned toward the hills where Carlos was still working and leaned heavily on her broom, until she abruptly angled the broom against the wall of the porch and clutched her stomach. Stooped over, she hobbled to the bench and delicately sat down. The bench creaked under her weight.

The weekend had gone by, the afternoon sun was thinning, and Petra was coming up over the hill, her head bowed in concentration. Her attention caught by Nonna's distress, Petra hastened to her grandmother's side and put her arm around her shoulder. Nonna's eyes lifted toward Petra, and a big smile that showed off the gap where her front teeth used to be greeted her. "You don't need to take care of everyone, *m' hijita*. You're turning into a young woman now. You don't have to be so strong and independent."

As if Nonna herself wasn't loath to let anyone help her.

"Someday soon a man is going to win you over and take care of you," Nonna continued.

Petra backed away. Her grandmother was always so obsessed with her delicate womanhood! Petra would rather continue to mull over the Deacon's words about taking steps toward her future than assess her femininity, or lack thereof.

The weekend had gone by; the routine of hopes and tensions began anew. She badly needed a bit of Nonno's wisdom.

Nonna might have learned from the experience of Sorelly, Petra's mother, that marrying at sixteen years old didn't always work out so well.

Maybe Nonna feared that she wouldn't be up to the task of caring for Petra much longer. She wasn't oblivious to what made her grandmother worry. Petra compensated by taking on extra household chores and keeping conversation as joyful as possible. She would not add to Nonna's burdens.

"That reminds me—I made you an appointment to get your hair styled by Pepa at the market next Saturday." Her voice held a hint of pleading.

"Ay, Nonna, you know I want to cut my hair short, not get it styled. So it won't get in my face when I'm playing soccer." She laughed.

"I've been meaning to talk to you about that soccer. I don't think it's safe for you anymore. And you know I don't approve of cutting your beautiful long hair."

"Ay, no, I have to play soccer. It's a big game that weekend!"

"You're a good, girl, Petrita. But don't forget you're a young woman now, and it's time you let the boys look at you sometimes."

"Nonna, *se lo ruego*. Let me alone about Emilio, *please*." Anything to change the conversation. "I'm going to get my chores done now. Nonna, will you come see my soccer game on Saturday?"

"*Niña*, I need you next Saturday. You need to go to the market for us, and you know your mother expects your call then from the Tienda Nuñez in town. She wants to talk to you."

It was so awkward, going to a store an hour from home to make phone calls. Grudgingly, Petra had agreed to go through the process about once a month when they were at the market in San Luis Hunahpu. If they could just count on regular money from her mother, they could buy a cell phone. "About what?"

"Well," Nonna hesitated. "*No lo sé*. Your mother has her own point of view."

"About *what*, Nonna?" Petra insisted, irritation in her voice.

Feebly, Nonna said, "Probably... *quizás*, about Emilio." Her tone rising, "And maybe about keeping yourself safe."

Petra ached to go now. Talking to her mother was hard, and she didn't know what to do about it. She'd rather not think about it.

Whose child was she? Children should have parents to wipe away the tears. She longed for a real mother. Not one who "sacrificed" by living so far from her daughter. Her mother couldn't hug her from so far away. She couldn't feel her mother's hand guiding her. Why did she give birth to Petra if she didn't mean to give her love and support?

A few months ago, when they talked, her mother cried again. "Oh, Petita, how I miss you," she said. And her mother bawled and sniffled into the speaker.

It happened this way far too often. Petra buried herself in silence.

Her mother tried to draw her out. "Petra, how is school?" she would ask.

But it was too big a question. How could Petra explain that the work was too easy? That she felt like she knew as much as her teacher? So she demurred. "It's okay, I guess."

"I'm sorry for crying, Petra. I know that's not what you need to hear. What's your teacher like this year?"

Petra fidgeted with the phone's wire, wrapping it around her fingers. "Nothing special, mamá. She's just a teacher. She's kind of quiet for a teacher."

An awkward silence. Petra tried to think of something to say, but nothing came. She wanted to hang up. In a feeble effort, she said, "How's work?"

Her mother said, "It's better now that I have my certification as a nursing assistant. I have more work now. But I'm tired, Petra. I lift older people on and off toilets a lot."

"Oh." Petra grasped for something else to say. "Why don't their children help?" she asked.

"Their children live far away, across the country in California." A pause. "Like I live far away from my children." Petra imagined the teardrops falling on her mother's phone again. She held the phone away from her face. Nonno grabbed it, and he took over the conversation from there.

Petra was silent the rest of the day after that call. She didn't know what to feel, so she decided not to feel anything.

Gravely, she said, "Nonna, I have to play. The team is counting on me. I can go to the market in the morning before the game."

A shadow dampened her grandmother's expression. Her grandmother loved her, but she loved Petra's mother, her own daughter Sorelly, too. "I'm sorry, Nonna. It's just, my mother seems so far away..."

Nonna said, "I know, *niña*, but remember that she has struggled." Nonna hung her head, heavy with her own burdens.

Unexpectedly, a warmth surrounded Petra. She couldn't fit under a platform bed anymore, but she remembered when she did. It was almost her only memory of her mother.

Misty brown eyes peered out at her world from a corner under her parents' bed. Petra's five-year-old eyes were so blurred with tears that she couldn't see the small details like the fleas hopping about or the dirt of the floor blackening her hands and smudging her dress.

Carlos's feet darted back and forth in front of her. Grimy toes jutted out from his *huaraches*. Petra squeezed her eyes shut to block out the scene before her and tried to turn her mind away. While she was searching for a happier memory, the *huaraches* passed by in front of her. Her heart gasped again. She hoped they would stop and he would bend down and show her his face.

Carlos was wailing while struggling to catch his breath. Petra couldn't hear what he was yelling because she fixed her hands firmly over her ears. The terrible sounds persisted, though, only muffled—yelling, banging, crashing, a series of thuds. She pressed her palms harder against the sides of her head.

The next time Carlos's feet went by, Petra stuck her hand out to grab his ankle, moving one hand from an ear for just an instant. If she could bury her head into his shoulder, then possibly her father's eyes could shine again, too. Even though Carlos was only eight years old, he shielded her from her father's rages. Now, though, his leg shook her off, and he continued to flounder unsteadily around the room.

The voices were smothered, but they'd be painfully loud if she uncovered her ears. Last time, her father had tripped over a chair when he was drunk and blamed her mother for putting the chair there. Actually, that had been Petra's fault because she had moved the chair to make a bigger space to play.

Petra suspected it would be a few days before her mother left the house, like usual when she had a black eye or a swollen lip.

When she tilted her head so her cheek touched the dirt, Petra could see her father's scuffed gray field shoes, with the gaping holes at the big toes, rush toward the shelves at the front side of the house. Then one foot positioned itself in front of the other, the back one raised up on his toes, and the weight shifted fast to the front one. A crash, then her mother's scream, and her mother's body joined her bare feet on the ground. Suddenly Petra could see almost all of her mother.

Petra screamed through her tears. Carlos's feet ran toward their mother, but then his back end was on the ground, launched along the dirt floor until Petra heard the crunch of his body meeting the wall. She wished Carlos would join her under the bed instead of pretending he was strong enough to protect their mother.

Carlos remained motionless against the wall for a minute. He shot Petra a reassuring if unsteady grin. She sighed in relief that he could still move as his body began to slide along the ground toward their father's feet.

Petra wadded up her eyes, closing even the little slit, so she could block it all out. Her hand came off her ears for a moment so she could smear the tears away and wipe her nose on her dress. As her grimy cheeks dried, her face tightened. The plastered mud on her cheeks cracked into small crevices when her eyes crumpled up in terror.

Her mother's voice came from the far side of the eating table: "An iron, Xavier! Stop now! Think of the kids…. Carlos, stay back!"

Carlos was crawling on hands and knees, trying to plant himself between their parents.

Then the iron lay inert, having bounced off the table leg back toward the center of the room.

Quickly, Petra slapped her palms back over her ears. She tried to think of good things. She thought of her brother sleeping next to her on their wooden bed at night, and the rolls of sugar cookies with just a little smattering of chocolate on top from Vicenta's store down at the road.

Her father's footsteps stomped out the door. Carlos's feet moved as if to follow him. She heard the wooden latch drop down across the doorway to secure them inside. Petra breathed.

She crawled out from under the bed and went to her mother. Her father had gone. There was an off chance he had evaporated into thin air.

Carlos began to pick up the objects their father had thrown about the room. A glass bottle was shattered on the table. Clay bowls and plates lay strewn about the floor. The parrot had flown up into the eaves, but now drifted down to its perch above the corn grinder. "*Buenos días! Buenos días!*" Squawking replaced the yelling.

She and her mother took hold of each other in a deep embrace. Her left ear savored the intense softness of her mother's stomach.

Her mother put her fingers to her swelling eye and said in a numb voice, "*Ya basta, no más*, Petra. No more."

Petra looked up beseechingly at her mother. Carlos said, in his boldest little boy's voice, "I'll kill him next time."

"No, Carlitos. I need to leave. I will go to the United States. None of us can live this way. I can get a real job there and send money for your food and school. You'll be safer without me here."

Petra's small voice trembled with dismay. "Mamá, you're going to leave us?"

Tears came to her mother's eyes. But her voice emerged strong and certain. "As soon as I get settled there, I'll send for the two of you. It will be better, you'll see. I will leave soon. Your Nonno and Nonna will watch out for you."

Petra turned away from her mother to hide the tear sliding down her dirt-smeared cheek.

Quiet seeped into the crevices of the house. With her father out, Petra could imagine what peace might feel like. She crawled onto her wooden bed and tugged the sheet up around her neck.

Her mother whispered. "Petita, do you like hummingbirds?"

"They're very beautiful, mamá."

"I have something I want you to keep, *m'hija*. Your Nonno gave it to me long ago, when I was your age."

Petra sat up with renewed attention.

Her mother drew something from her pocket, enclosing it in her hand. The hand stayed closed even though Petra stared hard. She thought she saw a faint light drift through the cracks between her mother's fingers. Her mother's hand lay in Petra's open palm. Petra felt a pressure, then a rough coolness.

"Close your hand around it," her mother said. But it didn't fit as well in Petra's hand as it had in her mother's. She touched her stretched hand to her cheek, and the object warmed. She looked. A simple clay hummingbird lay now in her own palm. One gentle eye flickered behind a broken beak. Only a small curl of yellow adorned its green wings. Petra kissed it.

"What is its name, mamá?"

"I have called her Alocinia."

"Alocinia," Petra mused. "Yes. That's her name."

"Here is her story. Listen now."

Petra slunk down into her bed, but her eyes tilted up to her mother's. Her mother's voice rippled like a delicate song.

Long ago," her mother began, "at the very beginning of everything, the people had a hard life. Their lives were even more challenging than your life, Petita. One year, a great drought dried up all the crops, and the people began to starve. They began to lose faith in the Earth Mother. In anger, they called on the Mother to help them. A great thunderstorm came that tore down trees, washed away the fragile land, and burned their houses. Then the rains stopped and didn't return for four years.

"The people noticed that the only creature that still seemed to thrive was the hummingbird.

Petra interrupted. "Mamá, I think it was a mistake not to respect their Mother."

"Hush, Petra, listen. People had already observed that the humming-bird was so fragile and light and beautiful that she could approach the most delicate openings of a flower without moving a single petal. Her feathers glowed in the sun like drops of rain and reflected all the colors. Her long tongue let it bypass the often tough and bitter outer layer to find the hidden treasures underneath. She lived on nectar and searched for the sweetness of life.

In her fascination with her mother's story, Petra forgot to worry about her mother leaving her.

"So the people watched the hummingbird to see how she lived. They found that the hummingbird had a secret passageway to the underworld, where she would go to gather honey. The gods had assigned to the hum-mingbird a job as subtle and light as the bird—she was in charge of car-rying the thoughts of humans between the earth and the gods.

"Some people tried to enter the passage to get honey for themselves but could not enter. Only the hummingbird had access because only she had never lost faith in the Mother. When they understood this, the people were inspired to regain their faith. Soon, the Mother took care of them again. The hummingbird opened people's hearts. When the hurt that caused them to close their hearts got a chance to heal, their hearts were free to open again.

Petra held tightly to the lingering specter, wrapping the beauty of the hummingbird around her like a colorful *rebozo*. Her eyes were closed, the clay hummingbird grasped tightly in a hand which caressed her cheek. Its heartbeat began to pulse against her palm. She would talk to this Alocinia. Later.

The wooden bed groaned as her mother stood. She gathered a few things together then ran over the hills to her parents' house.

Petra didn't need her mother anymore, anyway. At least she had Alocinia.

"Nonna, come see me play, please! You can go to the field with my uncle Tonyo. Please, Nonna." Tonyo would play the same day on the men's team.

Perking up a little, Nonna said, "It's still over a week away. We'll see. Go along now and take the clothes down to the stream. Go on."

"A quick question, Nonna? Isn't there something in the Bible about dust and ashes? What is it?"

Dust and ashes surrounded her life, threatening pure discouragement. How could she do battle against them so her legs didn't stick in the mud, like they did in her dreams? Last year it didn't even rain enough to create the mud that nourished the beans and corn, and in turn the cows and chickens. Did that mean the sorrow had gained ground?

Her Nonna's mind held verses of the Bible like a safe box. When asked, she could explain what they meant and make references from one Bible story to another. An amazing feat, since Petra was pretty sure Nonna was almost illiterate and couldn't read anything else.

Nonna said, "Job uses the phrase. God 'hath cast me into the mire, and I am become like dust and ashes. I cry unto thee, and thou dost not hear me: I stand up, and thou regardest me not.' His heart is in turmoil, and he worries that God has deserted him."

Petra smiled at the elegance of the biblical passage. "Don't you see dust and ashes all around, Nonna?" Petra asked.

Nonna scrutinized Petra, squinting her eyes. "You mustn't go down that road, Petita. Times are hard, but if you look for the right way, you will find it. Job is a good story, though. He was a good man, but God sorely tested him, subjecting him to one tragedy after another. He finally decided that God knew best, and he would respect God by following the path of goodness. Don't lose your faith, Petra. Your best defense to the problems of this world is a good heart."

From somewhere in the recesses of her mind, Petra recalled a story she had heard once about a hummingbird who opened people's hearts because she never lost faith in Mother Earth.

CHAPTER SIX

Under the mango tree, Carlos and a group of young men were hanging out and bantering with Vicenta through the doorway of her little store.

Now in late March, the summer season had turned the hill into a fine dust. By the time she returned, climbing the hill up to home again, momentarily clean and refreshed from the stream, a thin layer of mud, that mixture of sweat and dust that stayed with them almost constantly would again cover her.

Vicenta didn't sell much, but she had a few essentials – beer and cigarettes for the guys, candy and cookies for the kids. It was a close space—just a few shelves. But what really drew people to the store was the gossip. Vicenta knew everything that was going on.

Petra stepped into the store to get a bar of soap for the laundry. Carlos made an excuse to the guys at the tree and followed her inside. Carlos did keep an eye on her, Petra had to admit. With any luck, it was because he cared about her.

A musty odor lived in the old, damp floorboards. Petra paid her respects to a portrait of Jesus cradling the lost lamb above the shelf of beer, barely lit by the crack of bright light that came in through the doorway. Vicenta shifted to the side of the doorway so Petra could get through.

The hinges of the door to the storage closet in the back of the store squeaked. A set of fingers, the nails painted light blue, pulled the door closed from the back side. Petra's head cocked to the side to get a better view, but Vicenta shifted her stance and bumped against her. Vicenta always worked alone. Who was back there?

Vicenta was chatting with Don Fabio, their elderly neighbor with the fine house, when Petra got there. Her face broke out into a warm smile when she saw Petra.

About the same age as her grandmother, but a little more spritely, Vicenta found herself at the center of village talk. People came and went from her store all day, from as far away as San Luis Hunahpu. The gossip fed the people of the area, hungry for something beyond their immediate lives to munch on.

As far as Petra knew, Vicenta had never married or had kids. Some people thought that made her a loose woman, or at least eccentric. They couldn't figure why she didn't take on one of the men who always came and flirted with her at the store—like Don Fabio, for instance. She lived and breathed the store. It was her life. Petra admired her.

The old man carried on with Vicenta, while Carlos and Petra stood respectfully to the side. Vicenta was sighing a lot as she told Don Fabio that a young woman in Las Leches had been brutalized in the alley behind the church. Her father found her in the early hours of the morning when she didn't turn up at home. At least she was still alive. He found her fainted away on the ground, her dress torn, her body scratched and bruised; her head had a deep cut where they had hit her with a rock.

Quietly, Petra spoke up. She didn't like to interrupt two adults conversing. "Vicenta, who was the girl?"

Vicenta said, "It was Señor Menendez's daughter, Petra. Do you know her?" Everyone knew Señor Menendez, the pharmacist in the village, but Petra had never met his daughter. Everyone knew her reputation, though. She hung out at the dances held every couple of weeks in Las Leches.

Petra's head swirled, and she put her hand to her forehead. "I heard them in town. Guys in the gang were talking about using her to get money out of her father. *Ave María purísima.* They didn't mention they almost killed her."

Vicenta gently touched the back of Petra's head, and Petra draped her arm around Vicenta's shoulder. They clung to each other briefly in a hug.

Petra herself would never set foot at a dance. For one thing, she was a good girl, a good Catholic. Unless a girl went with a steady boyfriend, no good girl had any business at such places. For another, she wasn't interested. To go to a dance meant men flirting with her, trying to get her to dance with them, taking advantage as much as they could. She'd rather stay home.

Carlos didn't have to worry about his reputation. He could go have fun, and of course try to get what fun he could from the local women. A boy like Carlos did whatever he could get away with, and no one questioned. But Carlos also hoped to find a good girl for himself, so he sometimes hesitated to become known for hanging out in such places.

Don Fabio said, "That girl, she's been raring for a problem like this for months, hanging out at those dances by herself!"

Vicenta's deep brown eyes bore into Don Fabio as he spoke.

"But, Jesus alive," he continued, "they really fixed her bad last night."

Don Fabio scuffed his feet on the ground in front of the store as he talked, his shoulders hunched over with age. A whistle fluttered through the space between his front teeth. Usually he had a lot of life in him, this old guy.

Don Fabio said, "That's a sad thing, to see any girl suffer like that, no matter what she did. I wonder if anyone's going to get punished for it."

Vicenta answered, "Too dangerous for anyone to speak up. It'd be looking for trouble."

"Can't blame 'em there. We all got to look out for ourselves, can't be looking into the predicaments of people who aren't careful with themselves, or we'll be the ones to get it." The old man looked resigned to the reality of their lives.

Fabio changed the subject. "Hey, Vicenta, my son called from Los Angeles yesterday. Says there's no more white people left in his neighborhood, the last ones moved out last week. He'd never see a gringo if he didn't work in people's gardens around the city. Can you believe you can go so far away as the United States and still see nothing but us Spanish people?"

"Well, I guess there's so many of us, they're bound to keep floating across the border and take over the place eventually." She exhaled loudly. "Ay, Fabio, when's it all going to stop? I'm tired sometimes."

"What's bothering you, Vicenta?"

"I don't know, Fabio, it's just, well, that girl, she didn't deserve all that."

He swallowed hard and nodded. Vicenta counted up his purchases and put it on his tab. The old man hunched his way out of there, a little more weighed down than when he came in.

Carlos suddenly realized Vicenta was looking at him, waiting for him to do whatever he came for. "Vicenta, you worry too much," he said. "We'll be okay. All we need is a little of this here beer, and it'll all be all right, you know?"

"Yeah right, Carlos. Hey, good-looking, how much money you got for all this beer today?"

"Don't you worry, give me a six pack and I'll pay you back later."

"Can't do it. Sorry, boy. I got to put food on my own table, too."

He smiled at her. "Well, give me one beer then."

Carlos went back to the mango tree with his beer and his buddies. Petra watched Carlos for a few minutes from the doorway of the store.

Outside the store, the crowd of card-shuffling guys had grown. Carlos brought out all his cheer with his buddies. "*Hola, chicos!*" he said to a couple of friends who were just joining the group. "*Qué hubo?*" The sharp sound of hands slapping ensued.

"Hey, Carlos! Not much. Ay, where'd you come up with that beer? Give me some of that, *compadre.*"

Carlos handed it over to his friend Manuel, not because he wanted to share it, but because he couldn't deny a friend. Hoping her presence might tamp down Carlos's reckless merriment, Petra moved to stand behind Carlos.

"Carlos, after we soak up a little juice here, we're going over to hit some ball at the soccer field. You want to go?"

"Yeah, man, I'd love to. Love to whip some butt against those guys from up the road."

"All right, those pansies will crumble under us. Right after we consume some of this brew, we'll be fired up."

"One of those wimps walked by here with his mule the other day. Didn't even have the courtesy to say hello. *Qué coma mierda.*"

"OK then, we'll go right after we play a bit of these cards. You want to play for change?"

"Nah, I got none left. It's OK, man, let's just play." Manuel dealt out the cards to the six of them. "You go to that dance last night, *compa*?" Carlos asked.

"Not me, man. I was out late cutting cane, no energy left for that. Sure wanted to go out, though. My girl came by all melty-eyed, talking very nice to me. But then my cousins came over, and you know, I had to hang with them awhile, so she left."

The hot afternoon sun pelted down on the young men. They were drinking up the few available beers quickly. The mango tree drew people together and gave them the illusion of sanctuary. Its thick, dense leaves rained around the dirt clearing on the side of the road, cloaking bits of the cement wall around it and spotting the ground. The sweet smell of fruit hovered in the air.

Petra fretted about Carlos's bruised head, but Carlos seemed relaxed, oblivious to it. He laughed a bit too loudly, trying a little too hard to act the jovial friend in charge of the party. Manuel turned on the radio, cranked up the volume, and they kept talking, shouting over the music.

Alongside the pounding beat, Carlos finally perceived his sister standing behind him. His mood dampened. Petra glared at him. He tracked her glance to what were now a number of empty beer bottles, and the cards strewn about. He scowled back at her.

Petra's head turned back to the road at the sound of rumbling hoof-beats on the packed earth. "Carlos! Put yourself together! Don José is coming."

"So what!" he hissed at Petra.

"You want the world to see you being lazy and degenerate?"

"Sure, why not?" he said with mock enthusiasm.

One of the guys lowered the volume of the music. The beer cans dropped behind the stone bench. Carlos glowered at her.

Don José was headed in the direction of the plantation, Finca Anaconda, on a fine mare with a speckled roan coat. The brim of his black fedora was upright and unspoiled, his bearing proud. Petra's uncle Jacinto worked under José, the overseer at the cane fields. No one totally trusted him because he was so close to the owner, though he had yet to concretely earn the distrust. Carlos looked up and tipped his hand to Don José. Petra waved and wished him a good day. Once he was safely by, Carlos's friends hooted and guffawed in hushed tones.

Petra returned to the store. "Vicenta, you know Don José's son, right? Didn't he leave the gangs?"

Vicenta said, "Lucas? He tried to leave. He didn't want to be part of the gangs anymore. But they don't let people go easy, so he went into hiding."

"Did he do very bad things when he was in the gang?"

"Like they all start—he stole money from the stores and tried to lure kids into the gangs with promises of food and girls. But then it got more serious, and he realized maybe he didn't want to be in all that. When he told his buddies he wanted out, they scared the shit out of him. Excuse my language."

"Why did he join?"

"Good question," said Vicenta. "He used to be a good kid."

Didn't most kids start out good? Until they joined the gangs. Then where did all that goodness go? God is with each one of us—then even with Emilio?

Petra said, "Vicenta, I just wish the police would arrest the guys that hurt that woman."

Vicenta's eyes lit up with concern. Her tone became more intimate. "It may have something to do with the MS-13 delinquents coming into our village. I heard they're recruiting women to run with them."

Petra looked off into the distance, out the door, beyond the mango tree, to the new moon rising above the woods. "I'm afraid, Vicenta. It never really goes away, you know? It's in the pit of my stomach. I try to pretend it's not there, but it is."

"I understand, *niña*. You know I do."

"Some days I want to escape it all, Vicenta. Other days I want to dig in and help everyone, make it all better."

Vicenta probed her with her eyes. "You can make choices, Petra. Look at the options around you. Do you want to find a young man to protect you?" Her eyes twinkled.

"Vicenta, you know me better—"

"Or you could be like Carlos. Work yourself to the bones then slack off and have fun so you can bear it all. Or you could run to the United States and find your mother."

Petra laughed. "What do you do, Vicenta? How do you manage it all?"

Vicenta cradled her chin in a hand and looked searchingly at Petra. Her eyes darted toward the closet at the back of the store. She pondered a moment, then shook her head, as if arguing with herself. "There are other ways, Petra. Find your path, make it happen."

Petra frowned and pulled her upper lip between her teeth. Vicenta was apparently going to leave her with this mysterious advice. "Well... I need some soap. I better go do the laundry."

Petra slapped her grandfather Nonno's dripping overalls against the rocks to scare the dirt out. The coolness of the rocks that rose just above the coursing water soothed her backside. The crisp beat of the clothes could calm a sea of agitation.

Little fish swam by in shadowy clouds. She'd bring a batch home to Nonna to salt and fry when she was done. A small yellow bird rested on a branch just above, then flitted away.

The dusty earth mixed with rocks and the dense green of the forest around the stream. The water trickled in places, but larger rivulets flowed over the large rock where Petra set down the clothes and took out the bar of soap. Only a few years back, when she and Justina would come here together, the stream was a river—a narrow river, but everyone knew it to be a river.

As Justina's body churned in the ground and turned to dust, the dry, hot days worked on the water current and began to overcome the water. The river had slowly become a stream. So now the villagers were confused about whether to call it a river or a stream. People said the weather was getting warmer all the time, making the crops wilt under the sun, but in Petra's bones, she knew why the flow had slowed to a trickle. The tragedy of Justina claimed its retribution.

A lizard stole across the path, headed for the shade under Petra's rock. Two women from the village were already there, a few rocks upstream, with their babies. Boys were playing and arguing just below, where the stream widened out to a watering hole. Girls weren't welcome there, only boys.

Petra had been known to peek jealously through the trees to catch glimpses. Maybe she could learn to swim by watching the boys there.

Years ago, when they were still kids, she and Emilio picked their way along a path through the woods down here. Emilio veered away from the path, into the tangled vegetation, peering under brush, prying up fallen logs.

Before she knew it, he held out a big hairy spider in his hand. She'd never held one, but she immediately recognized the tarantula.

"Go ahead, hold it," Emilio pushed the tarantula toward her. Petra knew he expected her to jump back and squeal, and she loved to foil his ideas about girls.

Petra peered closely at the spider. The tarantula was a magnificent creature. Its long legs were brown and black and red, covered with robust hairs. Impressive pincers at the front of its head made it look like a distant relative of dinosaurs. According to Nonna, *chiwos* would pee on burro and cattle's feet and give them hoof problems, but Petra was skeptical. Nonna said the spider carried out surprise attacks by jumping an impressive three feet. Nonna had a lot of old Mayan ideas about the ways animals behaved and made people sick.

Emilio said, "Check out those fangs. Watch out, it'll bite you!"

But Petra was looking at its eyes. "She's wonderful, Emilio. Such amazing color. You can feel her power."

"You two are staring at each other like your eyes are passing secret messages." Emilio sounded jealous.

Petra reached out gently, and the tarantula climbed right onto her hand. Slowly, carefully, she touched the fur on its back.

"And what do you mean 'her'? I think it's a boy." Emilio stomped his foot.

"Nah, the males are smaller, and they die younger. Sometimes the females eat them."

"No way. Males are always stronger. Everybody knows that."

"You're wrong, Emilio. Lots of girl animals are stronger. Bees, too, and falcons."

"I think you should put it down now. Look, it wants to crawl up your arm." He awkwardly grabbed it to get it off her. "Ay! It bit me!" He flung the tarantula back to the ground and held up his hand, which now had a red mark spreading on it. "Petra, I'm in trouble now! What do I do?" His face was getting flushed by panic.

"Relax, Emilio. She didn't want to bite you, but you scared her. Don't worry. Her bite isn't so bad. You'll be OK."

"It hurts."

"You've gotten stung before by bees, right? It's no worse. You'll make it."

"Petra, how come you're not scared of things like most girls?" Emilio so wanted to impress her.

"Ah, there's no reason to be scared of little spiders. Next time, find an anaconda and bring that to me, then I'll be nervous, OK? I promise. But—I would like to see the anaconda. Maybe just take me to see it and we can look from a little ways away." They both laughed, and headed home, passing by the spot where she sat right now.

The pile of laundry had not gotten much smaller. Her hands were wrinkled with water and soap but moving at the speed of a river turtle. Her thoughts lumbered back to the present.

What happened to the good Emilio after the gangs took over his life? It must still exist in him somewhere. God is with each one of us—then even with Emilio? Perhaps there was a way to care about him without approving of what he did. But even if God's grace could heal him, he had to seek it out, right? Anyway, she had no role in it. Except to avoid him, because now he did nothing but threaten her.

The two sides of her mind kept thrashing the problem around. What happened to the good Emilio after the gangs took over his life? It must still exist in him somewhere. Really, his threats were those of a child whining, not serious, right? The Emilio who spun around her yard on the bike wouldn't seriously menace her.

Then a new thought came to her—or an old thought she'd had at the market the day years ago when she'd found Emilio stealing. What if Emilio was really begging her for help?

CHAPTER SEVEN

Carlos yelled at the cattle who stubbornly stood in his way. The sound of his frustration resonated over the hills. If she listened hard, Petra could hear the beat of a bass drum wafting out behind him.

Nonna and Petra stood together by the house contemplating Carlos. Nonna said, "Do you think Carlos is too hard? He seems sullen these days." Six days had passed since Emilio had battered Carlos's ego. Petra had hardly talked to Carlos since then, just the usual stewing of their morning walks together.

Carlos struggled, like Petra but in a different way. He was brooding and combative at home, but when it came to their meager farm, he had the will of a mule pulling itself out of quicksand. Soon enough, he'd be able to handle the work of a full-grown man. For now, though, a half-grown mule was in him, a wiry adolescent, so his determination played a major role in driving his body forward.

He looked so thoroughly at home, in his place, except—he kept looking around nervously, staring off into space, shifting uncomfortably as if uneasy in his own skin. Petra envied Carlos for the bond he felt with the land. He loved this earth and the produce that he wrested from it in a way she never would.

Carlos and Tobías, their fourteen year old neighbor, had cut the cane from two fields, and it was stacked up, slowly making its way over the hill to be pressed. In Petra's family, they didn't send the cane to be processed in town. They could get a few extra quetzals by pressing out the juice themselves and driving it to San Luis Hunahpu to be boiled down to crystals. It was back-breaking labor.

The pressing machine was on the other side of the neighbor's hill, so they hooked themselves onto harnesses and carried load after load of sugar cane down the side of the hillside and across the ravine. The cattle lapped at the water there, so they couldn't get past and haul the loads up the other side until they moved on. They shared the work, but Carlos positioned himself as the leader.

One more task remained before Petra could sleep this night: She had to deliver dinner to Carlos and Tobías. She suspended two jugs of water from each end of a yoke across the back of her neck and hung the food in a sack on her back, then trudged up the hill to find them.

As she crossed the barren landscape, a woman's raspy voice emerged, belting out rap lyrics, backed by electronic keyboard and that drum. Carlos carried the radio in one hand, while the burden of the load strained against the strap on his chest. His forehead was deeply furrowed, but his fingers tapped the rhythm of the music against the straps. Blisteringly fast lyrics set off the groans of effort. "Pumping, yeah," he said to Tobías.

The top of that hill was the best view around. The earth there hardly sustained the maize and other crops planted in patches. The grass the cattle fed on could barely be called grass, and it showed in the bones of the cattle.

The heat overwhelmed Petra, though she didn't labor as her brother did. Sweat poured from his armpits and chest. The cuts and bruises from the confrontation with Emilio had evolved into dark colors around Carlos's eyes.

The beat suddenly clipped off when Carlos spotted her.

"Hey, *señores* workers, time for dinner." Petra unwrapped a pile of tortillas, with bowls of rice and beans for each of them while she caught her breath.

Carlos said, "A man could starve up here waiting for you to bring dinner. It's late, *sister*."

The snide tone of "sister" wounded Petra. "Do you think you're the only one who works around here, Carlos? I'm doing my best, *sabes*?"

Tobías eased himself between the two of them, and said, "*Hombre*, food is here! Thank God the tortillas have arrived! Let's dig in!" He raised one of the jugs to his mouth. "Hey, our water was running low, man. *Gracias*, Petra." The water splashed into his mouth and overflowed down the back of his neck.

"Hey, yo, *amiguito*," Carlos said, "don't take all the water. Let me have some of that."

Petra gently touched her hand to Carlos's forehead, where the gash Emilio left was mending well. Carlos pushed her away. "Girl, keep your hands to yourself!"

"Carlos, cool out," said quietly. Carlos gave him a sidelong glance, then grinned.

"Are you okay, Carlos?" said Petra.

"I can handle myself. You don't need to think about me." He gazed around. Petra wasn't sure if his eyes were worried or dreamy. Maybe both. "That Emilio, he thinks he's a hotshot now in that little gang of his. They think they're so cute naming themselves the X-14, like they're first cousins with the MS-13."

"Vicenta said the MS-13 is on its way here from its base in Mexico," Petra said. "The X-14 is going to deal with them one way or another. It can't be good, Carlos. And Emilio, *púchica*, he wants to be mister big man by the time they get here."

Tobías added, "I heard the X-14 is pushing hard to raise a bunch of money and recruits before they get here, so the MS-13 takes them seriously. They want to get the protection, and the action, by getting friendly with the big gang."

Carlos told Tobías, "Yeah, now they're after Señor Picardo at his little grocery store in Las Leches, demanding 350 quetzals every two weeks. Anyone doing a little business is getting hit." Carlos grabbed a tortilla and loaded it with rice and beans, while his eyes flitted around them nervously.

"What?" said Petra. "Oh my gosh, nobody could pay that much!"

"*Sí, claro*," said Carlos. "He doesn't have that kind of money, and he doesn't have any family in the U.S. to send it to him. He gave them as much as he could, but he'll go out of business with that around his neck. That doesn't stop them from demanding more, though. Everybody is nervous after they raped Señor Menendez's daughter. Almost killed her. Señor Menendez certainly caught the message. He's lucky to have a cousin in the U.S."

Petra hesitated before asking, "Carlos, do you know who it was? Who attacked her?" She prayed Emilio was not involved.

"No, I don't know, Petra." He hung his head. But his eyes looked up, still casting about in case someone unexpected could be around.

Petra never did tell him about Gorto and Chofo. It was safer to say as little as possible.

CHAPTER EIGHT

Nonna called to her from the back yard. "Petra, would you go fetch your grandfather for me? He's been up the way with his brothers all afternoon."

Petra had just found her place in the Bible and begun to read, her sandaled feet rubbing a furrow in the dirt under their table as she swung her legs back and forth. The light of the day was fading fast, casting long shadows through the house.

"*Sí*, Nonna." The fatigue crept into her voice but, with some effort, her feet raised her up from her seat. She wrapped a *rebozo* around her shoulders.

The path narrowed as she walked toward Jacinto's house, ever farther up the hill from the road. The forest trees rustled in the breeze. A coati scuttled across the path in front of her. The raccoon-like eyes locked onto hers for a moment, then the striped tail disappeared into the vegetation near the spring. She bent down to take a few swallows of the fresh water. The cold water cooled her feet as she stood in the rut where the water flowed out. The water split in two around her then converged to continue on its way. Like Moses parting the Red Sea. Miracles could be found anywhere, right?

Darkness crept down the trees into the path. Tree roots played and slithered about before her, doing their utmost to trip her. Her glance flickered to all sides, scanning the underbrush and overhangs for lurking dangers. People who trod blindly into the forest ended up tangling with a rattlesnake or confronting the dreaded anaconda. If she ever encountered that anaconda, she hoped to have an experienced protector by her side. Justina claimed to have seen the beast, from a thankfully safe distance, in its full twelve inches of breadth and twenty feet in length, on the path between home and school. It seemed prudent to trust in God but remain vigilant for that green monster.

She rounded the bend at the old banana tree, which didn't have bananas anymore, but did have immense leaves which obscured the view of the Sibalq'aq volcano off in the distance. She pulled a branch back so she could look beyond the tree, as much as she could make out in the dusk. That volcano called to her and enticed her to its slopes. Someday soon she would see what it looked like up close.

Candlelight, nebulous behind the foliage, leapt in spirals at her feet. As she came upon the house of Jacinto, Nonno's older brother, she heard a booming, almost threatening, voice pierce the music: "Who dares come to this house!" Men snickered quietly, then broke into full laughter. Her grandfather's younger brother Arnoldo was playing sentry this evening.

Cracks in the surrounding trees gaped wider as the booming *rancheros* penetrated their defenses. Branches hanging above the men crackled with the tension, and blood pounded into her eardrums. *Conjuntos* of men were singing in broken harmonies about avenging enemies and judging the good women from the bad. The music coursed into her blood, streaming through the years of her life like the smell of sweat, spreading its crude values. Petra preferred the lessons of the Bible.

Beneath the music, from just beyond the banana tree, men's voices hummed in a familiar patter, broken only by frequent intake of alcohol. Like raindrops on the corrugated metal roof, the prattle fell amidst each other like they'd been holding forth there for decades. Which indeed they had been.

The house drew men like hogs were attracted to mud, and a large group of them were now perched on uncomfortable metal chairs and logs strewn about the yard. Each man had his cup of alcohol, his hand of cards, and a mouthful of gossip. But a few were also scrupulously alert. So far, the local delinquents hadn't bothered them, but in their moonshine habitat, they didn't forget to be cautious, not ever.

"Petra, *mi sobrinita*! Have some *chaparro* with your family!" With a wry grin, Arnoldo held out an old, cracked cup to her. Nonno's brothers,

Jacinto and Arnoldo distilled the local concoction from the corn and sugar canes of the nearby fields. Which explained why the men gathered at her uncle Jacinto's almost every afternoon.

It was also why her Nonno sometimes had to be retrieved and encouraged to return home in the evening.

"Mmmm, thanks but no thanks, *tío*. Not today."

Petra stood off to the side to take in the atmosphere a piece at a time. Her favorite horse, Chancho—her little niece Julina had likened its flaring nostrils to a pig, and the name stuck—nickered his welcome to her, and she answered by wrapping her arms around its neck and withers. Her uncles could afford the beautiful liver chestnut horse because of their second business selling the *chaparro* to locals, which was somewhat more lucrative than their first job. All day and many nights, her uncles gathered sugar cane at Finca Anaconda, the biggest plantation and principal employer in the area. The men lucky enough to get hired got to sweat and break their backs there every summer, the dry season.

The scene repelled her, but in a comforting, familiar way. The men got together before work, after work, during work, while looking for work—whenever they could—to gossip, stir around their thoughts on battling *la lucha diaria* of exhaustion and survival.

Chancho reached out his neck and threw his head high, then snorted so his nostrils vibrated until Petra reached to rub him behind the ears. While the horse nuzzled her shoulders, she obscured herself behind the horse's solidity.

"*Oye*, Jacinto, *tío*, put your attention here, *hombre*. You want this card? Put out your *centavos* if you're in."

"Bachito, put it here." Jacinto pointed to the pile of cards in front of him. "Here's my two *centavitos*."

"Cheché, another *copa*, 'mano?" Arnoldo piped up.

"*Sí, compadre, gracias*," said Cheché. Cheché leaned his torso across the card table to grab the new cup, making the table lean precariously. Bacho's drink spilled.

Bacho objected. "Eh, *muchacho*, look what you're doing! Watch yourself, or I'll come over there and sit you down myself."

Jacinto's girlfriend Leila ambled up to the table with a bowl full of chips. As she leaned over to put them down, Jacinto said, "*Mujercita*, you're blocking my view of Bacho with those big breasts. Make yourself decent, woman." He flapped his arm in front of his face as if to wipe her away from his view. Leila retreated, but not before she stuck out a finger at him.

Jacinto stood up with an angry clatter, knocking his chair backward. Arnoldo pushed the chair back into his knees, and he sat again.

Chancho gave a loud squeal, his nose pointed toward Jacinto. Petra patted his withers, then moved in the direction of home. Arnoldo blew the sentry whistle, and Nonno looked up. He gestured for her to sit next to him. He said, "Petra, come, we also have tamarind juice. Go fetch yourself a cup, over there. You must stay close to me. Your presence makes my heart sing."

With Petra's arrival, the atmosphere in the yard softened. A lighter, tropical song sang out from the radio, and the men toned down the volume and raucousness of their talk.

Petra gave Nonno a peck on the cheek. A whiff of alcohol made her shift away. The candlelight caressed the shaggy gray hair atop his round head.

Arnoldo sang out, "Ah, what the presence of a young woman can do."

"*Gracias*, Nonno." Petra caressed his furrowed forehead briefly. Crinkling her nose, she turned toward the edge of the yard. "Nonno, look, the yellow jasmine blooms are opening up for the night. Can you smell them?"

The moment ended. "I got the queen of spades, *amigos*. See her and weep." Cheché put down the card and swept the handful of coins on the table to his side, a big smile showing off his gold-capped tooth.

Jacinto said, "Yet another bad woman, that queen." He straightened up the cards and began to shuffle. "Who's in? Put in a *centavo* if you're not too scared."

The men in her family shared an impressive camaraderie, almost always. Only occasionally, after too much alcohol, or a fight with the wife, the tensions boiled over.

Little Julina stepped out of the house. "Hola, *tía* Petra!"

Julina carried herself with a dignity unusual for her ten years. The little girl bangs still topped a slight physique which made Petra think she could use more food, but Julina communicated poise without even moving. "*Qué pasa*, Julina?" asked Petra.

"Come, come, *tía*, I want to show you." She signaled for Petra to go with her inside.

Thankful for the excuse to leave the group of men, Petra followed. Inside, Julina led her to a room, dimly animated with a kerosene lamp and its shadows. Three small pieces of cardboard lay on a wooden table, each covered with a painting. Petra was immediately drawn to an image of their volcano, painted in brilliant colors, the sun lighting up one side and washing down the other. Petra said, "Julina, this is amazing! I didn't know you could do this!"

"I haven't told anybody hardly. I really just started. It's not very good."

"Not good! Julina, how did you get all these colors?"

"That's what's so amazing, *tía*. You know, my uncle Oscar comes up with lots of good ideas while he lies in his bed. He showed me what to try. Like for yellow, I grind up onion skins and dandelions, boil them, then make them into a paint with egg yolks and a little vinegar. Same idea for green, using grass and spinach. The ingredients don't cost hardly anything."

"*Bueno, quién supo?* I have an artist for a niece."

"I'm still working on the shadows around the volcano."

"Julina, I saw your mamá a couple days ago at the store. She told me about the man who grabbed you and took the money. Are you OK?"

"Well… I guess I'm OK. I might quit school, though. I don't like going to Las Leches anymore. I'm thinking to stay here and paint. Along with my other chores, of course."

"Julina! You can't do that! Let's walk home from school together, so we can watch out for each other. But you can't quit! You need to know all about the world to make beautiful art," she said, pointing to the volcano. "You can't go along all ignorant and just hide in this corner of nowhere your whole life."

"My mamá doesn't want me to leave school either. I don't know what to do. Will you walk home with me tomorrow?" Her eyes lifted.

"*Cómo no!*" Petra gave Julina a warm hug. "As long as you keep showing me your pictures."

Jacinto burst through the door, his arm splayed across Leila's shoulder, her ample frame propping him up. Petra took Julina's hand and pulled her to the side. Leila did her best to keep him upright, but his body swayed like the ground was shifting under his feet. Leila said, "I'm going with you this time." She glared at him defiantly.

Jacinto's head cocked to one side and an eyebrow rose. His message was clear: Much as he was happy to have her in his bed for the time being, she shouldn't expect too much. He leered at her breasts.

Leila said, "Don't think I'm going to stick around and wait for you again while you mess around doing what you want with whoever you want in the United States, and I'm doing nothing but waiting for you to come back. You keep coming and going whenever you feel like it—well, this time, I'm going with you." Leila took a step back because Jacinto's hand was cupped and moving up toward her breast.

Petra, too, suspected that he had another woman, or several, in the U.S. Embarrassment washed over Petra. She didn't need to hear this conversation. Unobtrusively, she tried to lead Julina back outside, but Jacinto stepped in front of her.

"Now *you* I might take with me back to Rhode Island." He pointed a bony finger at Petra's chest and exaggerated the "R" of Rhode Island with a sarcastic roll of the Spanish tongue. Jacinto teetered, and Petra recoiled at the tipsy spectacle before her. Deep pockmarks etched his entire face, the way acne turns into red scarring in people who make a habit of drinking too much.

"*Tío*—" Petra stuttered.

"*Qué pues, chica?*" He was so crass.

Trying to return the conversation to normal tones, Petra said, "*Tío*, are you going back again soon?"

"Why didn't I think of this before? *Claro*, you can go to school in Rrrhode Island, and do a little cooking and housekeeping for me and my buddies in exchange for your room and board in the afternoons. Whaddya say?" The alcohol on his tongue gave his Rs an exaggerated roll.

What a horrifying image! She would never go to the U.S., not that way.

Leila's face was blowing up. "Give me that drink, Jacinto. You're being an idiot." She grabbed for the cup, but he snatched it away, and it splashed all over Julina's dress. He *was* a sloshed oaf. Petra moved into the corner with Julina. Jacinto choked on his intemperate bumblings and snorted *chaparro* out his nose. When Leila tried to haul him outside, he shoved her, and she tumbled to the floor.

The noise brought Arnoldo in to check out the situation. With a stern voice, he broke the tension. "*Muchacho*," he said to Jacinto. "Hey, we need you out here for cards. C'mon, '*mano*. Dolores just brought down some grilled *elote*, and they won't last long." He handed Jacinto another cup of *chaparro*. Leila dusted herself off and shot Arnoldo a look of gratitude.

Calm returned, and Petra returned to Nonno's side. Nonno soon began caressing his grizzly gray mustache, and she knew he'd had enough to drink. It was time. Petra leaned into Nonno and said, "To tell the truth, I am tired. It's been a long day." Chancho let out a gentle snort.

Laughing toward the other men, Nonno took a look at Petra and said, "My wife sends this charm over to bring me home at night. It works every time." He put his hand to his granddaughter's elbow. "Well, let's go home then."

Darkness enveloped the forest now, and Petra could no longer see the path once they left the haze of candlelight from Jacinto's house. It was soothing to have Nonno by her side. They walked arm in arm, as Nonno asked her about her day. "Why are you so tired, *mi nieta*?"

"My brain works too hard, Nonno. I can't stop mulling things over. I love you and Nonna so much, but I think and think about what the future holds, when the present is hard enough. I can't find the answers, and the thinking wears me out. I want to do something with my life, Nonnino."

He stood back and gazed at her. "Petra, you are getting older, and you're very sensitive to what goes on around you. You will struggle like all of us. You must keep your heart open. You'll need it to find your way." Nonno's voice was deep and serene, the sound of wisdom.

"I spoke with Deacon Eduardo on Friday last week. He wanted to help me."

"Don't underestimate the Deacon. He is an interesting man. You know he comes from Bolivia to help in our church, in this small corner of Guatemala. You might think Bolivia is just another poor, backward country in Latin America, but it is bigger and broader than Guatemala. Eduardo got himself a real education, and he has travelled enough to understand a bit about us humans. You would do well to listen to the Deacon."

"I was saying my prayers with Nonna, but the Deacon called out to me. He seemed to want to talk to me especially, although Nonna may have prodded him a bit, as well. Why do you think he sought me out, Nonno?"

"I don't know, *niña*, perhaps he sees something in you. I know I do." Her grandfather stilled for a moment, resting his head lightly on his callused fingertips. Contemplating her eyes, he said, "Petra, you well know that, though our family no longer follows many of the Mayan traditions in clothing and cultural ways, the ancient spirit carries on very profoundly in this community, and in our home."

Her grandfather was making an effort to slough off his tipsiness. "Yes, Nonno, you have made this very clear. Your parents spoke Quiché, right?"

"And before my ancestors spoke Quiché, they spoke Xinca. Hundreds of years ago, before the Spanish conquered this area, the Xinca people populated this corner of Guatemala. But there were many more Quiché in Guatemala, and they eventually pressed their language and ways onto the Xinca. By the time the Spanish came, the Xinca culture was already all but eliminated. Our history has intertwined with the threads of many different Mayan peoples."

"Do you know some of the Xinca language?"

"No, I'm afraid it has all been lost, probably many generations ago. Unfortunately, many in my generation lost much of the Quiché language and traditions as well. When I was growing up, like you, I thought about my future, and I saw only poverty and backwardness among the traditional Mayan Quiché communities. We spoke only Spanish in school, and I found that the Ladino boys would beat me up less if I acted less Quiché. So I tried to act more Spanish, less Indian."

In her genes, she was as Mayan as the Quiché kids in her school. But the Ladino boys didn't beat her up like they did the kids that spoke Spanish awkwardly, the ones with hunger in their eyes. No one thought of her as indigenous.

Nonno continued. "On the other hand, when life feels hard, gathering your Quiché heritage inside you can fortify you. It's like bringing together a whole people inside your soul. The ancients still make their presence felt through us. I feel them when I am gathering the corn, even sometimes while I am enjoying the *chaparro*." He sniggered.

Her utter separation from the Quiché kids in her school didn't quite fit with Petra's embrace of Mayan myth and cultural symbols. Those kids would never invite a girl like her over for dinner with the family. Yet the mischievous *aluxob* on the altar next to the cooking area stood watch over her family. The falcon god Itzamná lived above their altar, where he oversaw all of creation and infused her with the sense of unfolding time. The mysterious depths intrigued and guided her. But—there was so much more to a full embrace of Mayan ways. She was content to draw from the symbols and myths of the Mayans or meld them with a prayer to the Virgin Mary.

"Petra, do you know the story of the Siguanaba?"

"No, I don't think so. Would you tell me?"

Petra and Nonno shuffled wearily up to the house. The dark was deep and long by the time Petra pulled down her bed and lay down her head. Mysteries played in the night, spinning tales out of anxieties and fancies. There were no shadows for subtleties—just the absolute dark. Petra and Nonno sat next to each other, their backs against the wall, their legs splayed out on her bed, the pigeons chortling in the eaves above. He began:

"Some years ago, the Siguanaba sat on the bank of a slow-moving river—very similar to the river where you washed our clothes today— scrubbing laundry. With a bar of golden soap, she also washed her hair and bathed herself. On her long, lustrous hair, she used a comb that gleamed in the late afternoon light. Her head faced away from the path, and she focused downward toward the water and her scrubbing. However, from behind, one could still see that she was very beautiful. Black hair cascaded down her back, and a thin, sparkling white dress covered her thin build. Her presence seemed to exude a glow, an alluring lightness.

"She did not look up when a man appeared on a mule behind her, though of course she heard. When the man spoke, she recognized the voice from her girlhood. A foreboding tone marred his now matured voice. Hearing him made her shudder. She cherished her memory of the young boy, but no longer recognized him in the man he had become. He had often provoked her—and was now reputed to misuse women."

Petra shuddered, too. "Nonno! You're being too obvious." She slid down and pulled the blanket over her head.

Nonno lay a hand on the crown of her head. "The man said, 'Arise, Siguanaba, join me and we will ride together. Let us ride off and enjoy each other tonight. You are the woman I have dreamed about, and I will have you for myself.'

"The Siguanaba obeyed, and she flung herself behind the man on his mule. Together they rode into the forest, beyond the river. He held back the branches in their path so they would not brush against her. When they came to a clearing, the mule picked up speed. The night was falling and the full moon rising as they approached a canyon, the volcano rising beyond it. The man chose a path along the edge of the canyon, and they descended. All the while, clouds formed a halo around the volcano, lit from behind by the moon, forging a quiet but eerie light on their journey. The heat of the day dissipated.

"They reached a green valley, where streams converged into a river along the ridge of their path. The man quickly dismounted and pulled the Siguanaba down next to him, preparing to grab her by the waist and forcefully kiss her. He was able to see her face for the first time, and she allowed herself to be revealed to him. Her long black hair had become the splendid mane of a horse. Her face was that of a horse. Even her hands were horse's hooves. She held up her hooves, and he suddenly felt menaced by this formerly ravishing woman.

"The man startled and fell backward in his fright. His head hit a rock outcropping, and he died instantly. The Siguanaba gathered the mule and rode home."

"Oh, Nonno, why do your stories end with such violence? It would be enough if the Siguanaba was able to run away!"

"*Niña*, it is a myth. Myth is born from reality, as also reality is born from myth. They are easily confused, but they are not the same."

"Why did the Siguanaba go with him if she didn't trust him?"

"Petrita, it is late. I can see sleep about to overcome you. You must think about the answer to your questions."

The tin roof didn't prevent all kinds of weather from penetrating, but it did block the bit of light from the moon and the flock of stars over the house. Itzamná's wife Ixchel was out there looking after her, though, in the wink of the moon. Nonna had turned off the kerosene light an hour ago. Petra's chin flopped down on her chest. She struggled to stay awake.

"Nonnino," Petra said quietly, hesitantly, "something happened with Emilio. I need to talk to you about it."

"Of course, *niña*. Tomorrow is just around the bend. Join with sleep now."

CHAPTER NINE

The darkness turned circles around her thoughts. Tales grew out of the walls like ivy. She flipped back and forth, until sleep ensnared the stories. A monkey cackled and took hold of the Siguanaba's long dark hair in its teeth. Petra held the clay hummingbird tightly under her pillow. Somewhere between asleep and awake, Alocinia came to her. How Petra loved the green wings, the flicker of a black eye, her broken beak.

Petra: What do you think? Should we go?

Alocinia: I don't think so. It's dangerous.

- How do you know?

- I don't. But it's dark, we don't know what's there.

- Well, that's the whole point. You've got to take risks if you're going to go anywhere at all.

- That's what you say. I'm not so sure. You go if you want to.

- Ay. You're making this harder, Alocinia. I don't want to leave you out here. Maybe this is what we've been looking for all along.

- Yeah. Petra, I know what you mean. I'm just not ready yet. You go on.

- All right, I'm going through for five minutes. Just five minutes, okay? If I don't come out, you'll know you made the right decision.

- What? If you're not coming back, then I want to go with you. Let me think. Don't go, Petra, I'm not ready for either of us to go. Petra, are you going to leave me? I'm afraid you're getting ready to go off on your own.

- It's just to see what's there. We've got to decide. How about
  this—I'll just put one foot through, and we'll see what happens.
- … Okay.

Alocinia said it quietly. Petra heard it, though. Her heart screwed itself
into spirals in leaving Alocinia, but she had to; this was everything. The
future, the core, the principle of it all. She stepped back for a moment to
gather herself. The sky was sparkling blue, the grass of the mountaintop
shimmering in its light. She could hear the soothing rustle of the leaves,
the chirping of birds hopping about the trees. Her skin prickled. She had
to go forward.

So Petra took a step. The toe of her sandal eased into the shadow.
Resting her heel on the ground, she took a deep breath, swallowed hard.
At the last minute, Emilio ran forward, tried to grab her arm, but he
could only grab her shadow. Justina cried out. Where did they come
from?

- Could I have some of that tortilla?

Alocinia's wing beat against her cheek, and she giggled a little, then
reached into her pocket.

- Here you go.
- Thanks.
- I really have no idea what I'm doing, you know.
- I know. You won't find out until you're there.

She savored the tortilla, chewing it slowly. Alocinia wrapped her
wings around Petra's cheeks, until they were locked in a hug. They were
both terrified.

- This doesn't change anything, Alocinia. You know that, don't
  you?
- Yeah, I know. Maybe we should try to get this fear under control.
- I've never been so scared in my life. It's the unknown. And the
  need. It's so strong.

A warm wave of heat shimmered just around the grassy entrance.

- I love you. I've got to go.
- You're okay, Petra. Just know it, you're okay.

In a moment, Petra was gone. When her knee disappeared into the
hole, Petra lost track of the sun, too. Complete and utter silence.

A trail of Alocinia's voice, a whisper, followed behind her, and then there was nothing else. She closed her eyes, gathering together all of herself and everything else she could find. And then, she was alone, with herself.

Melancholy crept beside her, trying to find a way in, but not. She was caught in the space between her body and the breadth of the universe. Splashes of color dripped from the air around her. A jug sat patiently, spring water slowly dripping, dripping to fill it. There must be a way through. Which way should she go to part the waters?

Petra reached deep inside to see what was there. There, what she was searching for, it was there, under the skin that prickled, all the way to the depths. Light blue radiance, ephemeral, translucent, a presence without embodiment that calmed what screamed inside of her. She joined the stars, together with all the other mortals.

She was lost and needed to go up for air, to return to what was familiar on the other side. But she couldn't, not yet. She tried to grasp Alocinia's wing, but it was too far away. A rushing marimba cut through the atmosphere with its vibrating whistles, heavenly wind, and thumping wooden drums. It sent her to one side, then the other. She seemed to be made of music.

Petra awaited Justina as she drifted down from the stars, her face bright with a smile. Petra couldn't look away from her misty brown eyes. She put aside the quivering melody while she admired Justina. Sweaty hands gripped Petra's shoulders while Petra's lips pressed the soft skin made of honey, and all sense of place disappeared. Loving while fully present with herself. What was her self? Why did it pinch?

She was quiet, open, and alert. With Alocinia it pinched less. Somehow she knew how to smooth out the pricks. Petra's insides knew only roil and turmoil, a constant struggle between chaos and control. The slow beat of drums wrestled with reggaeton, the coyote with the hen. Struggle between, and among.

The quiet love fled. A charging bull came upon a girl dreaming into the distance on a dry hillside and threw her to the ground. A painter's colors fell to the floor. Music splashed on the ground and the running people fled over it.

She was in all of it, it was in her. When she turned away, it followed her to the edge, such a beautiful and dangerous place. It was exciting, but so close for jumping, or falling, or being pushed. Her future was just beyond reach.

The mournful passion of an unfamiliar music expanded. The woman's voice sailed like a rising storm, filled the air with questions of love and loss, with her powerful hold on the depth, her control in letting it out, up, throttle, down, breaking up, breaking out. She missed Alocinia, wanted to travel through this new place, but not leave her behind.

The music transformed into *rancheros* and blasted her back to her reality. Carlos's radio thundered across her dreams. The first howls of the rooster outside decisively roused the household. Disappointment filled Petra's mind. She couldn't pierce the barrier, couldn't pick out her future, not even in her dreams.

Nonna yelled at Carlos to turn down the volume, but he laughed instead, holding close to the music, letting it jolt him with willpower. Candlelight drifted through the doorway between the two rooms, and Petra stirred to the smell of coffee, and to the strident insistence of the parrot, who watched the grinding of the corn from its perch, repeating "*Buenos días*," several times. Nonna shoved her husband, so she could put away their bed and get on with the food preparations. "Wake up! Get some coffee to thicken the blood for the day's work."

Moments after rolling out of bed, Petra lifted the two empty jugs onto her shoulders. Only a sliver of subdued light found its way through the cracks to the darkness inside the house. Two pigeons fluttered away, woken from their perch in the eaves by the human stirrings. The chickens began their squawking. A few minutes later, the cold spring water she had retrieved splashed on her face, startling away the early morning daze. Carlos kicked the scrawny dog out of the way and sat down at the table.

While Carlos gulped down the coffee, their grandparents and Petra knelt down by the family's altar. Itzamná dwarfed the figurine of the Virgin Mary. Petra prayed to both as one, and to Jesus, whose picture was pasted to the wall behind the copal incense, for peace in the underworld and the heavens, for compassion for those who had lost their way, for the gentle passing of days into nights and back again. Then she placed small bits of masa dough at the feet of the *aluxob* to soothe their impatience. A wizened old woman only three inches tall, the *alux* looked at Petra with an attitude of amused resentment. Her patience with the burdens she had carried for centuries was wearing thin. Her *alux* partner's long pointed beard hung from his chin, his hands cupping his cheeks as his eyes glared forth. They fully expected those they protected to attend to their needs. Petra obeyed their command.

Petra and Nonna began to sing the daily Christian hymns. Carlos listened from a distance, but he considered worship to be the business of girls and little kids and old people. For a moment, she felt him drift toward the sound of their voices praying together. But he soon sloughed it off to toughen his skin for the day's labor.

Nonna brought in two fresh eggs, cracked them open into a bowl, and offered them to Itzamná. Petra could have sworn she heard the beating of wings against the early mistiness of dawn. Her head jerked toward Itzamná, turning questioning eyes upon him. She leaned forward to grasp the message of this great creator of civilization. She closed her eyes and cleared her mind, obeying the command to listen. It felt as if her head was being pried open.

A series of very mortal images filled her mind: She sat at a table in a dark room lit with a single electric lamp suspended over the thick book she was studying; then she was dressed in a green cotton shirt and pants, moving about purposefully inside a bright, sterile room filled with medical equipment; her mother stood in the shadows, calling out to her in a whisper. Blood coursed through her hands—warm, strong, pressing her to take action, rushing toward its source.

Surprised by the force of the waking images, Petra shouted out, "Nonno!"

"Petra," Nonno responded quickly. "What's wrong?"

"Do you see Itzamná's wings beating against the light?"

"Every day, Petita," he said. "Nothing to worry about. When Itzamná has been duly fed and respected, he tends to rise up."

"But—"

"Itzamná is a powerful deity. You would do well to listen if he is communicating with you."

"My mother is there, Nonno, watching me. There is a pressure inside, like I need to heed the images."

"Listen well to Itzamná, *m'hija*."

"How do I know what he's telling me?"

Quietly, he repeated, "Listen. You will know when you are ready."

Nonna, who had been kneeling in prayer, stood. She cradled the bowl of eggs in two hands and handed it to Petra, gesturing toward the fire. Petra threw the eggs into the fire which had warmed their coffee.

CHAPTER TEN

The sun had long since set, and the darkness found Petra and Nonno resting on the porch bench. The mangy dog scratched itself with its hind foot, sneezed, grunted, then plopped down in a lump on the ground. The palm trees murmured to the banana trees, and they hatched sylvan plots together. The humans spoke in tones hushed by the moral murkiness of the black night.

Petra could handle the situation with Emilio on her own. What could Nonno do to help, anyway? He only needed to know the part about him. "Last week, when Emilio beat up Carlos, Emilio told me to find out about a secret place you know of, Nonno. I don't know what he's talking about."

Nonno shuddered and his eyes jumped to the horizon. Suddenly he stood, then began pacing the porch. "What did he say exactly, Petra?"

"He wanted you and me to take him to this place. He sounded threatening, Nonno. Why would he say such a thing?"

The palm leaves whistled across the fields, and the hills devised their specters beneath the volcano. The dog rose to bark at the vagueness of the night. Nonno's discomfort was evident. His glance fluttered between the dog and Petra, weighing the moment.

"Petrita, you are young. Life is long by the time you reach my age. It has stretched through many episodes and stories. I don't believe you know much about my life when I was a young man. Perhaps you are old enough now to know more."

Petra nodded, looking at her feet. "I feel old, too, Nonno." Each fright she experienced had pushed her childhood away a bit further. She thirsted for Nonno's trust, and to fully share the Mayan ways he used to open doors.

Gravely, Nonno said, "The time approaches to pass some things down to the next generation. In her time, your mother carried the burden. Now I believe it falls to you." With little hesitation, Nonno began. His persona as the wise *anciano*, the old sage windswept by life, came forth. He gazed upon Petra with concern.

Petra was fifteen years old now, the age at which girls traditionally took on the mantle of adulthood. She had not enjoyed the traditional *quinceañera* celebration at her last birthday because of the family's limited circumstances. "Nevertheless, you insist on making the transition on your own," Nonno said.

Petra's fingers pulled on her lower lip, her eyes narrowing. Alocinia's wings fluttered.

"You are beginning to taste what is a long history—of our country, and of your family. It is time to share with you a piece of our family's history, my history. I have struggled much in my life with this past, my daughter. I found it very difficult to embrace my Mayan heritage when I was a child because of the prejudice in school."

"But the danger went much deeper than that." The Guatemalan military, he said, was convinced that the indigenous people supported the guerrillas, and massacred many thousands of them. In the name of standing for the rights of the poor and indigenous, the guerrillas, too, killed those who refused to join them. "Here in this community, many got caught between the two groups and died often horrible deaths." Nonno lowered his head and rested his thumb under his chin, his forefinger against the tip of his nose.

"My father died in this way when I was just becoming a man." When he slowly raised his head to look at Petra, she glimpsed a deep sadness in his eyes. He allowed the silence to hang over them.

"But before his death, by my early teens, I had already learned to pass as Ladino." He spent little time with his parents, moving around with friends, and never spoke the indigenous language. He denied his Quiché parents, forced himself to lose any indigenous accent, and he learned Spanish perfectly. He acted and dressed the part of the Ladino. "Things seemed a little easier that way," he said.

"My mother refused to do any such thing." She proudly wore the indigenous colors and clothing, she practiced many Mayan rituals, she spoke to Nonno in Quiché—but he would only respond to her in Spanish. His father remained silent in the background. He never confronted his son, though he was conscious of his disapproval, and he rarely saw him. "I felt terribly guilty about it all, but I believed my very life was at stake, so I snubbed their customs. I tried to dissociate myself from my own mother. And despite myself, I absorbed her Mayan pride."

By the time he was seventeen, Nonno was looking for opportunities to leave home—the same home they lived in today—to experience something new. "Mind you, I had already married and Tonyo was a little baby, but the three of us lived with my mother." The war was raging, and the future looked bleak. One day in 1980, he stopped in a restaurant in San Luis Hunahpu. At another table near him a group of men were eating and talking seriously amongst themselves. They were Ladino and American, all speaking English, a language Nonno had never heard spoken in person until then.

"Now you hear it on television, you know so much about other places, but then, there were no televisions in Las Leches, none that I knew of, anyway. Electricity came and went because the guerrillas blew up the transmission stations and cut the wires. Everyone lived in fear during that time, Petra, especially indigenous people. Conflict between the guerrillas and the military was perpetual, and gruesome.

"Anyway, I was very curious about these men. I must have been staring at them because they looked toward me and waved me over." He drew together all of his courage and approached their table. It turned out they were archeologists working in El Juyú, not far from the Sibalq'aq Volcano. Apparently, he said, he made an impression on them, because they offered him a job helping them transport equipment and tools, dig where they directed him, do whatever they needed. "It was an incredible opportunity, Petra, and I had just fallen into it without trying!"

It turned out that archeologists had been working at El Juyú for years, Nonno continued. Even though it was only a few kilometers from their home, he had no idea. They were uncovering one part of a vast Mayan civilization, dating back many centuries before the birth of Christ. The site had links to other areas, some in Guatemala City, some up north in

Tikal, in Petén. "They were finding evidence of a complex political and economic system, Petra. All so close by!" Unearthing all those treasures, learning about the rituals, the gods, all the Mayan characters. It must have been incredible, overwhelming.

Nonno began to learn about his Mayan past, when he had shunned it for so long in his own family. "Ironically, that very past helped guide me back to the past I had tried to escape at home. Leaving really brought me back to myself. And myths became real."

Nonno stopped, shivered, overwhelmed by his story. His eyes blazed, but she saw fear lurking behind. Her Nonno, her rock, was afraid. Of what?

"Nonno," said Petra, "I had no idea. What you said yesterday struck me: 'Myth is born from reality, and reality is born from myth.' I think I am understanding what you mean now."

"That's only a small part of it, Petra. You will continue to understand if you think on it." Nonno's eyes blinked in weariness, shutting down the story of his life for the night. Petra had learned to tamp down her impatience when she hoped for Nonno's wisdom or support.

"But this place, El Juyú, is not a secret. I have heard it mentioned at school. What did Emilio mean?"

"No, *mi amor*, El Juyú is well known. Tourists visit, there is a museum and a visitor's center."

"Could we go visit sometime, Nonno? I would like to see it." Apparently, he was not ready to tell her what Emilio had to do with this. It was not proper for the granddaughter to push the grandfather. She would wait until he was ready. Emilio would have to wait.

Nonno's face sagged with the weight of his narrative. A vagueness crept into his voice. "Of course, Petita. But I must sleep. I am tired now." He rose from the bench.

Nonno shuffled into the house, but rather than falling into bed, he headed directly for the family altar. Petra tiptoed behind her grandfather as far as the doorway, not quite ready to leave him behind for the night. He lifted Itzamná up in both arms, first raising the falcon over his head, then cradling him against his chest, muttering words she could not hear. When he turned to face Petra, he smiled knowingly. Of course he had felt her presence there. His eyes closed, and he whispered, "Heed the dreams." Or had he just taken a deep breath? He gently replaced the falcon and got into bed next to Nonna.

But Petra could not sleep. She lay awake for hours weaving images of her teenage grandfather digging in the volcano—the volcano she saw every day! The volcano that oriented her in the woods, that hid behind the banana trees, that called to her to visit, that burned in her heart.

After hours of tossing and turning, the night finally reached into her and released her consciousness. Her body rose up in dream. She was traipsing through the woods, the steaming heat, the spiders and snakes, arriving at the foot of the volcano itself. The lava hissed as she climbed up, speaking to her in cryptic poetry, beckoning her to climb.

Time pressed on her. She had to get down the other side before day broke, so she wouldn't miss school in the morning. Hauling herself ever upward, she strained to find her bearings. She craved a companion. As the thought dawned, her hand unconsciously went to her pocket. It was empty. A hummingbird alighted on her shoulder.

Alocinia assessed Petra from her perch. Red and yellow vines, nebulous in the night air, encircled the trees, dangling over the ground. Sparks ignited the night. The volcano hissed and spat out its riddles. The heat sought to overcome Petra, and she swiped at the sweat on her face.

Alocinia flew off her shoulder. Her voice sang out, bouncing out against the hills.

- Peeet-raaaa! Peeet-raaaah! We climb now. I can see from here
    where we are going.
- Is it far?
- No, not far. Of course, that depends on how you think about far.
    Is it far to the moon? Because the moon is just a thought-mo-
    ment away. Is it far to El Salvador? Which seems light years
    away when you're on the ground.
- Come down, Alocinia. We must walk together. It's not safe to be
    far apart like this.
- It's true. Day and night are separating. Time is pulling them
    apart. We must find the place. But here I am, next to you.

They continued to walk, cheek to wing. The quarter moon glowed just beyond the crater of the volcano. Lines of light coursed across the face of the climb before them. Clambering over sighs and forebodings, up and up. The light spread, and collapsed, the moon shone and broke into pieces. The dark night gained the upper hand.

Petra watched her feet as she walked, avoiding clumps of stones, stepping carefully over tree roots, fallen trees blocking her way. Hurry, move faster. She must find it before the dawn, before daylight severed itself from the night. Her grandfather's whisperings pushed her from behind.

Alocinia: Where are we going?

Petra: The secret place. It's on the far side of the volcano.

- What's in the secret place?
- The secret! How should I know?
- You don't know? Why are we going then?
- We have to find something, Alocinia. It's important!
- But you don't know what it is…
- No. I don't. I will know when I see it. My grandfather will tell
  me when I see it.
- Your grandfather is not here, Petra!
- He is. Just the same as you are here, Alocinia. And the ances-
  tors—especially the ancestors.
- Which ancestors are with you, Petra?
- The Mayan ones. Alocinia, this is a bad time for questions. Let's
  go faster. We must hurry. There may be others.
- Did you hear that noise behind us?
- No, what?
- A noise. Something moving. Bigger than a mouse.

A leaping and falling sound. A tree branch in front of them began to shake. This shaking was too insistent for the wind. It moved purposefully, regularly. Then a barking sound—eerie barking.

- Alocinia, we must get there soon. Look, I see the crater! See
  the dark furrow above there? It marks the border! Don't pay
  attention to the monkey. He is one of the bad ones, the men
  who fled to the trees when the gods punished them for their
  foolishness.
- That barking monkey is a foolish man?
- That's right.

Foolish men. On the branch there behind her, the shape of Emilio was laughing in the tree. If she held tight to Alocinia, he would go away. In a groundswell of movement, they heaved forward. They passed the crater and began to pour in a rush down the far side. Home had disappeared out of sight.

  - Where is home, Alocinia? I can't see it. I'm scared.
  - Don't acknowledge fear and it will dissipate. Home is just a
    breath away.

Petra noticed Alocinia's breath, misty, sparkling like the volcano sparks when she spoke. Her words were made of fire. She reached for Alocinia's body, and it burned hot. Alocinia drew her wings up, over her head, arcing them in a circle down to her sides, as if communicating with the universe. Petra caught sight of her wings glowing in the dark.

  - Petra, another noise!
  - What is it?
  - Don't know. Bigger than a monkey. It takes steps behind us, steps
    of stealth.
  - Alocinia! Watch out! There's a jaguar over there, behind the rock!
  - Draw in your breath, Petra. You also breathe fire, but it must be
    calm so we can listen.

Petra saw that her hands, too, glowed. The jaguar accompanied them, through a tunnel overlaid by a canopy of trees, across a clearing where they peered north into the void of darkness, and finally into the dense woods of juicy leaves and pine needles, treading quietly.

She felt the ancestors rising up through her blood, beating in her heart, shooting through her veins and into her hands. Her hands pulsed, alive to the past. The jaguar followed behind.

A sad moan sang with the wind. A moaning that lifted and fell, played rhythms of the marimba, rising tones of breath. Her own lungs rose and fell, weighing in her chest.

An intensity flooded into her heart, lifted her inches off the ground, then dropped her. She landed on her hands and feet, the glow penetrating the earth. The earth opened up to her hands. They touched the secret.

  - Alocinia, are we there?
  - I think so, Petra. What do we do now?

The marimba reverberated in the thickening fog, deafening her. Alocinia was talking, but Petra couldn't hear her. Alocinia fell to the ground, her broken beak in the earth, her wings stretched out to her sides. Her body sprawled on the ground, as if the earth powered her insides, pulling her into the ground.

Before Petra appeared a slight, wizened woman, much older than her grandfather, barely visible through the fog, sitting before a gourd, its sides wrapped by cloth brightly colored in geometric patterns, throbbing on a deer skin drum.

- Alocinia, Alocinia! Come back! I'm scared!

The woman's hand rose and beckoned Petra. Terrified, Petra froze. Slowly, she forced her feet forward. The throbbing reached into Petra's soul and shook her. She looked at the woman with frightened eyes.

The woman said, "You have come despite the fear. I welcome you and your friend." She continued to beat the drum. "You have come to meet the creator, the lord of the skies. And you have come to search for your own destiny."

Petra gave a slight nod.

"You seek answers at the place you know best in your heart, but you are not of this place. You will find your future elsewhere."

"Where, *doña*? Where must I go?"

"Peel off the layers of suffering. You'll find it underneath." The woman's skeletal finger lifted slowly to Petra's heart, then grazed the point where her ribs came together, and again just above the bridge of her nose. "And elsewhere. Keep your friend close by. There is great wisdom in her, for she tells you what you already know. Now go, find the creator. Follow him to beyond."

Bowing her head, Petra turned. She felt Alocinia's voice rise up through her lungs, entering her mind.

- Let the fear loose, Petra. It's here. Touch the ground.

- I don't feel anything! Where is it? What do you have?

- It's right here! Lie on your back. See the raptor above us.

- But I can't see it! All I see is dark!

- It's there. It looks like a falcon, with a snake in its beak. The
   snake has two heads!

- Alocinia, I see it! Itzamná! It's Itzamná!

The moment she saw the falcon, daylight broke away from night; night dissolved. The heavens got the upper hand over the underworld.

Petra lurched from the ground and began to run back home. She had an overwhelming need to get home and leave for school.

CHAPTER ELEVEN

"Scorpion!" Carlos shouted. Petra leapt from her bed. He shook out the hammock and clobbered a leather sandal into the dirt.

"You okay?" Nonna's voice drifted in from her bed in the other room. Petra scrambled over to Carlos to check.

"Fine, fine. Just a scorpion bite. I'll live." He shook his arm, his jaw clenched tight.

The scorpion unleashed an uneasiness to the morning that crept under her skin and stayed with her. She slipped on long pants instead of the expected dress before anyone could object. Nonna didn't approve, and she'd have to undergo chiding from Carlos, but today she needed the relative muscle of the pants.

Calm eluded her this morning. Even the fragrance of tortillas, eggs, and boiled plantain made her uneasy. The fire cracked like distant gunfire. She wandered from the back yard to the front courtyard.

The roosters were quiet this morning. She didn't remember hearing them sing out at dawn. And the dog was nowhere to be seen. An unnatural hush lay over the early mist. Beyond the edge of the forest, where the volcano rose behind the banana trees, she spotted the hens up a tree, too far into the woods. Why hadn't they come down yet and begun to cluck about searching for tidbits to gobble? The volcano whispered to her in foreboding tones.

Below the chickens, the dog stared up into the tree, as if waiting for them to come down. Or maybe he was trying to persuade them of his innocent intentions, like the coyote in the story. "You guys just hang out there," she said to the hens. "Don't you believe anything this dog tells you." She clapped her hands emphatically to make the dog relinquish his post.

Unexpectedly, without thinking about it, she understood why the Siguanaba went with the man voluntarily. She had seized the power of acting first. If she'd waited and he'd forced her to go with him, she would have lost the advantage of initiative. By not hesitating, she took control over the situation before he could prepare a defense. Petra would act to determine her own future.

The variation in the routine was throwing her off. Carlos wanted to finish up the cane processing over the next week, so they could pack the burro next Friday and all go into San Luis Hunahpu together on Saturday. So Petra would walk to school unescorted this morning and next week. It was no big deal to go alone for a few days. After all, she usually walked herself home. Yet that feeling of uneasiness was tailing her. Every day, this road.

Thankfully, she could look forward to soccer practice after school. There was only one additional practice before the big game next Saturday. Her steps lightened. Practice days couldn't come often enough for her.

Notions of heroically blocking balls headed for the goal failed to scare away the troubled mood that beset her. She rambled slowly but purposefully along the road to school. Hearing a noise in the woods, she swung her gaze into the shadows, but didn't see anything. She told herself to quit being so edgy.

"Tita, Tita, Petita!" She heard just a whisper of that singsong. She was ninety per cent sure it was her perturbed imagination, an echo of last week's encounter with Emilio. She spun around but saw no one. She was surprised to notice there was no one else on the road with her. That was unusual. She picked up her pace.

She approached the curve which bent around the grand ceiba tree. Its magnificent canopy dwarfed the nearby fledgling trees competing for a piece of the sun. People said the tree was at least two centuries old. The mighty roots splayed out along the ground, framing the road's precipitous turn. Some of the ceiba tree's famous spines projected out of its trunk above her head, but not so many because many had fallen off as the tree aged.

She lowered her eyes in recognition of the sacredness of the tree, a symbol of the universe in the Quiché tradition. The tree could help her find that missing link to her purpose. She would join with it, from the roots, said to reach down into the underworld, to its trunk in her world, to its upper branches flowing high into the sky and the Mayan heaven. She lifted her arms in harmony with the tree for a moment. Her eyes swept across the upper branches in search of a hummingbird. No luck. Later, perhaps, she would ask one to carry a message for her up to heaven. She would come up with just the right message and give it to Alocinia.

As she rounded the curve, her head turned upward and arms in the air, she didn't notice the three young men in front of her. A man's laughter compelled her attention back to earth.

"Petita, don't fly off yet!" It was Emilio confronting her, blocking her way, mocking her. Emilio out front, two more behind him, standing with their legs apart, ready and alert. So Emilio had his own bodyguards now. A knife hung from each belt. No more "innocent" machete. "Tita, I promised you the other day I'd be back, didn't I? Where's your skinny brother?"

"What do you want, Emilio? Why don't you leave me alone already? Go talk to my grandmother."

"Tita," he said matter of factly, "I keep telling you I can't live without you. You're growing up into the woman of my dreams." He drew curves in the air inches from her body.

"Emilio, shut up. I have to get to school. I'll be late." She tried to brush by him, but he grabbed her by the arm. The scene felt far too familiar.

"Petita, what's your hurry? School can wait. We have much bigger designs for you." That fake lilting voice infuriated her.

"Who are these two repugnant guys with you, anyway?"

The husky, short guy bristled at the insult and moved menacingly toward her, a hand caressing the knife at his side, but Emilio stayed him with a piercing glance. "Don't worry about them. They're buddies of mine. We hang together, right, Potoo? But I shouldn't be impolite to you, Petita—since our destinies are intertwined. Potoo, this is Petra; Petra, Potoo. So called because he does a lot of moaning, especially at night, and he swoops down from high branches to eat little insects. Do you know much about the Potoo bird, Petita? It has eyelids that have tiny holes in them, so it can see everything all the time, even when its eyes are closed. It's also kind of ugly, like my friend here. Right, Potoo?" Potoo nodded askance.

Emilio looked at the other guy, who had remained stock still. He was tall and skinny, his hair and clothes disheveled. "Gorto, meet Petra. Don't let his obesity fool you." He and Gorto smirked. "I watched Gorto just the other day defend himself against a character that wanted to take liberties, shall we say. He performed quite well for himself. I rewarded him with a promotion." He didn't say what kind of promotion.

As soon as she heard the name Gorto again, Petra bit her lip so she wouldn't react. He had been one of the gang members talking outside her school. So this was Gorto! Not short and fat at all, as she'd imagined when she overheard his name and the squeaky voice. He struck her as the kind of boy she'd find picking his nose in a dirty outhouse somewhere.

"Nice to meet your 'family,' Emilio," she said, dripping angry sarcasm. "Gotta go!" But Emilio tightened his grip on her arm.

"Petita, we're not done yet. Just trying to establish some courtesy with the introductions," Emilio said sarcastically. "But I'll come to the business at hand, since you're wanting to get on with it. So here's the point. We want you to come with us and join our little X-14 club. There's a bunch of us cute guys, and we need a few cute girls to make it even. I can promise you gold bangles, an iPhone, beautiful dresses, roses, meat to eat, and lots o' love and *endless goodies.*" He drew out the syllables of the last words.

"You've got to be kidding, Emilio. You know I'm not even a little bit interested in your life or your 'club.'"

"Tita, don't be so cocksure of yourself. This is serious stuff here. Serious stuff has serious consequences. One word from me to these vultures here, and you're—well, perhaps you can imagine, I don't need to spell it out for you. You might find a little of that church humility to be useful about now." He spit out the word "church."

He paused a moment, considering his options. "The thing is, we can do this nicely, or not so nicely, but it will be done. *A la buena, o a la mala.* Come to think of it, I've been trying the nice way, and *you,*" he coughed, "haven't been so nice. As I said, I need you, and I promised myself I wouldn't let you go so easy again. Leaving your bro' so alone and vulnerable like that." He shook his head slowly and clucked his tongue. "You know you kind of insulted me a couple days ago by running off like that. What am I supposed to do? I try nice, I try tough—all you do is run away from me. I don't generally stand for insults." He glared at her through a torrent of mixed-up desire.

She scowled back. She wondered what the Siguanaba would do in this situation, but she couldn't work it out in the fraught moment.

Emilio continued, "And Petita, you remember that little matter I mentioned about your grandfather? I need the answer now. I told you I expected an answer within a couple of days."

Petra began to object, but he slapped a hand over her mouth, while still holding tightly to her wrist with the other. "Not here, though. We will discuss this in a more private place. Very soon."

The image of blood leaking out of Justina came surging forward and gripped Petra's mind. The horrors rose in a deluge over the dike she had erected to control them. She tried to blink away the thought; her mind refused to look at it.

Her legs felt weak, and she was desperately trying not to urinate on herself. She couldn't sort out what she should do. What did he mean, in a private place? She had to get to school now. How dare he touch her and not allow her to speak.

But now she couldn't blink away Emilio. Petra felt a trickle of urine rolling down her thigh.

"Let's make this easy. I have this little drink I think you'll like. This little bottle here contains some yummy, sweet water. Come on, just a sip now." He pulled a tiny bottle from his pocket. Petra yanked her arm, but Emilio's grip was tight.

"You're hurting me! Let go!" His hand over her mouth muffled her voice.

"Potoo, get over here and help me."

Potoo put his sticky, ugly hands on her and held her so she couldn't move, while Emilio forced the "water" into her mouth. She snorted it out through her nose, so Emilio held her nose, too. Petra was falling to the ground now, her legs collapsing under the weight of events. She began to cry, hating herself for showing weakness.

"Gorto, get the bike." It was the last thing she heard clearly. Within seconds, a weird lightness came over her; even her worries were a little thinner. She suddenly wanted to lie down and grabbed hold of Emilio's arm to break her fall. His arm felt strong, warmly vile. She tried to shake off the web creeping around her head. What was happening to her?

Emilio laced his arms around her middle to pick her up, burying his face in her chest. She didn't expect him to handle her so gently as he seated her in front of him on a small motorcycle, wrapping his arm around her middle. She heard the roar of the motor as she was thrown back into Emilio, helpless now. His chest seethed against her back. Gorto and Potoo followed on another bike behind them.

Before she lost consciousness completely, Petra understood that they were traveling back down the road past the hill to her house, past Vicenta's store. Through a blur, she might have seen the shadow of Vicenta as they sped by. After that, she knew nothing.

CHAPTER TWELVE

Petra's mind swam in her skull. Waves washed away her waking senses. She was underwater, ripping at the water with her legs, trying to rise to the surface, gasping for air. Emilio's arm wrapped around her, and she fell into a well of protectiveness. A small arm, for he was only nine years old, she eight, but the arm of a friend. Then the arm was holding her, as she and Justina, next to her, kicked and breathed and tried to learn the miracle of swimming.

Justina had come running up their hill at the onset of dusk one evening with Emilio just behind. Justina said, "Petra, let's go swimming! It's the girls' turn to swim in the pool. Let's go!" It was a rare opportunity to get a taste of freedom.

"Are you sure?" Petra asked Emilio.

He stumbled over his feet. Justina glared at him and poked him in the ribs. "Yeah, it's OK. Let's just be sure there's no other boys there."

They'd barely gotten their shoes off on the wet stones of the riverbank when Emilio scampered under the trees and plunged into the water. Palm trees spread their fronds over the pool, giving them cover, heightening the solitude. Deep shadows penetrated the water, but the moon gave them light enough to see each other. "Come on, Petra. Justina, over here!"

The girls hesitated. They nervously considered the water while it lapped at their ankles. Petra said, "Emilio, watch out for the water snake!"

He had experience with her subterfuge, so he laughed the warning away. Emilio flipped back toward the supposed threat, then suddenly rose up out of the water with a long and slimy serpent hanging between his wet hands. He tossed it casually onto Petra's thighs.

She recoiled when the slime wrapped itself around her hips, but quickly grasped that it was only a thick vine. Emilio found himself covered with a torrent of splashes from both girls.

Emilio plowed through the wave of water toward them and grabbed Justina's ankles. He pulled her in, so water rose to her waist, but she flipped back out, kicking Emilio away. The way he dove back under the water, rising in the middle of the pool—it looked like he'd been born to swim.

Petra said, "Any idea how to do this, Justina? How do I know I won't go under if I go out there?"

"No idea. Nobody ever taught me how this works."

Emilio proudly floated on his back, smug in the knowledge that this was one place where he could flaunt his greater mastery over his friends. While he was stroking his pride, Petra calculated the possibilities. Suddenly, she landed on him near the middle of the pool, sinking Emilio so he came up spitting out water with his breath.

Petra held her nose, sank straight down into the water, then thrust up off the muddy bottom of the pool. The cool water parted as she rose upward, the sensation on her skin like nothing she had experienced before. It was like being reborn into new skin that was invulnerable. She landed on his shoulders from behind before he could get his balance, knocking him under water again. He surfaced, gasping for breath, but this time quickly looked around for warnings of further sabotage.

But in her abandon, Petra lost the fragile aquatic equilibrium she had attained, and her head went under the water. She got flustered and breathed in water, trying and failing to get her head above the water to cough it out. Emilio's arm wrapped itself around her stomach and lifted her out. She declared that she was willing to cede the advantage to him and was grateful to him.

Then the most exhilarating part of all. He gave them a lesson in swimming. Petra hung onto a root, softly covered with bright green moss, her fingers sinking into the spongy stalks. Legs kicked out; arms swung. Her head went under while she held her breath, then swallowed water as her head pulled out. She spluttered and tried again. She pulled in a huge breath, felt her lungs expand, and floated, her head under water. Her toes wriggled in the wet leaves on the bank, burrowing farther into the mud with an enchanting squish. She took a huge breath, jumped in feet first, then magically floated to the top. Justina splashed messily, noisily, kicking and paddling in a circle around Petra. Emilio smiled broadly.

If someone had passed by the path below, they would have heard the sound of pure abandon, the elated laughter of three friends whose lives were braided together. They wouldn't realize that one boy had just opened a new world to his two best friends.

An eerie quiet invaded Petra's dream. A buzzing in the trees. The moon hid behind the upper branches. Petra listened, trying to understand the murmurs of nature. It was very important to be still, to concentrate deeply. Her nerves rose to the surface of her skin. Distress clouded the happy moment.

The ominous undertone became a whispering in the background. Awareness washed back over her, while her nerves bristled under her skin. Was it the same day? Another day? She lay motionless, listening. Two men were speaking in clouded undertones.

"The next one is mine, right?"

"Sure, sure."

"I'm liking the way this works. We each get girls, we make more money, we impress Mago, and the MS-13 gives us *more* ways to make money. The future is bright, '*mano*."

The comforting arm around Petra fled, wrenched away by crude reality. Every bit of her froze.

"Emilio's got an angle on the famous Mayan bird, too. He told me this girl's going to lead us right to it."

"Say what? What Mayan bird?"

"Gusano says it's a piece some big-shot scientists have been looking for. They lost it or something, but she knows where it is."

"And I thought Emilio just had a thing for her. I'll be sure to give her the white glove treatment." Sputtering laughter.

"For real, that piece has got to be worth a fortune! Mago is the one to find the right buyer, bro'. Linking up with the MS-13 will give us all the connections we need. We'll make a killing off that one.

Petra was waking up, still trying to get a hold on reality. Her ears were fully alert now. What could she have to do with a Mayan bird? Why did she recognize that name, "Gusano?" She searched her memory for the name.

"*Oye*! Watch what you're doing! *Four* lines."

"What if I want two?" Petra placed Gorto's squeaky voice.

"One for each of us, one for the girl. We're starting her off slow. Setting an example for her. Mix hers into that vial there. The needle's in the bag."

"How's Milvia?"

"*Jumba! Chachacha!* Score four, 'mano. All I do is send her a text, tell her be there at eleven, and she's there. Once Chofo gave her the what's what, she knows the score now. *Very* nice ass."

"I'm due, Potoo. This girl is Emilio's. You got the last one. I'm next, *verdad?*"

"You're still a mere youth around here, don't get a pussy up your ass." Potoo screeched with laughter. "This one's gonna need some breaking in, though, little boy." Low murmurs. Petra strained to hear. "You get the coca in her, you get to break her open." She heard a bag crumpling. "Careful with that thing, *niño*, don't be swinging it around."

Ave María. What was she going to do?

Gorto whined, "I'm no little boy, Potoo. Knock it off."

"Okay, *muchacho*. But listen, I'm hatching an idea here. She'll work as exhibit number one for Mago. She just needs to be initiated with the coca and softened up a bit with a whang of this here willy so she accepts her place here in the operation. Maybe we oughta get a little bite before the favored son gets back. Then we'll hand her over to Emilio, more pre-pared for action, if you get my meaning. You up for it?" A chair scraped the floor, then fell over.

"*Joh* yeah, bro', she's primo. She's very fine, *very* fine."

"Share and share alike among us brothers, right, Gorto? If she wakes up before Emilio gets back...." She heard a knife flipping open and closed amidst low snickering.

Gorto's voice turned dreamy. "I'm ready to run my hand along that smooth *barriga*. Wrap my fingers around those long black locks. Fondle the sleek bronze skin up under the shirt to the *chichis*, man. Ay, this girl's got the curves going." Gorto smacked his lips.

A pause, then the sharp sound of hands slapping together." Maybe you should practice on something a little less fine first. Leave her to me, 'mano. I have experience in these things." Potoo audibly slurped back saliva. "My mouth is watering, Gorto. She's lying there provoking the heck out of me. That pretty ass is calling out to me. Let's get us a piece, muchacho, before Emilio gets back with the food."

Petra felt like worms were crawling under her skin. She desperately tried to still herself while they compared her stomach to a cow's and feasted sloppily all over her body. One of them wore heels. The footfalls surrounded her.

Petra cracked open her eyes, trying to understand her surroundings. She was looking up at them, which meant she must be on the ground. It was damp and musty under her, probably a dirt floor. As far as she could see, there were no windows, so she couldn't tell the time of day. She had to focus on what to do. She prayed for God to give her strength.

Potoo and Gorto sat on two battered old wooden chairs, with a squat table to the side, the only furniture she could see. Gorto was working on something on the table. Flattened beer cans and plastic wrapping lay scattered about on the table. Bags of chips and pretzels littered the floor around them. The smell was putrid, a mixture of stale beer and urine.

Potoo began to pace the small room. He said, "Hey, she could be asleep for hours. Why wait till she wakes up?"

Gorto stood up in a hurry, his chair clattering to the ground. "I'm in, man. How can a man resist those lush lips?"

Involuntarily, Petra's body jerked and stiffened.

"Yo, Potoo, I think she's waking up!" Anxious whispering she couldn't hear. She prayed they'd return to their conversation if she didn't move again. The pacing stopped, and she heard a shuffling inch closer to her. Now turned slightly away from them, she slitted her eyes again. Potoo's face was two inches from her!

Petra rolled over and bolted up and away from him, feet to the ground. She scanned the room desperately for the door and hurtled toward it but didn't get there fast enough. Potoo launched himself at her and slammed her against the wall.

"Goddamn, girl, control yourself! Get your precious ass over here!"

Potoo sat down at the table, his eyes glued to her.

"Where am I? Where's Emilio?"

"Just get over here, girl! You got to learn to obey!" He whipped out his knife and thrust it out toward her.

It struck her that he was probably only in his mid-twenties, barely a few years older than Emilio, but the scowl lines on his face made him look a lot older. She refused to turn around to face him. Her cheek and torso lay against the mud-straw wall, her nails digging into it.

"We's the authorities now, you better learn that quick." From the corner of her eye, she saw him swivel a chair under himself and clumsily sit down. He tapped a foot, covered with a scuffed cowboy boot, the pointed, metal-tipped toe absurd in its fashion statement, waiting for her to do as ordered. He patted his thighs, commanding her to sit on him.

She turned around but glowered determinedly to the side, refusing to meet his glance, and stood motionless, her back plastered up against the wall. She would keep her dignity, not cower before these creeps. Her palms were sweating, she realized, her heart beating up her chest from the inside.

"You got to the count of five to get over here, or you're gonna see how sharp this knife can be. I'm counting silently, so you might not want to wait."

Petra didn't move. "I asked," she said defiantly, "where am I?"

Before she finished the question, Potoo hustled toward her, pulled her up close to him, and swung the knife out toward her. Inches from her, he moved the knife from her chin, excruciatingly slowly, building his own suspense, along her ribs and between her legs.

Her eyes widened and her breath caught.

Holding the knife there a moment, he lifted and pulled. A slit broke out of her pants in the crotch. He held the knife menacingly in front of her nose for a moment. His beady eyes stared like bullets into hers. Then his hands went inside the slits of her pants, and he pulled, ripping the pants down to her knees. The sound of her pants splitting down the seams bounced off his ugly bird face.

Petra heard screaming before she realized it was coming from her.

He slapped her in the face and covered her mouth with his foul hand. Gorto spoke from behind Potoo. "Slow, my man, let's share now. Keep watch for Emilio."

Potoo said, "Screaming will get you nowhere, Señorita Tita. There ain't nobody around to hear you." A twisted smile swept across his face, then vanished.

So Emilio made them nervous. They had to watch out for him.

An image of Emilio's father interrogating Petra the night his mother died flashed through her consciousness. His father, and that tattooed guy, what was his name?

Potoo pushed her so her back flattened hard against the floor. He closed his knife. "Gorto, you got any rope? This girl is out of control. She's having difficulty understanding who's in charge here."

Gorto disappeared for a minute out the door and returned with some fraying rope. One wrist at a time, her arms looped tight with the rope over her head, he hooked her to a couple of metal stakes protruding from the cabin floor.

Twisting tattoos danced on the ceiling. Suddenly cold, her legs ached. Jolts of pain raced through her body. She wanted to run, and couldn't. The sensation was eerily familiar. Her forehead broke out in a cold sweat. She redoubled her effort to concentrate, to think out her choices. Her vulnerability hit her like a rock flung from a hayloft.

Potoo strutted around and over her, pushing his pelvis forward with each step, the veins in his neck pulsating. He crouched over her, one leg to each side of her hips.

She spat in his face.

Potoo recoiled instinctively. "*Desgraciada*, miserable wretch!" He slapped her again. She swallowed blood, then spit the blood into his face.

His face tightened; his breath came in snorts. When she pulled her arms to loosen the bonds, the ropes tightened and dug into her skin.

Suddenly he grabbed her pants where he'd split them open and pushed against her with his fist. The force slid her along the ground, and the ropes cut sharply against her wrists. "Ow, you're hurting me!" She felt his knuckles against the inside of her thighs and thrashed her legs at him.

Then he was on top of her, grinding at her through his clothes. "Gorto, take this knife for me, man. I'm taking off the pants. And load up the needle, man. Bring it over here."

Petra flailed at him with her legs, and he rolled off, but then Gorto was next to her with the knife. He was holding a vial of liquid in his other hand, waving it at Potoo. She couldn't hear anything now. A great chaos of static in her head blocked all the words. Potoo had his pants around his ankles now. With shock, she registered the nastiness of his member, engorged and bouncing up and down as he stumbled toward her. He pushed his thumb into the tip of her nose.

"I'm ready to teach you one of those important lessons of life, girl. With any luck, you won't bleed too much, because I have a feeling this is your very first time."

She felt flesh, ugly flesh, touching her between her legs. She tried to scream above the uproar, but now Potoo was covering her mouth.

Then, Petra's gaping eyes took in Emilio, towering over them. Through the commotion, no one had heard him come back in. His face was flaming red, his body splayed like a rooster in fighting position. He flung his arm at Gorto's hand, and the syringe went flying.

Emilio's voice cut sharply into the tense atmosphere. "Goddamn it, what the hell do you think you're doing?" He propelled the words furiously at Potoo. The spurs of his rooster claws swung out and ripped at Potoo, catapulting him back against one of the chairs.

Potoo grunted, and he settled on the ground to lick his wounds. He tried to pull his pants back up, but they stuck to his bony knees, tangled up in his befuddlement. Apologetically, he said, "Just teaching this whore a lesson, Emilio. She needs some taming, man."

"Fuck it, Potoo, I told you this one's mine. Leave her alone. I'll handle this my way! Both of you, get the fuck outside. I'll call you dicks when I need you."

Petra was impressed at how sharp they were to attend. They rolled out the door in two split seconds.

As soon as they were gone, Emilio slammed himself against the wall. A low moaning filled the room.

Petra stared, stunned. They sat looking at each other, motionless, for what could have been hours, but may have been only minutes. Then the fear began to spill out of her. She looked down at her hands and was bewildered that she couldn't control their trembling.

Twisting around, Emilio sat up, cross-legged. As he threw his head back, his nose flared, and that lower lip curled under. She was having trouble grasping the meaning of Emilio's contortions.

But Petra fastened on his eyes, which raced around, ricocheting off the walls, like a soccer ball hurled angrily between competitors. His hands grasped his temples, and he shook his head violently back and forth.

Finally, he stopped. He looked down between his feet, still again. Petra listened to the sound of their breathing.

As if forcing his voice out of himself, he said, "Petra, you ok?" He sighed deeply, then groaned. He clambered over beside her and slashed the ropes holding her. He held her arm with a degree of consideration, his eyes strangely serene, while he untied the rope from each of her wrists.

Petra stuttered, her voice quavering. "Emilio, everything is—is so screwed up. What—what's happened to you?" She grabbed one of her hands with the other to hold it still.

Emilio rubbed his eyes, trying to hold the sobs back. "This can't happen again." His eyes rolled back into his head as if dredging up something important lodged there. "It's got to stop." He wheezed and gasped for breath. "It *won't* stop, not ever. I don't know how—how to make it stop."

"Nobody makes you harass me all the time! Why don't you leave me alone already?"

"Nobody makes me," Emilio echoed grimly. He closed his eyes as pain washed over his face. "Yeah, I guess." He hung his head. "Tell me, Petra, what are my choices? Because I can't find any good ones."

"Why did you bring me here, Emilio? And where am I anyway?"

Emilio appeared to rouse himself back to awareness. "Petra, your pants! Oh my god, I shouldn't have left those animals alone here." He called out, "Gorto, bring me the duct tape, in the bag on my bike!" Emilio gently touched her on the cheek where Potoo had slapped her. The touch stung, and she winced.

The tape appeared momentarily with Gorto, who kept his eyes on the ground and quickly disappeared again. Petra realized the smell of the place had changed from sour beer and urine, to chicken and sour beer and urine. Emilio had brought chicken and rice to eat. Emilio handed her the tape and gestured to use it to tape around her pants legs, so they'd hold together.

"Heck, Emilio, what are you doing? You know, sometimes I still try to remember that we used to be friends, really friends, and it's hard to imagine! Emilio, reach deep and remember, remember who you were, just for a minute. With any luck, you're still in there somewhere."

The man with the tattoos. She remembered now, at Emilio's house, when she was nine years old, when his mother bled to death. His father had called the man—Gusano! So that was the man Potoo and Gorto had mentioned. Was Gusano the "boss" of the X-14 gang?

Then what role did Emilio's father have in the gang? If his father had already been buddies with Gusano so long ago, he was probably a big shot in the X-14, so he'd pass along corresponding status to his son, and raise him up for an important role. Six years had gone by, plenty of time to train his son and move him up the lines.

Emilio's body stood, staggered. With a certain tenderness, he handed her a glass of water.

Petra snapped back to the present. "Why are you doing this to me? Don't you remember when we were kids?" Petra was realizing she had to seize the moment here to shift the mood. The Siguanaba took the initiative—that was the lesson she had to hold onto. Maybe she could maneuver Emilio to a better place with her memory. Clarity swept through her mind, and she knew exactly what she had to do.

"Remember the time you and me and Justina went down to the river at night, when no one else was there?" Her voice smooth and low, she began to recount the events of that night as Emilio stared at her, his mouth slightly open.

"Do you remember, Emilio?" Petra asked.

Emilio said, "It was Justina's idea. I was afraid somebody would see us there and I'd get beat up for bringing two girls there."

"Shush, Emilio." Petra recounted the memory, her dream. As she spoke, Petra thought of her Nonno's voice when he spun tales for her. Focusing all her attention and story-telling wits, she brought the scene to life for Emilio, understanding that this was her best chance.

Emilio interrupted when Petra knocked him under the water. "Damn if it wasn't hard to just be in charge over you two. I was supposed to be stronger, you know."

Petra laughed. "That's why it was so much fun with us. You let it happen, though; you did. You let me be strong, too. I noticed." Her smile was filled with warmth for their youthful friendship. "Let me finish the story." Emilio watched her intently, his brown eyes searching her face as she proceeded. She sipped the water.

"You broke all the rules that night. The friendship we had, Emilio—"

A tear dropped down Emilio's cheek. Fondness for him cut across her.

"Remember that, Emilio? The three of us were a team. We had so much fun together."

Embarrassed, Emilio flung his arm to his face and wiped it clean. He sat down at the table and hung his head down between his arms. In a few seconds, his head sprang up again, and he lurched toward the food.

Nothing was slow and calm with him. Like pins pricking his mind, a bewitched doll jumping at someone else's command. He didn't seem to be master of himself.

He found a jalapeño pepper in the container with the chicken and put it whole into his mouth. His eyes narrowed and his mouth formed a bitter line until he spit it out on the floor. Then he bit into a raw onion, chewing it like he was washing down the jalapeño.

Such male pretense, just to give cover to any tenderness he felt. Why wouldn't he just talk to her?

Emilio held out the box of chicken to her, encouraging her to eat. She shook her head.

He reached into his pocket, then proffered his closed hand to her. Slowly, it opened. There were the same jacaranda petals, broken and flattened, but infused with life by their memory. This time, her hand closed over his, the petals held tightly between their palms.

He walked to the back of the cabin, swept away some cobwebs with his hand, and carefully pulled away a square chunk of wood that fit tightly into the wall around it. An escape hatch, carefully carved out and camouflaged. "Petra, go! If you stay, you're going to get hurt. Go now!"

CHAPTER THIRTEEN

"Emilio…." There was more she wanted to say. And especially more she wanted to hear from Emilio. For instance, how long had those jacaranda petals lived in his pocket? But their moment was over. He was offering her an opportunity that might not last long. "Emilio. *Cuídate*. Please."

She scuttled through the hole in the wall. Potoo and Gorto's voices continued to rise and fall as they jabbered obliviously next to the motorbikes. She fled into the woods behind the cabin.

Petra started to cry now. Her tears mixed with the smelly dirt from the cabin floor that covered her clothes, her hands, everything. Her pants pulled uncomfortably at her thighs, but at least they held together. Her face stung, the skin of her wrists was raw, and her gum was trickling blood in her mouth again now that she was running.

After a few minutes, she stopped and vomited. She hoped the ugliness spewed out, along with the poisons they had forced her to drink.

A few moments rest, and she ran again. All she could see were clumps of trees, barely penetrable branches—a morass of forest ahead of her. She couldn't see through them to the familiar mountains or the volcano. The late afternoon sun was sinking fast, so she thought it must be the same day she'd started off to school. It didn't matter, she'd work it out.

It crossed her mind that she was incredibly lucky. Emilio had just given her a very dangerous gift. She raced the falling sun.

For two hours, she pressed on in an arduous march through the woods. The sun had slumped below the horizon faster than she could find her way home. Only the stars and the crescent moon lit her meandering path.

Thorns and brambles in the woods had pricked holes in her pants, now haphazardly wrapped with duct tape, and her legs were scratched. Her hair was tangled and dusty and her face smeared with dirt, but she buoyed herself with the thought that she had escaped relatively unharmed.

She never thought she'd be so happy to see the dirt road. A pick-up driven by an old man with a rickety gray mustache stopped to pick her up. Despite her discomfort at the prospect of sitting in close quarters with a strange man in the dark of the night, she had little choice but to climb in. Her body pressed up against the passenger door, she stared out the side window. Every bump in the road jolted her body.

He glanced toward her several times as he drove. "Last time I looked that way, I was in Vietnam."

Startled out of her huddle by his voice, Petra said nothing. She squeezed her legs together, trying to hide the duct tape as much as possible. Hazarding a glance at his face, their eyes met for a moment. The man's eyes held kindness. She tried to relax.

"You see the scar across my forehead?" he asked abruptly. He flipped his gray hair to the side to reveal a ragged scar above his eye.

She nodded.

"Vietnam," he repeated. He didn't seem to expect a response. The corner of his mouth turned up in a slight smile.

For several minutes, they rode in silence. Then the man said, "I heard a story there. It has stayed with me for over forty years. Just to say—bad things happen, but maybe they're not all as bad as they seem." His eyes were fastened on the dark road ahead as he told the story.

"Once there was an old farmer who had worked his crops for many years. One day his horse ran away. Upon hearing the news, his neighbors came to visit. 'Such a setback,' they said sympathetically.

"'Maybe,' the farmer replied.

"The next morning the horse came back, accompanied by three other wild horses. 'How wonderful,' the neighbors exclaimed.

"'Maybe,' replied the old man.

"The following day, his son tried to ride one of the untamed horses, was thrown, and broke his leg. The neighbors again came to offer their sympathy for his misfortune.

"'Maybe,' answered the farmer.

"The day after, soldiers came to the village to draft young men into the army. Because the son's leg was broken, they passed him by. The neighbors congratulated the farmer on his good luck.

"'Maybe,' said the farmer."

Petra felt a tear in the corner of her eye. The man stopped to let her out at the mango tree. She pressed her eyes closed and pursed her lips in thanks to the old man. The man bowed his head.

Finally, she stumbled in the dark up her hill, her mind a blank.

It should have been pitch dark and quiet at her house, but a kerosene light, burning late into the night, sent faint rays of light out from the porch. Nonna met her as she came over the rise in view of the house. Her legs faltered as she ran toward Petra to embrace her. She caught herself short, holding tight to her belly, doubling over in pain. "Petra! You are here! Thanks to the Lord!" She crossed herself. Her voice was weak.

Petra held her Nonna in her arms. Petra would have to persuade Nonna to consult a doctor at the medical clinic in San Luis Hunahpu, instead of continuing endlessly with the village *curandero* she'd been visiting. For years, she had breathed in herbed steam and performed elaborate rituals at the behest of the decrepit old man, the traditional Mayan healer, but the stomach pain had only gotten worse.

Petra used her strength to brace Nonna, and helped her lie down next to Nonno, whose snoring announced his presence. In her discomfort, Nonna did not notice the state of Petra's clothes, the scratches on her face and limbs. Petra sat on the edge of her bed, keeping her company a moment. Her own worries moved down the scale in urgency.

"I'm sorry, Petita, I don't want you to see me this way. Are you okay? Your face is so dirty." Nonna looked up with sunken eyes, her skin folded in webs strung from the corner of each eye.

"*Estoy bien*, Nonna. You don't need to worry about me."

"Carlos is still out in the night looking for you."

"I'll wait for him. Go to sleep now, Nonna. It is late." Nonno spluttered and turned over in the bed.

Petra grabbed hold of the knife that usually cut the throat of chickens due for roasting from its shelf, and she stripped off her clothes. She glared at the duct tape on those pants like it was the only obstacle between her and the holy grail. Her nose flared, and she sniffed in great breaths of air. The veins erupted on her wrists as she clutched that knife in her fist. Then she began the process of slashing at her pants, thrusting, ripping, flogging them, until they lay in little pieces. The fabric gave way easily to the sharp knife. She severed each belt loop, then slipped the knife into each pocket, and sundered them, one at a time. Finally, the offending clothes were conquered. Petra wet one scrap with water from the jug and wiped her face, then buried the remaining fragments under the garbage pile of plastic bottles and cardboard containers in the back yard.

Petra sighed. Her breathing slowed. The evening approached midnight as Petra, now half asleep on her perch outside the door, waited for Carlos to return. Finally, she heard footsteps trudging heavily up the hill. Carlos looked worn, his body slightly hunched over, his expression anxious. Seeing Petra there at the house, his frown loosened a fraction.

The two embraced in silence. It had been such a long time since they had hugged. Her brother needed her, too. He had proved his care for her on this night.

Petra whispered, "Carlos, you are exhausted. Shall we sleep?"

The slump of his body confirmed her evaluation. He rallied and, conscious of not disturbing anyone, whispered, "Come, let's talk for a few minutes up at the spring."

As they walked the short distance through the dark and up the path through the woods, Carlos stared at the ground and brooded. "Petra, I'm so sorry, this is all my fault! I should never have let you go alone this morning. Tell me, what happened?"

"I'm okay, Carlos. I don't want anyone to worry about me."

"I looked all over, Petra. Don José even offered to take me on his horse, so we could cover more ground. But we found nothing. A bunch of people along the road told me they saw your head lolling about, sitting in front of Emilio on his motorbike. But no one could tell me where you were."

"He forced me to drink something, Carlos. I tried to spit it out, but they held me and made me swallow it. I don't know what it was, but my mind went so dreamy. I couldn't stay alert, as hard as I tried."

"Those people have all kinds of drugs, Petrita. They might choose one kind to stay awake all night, or another to enhance romance, or to make their victim sleepy, like you. They all mess with your mind. Lots of them get addicted. The victims, too. They want to get people addicted, because then they can control them better."

Petra's body recoiled. The syringe was meant to get her started on that path. "I'm no victim, Carlos, and they'll never do that to me!"

"Sweetheart, they did do that to you. They drugged you and did what they wanted to you taking you off that way. If you're telling me you didn't get hurt, I'm very glad. But it wasn't because they didn't try."

It wasn't necessary to tell Carlos all the details. He might think less of her if he knew she'd nearly been raped. She didn't think it was that close, anyway. She'd have found a way out of the situation, even without Emilio's intervention.

She needed everyone to see that she could take care of herself. If anyone could understand, Carlos could. He knew what it was like to have no mother, no father. By their age, they no longer needed parents.

"Emilio let me go, Carlos. He let me escape. The other two didn't realize."

"Who were they, Petra? The other two?"

"Emilio called them by their gang names—Potoo and Gorto."

"Cute names. I've heard of Gorto, I think. He hangs in Las Leches. Potoo must come from another village."

"I don't think Emilio would really hurt me." She looked up at Carlos's forehead at the bruises, now fading from black and blue to gray.

"Emilio is no choir boy in the church, Petra. And his father…"

"What's up with his father, Carlos?" she interrupted. "I remember his father…. But it's been so long. And another man he called Gusano. Are they involved with the X-14?"

"Of course they are. You didn't know that? Gusano is the local boss of the little X-14'ers. And Emilio's father is Gusano's right-hand man. Which makes Emilio —"

"Let's leave Emilio out of this, please." Her refusal to hear this bit of information offered Emilio just a bit of protection from Carlos's judgment. And it prevented herself from thinking too hard on Emilio's role. "I know all about Emilio. More than you do, Carlos."

Carlos shook his head. "Think about it, Petra. Emilio had to prove himself to become the boss of those thugs. How do you think he did that?"

How should she know? What did she know of thugs and advancement in gangs? But something clicked, despite herself. Justina. Maybe she was how he had to prove himself? No, she couldn't believe that. But why hadn't he let Justina go like he did Petra?

Carlos let it drop, but his forehead creased with worry. "Petra, I'm so sorry I didn't go to school with you today. If I'd been with you, he might have attacked me again, but he wouldn't have gotten to you. At least you're okay. From now on, though, you don't go out of our house without me or someone with you to protect you."

Petra guffawed. "What are you saying, Carlos? I won't be a prisoner in my home! Emilio let me go, and he's the one who's been bothering me. I'm out of danger now."

Carlos laughed. "Who are you kidding, Petra? If Emilio let you go, what do you think Potoo and Gorto are thinking? What do you think they're going to do to Emilio? Or to you?"

"No way. They're underlings. Emilio was clearly in charge over them, doing all the thinking. They were just his assistants. Disgusting, ugly assistants, but peons doing what Emilio told them to do."

She wouldn't say so, but Carlos's words continued to reverberate. True, they wouldn't be happy with Emilio at this point. She would pray for him in the morning. As for herself—she'd pay better attention on that road.

Carlos sighed. The day weighed on them both. Neither of them was going to think out all the implications at midnight. "All right. It's been a long day, I think. Let's try to get some sleep, eh?"

CHAPTER FOURTEEN

Nonna's face was bathed in the glow of morning as she ground the corn for tortillas. The same sunbeam reflected in Nonno's eyes as he reached up to the shelf by the kitchen doorway, readying tools for the day's work. The sunlight reflected off the knife that had possessed her fury. She blinked back the glare. Itzamná's wings quivered, and on his wings the faded green glyphs for daytime and night sparkled.

Petra turned over in the light, holding onto it as a constant. Jesus was encircled by luminescence. Grace would rise above her concerns. The one day held within it all days. The night contained daylight; daylight contained the night. Separation was as impossible as separating good from bad, the underworld from the heavens. There was a time before God invented sin and forgiveness.

Nonna insisted that Petra stay home for the weekend and miss school for a couple of days next week, to keep her close by. Petra resisted, but she softened as she realized that Nonna needed help. She gave in when they reached a bargain. There would be no thought of keeping Petra home next Saturday. She would accompany the family to the market in the morning, talk to her mother on the phone, then play in the big soccer game in the afternoon.

Her cousin Julina and her mother Dolores passed by on their way to church. Julina promised to apologize for her to one of the girls from her soccer team for missing the practice and to tell her she would definitely be at the next one on Wednesday.

Carlos went off to his work but shortly came home. He left, he returned, and left again, as if two beasts of burden pulled him in opposite directions.

Her thoughts flew off in different directions, and the various trajectories meandered in and out and across each other. Nausea kept circling around and through her. The image of that knife between her legs—she pushed it aside.

As far as she remembered, she had screamed for the first time in her life. She'd been desperate, out of control, and reacted as if her only recourse was to seek help. It was an admission of weakness to admit she'd screamed. So she told no one.

But she had taken care of it, finally. She'd gotten out, more or less unharmed.

Carlos had called Petra a victim of the gangs. He said they could have hurt her far worse. She couldn't reconcile the concept of victim together with her idea of herself—capable, independent, unfettered. Difficulties presented themselves to her, but what she had to cope with was hardly out of the ordinary.

If Emilio's father was the right-hand man of Gusano, that meant Emilio had grown up practically as the crime boss's son, or close to. But lots of people in the area liked Emilio, more so than the other gang-bangers—even if he did have a special position at the top of the local gang through his father. Even Nonna liked him!

Perhaps he deserved some credit. Emilio *had* helped her escape. But he had abducted her and filled her with drugs! Two personalities in Emilio warred with each other—and with her. Something still stirred in her, his imperfections deepened now, somehow rooted in his sweet fragility as a kid. Like the spider monkey, falling over himself up in the trees—the demonic clown, forever craving respect.

A few years back, when Justina, Emilio and she were the best of friends, Petra had dropped her notebook as they were walking home from school. Just as it smacked onto the ground, she spotted a sloth up a tree. Struck by how adorable it was, she started up the tree to get a closer look. As she climbed, she realized that Emilio was falling all over himself trying to pick up her things because he thought she'd tripped. By the time he looked up, Petra was way up on a high branch, crawling along next to the sloth.

Emilio yelled out to Petra to ask if she was okay, like he wanted to save her. Sure that she was scared up there by herself, he tried and tried to follow her up the tree, but he kept slipping back down. Petra, in the meantime, inched her way out the branch toward the sloth, hoping to cuddle with it. Emilio got smart and yelled to Petra that they looked so good together, like they were family. Petra answered that the four of them, including the sloth, should be cousins. Emilio objected that Petra moved too fast for the sloth and would probably knock it on the head when it came to her next soccer game.

What made Emilio change so drastically that he would take Justina and hurt her?

Once, she and Justina had talked about what happened to Emilio. Petra told Justina how his father accused his mother of using too much cocaine before she died. "His father was so mean and didn't seem to care at all that she had died." And then Emilio had turned on Petra. "I'd never seen him like that before. He told me to leave him alone. Why did he go that way, Justina? He could have turned to me—I was his best friend!"

"I don't know," Justina had said, "but his father seems pretty awful. Maybe Emilio had already seen things we can't imagine. Maybe his father made up that part about his mom using cocaine, or maybe not, who knows? Emilio was a great friend, but he did seem a little haunted sometimes, like his head was going in one direction and his emotions in another. When he was so awkward, I think he was trying to catch up with us while his mind was occupied with something else he never talked about."

Petra took that in for a moment. "Do you think maybe he'll snap out of it sometime and go back to being like he used to be?" Petra had always held tight to the idea that there was a real Emilio in him somewhere that he could let out again if he wanted to. That he'd finally share with her all those things he had never talked about.

Justina said, "I don't know, Petra. I don't think he's the same person he used to be. Something broke in him. He couldn't have joined those delinquents if his insides hadn't hardened up somehow."

These thoughts still roiled her mind. Her dreams, in the day and at night, danced endlessly around them, perpetually sucking delight out of her relationships with people.

At lunchtime, Nonno and Carlos came back hungry for food. It was high noon, time to break while the sun beamed down on them in all its magnificence, and all its humidity. Petra served them hot rice and beans, with Nonna's tortillas. From the adobe oven out back came the *champurradas*. Such were the benefits of having Petra at home, her energies applied to work around the house. Nonno and Carlos would eat up the crunchy sugar cookies within a day.

Petra itched to burst out of her seclusion. Every pore of her body resisted the confinement. It seemed that every time she looked up, Nonna was following her movements from just around the corner of the house.

No one should object if she just went down to Vicenta's store for a few minutes. She would bring Nonna back a can of peach nectar, one of her favorite treats. Ever so carefully, she reached into the can for a few centavos, but the slight jingle was enough to alert Nonna from the back yard. Nonna threw her a piercing look.

"Nonna, please, if I am going to stay home today, you must sit and relax," said Petra, feigning innocence.

Nonna's eyes flashed with temerity, and she confronted Petra, lifting a broom clutched in her hand. "*You*, my dear, are to stay home today. No sneaking off. Did you think I wouldn't notice? *Jah!*" The air rattled through the gap in her front teeth.

Standing tall and straight, Nonna gestured with her arm as she began to say something to Petra. But before she could speak, her knees buckled. She broke her fall to the ground by sinking onto the tips of her muscular fingers. The fingernails were brittle and broken from years of overuse, the backs of her hands covered with protruding veins, dark brown spots, and blotches. Nonna gripped the broom, protectively ensconced under her right hand, while her left cradled her stomach.

Petra ran over to her and put her right shoulder under Nonna's left arm. "Here, sit on the bench here." She bent down with Nonna and helped her sit up, her fingers still firmly wrapped around the broom handle.

"I am fine Petra, thank you." Nonna took several deep breaths to steady herself. "But I do wish to tell you something."

Concentrating on caring for her grandmother, Petra ignored the statement and ran inside for a cup. She scooped some water into it from the jug in the backyard and brought it to Nonna.

"Thank you for your help," Nonna said, sipping the water. "But you do realize that I make do every day on my own. I will continue to do so."

Petra looked directly into Nonna's eyes and said, "Nonna, you must go to the clinic. The *curandero* has not helped you."

Nonna visibly bristled. "I will go to the clinic when I say it's time to go. What takes place between him and me is a private matter."

Petra gently took the broom from Nonna and swept out the house, the front porch, and the back yard. The two contemplated each other in silence.

Nonna brooded for a few minutes, glancing between Petra and something far off beyond the trees that Petra could not see. Nonna rose, took the broom back from Petra, and leaned it against the bench. "Come, Petra. I must show you something."

Taking Petra's hand firmly in her own, Nonna left Petra with no choice but to follow. Together they walked down to the gurgling rivulet where the cows straggled about, then up the hill to the land now cleared of its sugar cane. When Nonna squatted down in the bare earth, Petra thought she was falling again and rushed to support her.

Nonna swatted Petra's hand away, and said, "*Mi nieta*, you have a kind heart, but I feel your mind stretching away from us. You yearn for something beyond this place." Nonna's broad, cracked toes clamped onto the earth beneath her feet.

Petra opened her mouth to object, but Nonna's hand went up to silence her. "I will speak now," Nonna said.

Stunned by Nonna's sudden forcefulness, Petra folded her arms against her chest and lowered her eyes in submission.

Nonna plunged her fingers into the soil and pulled out clumps of earth. She pressed the earth in her hand, and the clumps dissolved into dry dusty dirt that flowed from between her fingers back to the ground. "This earth," she said, "holds our ancestors. It holds all of time. Here—" she took a clump of earth in her hand again "is the meaning of our lives." Nonna, on her knees now, held the earth in her hands and rested her forehead to her wrists. When she looked up again, her coal black eyes bore into Petra. "There is nothing more important. Do not ever forget,

Petra."

Back at the house, Petra gathered and cut wood for Nonna to use to make the fire for lunch and dinner. She returned to the trickling stream, hauling the morning's dishes with her. When the cows paraded through without regard to her presence, she leapt to the side, flapping her arms, and glaring at them. Ignoring her, they took their time to drink their fill before moving on. Only then could she wash and stack the dishes and lug them back up to the house.

The puzzle of Emilio and Justina again tangled her mind. Emilio looked like demons were attacking him after he returned to find Potoo attacking her. Something he'd said came back to her: "Tell me, Petra, what are my choices? Because I can't find any good ones." As much as she'd wondered about his life since his father took over raising him, she assumed he could just choose to walk away from his role in the gangs. But she hadn't put together his father's role with the gang until Carlos talked to her last night. Something had happened to change Emilio, perhaps something terrible. Maybe he really was calling out for help.

Sweet Justina. If only she could talk to her now. They could have figured out what to do together.

About nine months before, only a week before he took Justina, she and Petra had talked about Emilio. She had come home from school with Petra. Nonna wanted Petra to take lunch to her uncle Jacinto, who was working brutal hours in the unstinting sun cutting sugar cane at Finca Anaconda. She and Justina went off together carrying plastic bottles of water and a bowl of rice, beans, and tortillas. At the familiar rough, rocky road leading to the big plantation, three trucks—each skewing to one side or the other, balanced precariously over their wheels, as if one more bundle of cane thrown on top of their loads might bring the whole truck tumbling down—pulled ahead of them onto the main road, raising clouds of dust behind them. Petra pulled her dress up to cover her nose.

Petra and Justina wended their way past row after row of standing cane. Then rows of cane slashed to the ground. The men, many dozens of them, spread across the acres like multiplying rabbits, their muscles gleaming with sweat, some swinging machetes, some collecting the cane from the ground and heaving it up onto a ramshackle truck, wiping their foreheads, some sitting for a few minutes, swigging water.

Young men little older than her looked desperately thirsty. Envious eyes tracked the two of them with their water bottles and plates of food. She could feel the men appraising them. How cool and steady on their feet they must appear. Cat whistles pursued them. Young kids trolled the narrow paths, selling *chicles* and cigarettes, while others gallivanted through the rows chasing each other. Petra and Carlos had both sold the little packages of gum for years until Carlos got old enough to work his own fields and toil even harder, and Petra took up most of the household work to help Nonna.

Justina jumped up and waved her hand to get the attention of Don José, the overseer. He was wending his way in and out of rows, attending to the workers. José scanned intently across several rows, and Petra followed his eyes to his son Lucas, who seemed to be giving out orders much more freely than his father. Petra had seen him hanging in the village with the X-14 guys. She couldn't hear what Lucas was saying, but Don José clearly wanted to keep tabs on Lucas's activities. Don José pointed them in the direction of Jacinto.

Jacinto slumped to the ground at the spot where he was working. In a matter of seconds, the water from one bottle—and in short order the second—vanished down his throat. Within minutes, the meal was consumed, and Jacinto returned to work. Time lost meant less cane cut, and fewer quetzals at the end of the day. Petra felt sorry for these men. The work pushed the limits of human endurance.

On the way back home, as they were about to cross under the jacaranda tree, the heat surged around Petra and she lost her footing. Memories of the day with Emilio when they had flown past that tree on the bikes surged like vomit in her throat—the way they teetered on the bikes, laughed as they fell onto the ground, soared down the road like birds, then the shock of seeing his mother die on the ground.

That familiar feeling began to take over—her mind loosened its ties to reality. She tried to grasp Justina's hand, but she couldn't find it. The nightmare that had begun when she was nine took over. Bikes hung in the trees, swinging with the gesture of the branches; they threatened to fall, aspired to run away. Wisps of red ribbons blew by in the suddenly cold air. Petra wrapped her arms tightly around herself as the fear took hold of her.

In horror, Petra remembered the streaks of red that had pursued Emilio into the woods, lining the ground like shining blood. He fled from his mother's lifeless body, while the bicycle tires turned uselessly. The spokes sighed in the breeze that rattled the leaves.

Bottled up screams had followed Emilio, and now Petra cowered next to Justina, her arms aching from the effort of holding herself so tightly. His slight, child's body had hurtled silently through the woods, but the twigs shrieked as they broke under his feet, the undergrowth howled as he flattened it beneath desperate footfalls. The redness spread out in frightening threads along the charred vegetation.

She became aware of Justina's hand pulling her, guiding her to sit down on a rock under the jacaranda. Before she let them go, she marveled at the red ribbons encircling the purple blooms, a bounty of awe-inspiring color. She tried to creep through the maze back to Justina, but the passage wound through the quaking trees, the shadows of decaying matter holding fast to her. The gruesome stickiness clung to her dress under her arms.

Justina said, "Petra! Where are you?" She touched her gently on the shoulder.

Petra tried to blink it away. "Sorry. The heat got to me. The tree—it reminds me of Emilio." Petra and Justina stood at the foot of the jacaranda tree, where the path turned off to Emilio's house.

Her eyes refocused and landed on Justina's eyes, which were searching her face for consciousness. "Sweet girl, come back to me," she said. She laid her head on Petra's lap, and Petra stroked her hair. A pick-up truck loaded with men clattered by.

Hoping to find a moment of solitude, Justina took her hand and led her along the path next to the tree. It turned this way and that, but generally made its circuitous way toward the same stream where, farther up, Petra did laundry and boys swam. "I think we need to get away from the road for a few minutes," Justina said.

Petra began to realize that she had gone off somewhere strange in her head and felt embarrassed by the grief betraying her. "I think I'm okay now," she said. "I think the heat got to me for a minute."

"That's great, Petra, but let's just hang out for a few minutes and talk."

They spotted the boulder that rose out of the ground as tall as a house. On the back side they found a crevice where they sat down together out of sight from anyone heading down to the stream.

Justina said, "Girl, you're scaring me."

"Justina, what would I do without you?"

"Me, too. Let's be friends for a long, long time, okay?"

A warmth came over Petra, and she swooned, her head lolling to the side, grazing Justina's soft hair.

Justina said, "Petra, let's talk to Alocinia again."

"*Bien.* She will come if we ask." Petra leaned on her side, her head resting on her hand. Justina's cheekbones rose high and broad. "You tell a story this time."

Justina closed her eyes. Alocinia hovered between Justina and Petra. Slowly, Justina began. Petra forgot herself in Justina's soft voice. "*Había una vez*, years and years ago, when a raging fire threatened to take over a forest. All the animals fled their homes. They stopped at the edge of a stream and watched, feeling helpless and scared. They began to bemoan the destruction of their home. The smallest among them, a little hummingbird, swooped into the stream and picked up a few drops of water. She flew over the forest and dropped them onto the fire. Then she returned to the stream and did it again, going back again and again. The other animals watched in disbelief. The elephant, who had a big trunk and could have carried much more water, said, 'Don't bother, it is too hard. You are too little; your wings will burn and your beak is too tiny. You can't put out this fire with only little drops.' As they stood around disparaging her efforts, she noticed how hopeless and forlorn they looked. Then the tiger challenged her in a mocking voice. 'What do you think you are doing?' Without hesitation, the hummingbird responded, 'I am doing what I can.'"

Justina lay her head on Petra's shoulder. Petra felt her friend's lips brush against her neck. Petra's stomach swooned unexpectedly. She tried not to move, so the moment would last.

"Sometimes I do miss Emilio, though," Justina said. "Remember how he fumbled around us? How he'd try to be all macho and take care of us, and end up looking kind of foolish instead?"

Petra smiled at the image. Justina spoke to her softly, almost whispering into her neck.

"Justina, promise you'll never get lured in by some boy who wants to use you. Promise you won't change like that. We'll always be friends, right?"

The two girls looked at each other across centuries of girls promising their everlasting affection to each other, through eyes that had seen violence and betrayal, and heard about much worse. The tree branches writhed above them. Petra touched her fingers to Justina's cheek, and Justina leaned very close, whispering in her ear, "I promise."

Justina turned to face her, and her lips touched Petra's. Moments passed, and their lips still touched. The blood supply to Petra's brain must have dropped given how weak she felt. She was excited in a way she had never dared to dream about. Slowly, deliberately, she leaned in, and they kissed. Lips wet, tongues exploring, calm but tentative, hands hanging limp by their sides. Petra was afraid to move in any way that might interrupt.

The moment was endless and instantaneous. Warmth flooded through her. She never imagined how sweet lips could be, how every part of her body would yearn to join with Justina's. Her breasts rose in her chest and craved Justina's touch. Petra held Justina's cheek and jawbone in her hand, her tongue gliding along Justina's.

Then Justina had to breathe. She pulled back a little. Petra swallowed and tried to slow the breaths overtaking her, her hand awkwardly dropping to the rock beside her. They looked at each other questioningly. Petra's heart was piercing the ribs trying to hold it in, her insides churning.

She saw a cloud pass by Justina's eyes, a cloud of doubt and confusion. Her graceful eyebrows pulled together ever so slightly in a question. Petra's heart skipped a beat. She told herself to keep breathing.

"You okay now?" Justina asked. Petra laughed, then Justina laughed, and for a couple of minutes, they were caught in laughter they couldn't stop.

Just a week later, Petra was giddy in the company of her friend. The cool air and babbling waters down by the stream were exhilarating. Petra lowered the basket of her family's dust-stricken clothes from her head, Justina by her side with a load of her own to wash.

Petra reached over the edge of the rock to rub a shirt against the stones at the stream's bottom. Water caught the hem of her skirt and began to inch up the fabric. She flipped the wet shirt at Justina, spraying her with water, soaking Justina's blouse. A handful of tiny fish got caught up in her grandmother's underwear hanging halfway into the water, and Petra took a few in her hand, offering them solemnly as if on a golden platter to her friend. Justina knocked them away, giggling.

Her friend's smile lifted her cheeks and narrowed her eyes. They splashed at each other, laughed at far-flung jokes. How she loved Justina. When Justina laughed, her eyes twinkled directly at Petra, and Petra's insides burst with the attention. The corners of Justina's lips crimped in an enchanting, elfish curl.

Justina's dripping shirt barely constrained her robust breasts. Petra could swear they swelled when she gazed at them, all the while trying her best to look away. She hated it when she saw boys noticing Justina's figure. Petra didn't want her own breasts to grow as large as Justina's. The boys paid too much attention. And they would interfere with her playing soccer. So far, at fourteen years old, they hadn't, so maybe they wouldn't. Nevertheless, Justina wore them nicely, she had to admit.

Distracted by Justina's attention, Petra dropped her soap into the water. She leaned down beneath the rock to catch it. Justina grabbed a wet t-shirt and wrapped it around Petra's eyes from behind. Water dripped down her t-shirt, and she looked blindly into the sky, laughing and shouting at Justina.

Abruptly, Justina's laughter evaporated. There was no response. The shirt loosened around Petra's eyes. Then shadows fell across the water, and the crunch of boots bore down on them. Petra threw off the shirt, and there stood three of them—including Emilio. She relaxed slightly. If Emilio was there, nothing bad would happen.

Justina was standing, dumbfounded. Emilio was the youngest of the three, only fifteen years old then. Petra didn't recognize the other two men.

Emilio stood back, his legs slightly spread, feet definitively planted in the ground, his arms crossed, his eyes darting in every direction.

Savage eyes stared out at them from the grisly face of a man roughly thirty years old. Over his burly frame hung a black cloak and black pants. The gold outlining his front teeth caught the sun, and they protruded over his lower lip. He looked like the devil himself.

Rings covered the fingers of the second man's right hand, which he slapped into the palm of his left hand in a show of machismo. Flecks of gold on the rings glinted in the bright light like small daggers. He appeared only a year or two older than Emilio. A fingerless glove covered an unusually rigid left hand. When his hands separated, she understood. Metal spikes lined the palm of his glove.

This was not Emilio their old friend. This was lethal danger. Petra's spirit sank into a swamp of dismay. Justina looked unresponsive, her eyes vacant pools.

Buck Teeth gripped Justina from behind, holding her close. He wrapped a hand over her breast, squeezing tightly. "Let's go quietly, my sweet girl. Not a word," he said under his breath.

Justina's mettle rose momentarily. She flailed and tried to scream, but Ring Man slapped her on the face with the rings. Parallel lines of blood appeared on her cheek.

If only this demonstration had been mere bravado. Their charmed afternoon had changed drastically. The rings must have had sharp edges, too, making both his hands toxic. Petra swung her arm, aiming for Ring Man's head, but her arm flapped uselessly through the air.

Emilio shoved her aside like a hurricane propelling a feather, and she fell into the water. Pain shot through her as a rock tore into her hip.

Within a minute, they had marched off with Justina held tightly between Ring Man and Buck Teeth, Emilio trailing behind.

Petra could only watch them disappear into the pine forest. The group had barely spoken. Evil had just stormed through and away, and Petra had merely swung out uselessly.

Petra gulped for air, panic rising up her spine and clogging her mind. She ran away from the river, up to the road, up to her home, running fast, her body weightless.

Alocinia helped Petra breathe.

- Run for your life, girl. When hands become claws, the vulnerable flee.
- How do I save Justina if I'm running?
- We can't save right now. Guilt is not yours. It belongs to those nasties below. Run home, Petra.

Tears blackened by dust covered her face by the time she crested their hill and saw Nonna in their front yard. Petra collapsed into the arms of her grandmother, panting through her anguished words, so frantic that Nonna strained to understand her. When she finally grasped what had happened, Nonna simply covered her mouth with her hands and closed her eyes.

Carlos ran to Justina's house to tell her family what had happened. Nonno came back from the fields. They all sat together at the dim table by the wood fire. In silence, each holding tightly to themselves, reverberating with the impact. Petra said, "But she'll be okay, right?" Carlos's head dropped a notch below his neck. Before long, he laid his forehead on the table.

Nonna offered a prayer. Petra's mind went blank.

That evening, Nonno visited his brother Jacinto's house up the hill, the place known throughout the community for comradeship and debauchery. When he returned, he sat on the bench, staring at the ground, twirling his mustache. Perhaps he was deep in thought, or perhaps too drunk to think, Petra didn't know. She yearned to cuddle up to him and talk, but, once again, he wasn't accessible to her in that state. She held in her disappointment, then took a deep breath and went to bed early.

The next morning, Carlos began the routine of accompanying Petra to school. He was only seventeen, but two were less vulnerable than one lone girl. There was little to be done, so they did what they could.

No one considered calling the police because, as Carlos pointed out, that would only increase the peril. To contact the police, they would need to take a trip to San Luis Hunahpu, give a report, drown in the petty bureaucratic non-response. If they decided to act at all, the police might ask a few questions around their village, enough so the gang would know that Petra had informed the police. That would be sufficient to bring the wrath of the gang to bear against Petra—any time, any place of their choosing.

No, it was better to keep it to themselves and pray to God for Justina's safe return.

Days of confused misery followed, of fright bottled up and shaken but unable to explode. But then, a murmuring crowd drew her and Carlos out of the house. As soon as she and Carlos approached the road, they heard the rumble of voices from the river below, so they slowly followed the trail of sound, each step a descent into a morass of stupor. They didn't look at each other, each buried by thoughts too heavy to decipher. The cackle and chatter of grackles above mixed with the voices at ground level, some hushed, some angry, as if they were surrounded from above and below by life churning out of control. The black birds flew about, creating trails of black smoke in the air.

Petra saw her first. There on the ground, a group of people stood over her nervously but at a distance, as if she were emitting a poisonous gas. One woman had dared to lean down and touch her face, testing for life, while the rest gawked. Petra rushed over and kneeled beside Justina.

Blood pooled beneath her, beside her. The dress Petra had splashed with water a few days before was torn, soiled, covered in dark brown stains. Petra threw herself forward onto her hands, on her knees, on the dirt and blood. The parallel cuts on her face were inflamed. Blood trickled down her thighs. Petra turned her head away.

Justina's hand ticked with slight movement, then lifted to touch Petra's. Petra glanced up quickly. Justina moved her mouth, but no sound came out.

"I love you, Justina," said Petra. "*Ay, Dios,* what have they done to you?" To think they had held her Justina captive for three days! What she must have gone through in those days. Justina's hand felt damp, warm on her skin. "Justina, you will be okay. My brother is here; we can get you to a doctor."

Petra bit down on her lip and grasped Justina's hand. It was cool, like a wilting flower, not like her strong friend at all. Petra sank into her own wretchedness, the obliviousness of her words. She combed Justina's hair gently with her fingers, tears filling her eyes until she couldn't see through them to Justina anymore. The damp hand became limp in Petra's fingers.

Sobs wracked her body. She struggled to regain control over her limbs. Her muscles had fled and left her in a puddle next to the form that had held Justina. How could her friend die? Only a few days before they had been laughing together. Petra's mind shut down. For the next month, she stayed at home.

At that moment, she had determined she would never let herself feel so helpless again.

She wiped her brow and set herself to pat out the tortillas for the evening meal.

CHAPTER FIFTEEN

In the early evening, Petra gathered her Nonno up to speak with him again on the porch.

"Nonno, will you tell me about Itzamná?"

Nonno was visibly startled. "Why do you ask about Itzamná, little girl?"

She told him about her dream and how she was left feeling that it held something fearful but very important. "I have prayed to Itzamná here at home since I remember, but now it feels urgent to understand."

Petra waited while her grandfather considered this. Softly, she said, "Nonnino, does Itzamná have something to do with the secret place Emilio asked about?"

"I am going to have to reconsider you, my daughter. Your questions hold more knowledge than I was prepared to share." He looked at her in a new, deeper way. She tried to bear up to his searching eyes.

"When you are ready, Nonno, I am here. You know I respect your decision."

"You are a good girl, Petra. Sorelly does not know what she is missing. You must come to know your mother better. The two of you have more in common than you realize. There is a joining that must take place. I see that more clearly these days. The separation is impossible—a crack through nature—which must mend."

Petra didn't know how to talk to her mother, but she had determined to make a renewed effort on Saturday.

"You must bring her closer, Petrita. She is in your heart, much closer than you think. Reconcile your beginnings with your future. In order to accomplish your dreams, you must retrieve the seeds of your soul. And you will need a full soul to experience Itzamná."

Loudly crunching *champurradas*, and leaving behind a trail of crumbs, Carlos came clomping out the door. He glanced at Petra as he headed down to the mango tree. "You okay here? Nonna will be here. I will hear you if you scream. Do you know how to yell?"

"Not sure, Carlos. I'll try. If not, I'll throw *champurradas* down your way if I need help." They laughed. There would be no more talk of her abduction yesterday.

Shortly after Carlos disappeared down the hill, Nonna returned inside to rest. Nonno retreated up the hill to his brothers' house.

Evening closed in and her family sank into their beds. Petra still ached to get out of the house. She couldn't be bottled up all day and then all night, too. She didn't know why, but she really wanted to see Vicenta. Only in the dark could she get away with it.

Her sleeping platform creaked slightly when she put her feet to the ground. The door latch only rattled a little when she lifted it. She waited until she got off the porch to put her sandals on. The breeze whistled through the palm fronds.

At this late hour, there were no customers at the store. She didn't see anyone at all. She started for the door to the stairs, up which Vicenta had a small living space.

Music seeped under the threshold of the door to the storage room in the back. The unusual hip-hop rhythms pulled her in, and she stopped to listen. The woman's brash voice enthralled Petra:

Cuando caminas con las ancestras
La selva camina contigo
La energía curativa de las ancestras
La energía de la Maya antigua
A los que sostengan el cielo
Los que viajen por los bosques
Que cuiden el cielo, la tierra, el fuego

Los que levanten la noche y la mantengan en las manos
Preste atención a los que escuchen el espíritu de los ríos
Que devuelvan al espíritu de las montañas
Caminen con las ancestras Mayas.[1]

She'd never heard anything like it. The blood in her chest pulsed with this new sensation.

She heard a barely audible rustling in the back room. Expecting to greet Vicenta, she rapped lightly on the door, then pushed it ajar. In the kerosene half-light, she saw two women disengaging from an embrace, and she recognized Vicenta startled out from behind the two.

In a quick moment, before self-consciousness arose, Petra glimpsed ample breasts, cradled in loving hands. Hands wrapped tenderly around a neck. A pursed mouth backing away, a pink tongue reaching to moisten lips. A skirt pulled up to disclose undergarments stretched down over thighs. Pubic hair, black and gray entwined, open to the air. A glimmer of light from the dingy bulb hanging above caught in languid eyes.

Petra's own breasts swelled. Her stomach tingled with illicit discovery. The brutality of her experience the day before dimmed.

Vicenta's face lined with age and concern, she hopped down from a stool and quickly fumbled with a stained white dress, yanking it, then a thin sweater over her heavy frame. Petra noticed the hang of her stomach over baggy underwear as she stood frozen to the spot, mouth gaping wide. Vicenta motioned to Petra to turn away, indicating that she would follow her back into the store.

"Petra! *Gracias a Dios*, it is so good to see you here again." Petra composed herself, confronted now with the Vicenta she had known all her life. Her pleasantly fleshy arms, her cheekbones high in a smile, all now stretched toward Petra to embrace her. "*Mi amorcita*, my love, where have you been? What happened to you?"

---

1. When you walk with the ancestors
   The wilderness walks with you
   The healing energy of the women ancestors
   The energy of the ancient Mayans
   To those who hold up the sky
   Those who travel the forests
   Who care for the sky, the earth, the fire
   Those who lift the night and hold the sun in their hands
   Take heed to those who listen to the spirit of the rivers
   Who give back to the spirit of the mountains
   Walk with the Mayan ancestors.

Petra opened her mouth, expecting to form words of explanation, but her thoughts wouldn't come together. Petra said, "Can I sit down, Vicenta?"

Vicenta rambled on, ignoring the request. "I saw you go by with Emilio, and I wondered. Going so fast, I could barely wave hello. But then I saw two other creepy-looking guys following on a second bike, and I got really scared. After what just happened to Sr. Menendez's daughter... Petra, I ran up to your house faster than I ever ran up a hill in my life to tell your grandparents."

Her voice slowed. "Your Nonna is not well, though—you know this." She regained the faster tempo. "Thankfully, Carlos was just coming down from the hills. He took off running down the road to look for you. Carlos and you both were gone so many hours!" She paused for breath. "Carlos told me today you were home, but... Peta, I've never worried so much!"

Petra nodded silently throughout Vicenta's torrent of words. Vicenta's life and business revolved around her conversations with people. She was practiced in covering over the awkward moments with dialogue.

"I got home late last night. We're all okay now." She barely uttered the words before her legs buckled from under her, and she fell to the floor. Vicenta scrambled for a chair she kept in the storeroom and helped Petra into it. Briefly, Vicenta lowered herself to the floor on one knee before her, her hand reaching to wipe Petra's brow. Her eyes glistened with tender feeling toward Petra.

"Thank you, Vicenta. I don't know why I fell like that. I'm fine."

"Petra, I don't know what's happened, but I thank the Lord you are here and not with those nasty boys. What can I do? Here, drink some water." Vicenta scurried about, handing Petra a plastic water bottle. "*Chica, Dios mío*, what's happening in our little world? Here, open up this package of crackers." Caressing Petra's cheek, she said, "Thank God, Petra, you are okay."

Petra sank into the chair, cherishing Vicenta's care. She knew Vicenta was too respectful to press her about what had happened, and she had no desire to talk about it. In the back of her mind, Petra was trying to work out the scene she'd glimpsed in the back room. Those fingers she had seen closing the door a few days back! The fingers caressing Vicenta's neck wore the same light blue nail polish she had noticed then.

The second woman, complete with blue nails, emerged from the storeroom. A gripping desire to understand what she had seen led Petra to contemplate the woman. It was immediately apparent that she did not come from the surrounding area. She cultivated a distinctive style which included conspicuously short hair, high cheekbones indicating Mayan ancestry and reinforcing her upright composure, and a noticeable assurance in her stance—all of which belonged to a more sophisticated setting. The short hair meant she was willing to defy norms. Petra's deference to Nonna was the only thing that stood in the way of getting her own hair cut.

The woman's penetrating eyes turned graciously to Petra. Vicenta said, faltering, "Petra, this is not the best time to introduce you to someone new, but under the circumstances…"

Petra interrupted, "Vicenta, you don't have to explain anything."

"This is Novina, Petra. She is a very special friend to me. She visits with me when she comes this way to see her sister in Las Leches. Novina, I have known Petra since she was a baby. She is a local soccer star, and a young woman rising with care and integrity in her bones. She lives just up the hill here." Petra received a beam of affection from Vicenta.

Novina nodded in recognition but stepped back to allow Vicenta to handle the moment. She had said nothing at all before retreating with an air of mystery.

Vicenta gazed out the door to the darkness which utterly obscured the world outside. "But, Petra, why are you here? It's so late."

"Something pulled me here. I'm not sure myself." The music continued, the bass drum pounding at Petra's heart.

Vicenta focused her full attention on Petra, searching her eyes for clues. Vicenta began, "Peta… I wanted to say…" It was not like Vicenta to fumble for words. "Justina was a good friend." Her eyebrows twitched.

It seemed an awkward transition in conversation. There was a question behind the statement. The moment gathered strength, and Petra's eyes welled up. "I miss her so much, Vicenta." The older woman stepped close to her. From her stool, Petra put her arms around Vicenta's waist and buried her face in Vicenta's breasts. Her tears poured out. She clung to Vicenta until it was over. Novina stood at the doorway to the closet but didn't budge. Petra was glad for her presence there.

Vicenta began to pace about uneasily, shifting her glance between Novina and Petra. She continued to cast about for words. "Petra—I have kept my personal life very private."

Petra wiped her eyes. "Vicenta, you've been a wonderfully steady rock in my life. Nothing will change that. Please don't worry about me." Petra searched her reaction to seeing the women in that intimate pose and did not find shock. On the contrary, it felt both shockingly new and decidedly natural. She hoped it meant that Vicenta was not as lonely as she had feared.

Vicenta sighed in some relief. "You have no idea what that means to me, Petra. You have an uncommon spirit living in you. I don't know if you realize that."

Petra was ready to go home now, but she had to ask about the music she had heard before she left, for fear she might never chance upon it again. "Vicenta, what is that music? That woman rapper? I never heard that before. I feel it deep inside, under my ribs."

"Ah! Yes, I know what you mean. Novina brought it with her CD player. The music is practically clandestine, even though the singer is from Guatemala. They don't play this kind of music on the radio. There's a lot about the power of women in her songs."

"I also heard something about indigenous spirit, I think, and connection to the earth. I'd like—" Petra broke off suddenly.

Then they all heard it. Footsteps outside. A twig broke. Heavy breathing. A man's hand pulled the front door wide open. Novina looked at Petra with alarm.

"Carlos!" Petra exclaimed. "What are you doing here?" Her nerves bristled as she realized she'd been caught slipping out.

"*Hermanita*, if you just *had* to disobey orders to stay home, you could have snuck out during the day. That would be much safer, *chispita*."

Petra smiled. If her brother was calling her a little spark, it couldn't be all bad. "I didn't mean to light any fires, *hermano*. But I am ready to go home. Would you be so kind as to escort me?" She offered an elbow to him, hoping against hope that in the lightness of the moment he would accept her arm.

Carlos glanced around quickly at Vicenta, registered Novina standing in the back, then looked at Petra in the face, and finally peered at her elbow extended out by her side. "Darn. Why did I have to be the older brother?" At least he was joking around this time. They walked out the door toward home arm in arm.

Petra glanced over her shoulder at Vicenta. "Thank you for the crackers. You have given me some things to think about."

"Don't think too hard. I am right here if you want to talk again." Lightly, she laid a hand on Petra's neck, guiding her part way up the hill. Petra counted her blessings to have her brother on one side, Vicenta on the other.

CHAPTER SIXTEEN

After four idle days at home, her muscles felt weak and weary. They screamed at the end of the first lap around the field, with two more to go. The exertion was shaking the tension loose from her body. She couldn't wait to play the real game with Los Poblanos. Just a couple more days. Their field in San Luis Hunahpu had real grass covering it, not the dust that clogged her lungs on their dirt field. Six of the girls fell from exhaustion at the finish of the third lap. She loved every moment.

They conspired against her, four teammates passing the ball among their airborne legs, the ball getting closer and closer to her goal. "Guide it, not too fast, work together!" the coach yelled out. She stretched to her side, leaped upward, took the ball hard in her stomach. "Great work! Pull in a deep breath." Her hair flew up around her head despite the band trying to hold it back. Everything was concentrated in the moment. The game set her free.

Nonna had released her from her confinement for this last practice before the big game. Win or lose, the team was an island of support, a cocoon of security.

Petra retrieved the ball and went to the corner, bounced it off her head to Sara. Sara kicked it high into the air, then off Claudia's head and back into Petra's arms. Then Laura was rushing toward her, dribbling the ball, completely in control. Petra came forward from the goal, blocking her path, until they collided. The ball flew off into the woods that formed the boundaries of their field.

A few gawkers hanging around the edges of the field moved aside to let Petra through. A woman raised her hand, inviting Petra's high five. Novina! What was she doing here? Petra threw her a questioning look. Novina smiled back. Befuddled for a moment, Petra forgot where the ball had gone. María shouted to her, pointing. "Afterward," Novina said to Petra.

The energy still coursed through her limbs when they ended practice. Her steps were lighter than she remembered.

Behind her net, the statuesque figure of Novina waited. Some of the girls on the team milled about chatting, casting stray glances toward her.

Petra scrambled to make herself presentable. "Novina! Welcome to our field. Is Vicenta with you?" She searched the path beyond Novina for Vicenta.

"No, no, I'm here in my 'professional' capacity. You probably don't realize I'm the coach of the Poblanos team you're playing this weekend. So I'm checking out the competition. Maybe recruiting. But we can talk about that later. You're quite the hot shot out there."

"What?! You're a soccer coach?"

"Indeed. One of the best! I too was a star goalie when I was your age. The Poblanos know they will have a difficult match this weekend. We want to be as prepared as possible."

"But a woman! Surely there is a man who would be willing to coach the team."

"But Petra, I am very willing." Novina laughed at Petra's astonishment. "Watch out, I may just be such a good coach that we will beat Las Lechitas."

"So—you're spying on us?"

Novina laughed. "Actually, it's pretty standard operation. The more established teams usually spend some time getting familiar with the rivals so they can better prepare. We probably have a few more resources than you guys. Sorry."

The way Novina carefully articulated her words, her tone bearing a certain solemnity, revealed a well-mannered upbringing. Once again, her presence fascinated Petra. The long pants she wore today were strange in her village, made of a flowing light cotton, crinkled and bagging out around her legs. Her gray-red hair flounced about, but she never had to push it away from her face. She carried herself with an unfamiliar buoyancy, as though unencumbered by the burdens other women lived with. Her arms swung higher when she walked, her legs pivoted without hesitation to take in her surroundings, her shoulders seemed only loosely connected to her arms. She smiled kindly at Petra.

Her manner put Petra at ease with Novina—a rare sensation with someone she had just met. Her association with Vicenta—whom she trusted implicitly—helped.

Novina continued, "Also, I have to admit Vicenta asked me to talk to you. It is hard for her to leave the store. A customer might appear at any moment. Petra, we do not know each other, but I found myself thinking about you a lot since your visit Saturday night."

The moment she had witnessed in the storeroom flooded through her gut. The two women's bodies pressed together. Vicenta's hands cradling Novina's breasts before she jumped off the stool. Justina's silky-smooth lips caressing hers. Suddenly embarrassed, Petra saw goosebumps rising on her skin. Confused, she tamped down the feeling.

"Well, it's really nice to see you, but I feel much better now. The few moments with you and Vicenta that night helped so much."

"It is good that you have been staying close to home. I have an idea what life can be like for young women these days."

Petra lifted an eyebrow skeptically. "Is there more help for women in San Luis Hunahpu?"

"It's not much different there. You would think the police would help, since they are stationed right in the city. But they do nothing, Petra. The gangs intimidate the police just like they intimidate us. Sometimes they work hand in hand. The police supplement their meager incomes with pay-offs from the gangs." Novina leaned down to pat a dog's head. "Cute dog." The dog curled up by her feet.

Novina continued to stun her. Most people would have kicked that dog away. Dogs lived flea-bitten lives, hunting for food and sleeping in the dirt, with their own jobs of chasing rodents away and guarding homes. Or they lived completely on their own. Petra barely noticed the existence of dogs. Spiders and sloths drew her attention more than *chuchos*. This giving affection to a dog—she tucked the image away in her mind to consider it again later.

"Petra, I don't know what happened to you last week, but Vicenta and I want to do anything we can to help you stay safe."

Petra was struck that Novina seemed genuinely troubled on her behalf. Novina had only just met her, and already she was concerned about her? The inclusive language gave Novina and Vicenta the guise of a real couple. "I'm in no real danger, Novina, but thank you for your concern. I stayed at home for a few days out of respect for my grandparents, who can be overly anxious. But I am not worried."

"I defer to your strength. For such a young woman, it is very admirable. At times, though, there is even greater strength in showing weakness. You do realize that these gangs are playing with serious weapons. They kill people, kidnap, and rape when they have a whim to do so. Vicenta has told me that sometimes you do feel afraid. Perhaps you mentioned this to her recently, yes?"

She didn't want to tell Novina that she was more likely to feel a foreboding when there was nothing at the moment to fear. When something did happen, she blocked out the anxiety and became all strength. Spirit kept her going. Surely her determination to carry on was not cause for concern. "It's nothing I can't handle, Novina. Please tell Vicenta she doesn't need to worry about me. It was a childhood friend, Emilio, who took me off that day. But he is still young, like me, and he values the memory of our friendship too much to harm me."

"That's fine, I hear you. I want to offer you an option, though, in case you should decide you need one. I have a small apartment in San Luis Hunahpu. I live there alone, and there is plenty of room for one more. It can be a little more anonymous in a town, you know, even if it is still small. So many more people, so much going on. It can be harder to find any particular person. If you need a place to go for a while, I'd be happy to have you."

Petra was taken aback. "But why, Novina? You don't even know me. Why would you want to help me like that?"

"I know you through Vicenta, who can't stop talking about you and all the things you've done since you were a little girl." A corner of her mouth lifted in a bemused smile. "Perhaps by offering a safe place to you I open a safe place within myself. Somehow opening this particular door and welcoming you feels right, Petra. Without knowing you, there is a bond between us. Is it possible you also feel this?"

Petra suddenly felt very shy. No one had ever reached out to her in this way before, with a plate teeming with kindness and concern. She hesitated. "I don't know…"

"There is a vast space between us, perhaps, as between any two people. But I am open to traversing that distance, if you choose." Novina hesitated before adding, "Please do not mention the special relationship you have observed between Vicenta and myself, Petra. If people learned of our relationship, it could create great danger for us."

Petra became aware that her teammates Sara and Claudia had stopped conversing nearby. Sara quickly turned away when Petra glanced toward them.

"Would you walk with me?" With a slight nod of the chin, she signaled the presence of the girls behind Novina. They walked back toward Las Leches. "Do you think the other girls on Las Lechitas know you are the Poblanos coach? They seemed curious about us talking."

Novina's eyes narrowed slightly, but she said nothing.

Petra said, "About you and Vicenta, I do understand, Novina. You can be sure I would do nothing to put Vicenta in any danger. I will not share Vicenta's private life with anyone. Me and gossip stay miles apart."

Though so many kids at her school whispered about each other, gossip had always been repellent to Petra. One of the first lessons Nonna imparted to her in their nightly prayers had stuck with her. "…shun profane and vain babblings: for they will increase unto more ungodliness." Girls inclined toward endlessly analyzing other girls' behavior with boys, and she'd witnessed the serious consequences, whether or not the facts were true. No, she would never peddle talk about people's personal lives. A year or so ago Justina had been the center of gossip.

Enzo, an older boy from school, had followed Justina, who was walking home from school with Petra. He managed to stop her and asked, "Do you want some help? I can carry that for you."

"No thanks. I'm fine." As soon as Justina opened her mouth, the boy quickly hoisted his eyes from her hips up to her eyes.

They had been running along the path through the woods, on their way back from school, when Justina dropped behind. A crude whistle had ricocheted through the forest—some boy trying to get their attention—but Petra ignored it. Now Justina was back chatting with the whistler. Petra glared at Enzo. All she had was a little writing notebook. *Púchica*, it wasn't like it was heavy.

"What are you doing here?" Justina asked. "Don't you live on the other side of Las Leches?"

"Yup, that's true. About a half hour walk from school." He demurred a moment. "*Bueeeno*, well… I guess I just wanted to see what's on this side of the village today. Sometimes you never know who you might run into when you go places you don't usually go." His smile sidled up to her. His eyes dropped down again around her thighs. Justina's adolescence had started on the early side.

The boy acted polite enough, but his eyes got out ahead of him. As they talked, his big eyes kept drifting down her body, lingering especially at her breasts.

Petra stared right along with him. She, too, was fascinated with her friend who was developing so quickly before her eyes. She told herself she was looking out for Justina and gauging the boy's intentions toward her, but it was also a chance to gaze on Justina in a way she didn't dare when they were alone.

A new intensity was bubbling out of Justina's skin, spilling onto anyone paying attention. Petra paid attention, and lamentably, so did a lot of boys. For Petra, it was warm, comforting, and exciting; she grasped close their time together. Naturally, Justina absorbed the compliments and carried herself with a little more confidence.

Justina grinned back at him. When she saw the twinkle in Justina's eyes, Petra's stomach clamped tight. What was all this cheerfulness going back and forth between them? Justina said, "It happens that I don't so much go places I don't usually go because I have places *to* go. Don't you have places you need to go?"

The boy looked up at her again with a dumb grin on his face. "I think right here is the place I really need to go. So… can I walk with you a little ways?"

But *Petra* was walking with Justina. They were going to walk home together and play together at Petra's house. Justina was on the verge of forgetting that the two of them already had a plan. Justina said, teasingly,

"Why do you want to walk with me when you live the other way?" Petra exhaled in relief.

"These woods are pretty dark. You never know what might lurk in here. I'd be happy to protect you." Yuk, so gallant! Why wasn't Justina throwing up yet, or at least telling him to leave her alone?

"That's sweet. But really not necessary." Sweet, Justina, really? How about ridiculous and presumptuous, and you're perfectly capable of taking care of yourself.

"Justina, how about this weekend? Will you meet me in Las Leches? We could just sit on the fountain and talk for a while."

"What do you want to talk about?" Horrors, Petra noticed that Justina was looking at his bare shoulders. He was wearing a tank top to show off his just-blooming adolescent muscles.

"Well, we can plan out the conversation now if you want. I'd start by asking you how you feel about the weather. That's a good, safe place to start. Then I'd tell you about the soccer ball I found in the woods behind my house, so now I can practice anytime I want."

Justina laughed. "Really, you found a soccer ball? Is it a good one?"

"It is! It's blown up tight, it's white and red and black, hardly worn down at all. Well, maybe a little, if truth be told, but it's good enough to practice with."

"Will you bring your soccer ball with you if I agree to meet you?"

He smiled. "You bet."

Justina lowered her eyes, pretending to be all demure and shy—too late in this little encounter, in Petra's opinion. "Well, okay then. I'll see you there on Saturday after the youth bible study at church." At least she let him know where she's coming from.

A huge smile—way too huge in Petra's opinion—cracked open Enzo's face. She thought she heard him simper, in a groveling sort of way. But he finally turned back (yes!) and left them. At long last Justina turned around and remembered Petra's existence. Justina sighed and floated back to earth.

Feeling petulant suddenly, Petra said, "I don't like that guy, Justina."

Justina looked surprised. "Why? I think he has an adorable way about him. He makes me feel happy. He's kind of cute, don't you think?"

"If you like sunken cheeks, and hairy chins, bulging shoulders, and that kind of thing, sure."

"What's wrong with you, Petra? He was perfectly nice."

"You deserve better than him, Justina. He's just not your type."

"I'm not about to marry him! But it could be entertaining to hang out for a few minutes. Maybe kick around his soccer ball."

She made it sound so innocent, but Petra knew a threat when she saw one. "Let's go climb that huge pine tree behind my house, Justina! You know the one where the branches start above our heads? Sometimes there's snakes up there!" She proposed the absolute best climbing tree to lure in her best friend.

"I don't know, Petra, I kind of feel like relaxing in the sun. Maybe we could set the bench out in the yard and let the sun heat us up from head to toe."

Anyway, they headed for home.

That weekend, Justina and Enzo sat together on the fountain where lots of other people saw them talking, and flirting. Petra heard about it from Carlos, who was hanging on the corner with his friends and watched the whole episode. Other girls from school saw her head in Enzo's direction when they all came out of church together. One girl kept an eye on them while she was working at her mother's store by the plaza. And that's the girl who told other girls, and other girls told more, until it became the big news at school.

Pretty soon they were saying that Justina and Enzo had been kissing. Supposedly, they'd gone off into the woods to mess around, and Justina had let him take advantage of her.

But none of that happened. Justina told Petra all about it because Petra grilled her the next day after mass. Justina said they had fun. They talked a little, laughed together, played a little soccer. Then she had to go home to do her chores, so that was it. Nothing raunchy, nothing disrespectful, nothing tantalizing.

Justina was pretty, and getting prettier each month. The boys noticed when a girl was growing up that way and curried favor with her. She started to get a reputation, and it all started with that gossip. The reputation, along with her maturity, made the X-14'ers take notice. And a few months later, tragedy happened.

Petra figured that was as good a theory as any about why they took

Justina. In Petra's estimation, it all started with the gossip. Gossip caused nasty things to happen, and she would never mess with it. False rumors contributed to the demise of her best friend, as far as she was concerned.

Petra preferred to keep her problems to herself. There was too fine a line between sharing personal happenings and feelings with friends and flipping them over into rumors. So she opted to hold things close to her chest. No matter if it meant she had few friends. She had no illusions about the harm revealing one's inner life could cause.

Her attention returned to Novina. "And I would never do anything to hurt Vicenta." Time was running. Petra needed an excuse to rest for a while. "My grandmother is not feeling well today, Novina. I should go help with dinner."

"It's been a pleasure to speak with you. I expect to see you perform well at the big game on Saturday."

Petra ventured, "Could I come over to your apartment for dinner after the game?"

"Perfect. Vicenta will be there, too. You will stay for the weekend, *sí?*"

CHAPTER SEVENTEEN

Her uncle Tonyo leaned affectionately toward her. Her little space on the bus seat, squeezed between Tonyo and her grandfather, got even smaller. "Little Petrita. You are not so little anymore. Come to think of it, I haven't seen you chasing the mice and pacas by my house for some time! Are your legs too long for that now?" Out of all the kids running around their part of the hamlet, Tonyo had always picked her out to tease.

"Now I run on the soccer field instead! Tonyo, you are coming to the game this afternoon, right?"

"I wouldn't miss it for the world, *guapa*. Our game is right after yours." The bus bounding in and out of potholes made Petra sound like she was talking through hiccups. "Are you going to stop all the balls at the goal? Because I might have to leave if you let one go by. My stomach can't handle a miss." Tonyo's eyebrows always lifted high into his forehead when he was teasing.

The coins Nonna had given her for market purchases, concealed in a plastic bag tucked into her bra, jingled happily as she boarded the bus and shuffled quickly to the seat next to her uncle Tonyo. Nonna always said her mother and Tonyo had been the closest of the siblings when they were growing up. Bowing to Nonno's advice that it was time for her to open up to her mother in today's phone call, she hoped talking with Tonyo might put her in the mood.

By the time they arrived in San Luis Hunahpu, people would be hanging out the doors of the bus, holding onto whatever hardware they could find, on for the ride no matter the conditions. So many times, the bus had passed her by as she travelled her well-worn path between home and Las Leches. She wanted nothing more than to get on it and follow it to new adventures.

Besides the difficulty of paying the fare, trepidation held her back. Gangs preyed on buses, forcing them to stop, ripping victims out of the bus and into the anonymous woods, stealing the drivers' and passengers' meager coins. Ruthless gang members were known to kill the driver on the spot if he didn't pay the requisite "tax." Riding with her family, at least she wouldn't be a lone and vulnerable female teenager if they encountered a roadblock.

Troubles had a way of falling away amidst the buoyant colors and sounds. And the noise multiplied as if it was contagious. Everyone on the bus seemed to talk at once, and the chickens joined in with continuous cackling. Repainted to inspire its passengers in a glory of colors, the bus resembled a monstrous quetzal. The sides were streaked with greens, yellows and reds, the edges sprinkled with geometric designs. The lettering above the driver announced "SAN LUIS HUNAHPU." Joyful music— *playeros, cumbias*—flooded out the bus door. Colored tassels, scented ornaments and prayer beads hung from the dashboard, while a velvety picture of Jesus looked down at the passengers from above.

Just the usual local bus in Guatemala.

Carlos had worked through most of the night filling the barrel with cane juice and collecting from Uncle Arnoldo the burro which would carry it to the city. Bleary-eyed, Carlos emerged from his hammock, shaking his head sharply to throw off sleep. He prepared to load up the burro and set out before the first glimmer of dawn on the nearly two hour walk to the market in San Luis Hunahpu, accompanied by Nonno's brothers Jacinto and Arnoldo, and their handsome steed Chancho.

"I recently met the coach of Los Poblanos. The coach is a woman, *tío*!"

"Well then, I guess if fifteen-year-old girls can be goalies then we'll have to let women coach."

"Yeah. I guess so. I never heard of it before though."

"Life just keeps changing, with or without us. Sometimes I think it would be okay if it changed a little faster. But I might be able to live with that particular change."

"Hmmm. Tonyo, can we talk about my mother?" Tonyo was always willing to tell stories about her mother. If she was going to work on having a better phone conversation this time, it might help to get another taste of his love for her. Whenever people talked to her about her parents, there was always a new tidbit of information.

"Are you kidding? She was the best sister a kid could ask for. I could talk about Suri for hours—days, if you give me the chance."

"You and Nonno seem to admire her so much. When I talk to her on the phone, she always gets all sad and says how she misses me, but I hardly remember her."

"I haven't seen her for about ten years either, *mi sobrinita*. I miss her terribly. Your mother was unusual—like you. You remind me of her every time I see you." Petra could see his eyes searching back in his head, touching the memories.

"Tell me, *tío*. Tell me about her."

"Suri seemed different from other people—better. I remember a time. It was when the war was calming down, she was about five, I was seven or so. We were very poor then, more than now, and we were lucky to get a few beans for dinner. I was going around whining to everybody about my empty stomach, and my mother lost her patience. Your Nonna kicked me out of the house and told me to make myself useful getting wood or cleaning the porch or something. Suri followed me outside and laid her hand on my stomach. Looking right into my eyes, she pretended to be a sorceress and made up an incantation: 'Suki, soki, I am the magic Suri. Away away fly the tummy goblins!'"

"Really, she said that?"

They laughed. "She was adorable, and I savored her attention. And you know what was the strangest part? The hunger went away! I think she scared away the hunger with her care. That's the thing: your mother knew how to love. She had these big, sweet eyes, just dripping with benevolence. She looked up at me and, even when I was in a terrible mood or something happened that had 'ruined' my day, my heart would melt." His eyes lingered sadly as he met Petra's eyes.

After a short pause, he continued, reveling now in the memories. "I remember another time: I quit school when I was still pretty little so I could help my father, your Nonno, build up the corn field. We worked hard clearing new earth. One day we pried a big rock out of the ground, just small enough so we could do it between the two of us. My papá, your Nonno, went off to clear another area, just over a hill, and told me to keep pushing the rock off to the side of the area we wanted to plant. So I pushed it and pushed it.

"Being the ten-year-old boy I was, I worked myself up and started dancing around it while it rolled down a slope, and then it rolled onto my foot. Suddenly I was in huge pain, and I couldn't move. I yelled for my papá, but he couldn't hear me. I lay there crying for a few minutes, and when I looked up, there was my sister Suri! She said she'd heard me yelling, but Petra—she was at the house, a whole lot farther away than our papá. She brought me water from the well and held me until I calmed down. Then she went to get our papá for help. It turned out I wasn't hurt too bad. My foot, and my pride, were bruised, but both got better after a while. I still don't know how she knew to come for me."

"With all that specialness, why did she get involved with my father, when he treated her so badly?"

Tonyo glanced around the bus, considering his answer. "I guess we have a little while here. Shall I tell the story, as far as I know it? You've never heard it before, right?" His eyes flashed at her, knowing she had, and knowing he would tell it again anyway.

"Little Xavier... Unfortunately, too many people—and I have to say especially young women—start off pitying men and are drawn into loving them when they should keep it at pity. Suri got drawn too far in, and it ended up almost ruining her.

"Xavier was my age, just a couple years older than Suri. We were maybe three or four when the military came rampaging through our neighborhood looking for guerrillas. We were scared out of our minds because they liked to round up all the indigenous people, accusing them of supporting the guerrillas, and shoot them, or worse. So the day they came to Xavier's neighborhood, his papá picked him up in his arms and ran into the forest. A couple of soldiers ran after Xavier and his dad, though, and they shot at them from behind. A bullet grazed Xavier's right ear and cheek, right there in his father's arms. They took him to a *curandero*, but it never healed up right.

"From that time on, he had a huge scar on his cheek, and he couldn't hear at all from his right side, and not too well from his left. Somehow the loud noise affected the hearing on his left side, or maybe the shock to his system made the hearing on both sides go, but from that point he changed. He tried to compensate for the loss by being tougher, especially once he experienced other kids teasing him or shunting him aside when he didn't hear them. He lashed out at guys who asked him about the weather. He started fights and got angry over nothing.

"He lived just over the hill, up toward Las Leches a tad, so Suri ran into him from time to time. Seems like she had a way with Xavier that made him quiet around her. She sympathized with him, grieved how hard it must be for him to make his way in a sound-dampened world. He listened to her, and when he got in a mood, she helped him let go of the rage. She didn't reject him or yell back at him.

"He fell in love with her quick once she grew up to look like a woman. She was still young, though—only your age, Petra, only fifteen short years old. She didn't know much how to tell the difference between a man who would make a good lasting partner and one who might create problems.

"And your Nonna, you might say she was naive, too. Probably she still is, because I hear she thinks you should marry that Emilio, who's definitely not proved himself worthy of my niece! Your grandmother saw Xavier fawning over her daughter, and she was happy that rugged, handsome man wanted to marry her daughter. She's proven to go a little weak in her judgment in the face of young romance. She approved the relationship, and they got married at the church in Las Leches before Suri was sixteen years old.

"It was downhill from there, Petra. Once they got married and the shine wore off the relationship, inside of a couple years Xavier was treating her as badly or worse than he did everyone else. He tried to keep her home all the time, and got jealous when she went to church, even when she came to visit me. I saw what he was doing to her, but I didn't think I could intervene. People said it was between them, let them work it out, he has a right to control his wife.

"But that kind smile she always had wore thin. I saw the glow seep right out of her eyes. By the time she got pregnant the first time, her shoulders bowed down, like she was tired from carrying the world on her back. She lost that first baby. Probably Xavier kicked her when the baby was still inside. But then she got pregnant again with Carlos, then with you, Petrita. He did what he wanted to her during those years. Beatings, calling her trashy names, keeping her at home all the time. I don't know too much because she was living next to his parents during those years. I hardly got to see her. None of us knew the details of Suri's torments at the time. Now I know—by the time Suri ran away to the United States, he was on a road toward killing her.

"When she had a chance to escape, she grabbed it. He stomped out of their house one evening saying he was going to go visit Guatemala City with another woman he was fooling around with. Within an hour after he left the house, Suri arranged for your Nonna to take care of you and Carlitos for her, until she could bring you to join her. Nonna knew enough about what was going on, and she'd been sick with guilt about pushing her to marry Xavier.

"I accompanied her to Guatemala City. I'm thankful I got to take that trip with her, because hope reentered her soul that day, and I was reminded what a wonderful sister I had. I saw that she got on a bus going north. When she waved at me through that bus window, she was sitting up straight, calm and decided. Tears fled out my eyes, though.

"Her determination got her all the way to the United States. None of us have seen her since."

Petra stayed quiet. She had heard parts of this story before, but not all put together. "Do you know where my father went?"

"I hope he left for China, Petra. I never saw him again. He's long gone."

"I barely remember either of them, Tonyo. I only remember hiding under the bed and crying in fear." She looked longingly at Tonyo. "It seems like I should remember what happened when I was five years old, but I don't."

"Don't fret, Petra. There's still a long life ahead for you all to get to know each other. Maybe one of these days she'll come back to visit, and I can hug her again, too."

"Tonyo, my mother is expecting us to call this afternoon. Me and Nonno. I'm nervous to talk to her, but—I don't want to run away from her anymore. I get all muddled up every time she's on the phone. Mostly I don't say much of anything. I don't know how to talk to her."

"Petra, there's no how. Just be yourself. If you're nervous talking to her, maybe tell her that. There's nothing like sharing a difficult thing with someone to shake it right out of you."

Petra tapped her foot, feeling suddenly shaky. Tonyo looked at her intently. "Do you realize," Tonyo said, "how like my sister you are? That people love you the same way they loved your mother? Which means the two of you can understand each other in a unique way. There's a second wind behind you, Petra, an angel riding on your shoulder. Just ask the angel when you need help. And don't get married anytime soon."

"That's definitely not happening," Petra laughed. "Emilio can jump off a cliff before he'll get a hold of me, in any way, shape, or form."

Leaning on Tonyo's arm, Petra made an effort to pool her courage to face her mother.

At the market, stretching as far as her eye could see—though all the people and canopies admittedly interfered with her sight—narrow aisles defined row after row of vegetables and grains, baskets and blankets, textiles and bags. The endless panoply of colors washed over her.

Conversations in English, Quiché, German, Kakchiquel filled the air with signs of life beyond Las Leches. She leaned toward the English words, trying to pick out a few meanings, while she chose vegetables the family would eat for the next weeks. A program on Tía Dolores's television about an international medical organization had featured those crisp sounds of English. Apparently, the group helped victims of domestic violence in Guatemala City. Someday Petra would drop in to volunteer her services.

A thin blond woman with narrow glasses and a little leather handbag dawdled over colorful Mayan cloth as she tried to balance her already bountiful purchases on her shoulder. In thickly accented Spanish, she asked a vendor, "*Cuánto es?*"

A heavy-set peasant woman stood behind the piles of fabric. Her wide, cracked feet, the color of the earth they had walked on over many years, didn't fully sustain her, and she leaned on her teenage son. The boy suggested a price that was three times the usual amount. The American's eyebrows went up, but she reached for her purse.

Petra decided to try out her few words of English. "Can I help?" Nonno had found opportunity by a chance encounter with foreigners. Maybe she could, too.

The boy stood tall next to his mother, but his eyes leapt across several rows, meeting the inviting expressions of a couple buddies. They gestured for him to hurry up and go off with them.

The American woman smiled appreciatively at Petra. In English, she said, "Is that the usual price? It seems a bit high." Petra looked confused. "*Mucho dinero?*" the woman simplified.

"*Sí.* Too much." Petra and the peasant woman exchanged a few words, the boy now otherwise engaged with his friends. The American paid the much-reduced price and stuffed the fabric into her bag.

"*Muchas gracias,*" the woman said to Petra as they moved down the aisle. "*Tu vives aquí?*"

"*Un poco por allí.*" Petra pointed down the road. "Are you visiting Guatemala?"

"We're going to see the Mayan ruins at Juyú tomorrow. Do you know the place?"

The idea came through, if not all the words. "*Qué bueno!* I want to see soon."

Petra turned to buy a sack of rice, and the woman was off down the next row.

Maybe her mother worked with someone like that. But English would come naturally to her now, since she'd been in the U.S. years now. Petra picked out one woman, then another, to assemble a picture of her mother. She probably stood tall with a certain elegance. Generous, soft breasts, like the woman buying plantains there. Her mother would wear a heavy sweater, heavier than the one worn by the woman selling corn, because it was colder in the United States. Full lips, like Petra's, with eyes warm like a doe. The way that woman's long, dark brown hair, tied loosely, flowed across her forehead and down her back. That's the way her mother's hair would be.

Petra quickly let drop the *quetzales* and *centavos* at one market stall after another, and she emerged with a bag full of vegetables. She would be happy to indulge at dinner that evening. Tonyo appeared to relieve her of the load. She reserved a few quetzals for herself, for a *licuado* after the game. If they won, Nonna said, the drink would boost the celebration. If they lost, she could wash down the disappointment, and take comfort in her teammates.

Now she had only a little time to get to the shop where Nonno was meeting her to talk to their mother. She ran.

The heart of the town began to encroach. A neon Coca Cola sign emblazoned the first store on the block. A sea of signs, banners, and activity blurred together as Petra sped around a corner. A young woman carried a baby swaddled in a colorful *rebozo* on her back. Motorized scooters zipped in and out around the people, lurching to the side as they took precipitous turns, one after the other. A group of young girls jumped excitedly on each other. A man with a severe frown stared gloomily at passersby, apparently disapproving of the sights before him, then began to intone Christian messages of doom and reproach.

Small flashing lights attracted her to a storefront. Words in English floated out the door, and people's hands swiped computer screens. She pulled herself away from the window of the internet café when she became conscious that she'd been staring too long. What different worlds came together on this street!

An elderly man entered the meat store, both of his thick, worn hands wrapped around the necks of three or four chickens who struggled and squawked. In the store window various cuts of a cow hung, apparently recently butchered, judging from the blood dripping on the floor below.

A boy about twelve years old exited the store carrying a bag. Dressed from head to foot in white, the pointed toes of his boots were conspicuously stylized. He sauntered along the edge of the street with the erect stride of a well-off rancher's son. He disappeared around the far corner.

Adrenaline was beginning to flow in anticipation of the soccer game, which would start in about an hour, but she had to focus on the call with her mother first. She turned into Tienda Nuñez, a small food market. Nonno was already on the phone. Petra swallowed and tried to remember to keep breathing.

Nonno said, "Are you ready?" The calling card would give them a half hour of talking time.

She took the phone but covered it with both hands over her stomach. "Nonno, tell me what to say to her. Just to start off. How should I start?"

"Oh, Petra, I'm sorry this is so hard. Remember this is the person who gave birth to you fifteen short years ago. As much as you struggle to make the connection, your mother has felt the connection since that day. Remember that. It may help. Tell her your hopes for the soccer game. Tell her your dreams of becoming a doctor." He paused, then added, "I'm sure she'd be quite interested in your dream about Itzamná, as well."

Petra closed her eyes to digest the thoughts, to get a hold of herself before cradling that phone next to her ear. So her mother knew about Itzamná also? And her grandfather was encouraging her to talk to her mother about it? She remembered every bit of her dream. Alocinia kept stirring the images around in her mind over the last couple of days, so she kept mulling them over. Perhaps she did have a real bond with her mother.

Before she quite found herself, though, Nonno nudged her. Her mother was waiting on the other end.

"Petita, I have so many things to tell you, but first, talk to me—how are you?" Her voice held out a cup of love to her. Petra instinctively pulled herself inward. Petra had rejected that cup in their last conversation, a couple of months ago. Now, she wanted to accept it but wasn't sure if she could. Her heart and mind battled for her voice.

"Mamá, everything is crowding at me this week. My insides want me to grow up, but my skin is stretching tight, holding back. So many things are happening to me."

With concern, "Start with one, Petita. Tell me."

"The Deacon at our church, his name is Eduardo. He's from Bolivia. He likes soccer, and says he's coming to our game today! He pulled me aside a couple days ago and talked to me about finding hope in God and forgiving people who hurt others." Petra was struggling to find the words. "Mamá, he made me think a lot…. But—I told him something I hadn't told anyone besides Nonno. Now I want to tell you, too." It was a question.

"Do you know, Petra, that I feel your heart beating right next to mine, as if you are still inside me. Perhaps you are, I think. Please, I want to know this something."

"I want to go further in school, mamá. I want to study through high school, and college, and maybe, if I do well, become a doctor." She stopped, afraid of how her mother would react.

"Don't you ever—ever—give up on your ambitions. As long as you have the will, you will find a way."

"Really? Eduardo said the same thing."

"You're afraid you won't be able to continue to high school, aren't you? It's not so much the money, Petra, because I believe I could help you pay for it, but the trip on the bus every day. It's so dangerous, I know it is."

"I know, mamá. I am afraid." Petra suddenly began to weep. How many people had she talked to about her fears, about her desire to continue to high school? Why was she crying now? Her tears ran down her cheeks. Her grandfather came over to where she stood and put his hand on her shoulder. She shook with sobs, her chest swelling and pushing at her ribs. She buried her eyes into Nonno's shoulder. Nonno patted her gently on the head, then wandered off. He was right; she needed the moment alone with her mother.

"Are you there, Petra?"

"Mamá, I don't know if I can talk." She sniffled and knew her mother heard her tears. Embarrassment made her cheeks burn. She tried to push back the feelings so she wouldn't disturb her mother.

"Petita, let me talk to you. I know you're dealing with a lot right now. I can imagine the pain. I grew up much like you. You can tell me more after. What I want to tell you may help. Petra, I have married a man. His name is Wyman. Wyman Sibley. I have taken his last name, so now people call me Sorelly Sibley. Sounds strange, doesn't it?"

"Mamá, no!" A man would take her mother even further away, when she'd only just begun to consider a new relationship with her.

"Petra, stay with me here. He is very kind to me, *mi hija*. But imagine this! The day we got married, he made a wonderful meal for his daughter, some friends, and us, to celebrate. You know what he made? Tamales! They were even wrapped in real banana leaves—and they're not easy to find here in Rhode Island! He learned how to make them because he knew I loved to eat them on holidays as a child. Can you imagine a man doing that in our village, Petita?"

Her mother was going on about herself again. Even though Petra had just laid bare her deepest dreams to her. She laughed. "No way, no man here deigns to cook, and never for a woman! I can't picture it! Tell me more, mamá. What is he like?"

"It's very new for me. He is so kind and yet, it's different. He is American. I'm learning English faster now because he doesn't speak Spanish. Just a couple of words. So it's hard for us to communicate sometimes. And Petra, there's another thing. He's an old man. He's 68 years old, and he gets around in a wheelchair. He fought in Vietnam and suffered an injury to his spine in the war there. This might be hard for you to imagine, Petra, but he's full of life, more than most men I've known, despite his disability and his age. I'm happy to help take care of him now, and he treats me with a kindness I've only dreamed of."

Petra struggled to absorb all of this information. The distance she always felt with her mother surged forward, rising from under the rock where Petra had tried to quash it. "But that means he's thirty years older than you! How will he take care of you?" If her mother wanted to marry an old man, an invalid, well, it was no concern of hers. It wasn't as if Petra was a part of her mother's life, after all.

"I don't think I can give you a complete picture over the phone, Petra. But there's more. He has applied for me with Immigration. In a few months I will have a green card, so I can be legal here finally! He wants me to stay with him and be my husband, Petra, and I believe he truly cares about me. You can't imagine what this means, Petra. It hasn't been easy here, and I've wanted to help you so much more than I have been able to."

"But —," Petra hesitated to ask, nervous about the answer, "does that mean you'll come home to visit?"

"Oh, Petra, you have no idea how I long to see you, and Carlitos, Nonno and Nonna, Tonyo…"

"You'll probably be too busy with your new husband." It crossed Petra's mind that her mother and this man might have a baby, and then she really would be irrelevant to her mom's life.

"Wyman wants to meet you, Petra. Of course I talk about you all the time! I think he begins to love you as I do. He has also filed papers for you, *mi amor*. It means we can be together again! I will go visit, I want to see everybody, but *you*—I want to be with you all the time, Petra. I want you to come here and live with us in the United States, here in Providence." Her mother paused and sniffled. Maybe her mother was as unsure of their relationship as Petra was. "You can go to high school here, Petra. And there are so many more opportunities for a young person here. If we work hard, and you still want to, you will become a doctor in the U.S."

"*Ay, Dios*, mamá, you're trying to kill me. My mind is spinning. I don't know what to think."

"Think positively, *m' hija*." Her voice cracked.

"But what about Carlos? Don't you want him to live with you, too?" The promise her mother had made to them when she left Guatemala ten years before simmered in the back of Petra's mind. Petra had despaired of the fantasy of joining her mother in the U.S. sometime along the way.

Her mother said, "I fear that I have lost my chance with Carlos. He is a man now, and he is committed to making his life in Guatemala. I believe he has a strong bond to the land there, whereas you—you have a connection to my heart, and perhaps to an ambition very difficult to fulfill in the land of our ancestors."

"You know us pretty well considering how far away you are. How do you know these things?" Petra paused. "You might just be right about Carlos." She wasn't sure whether her mother was right about herself, but she put it in her mind to think about later.

Her mother laughed. "Petita, you do realize that I love you both so much. Your Nonno and I have spoken by phone every week for ten years now."

"But how can I leave Guatemala? Nonna and Nonno—who would take care of them? Nonna is ill, mamá. Her stomach hurts her. I don't believe she even knows what's wrong. How could I leave her?" Petra's head was swimming.

"Petra, Nonna will always be cared for by our family there. Carlos works hard and will help support her. Julina is growing up every day. My brothers Oscar and Tonyo are nearby. And your Nonno is still strong, Petra. I know this is a lot to take in, but you have a life ahead of you. A mother and daughter should be together. You must take some time to think about this. In the meantime, Immigration has the paperwork, and we will wait a few more months. Perhaps by the time you finish ninth grade in October…"

Petra wiped her face, the tears drying now. "I know we will have to hang up soon. Our time on the card is running out. But Nonno has given me an idea that I should ask you about something else. Mamá, do you know something about Itzamná? It is important, mamá. Will you tell me?"

The question met silence as her mother faltered. "You would see the look of shock on my face right now, Petra, if you could see me. I'm thinking this is a long story but tell me quickly why you are asking this question."

"You remember Emilio, mamá? He was my friend when I was a child, with Justina, too."

"Of course, Petita. Emilio's mother was my best friend. I held Emilio when he was a few hours old."

"Seriously? I didn't know! Oh, mamá, the way his mother died…. It was so awful."

"I know, sweetheart," she said solemnly. "I do know something of how hard your life is there."

Petra rallied. "Well, Emilio's in the local gang now. He's threatening to hurt Nonno unless we take him to some secret place. Nonno has not told me much, but I think it has something to do with when he worked at Juyú with the archaeologists. He said I should ask you about Itzamná. I don't really believe Emilio would hurt us, but… I'm not sure. I need to understand what he's talking about."

"*Ay, Dios mío.* I will speak to my father before we hang up. This sounds like a dangerous situation." She paused. "Your grandfather will understand this, Petra. When I was about your age, he took me to the place where Itzamná is. The experience is carved into my psyche. It is not at Juyú, but close—near the volcano. He found an old stone carving of Itzamná during the time he worked with the archeologists there—a figurine made by the Mayan people thousands of years ago. It's inscribed with all kinds of symbols and meaning in Mayan mythology. And very valuable. I have seen news reports of gangs selling ancient artifacts for their own profit. But it must be protected, Petra. Your grandfather wanted the ancient Mayans to keep it, so he left it right there where he found it. If it is in danger, we must get it to people who will protect it the right way."

"If Nonno found this figure so many years ago, how would Emilio's gang know about it?"

"This I don't know, Petra. But your grandfather can help. He will talk in circles. You must follow him into the center of the circles. But don't ignore the import of the circles. You won't grasp Itzamná unless you understand the spiral. Mythology is not so well understood in a straight line. Talk to Nonno."

"I will, mamá. I don't really think Emilio will do anything to us. Don't worry."

"Petra, be careful. Many people who don't worry end up dead. Things can change from one moment to the next. *Ay Dios*, what would I do if something happened to you, or to my father? Please, Petra, you must take great care, for our whole family as well as yourself. Understand, this is not just about you."

Swallowing hard, Petra said, "OK, mamá. Perhaps Nonno will tell me the rest of the story tonight. Mamá, I need to go now. Mamá…" She searched for the words she wanted to say. "Mamá… it is nice to talk to you. It's been so long. I want to touch you, to know who you are."

"Petita, that sounds sad, but honestly, you make my heart sing. You *are* growing older; I can hear that. Think about coming to the U.S, *m' hija*. In a few months, you will be able to come legally, on a plane. Can you imagine? I have never been on a plane, but you will do so many things in your life."

Petra choked back a sob and forced herself to say the words bubbling up in her. "Mamá." She hesitated. "I love you, mamá. I miss you."

"Ay, *m' hija*, how I will cherish those words in the next weeks. Now go win a soccer game!"

The score was one to one, and the second half had just begun. It was a battle of the defense. Petra was at the peak of her performance, but so was the Poblanos goalie.

The ball plunged toward Petra high up above her head. She leapt up toward the frame of the net, an impressive jump, just tipping the ball with the end of a finger, sending it soaring above the net. Tonyo hollered out amidst the fervor of the crowd.

Las Lechitas's Laura threw the ball in and passed it down the field toward the Poblanos goalposts. María kicked hard to her forward side, and it flew like a juggernaut off Sara's forehead. Claudia sent it speeding back to María, their best goal kicker, who booted it straight toward the middle of the net, where the Poblanos goalie picked it off and sent it back into mid-field. On the sideline, Novina's arms raised above her head in celebration of the masterful defense.

While the ball tarried at the far end, Petra watched how the Poblanos team moved the ball, which players had the most control, who used her teammates to best effect and who wanted to be a lone star. She carefully positioned herself just in front of the goal area, inching this way or that as the ball's position on the field shifted.

The Poblanos forward held onto the ball, deftly moving it around the Lechitas defense. She danced down the field like a ballerina with tight control over her graceful movements, putting the ball into the air, then head-butting it to Petra's close left side.

Petra moved into the field to block its momentum, and the ball headed fast toward her gut. The ball pounded her chest, and she sucked in a breath.

A sharp whistle broke her concentration. Half-time. Petra headed toward Tonyo and Nonno on the bleacher seats. Carlos was probably hanging with friends at the men's field. As she reached for Laura's hand to give her a congratulatory slap, Laura abruptly turned away. It slowly dawned that all heads had turned toward the sideline behind Laura. People were climbing off the bleachers, and a crowd had formed next to the seats.

A pair of cowboy boots with pointy toes was moving fast toward her, a young boy dressed all in white just behind him. Potoo again! Suddenly a blur of activity. The man was waving a knife, his arms thrust forward. He closed in on Petra before she could collect her wits.

The crowd parted, and Deacon Eduardo appeared out of the fold, trailing Potoo. She had forgotten that he'd planned to come to the game. A smile circulated inside her at his presence.

As Potoo lurched toward Petra, he flashed gang hand signals, and his blue and white shirt blared "14" on his back. Almost like he was advertising. He glared at her through slit eyes, but also fearlessly scanned the people surrounding the field. Emilio had warned her about those slit eyes when he introduced Potoo to her. The ugly bird that could still spot its enemy below even when its eyes were closed, through a slit in its eyes. The potoo that hid itself in trees during the daytime, its coloring blending seamlessly with branches, making it almost invisible. Venom seemed to rise from his body and cover Petra in slime. His long arms reached out and grabbed hold of her waist, pulling an arm behind her in a painful hold.

He spat out, loud enough for others to hear, "Girlie, you've played your last hand. Your shit-faced boyfriend ran off with his tail between his legs, and you are going to pay for the sins of you both." He held the knife to her neck.

"Shall I spit in your face again, you ugly bird? That might be embarrassing in front of all these people," she said.

Eduardo led a group of five men who were closing in on Potoo, with others gathering on the field on all sides. Out of a corner of her vision, she spotted Tonyo and Carlos pushing their way toward her.

"Whatever happens here, Petita," he spat out her name, "your boyfriend is a dead man. He won't be able to help you anymore."

Despite herself, Petra felt her stomach tighten. As bad as Emilio was, she didn't want him to die.

"And you, my precious, have just moved up in the ranks. Your situation only gets more serious when you cross us. Gusano wants to see you, tomorrow at noon, at the jacaranda tree. Put that in your little brain. Families suffer, too, *chiquilla*. Girls come when we summon them, or worse awaits. *Comprende?*"

She squirmed amidst the nausea that rose in her from sharing the tight space with Potoo. The knife felt sharp against her neck.

Potoo shouted at the group nearing them, "Keep back or the knife will open this pretty young flesh. You'll see some fresh red blood flow down and ruin her handsome soccer shirt."

Eduardo said, "Young man, there is a better way. The girl is innocent."

Potoo threw his head back and scoffed, "Innocent! What do you know about it?"

Tonyo pushed forward. "Drop the knife, *cabrón*. Can't you see you're outnumbered?"

Apparently savoring a warped pleasure from the attention of the crowd, Potoo waved a hand up in the air, as if to celebrate his own prowess. He kept the other wrapped around the knife at her throat, using his elbow to restrain her shoulder.

Petra saw Carlos stoop down to crawl, hidden amongst the legs, toward her. But Petra didn't wait. She thrust her arms up to get the knife away from her and pivoted swiftly to face Potoo. Her raging eyes glared at him. Without a moment's hesitation, she kneed him in the groin.

Potoo doubled over in pain but managed to hold onto the knife. In no time, he looked up at Petra, his eyes narrowed, burning with fury.

Petra raised her leg and kicked out toward the side of his face as hard as she could. Potoo fell backward, and the knife skittered along the ground.

Suddenly everyone was shouting. Pandemonium reigned. Eduardo leapt toward Potoo and clamped him to the ground. Little did Petra know about this Deacon! At least three men grabbed Potoo. Eduardo and the men dragged him up to standing position while one paralyzed him by bending his arm behind his back. They hauled him around behind the bleachers.

Eduardo returned quickly to her side and leaned down on a knee to speak to Petra. "Petra, you're bleeding!"

Petra touched her neck and looked at her bloody hand. "I think it's just a slight cut." She was taking shaky, shallow breaths now. The grease from Potoo's hands stank on her skin, and the nausea crept inside her. She twisted to the side and vomited.

Eduardo shouted out, "She needs help here!" He was a hero, but he didn't know what to do next.

Tonyo and Carlos helped her up and began to carry her, one arm under each of her shoulders, but she rebuffed them, craning to see what happened with Potoo. She wanted to thank Eduardo.

Her legs had a different idea. When she collapsed to the ground, she gave in and leaned heavily on Tonyo and Carlos. A local man guided them to the medical clinic amidst the stores and noise of the city. Closing her mind to the confusion, she was nonetheless overwhelmed. Tears came to the fore, but she fended them off.

A graying doctor, prompt but officious, fixed her up with a couple of stitches on the right side of her neck and a gauze bandage that stretched from her throat to the back side of her neck.

Carlos was negotiating with a clerk at the counter about the bill when Vicenta and Novina came through the door. Vicenta rushed to Petra. "*Chica*, are you okay?" She touched the bandage on her neck, which seemed to reassure her a bit.

Novina said, "Petra, that was a great catch at the Lechitas net there, but the game seems to have aborted. I guess we'll just have to say that the hometown team wins, eh?"

Petra smiled awkwardly but looked beyond everyone to the door. She yearned to make a break for that door and run out of there. Run until no one could find her. Until she couldn't find herself.

Carlos and Tonyo shifted over to sit next to Petra. Introductions were accomplished.

Carlos crossed his arms tight over his chest, and a serious frown descended from his forehead, covering his face with gravity. "Petra, this Potoo…. He seems to have it in for you. The way this guy sees it, when Emilio saved you, he betrayed Potoo and the gang. And your escape wounded the gang ego. We need to protect you now. We need to get you home as fast as we can."

Novina offered, "Perhaps she would be safer if she stayed in town here. My home is open to Petra if she wants to stay for a while."

Carlos looked back and forth between Petra, Vicenta and Novina with a questioning look.

Before he could say anything, though, Petra said, "Novina, thank you. But I need to be with my family. Honestly, I can't wait to get out of this town right now." Petra's feet tapped on the floor, generating a rhythmic anxiety. Tonyo's ears perked up, trying to locate the sound.

The clinic door chime announced the arrival of Deacon Eduardo. Petra stood to embrace the Deacon. She got up a bit too quickly, as it happened, because her head spun, and she stumbled into him instead. The two found themselves in an unexpectedly close hug as Eduardo sought to right Petra. Embarrassed, she hastily stepped back and sank into her seat.

Carlos, taking up the mantle of the man of the family, extended his hand with exaggerated solemnity, and the Deacon stumbled forward to shake it.

"Deacon," said Carlos, "your talents exceed your calling. Savior of young women, counselor to wayward gang members, soccer fan. Should we know of any other vocations?" He smiled at Eduardo. "Sir, it is possible you don't know me, as I have failed to frequent your church as often as I should. For this I cannot justify myself. However, I see my failure has led me to disregard a man of great stature in our town. I am Petra's brother, Deacon. Carlos. Very pleased to meet you." It had been a long time since Petra had heard her brother speak with this kind of formality. She looked at Carlos with fascination.

Red-faced in receipt of this admiration, Eduardo responded with corresponding propriety. "You must know it is my pleasure to meet the elder brother of one of the bright lights of our church." He turned the admiration on Petra. "I apologize for interrupting. I see Petra is well-attended," he said. Conscious of the numerous friends and family members all training their eyes on him, he loosened his shirt collar to sweat more freely. Each in turn stood to shake his hand.

Carlos said, "Please accept my sincere thanks for your intervention on my sister's behalf. You may have saved her life today." His eyes were gleaming with pride as he turned to Petra. "Though I must admit she did pretty well for herself, too."

Petra blushed at the complement from her brother.

Eduardo said, "I am only chagrined that I could not see the exciting end to Las Lechitas's victory over the Poblanos." Novina raised a finger, then thought better of interrupting. "Petra, I'm not sure I've ever seen a goalie jump with such determination to block a goal. Very impressive." He nodded with respect toward Petra. "The police did come to arrest the man who threatened this young woman. Two officers handcuffed him and took him away."

"What I don't understand," said Tonyo, "is why the gang would threaten Petra in such a public place. It does seem that the man is a well-connected member of the X-14 gang, Deacon. Given that, it would not surprise me if the police release him, and he is back on the streets by tomorrow."

"Yes," Eduardo responded, "I understand such a result is unfortunately quite common."

"Of course!" Carlos said. "The gang must have decided that making a public statement was more important than any risk to them. Gusano and Potoo knew there would be no consequences because they have the police in their pocket." He paused to reflect. "Or, *quién sabe?* Maybe he just saw Petra there and acted spontaneously. These guys can do whatever they want, I guess."

Eduardo nodded gravely. "Members of the congregation, who know more than I, have told me the MS-13 is taking our local X-14 gang under their wing, which will undoubtedly give this man great leverage over our weak and corrupt police. In light of this, we must consider how to best protect your sister."

Carlos said, "In fact, we were just on our way out of this clinic and heading home, where our family will watch out for her."

Petra's feet continued to tap out perturbed rhythms. Her discomfort was increasing by the moment, and she was beginning to boil over. She said, "Sorry to interrupt your plans for me, but I do not intend to sit around at home while my older brother tries to fend off the MS-13 in some gallant attempt to protect me. I have plans, which don't involve hiding behind my family."

Eduardo looked staidly upon the clinic ceiling, then lowered his gaze as humbly as he could upon Petra. "Petra, you and I have spoken about your future, and I told you I would see if I could help in some way. A Catholic minister of my acquaintance in Guatemala City has suggested to me that you might live with his family there in exchange for doing some housecleaning. He has the ability to obtain a scholarship for you to attend a good private school for girls in the city. If you do well at a such a school, you may find that other opportunities follow. This could present an opportunity to you to remove yourself from this environment of delinquents and shadowy figures."

Petra's teeth clenched involuntarily. She had the sense that her body could not contain her emotions, as if her blood was boiling in her chest.

CHAPTER EIGHTEEN

Tears of frustration formed in the corners of Petra's eyes. It was all she could manage to respond appropriately. She nodded to Eduardo in respectful acknowledgement, and said, "I need to go home. Right now. I'm sorry." She fled out the door.

With only a moment's hesitation, Tonyo took to his heels in pursuit.

Petra still had coins in her bra that she had intended to use to celebrate with her teammates after the game. She ran toward the bus stop, her legs flying, her mind shut down, the tears wiped away and stopped in mid-flow by force of will.

The Deacon had taken her aside for that talk in the church, singling her out for some unfathomable reason. People kept telling her that she was special. What was so special about her? She didn't want to be "special."

Novina and the Deacon were both reaching out to offer her safe haven. And then, out of the blue, her mother had paved the way for her to immigrate to the U.S. and change her life around completely. After abandoning her for so many years!

About this time a year before she had walked from the soccer field to the bus stop with her family. If she concentrated hard, she could remember the route. But she was having trouble concentrating.

People turned to stare at her as she hurtled down the middle of city blocks, past stick figures going about their business, shopping, exhorting, begging. Music blared and shop signs fought for attention. Blind to everything but her sprinting legs and steady breath, she turned corners, searching for familiarity.

Slowly she tired, became distraught, and realized that she was hopelessly lost. Finally, she stopped, out of breath, on the verge of fainting. Her neck throbbed. Her bandage felt wet to her touch. She wasn't sure if it was from blood or sweat.

The scene might have played out very differently. Potoo, keeping everyone back with the threat of his knife to her throat, could have dragged her aside him to his waiting motor scooter. The humiliating spectacle of her as hostage, weak victim to macho man, might have held everyone back. He could have forced her onto the bike, taking her off who knows where. Surely friends of his waited. The group of them could have overpowered her. Perhaps drugged her again.

Gusano, whom she now understood to be their boss, would have directed the attack. Potoo would take over the high role in the gang hierarchy that had been played by Emilio, who had now been disgraced, dethroned, and fashioned into an enemy. Emilio's father, having beaten Emilio to a pulp after he learned of his role in letting her escape, would encourage the gang's retaliation against her. What had she done to become such a focal point?

The protectiveness of Carlos, Novina and the Deacon suffocated her almost as much as the gang's insidious intentions intimidated her. Her mind closed off consideration of what would have happened next.

But while she willed her mind to block out her fears, past events came flooding forward. The dike had already been lifted a bit. Now the waters came plunging through. What had happened to Justina could happen to her, she didn't doubt. Tucked into an alley between two flimsy storefronts among the stench of garbage, she gave in to the memory.

There was that time when her joy got away from her. Sitting on that huge rock with Justina, she had leaned into that smile, become one with it. Her lips became moist and parted as she entered the magnetic field of Justina and their lips entwined. That day, just days before she perished, Justina had promised never to leave her, to stay friends forever.

How she wished Justina were here with her now. Petra had always been able to make her laugh. Until laughing together killed her friend. She'd never lower her defenses that far again.

Petra's heart was pounding. She tried to force herself back to the present. The bare feet of a gaunt, stooped, dark-skinned indigenous man passed by, crying out, "*Refreeeeescooos!*" He hauled a crate of soft drinks atop his shoulder. Rugged, stained an earthy, ashen brown, toes splayed and deformed, the feet had probably never seen shoes.

The frightful image of the man dressed in black, gold teeth glinting in the light, his partner's hands dressed in murderous blades, carrying her beloved friend off into the forest. Nonna had offered a prayer. Nonno had gone off and gotten drunk. Emilio had betrayed her.

And where was her mother then? Her mother had never asked her about what happened. Had Nonno told her? Her mother had stranded her in this god-forsaken dustbowl to cope with it all alone.

Petra was already repelled by this new husband, the old man her mother claimed to care about. But Petra didn't care about him. Why get involved at all? She could figure out her life in Guatemala. It wasn't easy, but at least she understood it. Here was her life, her language, her people, her family with Nonno, Nonna, and Carlos. Leave her uncles and Julina up the path? The well where she drew water? The tarantulas, the dust, the volcano, the gangs? She had to admit there were down sides to her life and her prospects in Las Leches.

Petra shook her head to stop the flood of outrage streaming through her. She peered desperately at the blue sky of San Luis Hunahpu. She was ready to throw it all away.

Blood pounded in her ears. Justina had a hold on her thoughts now, and she wouldn't let go.

But why? Why did they kill her? What did they do to her during those three days? And why Justina, why *her* best friend, why the person who had so recently been Emilio's friend, just a fourteen-year-old girl?

The questions lay with her during the long nights after her death, but she never found answers. And one more that she held underwater as much as possible: Would she be next?

An image grew in her mind, the final piece of Justina's death. She wanted to stop it like she always had, but this time, she couldn't. The image had lived there, in the recesses of her consciousness. The festering scratches along her cheeks. Her limp hand. The blood everywhere. Her mind's eye followed the path of the blood.

A lot of blood, pooling—she could see it through a haze of dread. And the dried, rusty blood all over her. There on her stomach, she had wiped bloody hands. At the shoulder hem of her sleeve, a bloody hand had pulled, leaving crusty fingerprints. But the dried blood on Justina's dress was concentrated between her legs. It was still pooling on the rocks—between her legs. They had violated her beautiful Justina. Petra felt a trickle of sweat dripping down her neck.

After the killing, she began to suffocate the questions. She never wanted another friend like Justina. If a friend could be taken away like that, she didn't need any more friends. After that, she did her work at school, smiled when appropriate, but didn't give out so much of herself.

Petra urged herself out of her hiding place and turned down the street away from the restaurant. Where she all but collided with Tonyo.

Tonyo pulled Petra to him, simply held her close, without words. Relief flooded through her, and she allowed her mind to shut down and Tonyo to guide her. Together they walked to the bus stop. Within a few minutes, they were riding together back toward Las Leches and home. Petra leaned her head on Tonyo's shoulder and slept until they arrived.

CHAPTER NINETEEN

"No, this can't be the solution! I won't stay shut up here again!" Petra yelled at Carlos. The storm of words sent Nonna retreating into the back yard.

But Carlos stood firm. "Peta, when Gusano realizes you're standing him up, what do you think he's going to do? Slink home with his tail between his legs? All hell may break loose. Being here gives you a little protection. He may not be prepared to deal with all of us together."

Petra's mind was racing. She needed time alone to think. When she got home the night before, she'd collapsed into bed. With the arrival of a bright new morning, Petra was sure there was a better solution.

While Petra was stewing on the front porch, Julina came skipping down the trail, Dolores close behind. Petra's heart relaxed. "Julina, *sobrinita. Qué tal?*"

They chatted for a few minutes. They were on their way to visit Julina's godmother in San Luis Hunahpu.

"*Tía!* Can I ride to town with you?"

Carlos's eyes went wide. His elbow lifted over his head as his hand rubbed the back of his neck.

It was perfect. She would take Novina up on her offer and stay with her, just for a couple days. "Carlos, I'll go crazy if I can't leave home again." At the moment, it didn't seem so safe at her home either. Maybe things would calm down after a couple of days. At last she would be able spend time with Vicenta and Novina without Carlos arriving to haul her back home.

Nonna stomped through the house from the back yard wild-eyed, hollering that the trip was dangerous, that Petra needed to be with her family at this time, this and that reasons why she couldn't go. But in the end, she relented.

Carlos said, "What's with this Novina anyway? She's... different."

"She's more urban than people around here, that's all. I like her. And she's a good friend of Vicenta, so we can trust her."

"Seems like she and Vicenta became close friends awful fast. I never saw her around before now."

Petra shrugged her shoulders, and Carlos thankfully dropped the subject. A few minutes to get herself ready, and she headed down the hill with Dolores and Julina.

Petra quickly learned to sprawl on a couch. Novina played not just the CD she had heard at Vicenta's store but several like it, while Petra inspected the covers, reading every detail about the artists and the lyrics. Vicenta wandered about the apartment, offering Petra a bag of corn nuts, a bowl of cut up mango, a roll of sweet *Galletas Marías*. She'd never been so indulged.

"It's so deliciously soft on this couch," Petra said. "How do you ever get anything done?" Within an hour of her arrival, the sun was at its peak, its warmth washing across her, and her eyelids closed. Was she really allowed to sleep in the middle of the day? In her life, only little kids had the luxury of a nap. In the back of her mind, she was endlessly trying to tunnel her way out of the danger that seemed to be surrounding her, caging her in. She made only a feeble attempt to resist the sleep that shut everything down.

Novina's new kitten settled at Petra's feet. Her toes vibrated with the exuberant purring. There was some potential in this new relationship with the animal world, with animals who didn't have their own jobs, who belonged to people for no reason other than their enjoyment.

Two hours later, the aroma of garlic and chicken roused her. Little paws jumped on her feet when they moved. She bolted up and, without missing a beat, offered her services in preparing the food. Vicenta shushed her quietly and motioned for Petra to relax. Vicenta sat on an armchair, her legs slung over the arm, her skirt not quite pulled down all the way around her legs, conversing in subdued tones with Novina, who was stirring a pot of food on the stove. She had seen something like this scene of domestic tranquility in *telenovelas* on her *tía* Dolores's television.

Petra stared in turn out each of the glass windows, three of which split up the living room's longest wall. What was left of the sun cut across the building and cast a shadow that divided the empty lots across the street into geometrical shapes of dark and light. Smatterings of light broke into the living room, crossed the brightly tiled floor, and disappeared into a a set of shelves lined with books. Novina lived on the outskirts of town, close enough to get to the stores of town within minutes, far enough to be able to glimpse neighbors passing by trees and open land on their daily wanderings. How had Novina come by so much money to live this luxurious life?

Novina pulled out a book and handed it to Petra. "It's about a Chicana woman in the U.S. who has a torrid love affair with a female nurse. Not a work of literature, but it's fun."

"*En serio*? There are books about romance between two women?" Petra turned the book over from front to back and flipped through its pages.

Novina laughed. "Petra, there is a whole world of things to discover out there. You can read the book tonight. Or anything else you see here that catches your eye."

"*Ay Dios*. I am so ignorant."

"Not at all. You cannot learn what no one shows you."

Vicenta said, "*Mi amiga*, you are only a step behind me. I have learned so much since I met this woman."

"I have a feeling you will finish reading all of my books here by the end of the week."

Petra's throat caught, and she coughed. "Novina, no. I can't stay that long. I just need a couple of days for the X-14 to cool down around my house. I have to go back to school in a couple of days."

"However long you wish to stay, *mi casa es su casa*." Novina nodded toward Vicenta, shrugging a shoulder. Vicenta turned toward Petra and pursed her lips tightly.

"What? Why are you looking at me like that?" Petra asked Vicenta.

"I wish you would stay longer. I am worried about you, Petra. First Emilio whisks you off somewhere, and now this man—what do you call him—"

"Potoo." It was hard to say the name without spitting.

"Potoo, yes. How is the cut on your neck, Petra?"

Petra touched her fingers to the bandage. It was much less sore now. "I'm fine. It's not as if—" She trailed off, gazing out past Vicenta. Petra's eyebrows came together, and she crammed her hands into her pockets. Again, people were rushing toward her, wanting to help.

Vicenta said, "Petra, I know this lifestyle here—it's all new to you. Please feel free to share your thoughts. It would help us, too."

Petra contemplated Vicenta. "I will. Thank you, Vicenta." She nodded. Dimples dented her cheeks. "When do we eat?"

The meal was a feast, the kind of food reserved at her house for rare special occasions, like Good Friday, or the time the minister from their church had come to visit, years ago, before Deacon Eduardo and the new Bolivian minister had come to town. This chicken was a little dry, but meatier than the freshly killed chicken they would have had for such festivities at her home. This was the kind of chicken people bought at the butcher in San Luis Hunahpu, along with the fresh tomatoes and peppers from the produce store next to it. The garlic, and the green herb, whatever it was, sprinkled on the skin, was a real treat, the kind of extra that was thrown in just for the taste, not to fill you up.

Electric lights, flushing toilets—it was all so luxurious to Petra, the stuff of rich people's houses on Dolores's television. Who was Novina anyway?

Vicenta said, "Petra, ask. It's okay. I can see the questions burning in you."

Petra bit her upper lip. "Well, maybe one question?"

Novina nodded. "Anything."

The kitten's tail flicked into Petra's face. It turned upside down and batted its legs at Petra's hand. "You don't have to answer. I don't mean to pry into your life."

"I don't mind, Petra. I want us to get to know each other."

"Who is your family? How can you afford all this?" Petra indicated the apartment around her.

"That's *two* questions." Novina laughed. "Very understandable ones, though. Let's make a deal. I will answer your questions, but then I get to ask you two questions. Deal?"

Petra's eyes sparkled. The lines in her forehead disappeared.

"You are familiar with Finca Anaconda?" Novina began.

"Very funny. My uncle works there. I used to sell the little packages of gum there."

"Right. Of course." Novina shook her head. "My father owns it."

"*Jesucristo! De verdad?* Your father is Señor Velasquez? I know his name, but I have never seen him in person."

"Yep, that's him. He owns Anaconda and three other plantations in the southern lowlands. Lots and lots of sugar cane. I haven't seen him myself for a number of years."

Not having seen her own father for many years, Petra could imagine this. "Is he a bad man, Novina? I haven't seen my father either, since I was five."

"It's a little different, I imagine. My father is nearby. He is the one who doesn't want to see me. I am the black sheep of the family. He has agreed to support me if I disappear from our family and don't contact his acquaintances. He doesn't want people to associate me with him."

"Black sheep. Because of—?"

Vicenta raised her hand in the air and smiled. Novina said, "Before I met Vicenta, there were other women. I was not always as discreet as I am now. And I no longer live in the town I grew up in, where I broke all the rules and attracted some unpleasant attention."

"And your mother?"

"She is very timid. She bows to the will of my father. Occasionally we arrange to meet at a café in Guatemala City, when my father takes her there and goes off to meetings. A café which is not frequented by members of their society, so there are no unexpected reunions."

"I'm so sorry, Novina." It was hard to imagine living without the support of one's family. Then again, Petra did not have the support of her parents, either.

Novina shook her head. "No need to be sorry. I have the life I wanted. I am aware that I am very lucky to be able to live without financial hardship. And I borrow some pleasure from your friend Vicenta as long as she'll have me. As often as I can tear her away from her store."

Alocinia whispered in Petra's ear. "These are good people. We like Vicenta's friend." Petra swatted at her ear.

A light knocking at the door interrupted. Worry crept across Petra's face.

Vicenta said, "Are you okay?"

Novina rose. "Who could that be?" She slowly moved aside a curtain to peer out the window by the door. "It's Ariela, from the team." To Petra, she said, "She's one of our best players." Quickly she pulled the door open.

Ariela was winded, her face red. "Novina, I'm sorry to bother you, but I have to talk to you. Can I come in?"

"Of course, Ari."

Ariela's eyes immediately fastened on Petra. Novina introduced them, putting her arm around Ariela's shoulders. "It's okay, Ariela, she's a good friend. You can talk in front of Petra."

"So it's true, then," Ariela said to Novina. "Sara said you were looking pretty friendly with members of the other team."

"Sara?" Novina asked.

"Sara is a friend of mine. She's on the Lechitas team."

"What did she say?"

"She said you were all cozy with their goalie, and she thought it was weird. She heard you say something about having an unusually close relationship with Vicenta."

Vicenta fell back onto the couch. Novina rubbed her temple. Petra said, "I saw them watching us, Novina. I guess she *was* listening to our conversation."

"Maybe it's nothing, coach, but I thought you should know. I got a little worried." Ariela twisted a finger around the strap of her sleeveless shirt. Her shoulder muscles were dazzlingly bare.

Vicenta reached a hand up to Novina to encourage her to sit on the couch next to her. Novina said to her, "*Mi amor*, let's not worry about every little suspicion about us. What can one girl do to hurt us?"

"Tell her the truth, Ari. I was doing my job as Poblanos coach and looking to recruit their top player." Petra blushed. "I just have to persuade

Petra here to move down to San Luis Hunahpu, so we can add a new top-notch goalie to our roster."

Petra thought about the gossip about Justina, how it had turned her into prey for those in Las Leches inclined to believe the lies, including young thugs. She shivered.

"I don't want to scare you guys," Ariela said, "but—everyone knows Vicenta. Well, more up toward Las Leches, but still. And everyone wonders about her being so old and still single. Sorry, Vicenta, for being blunt, but I am a little worried about this. Sara's brother is still kind of a kid, but he's unpredictable. Their parents are trying to get him under control. He's been stealing little things from the shops and showing up with too much cash. If he hears about the rumor—"

Petra said, "This is my fault. I'm attracting bad luck everywhere I go."

"Stop, Petra," said Vicenta. "Hatred has been around since well before you were born."

Novina stood to open a bottle of red wine, pouring the first cup for herself. Ariela rose to fill a glass for each of them. Somehow, in this new context, Petra didn't even consider turning it down. Novina said, "We'll be more careful for a while. I'll avoid the store and Las Leches. If the mobs have nothing to feed on, they'll calm down."

Ariela's nose lifted to sniff the air. Petra said to Novina, "I think there's some extra chicken and rice, no?" Filled plate in hand, Petra held it before her and bowed slightly to Ariela. "Platter for you, miss?" Ariela had a charmingly goofy smile.

Music slid into the background. The four women, two younger and two older, chatted into the late night. Petra owned her corner of the cushioned couch. The wine coated her throat with warmth on its way down. The company entertained and eased her spirit. Every part of the experience was a first for Petra.

Vaguely, Petra sensed a slight breeze when the door opened to let Ariela go home for the night. A blanket floated over her, and she stretched out on the couch. Whiskers tickled her cheek, and a soft mewing wished her safe sleep.

Petra woke with the morning light, which was to say, hours after Vicenta had caught the bus to her store in Las Leches. Other than a crumpled paper bouncing across the floor, followed by a leaping kitten, all was quiet. Petra rose to make breakfast. She searched the refrigerator for food and fiddled with the many knobs on the mysterious stove. She had to admit she had no idea how to put together a meal in this new environment. Instead, she grabbed the book Novina had recommended, pulled the blanket up to her shoulders, propped her head on the supple pillow, and lost herself in the story.

"*Buenos días*, Novina," she offered when Novina emerged from her bedroom. "I wanted to make breakfast—"

"Don't even think about it. This is vacation for you. I bet you haven't had a couple of days off from your chores for a long time."

"Days off? Meaning?" Petra laughed. She would clean the dishes then. That she could do, she was pretty sure. "Anyway, I have been working. I've been babysitting your kitten for the last hour. She seemed very willing."

"You have found something to occupy yourself, I see?" The book was lying open on the floor next to the couch.

"*Dios mío*, Novina! This story is very—provocative. I'm not sure I should be reading it."

Novina raised her head high in laughter. "Think of it as education, since you're missing a day of school today."

Petra absorbed new worlds in those books like someone who had been denied water for too long. When she finished the raunchy romance, she read another about a girl who had immigrated to Los Angeles from Mexico, and then some short stories about the childhood of a gay Cuban man in Miami. Novina went out for a couple of hours to her volunteer job as assistant at the local orphanage. The kids, she said, fed her heart. From the moment she arrived, they jumped on her, hugged her, made up stories for her, and vied for her attention. She struggled to give as much to them in return.

When Vicenta returned, the sun had long descended from its perch in the sky, and her steps dragged with fatigue. Vicenta was keeping long hours and traveling back and forth so she could spend more time with Petra. Normally, she stayed on her cot above the store during the week.

Petra would return home on the bus with Vicenta early in the morning and get back to school. It was now clear that if Petra stayed with Novina for more than a short visit, her presence would increase the danger of exposing the relationship between Vicenta and Novina. Petra would not take that risk.

"Perhaps you are right, Petra," Vicenta admitted. "There is a reason, after all, for my secrecy."

"*Pues sí.*" Novina ran her fingers through her short hair. "If it has to be that way, I must press forward with my two questions then. Are you ready, Petra?"

"Ready and willing, Novina," Petra smiled. Quietly, she hoped the questions would give her reason to be more open with these women. She couldn't remember the last time she felt so excited to get to know some-one beyond her family.

"First question then: Where do you want to attend high school?"

Petra grinned. They could have guessed this was on her mind. The question assumed that she had control over the matter. This dilemma looked different when she was at home in Las Leches, surrounded by all of the fears and limitations imposed by that life. But here, her imagination was bounding ahead, excited and free. "I want to go to a school where teachers have advanced education in the subjects they teach, where the students are motivated to learn, where I can study biology, and English, and mathematics, and history of the world."

"What about books?" Novina prodded, smiling.

"I want to go to a school that has a huge library full of books, where I can curl up in a chair and read until it is time to go home; a school that has textbooks for every class."

"And the gangs? Let's get rid of them, too." Vicenta said.

Petra continued without hesitation. "To a school where I can arrive and leave and study without worrying about gangs outside recruiting the students. Do you know where this school is, Novina?" She looked up at Novina as if she had the answer.

"Mmm, *pues*," Novina stalled for time. "*Así que* probably not here in San Luis Hunahpu. Didn't the Deacon mention something about a school in Guatemala City? There are several good private schools in the capital. Or in the States, of course."

The image of this education had taken hold in Petra's mind as she spoke. Petra was surprised to realize that the school in her mind was in the United States. A flush spread across her cheeks.

"Well, that just proves what a person wants is not always what a person will get," Petra said. That inkling of a life in the United States was just selfish; she wouldn't give it force by mentioning it. "I will stay near home to help care for my grandparents."

"I hear deeply conflicting desires. Do you hear that, Vicenta?"

"I hear a very intelligent girl who does not fully appreciate her own value. Or maybe just begins to understand."

"You guys are hilarious," Petra said, without laughing. Her own value—what an idea. "And believe me, I get the message. Let's hear the second question."

Novina perked up. "Second question is a good one." A look of mischief spread over her face. "Have you kissed a girl yet?"

Petra's eyebrows went up, and she grinned at Vicenta and Novina both. "Somehow I thought you might ask that one. I've never talked about this with anyone, you know."

Vicenta looked wryly at Petra. She didn't need to say a word.

"But—clearly that's over." Petra's eyes flashed with amusement. "There was that *one* time..."

Vicenta said, "I knew it!"

"Shhh, woman, don't distract her." Novina gave Vicenta a mock stern smile.

"You want to guess who the girl was, Vicenta?"

"I think I know, *cómo no*. It was Justina, wasn't it?"

Petra's hand went quickly to cover her mouth, and she looked down. She had no right to divulge Justina's secret. It was not just hers.

"You may not feel shame, Petita, not in this house," Vicenta said.

Before Vicenta completed her admonition, an immense relief flooded through Petra. To think she could actually share this experience with someone. It was possible to separate the delight of Justina from the tragedy of her death. Suddenly Justina became a source of pride that made Petra feel warm all over, a thrill that spilled out through her every pore. The deliciousness of their intimacy grew bigger inside her.

A tear squeezed out the corner of her eye and dropped onto the tile below. Her eyes burned. With the motion of a little girl, she balled up a fist and rubbed away the tears. "It's just—I'm not sure what Justina would think. Boys paid a lot of attention to her." More tears formed.

Novina offered, "I did not have the pleasure of knowing Justina, Petra. But I know she is no longer with us. It is your experience, your feelings that matter most now."

The kindness in Novina's gaze flooded Petra's insides and pushed her nerves to the surface, where they tingled, then itched, and it pushed heat from her heart up into her head and turned her face red. She covered her face with her hands. After a moment, she looked up, and her face lit up. Petra talked and talked about Justina as her friends listened with rapt attention.

For a good ten minutes, Vicenta sat on the couch next to her, her arm draped around Petra's shoulders. When Petra finally ran out of words, Vicenta said, "Life is long, my friend. Allow these trying times to make you stronger because they will make you stronger. Novina and I can both attest to that. Petra, you have a home here in my heart. Come lean on it whenever you have the urge. In the meantime, find your path and grab it."

The kitten scuttled off Petra's new favorite couch when Petra, readying it for sleep, threw the blanket on top. With a determined and vengeful demeanor, the fanciful feline then leapt high, pouncing with all four feet directly on the offending usurper. The bathroom light reflected off the mirror and landed squarely on the kitten's back. Whispers, then a sound like the slippery sloshing of a cloth in the sink made her open her eyes. In the mirror, she saw Novina and Vicenta entwined in a long and passionate kiss. Petra breathed deeply and rolled over into a magically swift and restful sleep.

CHAPTER TWENTY

Nonna was intoning verses from the Psalms as she crested the hill. The gentle tone of her grandmother reciting one of her favorite prayers reminded her of the joy and tranquility of home that she loved. Then the prayer took an unusual turn—Carlos's voice joined Nonna's. But Carlos usually scoffed at their prayers! He always found something else to occupy him. But as she stepped into the house, there was Nonna, with Carlos and her grandfather joining in. "Yea, though I walk through the valley of the shadow of death, I will fear no evil: for thou art with me; thy rod and thy staff they comfort me."

A piece of God's love could appear inside her if she could absorb celestial blessing and divine love through the caring of her grandparents, whom she loved so dearly. Perhaps there was a similar art to accepting gifts from others, allowing herself to depend on someone, at least for a moment. Maybe relying on other people could help her find that bit of God within herself.

Nonno rose to embrace Petra. His frame trembled slightly. As Petra peered around Nonno's shoulder, she gasped at what she now saw more clearly. Nonna! Her cheeks were bruised, her eyes bloodshot. A towel with spots of dried blood draped over a chair. A chair was pushed back to the wall, and the family's machete lay on a chair. The eating table was askew, and what had been a small pile of firewood waiting to cook their food was scattered around the room.

Petra ran to Nonna, throwing her arms, gently, around her. When they stepped apart, she looked closely at Nonna—the dark brown eyes moist with tears, red marks highlighting the bruises on her temples, on her sagging cheeks. "Nonna! What...?" Nonna remained silent. The bruises seeped inward.

Carlos retrieved a note, wrinkled and smeared with stains, from the altar next to the Virgin Mary and handed it to Petra. He told her what had happened. The night before, he and Nonno were both out when Gusano and his men came and tied Nonna to the chair, put a cloth in her mouth, and left the note, sticking it to the back of the chair with the machete. "We left all this the way we found it. I thought you should see it for yourself." Lines of concern rippled across his forehead.

She read: "You've broken the rules one time too many. If we don't get cooperation in obtaining the secret treasure, the old man and the little girl will suffer. Be ready for a trip Wednesday morning." It was signed, "Gusano. *El Jefe*."

"*Ay, Dios mío*, that's tomorrow." Petra slowly breathed out. "Nonna, I'm so sorry I wasn't here. I didn't want this to be serious, but it is. I see that now."

Now that it affected her grandparents, it was easier to see. When she was the only one in danger, it hadn't been so obvious. She would do anything to keep her grandparents safe. It occurred to her that her mother had warned her on Saturday not to minimize the danger, that it was not just about herself. Maybe her mother was not so distant from her life after all.

Nonna said, "They hit me, Petita. Two of them. The one who did most of the talking had a shiny bald head, but it was covered with tattoos, all over. I vaguely remember him from Emilio's house, years ago, when Liana died. But I didn't remember so many tattoos! They were all over this man, down his arms, disappearing right down his chest into his clothes. I don't know who they are, or what they want!" Her voice cracked with age. She had grown older this day.

The image of Gusano's tattooed face came alive. The day Emilio's mother died, his father Fernando lumbered out of the woods with Gusano, the very picture of fear. Petra began to tremble. An overwhelming image of sticky red ribbons flooded through her.

Petra said, "It's suddenly so cold!" She draped a light sweater around herself and folded her arms against the air. The lightness she had absorbed in Novina's home dripped away.

Fernando's words had been so ugly in her child's ears, and he had hurt her by grabbing her small frame, pushing her like a shovel into the ground. To a nine year old raised on stories of hell and the devil in the Catholic Church, he had seemed like the incarnation of evil.

Carlos turned to his grandparents. "Petra is right. The danger is real now. Gusano has a bad reputation. He's the head of the local gang here around Las Leches, even as far as San Luis Hunahpu. He runs drugs, extorts money from businesses, kidnaps girls, kills people when they get in his way. Worse, he's ambitious, because he's trying to join the local gang with the MS-13, a bunch of soulless murderers who have overrun all of Central America, into Mexico and the United States."

Half-consciously, Carlos had picked up the machete and was waving it in front of him for emphasis. "He must be buying off the police, because they leave him alone. If he came up here personally to do this —" he swept the machete across the room, "it is definitely serious." Petra was thankful that he didn't mention her own abduction—and happy when he put the machete down again.

Nonno bowed his head. "I may know who this Gusano is. Let's eat some dinner, put some space between this terrible attack and the conversation which we must have. Petra, you and I need to sit together tonight."

"Yes, Nonnino."

Nonno added, "And Carlos, you know a lot about what's going on around here. Will you stay close tonight? We need to come together on this."

Carlos said, "I'll be around. I need to get something down the hill for a few minutes, then I'll be back."

Petra averted her eyes, ashamed of her brother's base instincts. The only thing that lured him down the hill was beer and the banter of his stupid friends at the mango tree.

Then she remembered how much concern Carlos had shown for her this past week. Nonno, too, had his stash of alcohol out back, and drank too much *chaparro*. They all knew that. She turned her gaze back toward Carlos, and said, "Carlos, just come back soon, please. We need you more than ever."

"Sure." He struggled to articulate another thought, frowning with consternation. "Do *you* need me, Petita?" He searched her eyes, then self-consciousness cast them down.

So he had noticed her aloofness from him. They were so alike in their desire to be strong and separate. He kept his feelings to himself as much as she did. They had grown up taking care of their grandparents as much or more than their grandparents took care of her and Carlos, so they were both tough and resilient, never giving in to feeling sad or weak—especially with each other.

Actually, now that she thought about it, Carlos had also taken care of her. He never forgot that he was three years older than her. They had both been through a lot this week. Everything was changing so fast.

Despite all his gruffness, Carlos wanted her to need him! She nodded at Carlos and cast a small grin toward him. "Well," she said, "I guess I might need you. I'll need you if you'll need me. Sometimes anyway." She laughed at herself.

Carlos must remember their mom more than she did. He was eight when she left. She hadn't really considered how it might have impacted him, maybe even worse than her. They had barely talked with each other about their mother.

Carlos smiled. "*De acuerdo, patoja.*" She noticed a levity in his step as he left for his mango tree.

Her own heart felt a little lighter, too. She would open her moral door just a bit for Carlos and her grandfather to soak up some of their burdens in alcohol. As long as it wasn't too excessive. As long as they didn't turn angry, like some men did.

Petra cleaned up the cooking and eating areas and put together the rice, beans, and tortillas with some of their new vegetables from the market.

"God bless this food and may the Lord protect this family," Nonna said.

Petra watched her grandmother eat. She held her fork loosely, as if she had no muscles in her hand. She looked up and gave Petra a wan smile. It seemed that the ash had flown from the fire pit and covered her grandmother's spirit.

Petra kicked at the dust on the floor below. The dog, who had been sleeping under the table, yelped and ran out of the house.

Alocinia piped up.

- Petra, you've got to tell me. Are you leaving me? Like that other night when you went off through that hole by yourself. You left me alone. I'm worried.
- I was scared.
- You were scared, but I was even more scared.
- You gave me a tortilla. That helped.
- You're growing up. I'm not sure whether I still have a place in you.
- Alocinia, I love you like my soul! You may even *be* my soul.
- You've got to get past this dust and ashes thing. They're nothing. They're so lightweight.
- But every time I try to get rid of them, they float right back and cover everything up again.
- Raise your mind up here, Petra. Consider the contrast between the *guaco* and the potoo birds. Itzamná the *guaco*. Your nemesis the potoo. Some people call the *guaco* a "laughing falcon." So you know it has a sense of humor.
- And the females are bigger. All female birds of prey are bigger and stronger than the males.
- You should hear it talk! It laughs, or screams, but loud and long! No missing it.
- Alocinia, I think if the Siguanaba were a bird, she'd be a *guaco*. Wise, assertive, powerful. And beautiful, too.
- Remember, Petra, Itzamná is a guaco. So the Mayans are behind it.
- Itzamná and the *guaco* both kill poisonous snakes and cure people if they are bitten. Mayan healers imitate the *guaco* call in order to cure snake bites.
- If only Potoo were a poisonous snake, Itzamná could take care of him. Maybe Itzamná is meant to counter Gusano! A worm is pretty close to a snake, don't you think? Which brings us to the potoo. This bird is *not* a vulture. It's a frogmouth, whatever that is. But it sounds ugly.
- And its call is haunting, Alocinia, not powerful like the *guaco*. As

if its purpose is to scare people.

- Its eyes have slits in them, so it can see even when its eyes are closed. During the day it imitates a branch—that's exciting and romantic, right? It doesn't move, it just sits there blending right in with the tree. At night, it attacks its prey, sometimes gathering a mob of birds to chase down and attack its enemies.
- It sure sounds like my nemesis, as you say.
- Find your Itzamná, Petra. Protect it, and it will share its powers with you.
- I need to do some asking and seeking. Maybe I should ask for help.
- I'm here whenever you need me.
- Thanks, but I need to branch out and trust other people, too.
- See, what did I tell you, you don't need me anymore!
- Alocinia, you're my little hummingbird. Don't leave me. Ever.

The bench out on the porch felt like an old friend. Rotting gray wood, though cracked in places and spotted with the years, still held them with confidence, despite a sag here and there. From time to time, her fingers flinched when they touched the aging gum Carlos had stuck underneath the seat years ago in a fit of rebellion when Nonna had insisted he clean up the house. Emilio had carved his initials with a kitchen knife onto the side edge when he was eight, after enjoying Nonna's *champurradas*. And Petra and Nonno had sat on it in a bond of quiet communion ever since she could remember.

Tonight, the breeze of a warm evening drifted across her face. Her toes ran through the fine dirt. Before her was the yard where she'd learned to ride a bicycle with Emilio. The bench remembered. The bench digested the scene with her—the banana trees, the bright red and yellow flowers mixed in with thick green leaves, the volcano beyond, the good and bad that passed through.

Nonno dispensed with the formalities of easing into a conversation. "I owe you an answer to your question about Itzamná." Nonno's eyes looked inward, while he put words to what he found there. Petra listened with an intensity that deepened while the rest of the world faded. He began by circling around.

"When Itzamná was young, he fell in love with Ixchel, a beautiful and wise woman. They married and had thirteen sons. Together, they worked to brighten the skies. Then he learned that she was having an affair with another man. Ixchel fled in fear of his anger. But Itzamná loved her very much, so he forgave her and asked her to come back.

"They were so happy together that the skies became overly bright, and the sun blinded Ixchel in one of her eyes. She continued to light the skies, but her light had dimmed. The Mayans told that for this reason the moon, created by her brightness, was softer than the sun. Mayans worshiped Ixchel as a goddess of healing.

"Itzamná was an important deity to the Mayans. Like many Mayan gods, he had both a mortal and divine form. He was the son of the creator god and taught the Mayans many of the skills they became famous for, including writing, medicine, sculpture, agriculture, and the Mayan calendar. He healed the sick and wounded, and he resurrected the dead.

"He could see things that others couldn't see, often foretelling the future. People believed he was a universal spirit of life who could make the world collide with chaos to create living things. For this reason, many considered him the god of creation.

"Itzamná lived in the upper skies. His wings were inscribed with symbols for daylight and night. In flight, he bore witness to the unfolding of time. There is much, of course, that is unknown about these myths and the meaning Mayans gave to them.

"Petra," he said slowly, "I believe Gusano and I know each other." He paused to let Petra absorb that information. Petra's eyebrows shot up.

"Something very important happened while I was working with the archeologists in Juyú, and it seems to have returned to challenge me." He hesitated a moment to collect his thoughts. His bushy hair flapped about like an old shirt drying in the breeze.

"One day the archeologists were all concentrated on removing the dirt and rock around a skeleton they had found," Nonno said. They sent him off, saying they wouldn't need him for a couple of hours. A young helper named Martín followed him, as he often did. He was only eight or nine years old, but he did little chores around the worksite. Nonno went exploring in the woods, picking his way through thickets of bush and trees. He went far that day, probably a couple of miles from the site. Martín tailed after him.

They came upon a cave that intrigued her grandfather. He entered through a small crevice above ground and descended a few yards, where it opened up into a spacious cavern. There he sat down on an old log to adjust his eyes to the surroundings. He began to poke around in the ground, thinking he'd find some bug or snake to scare Martín with.

"But instead, the head of a figurine appeared. I thought it was funny that I was looking for a snake, then found one, but made of ancient clay. It was so close to the surface! I pulled it out carefully and went back up to the daylight to inspect it.

"I quickly recognized it as Itzamná, with that two-headed snake in its mouth." The archeologists all knew about Itzamná and had talked about his importance to the Mayans. "I knew it was important."

By that time, Nonno had come to revere the ancient Mayans and their mythology. He decided that the ancient Mayans had left their creator there at that spot in the cavern for some reason, and so it belonged there. Any disturbance to such a powerful figure could agitate the spirits and disrespect the ancestors. Perhaps its residence served to maintain a delicate balance of forces they knew nothing about. So he left it where he'd found it.

"Martín wanted it for himself, to fondle and play with, but I refused. He shrugged, and we left. I never spoke of it again—except when I mentioned it in passing to your mother, and she begged me to show it to her. Something there is unfinished. It seems to call out to one person in each generation. Now it calls to you."

Like kids will do, Nonno said, Martín was always running off into the woods when he was supposed to be doing this or that. Several times, he found him digging in the ground, looking at ants, or worms. "So we gave him the nickname 'Gusano.' Once the project was over, I heard nothing more about Gusano. He lived in a different area, I believe somewhere between here and San Luis Hunahpu." Nonno was quiet for a moment. "Gusano would be about 46 years old now."

"Your Gusano used his childhood nickname for his gang name and became the boss of the X-14 gang here." Petra put together the pieces.

That explained why Emilio thought Nonno and she could lead

him to some secret treasure. And now the threatening note by Gusano. Martín must have remembered the Itzamná figurine, but hadn't been able to locate the exact spot. And he still wanted to play with it, to use it for his own selfish purposes.

"If we're to believe Carlos, he may be willing to kill in order to get it." Nonno paused. "Fortunately, my memory is slipping, and I no longer know the way to Itzamná's cave." He winked at Petra. "As far as Gusano knows, it has been more than 35 years since I found it. And an old man's memory is unpredictable."

"Of course, *lo entiendo*, Nonno."

"By the way, you acted with great bravery against Potoo the other day."

In a corner of her heart, Petra felt ashamed that she had not told Nonno about Emilio abducting her. It was starting to sink in just how much danger she had faced in that isolated cabin.

She would not burden her grandfather with her own problems, though. She said, "Nonno, I am not brave. I broke down over nothing when I talked to mamá on the phone."

"My daughter, on the contrary, crying is often a sign of great strength. You presented yourself to your mother in that call. You've hidden yourself from her in the past. Revealing yourself made you vulnerable, but one must have strength to allow weakness to emerge. Don't think I didn't notice this.

"Petra, mysterious forces make us grow up quickly sometimes. Your inner being has risen in you recently. It strives to ascend. Rather than give a growing and curious girl advice, I now find myself trying to catch up to you."

The Siguanaba did not hang around waiting to become a victim. She drew on her own capacity to protect herself, to turn away evil.

"There is a reason I gave in to your mother and showed her the Itzamná figurine, Petra. And when I say your mother is connected to you, I am not guessing. I know. I know what I see in your eyes, and what I saw in hers. You were able to talk to her, then?"

"I did, yes. I guess she's a real person, even though she's my mother, right?"

Nonno chortled. "She suffered very much from bad decisions she made as a teenager. We make mistakes, we learn. Sometimes there is an essence which will creep into one's life no matter what struggles are placed before it."

"She wants me to go to the United States to live with her, Nonno," Petra said. She expected Nonno to react to this news, but Nonno just watched Petra, unperturbed, waiting for more. Did he already know this? "But there are so many reasons I need to stay here."

"What are these reasons, Petra? It will be very difficult for you to become a doctor here in Guatemala. You know that, I think."

"But look at everything that's happening! How can I leave you and Nonna? Nonna needs me more than ever! And I need to settle this problem with Emilio and his gang before they carry out threats against our family. I feel responsible for this mess, Nonno."

"Petra, you must seek answers within yourself. But I repeat, there is an essence which will creep into one's life no matter what struggles are placed before it. This is as true for you as for your mother."

The passage repeated itself in her head. The message had greeted her upon arriving home, and it flooded through her now. "Thou preparest a table before me in the presence of mine enemies: thou anointest my head with oil; my cup runneth over. Surely goodness and mercy shall follow me all the days of my life: and I will dwell in the house of the Lord for ever."

The Deacon had told her that she needed to do her own work to realize her dreams. Then he came forward with an answer which seemed to make irrelevant any measures she might take. The option to go to Guatemala City to work and study was all his doing. What effort had she made toward realizing her dreams? What could she do on her own? Her grandfather gave her hints, but she could not pull it all together.

Freedom comes through acceptance of the grace of God, the Deacon had told her. The Siguanaba found her strength within. Her grandfather spoke of her listening to some inner essence. And then there was Itzamná.

Nonno interrupted her thoughts. "Petra, you dreamed about Itzamná recently. What did you discover about Itzamná?"

"Only the feeling of it, Nonno. It flew over me with such great power. It held a snake in its mouth. And it seemed to have something to do with day following night, the heavens separating from the underworld.

Its passionate flight pushed me out of the dream. The intensity overwhelmed me."

Nonno continued. "It is possible that in Mayan mythology, daylight and night also stood for the heavens and the underworld, as you say, Petra. The Mayan underworld, Xibalba, was a dark and ghastly place. Although Itzamná created the brightness, his flight connected the two. Between light and dark, between good and bad."

The ancient Mayans, he explained, believed that in death a person had to find his way through nine levels of Xibalba until she reached the middle world, our earth, then continue to ascend thirteen further levels to reach the heavens, in order to finally settle closer to earth for eternal happiness.

Certain honored individuals were exempt from this fraught and perilous journey, however. Humans selected for sacrifice in Mayan rituals were among those greatly honored individuals. They were chosen for sacrifice because of their perceived worthiness to become messengers to the gods. "Perhaps our hummingbird received such an honor."

Petra mused, "The hummingbird flutters inside me, carrying messages from my heart to my soul, from my daily life to my hopes."

Alocinia responded:
- That is my sincere desire.
- I thought you were my friend. Who are you?"
- Find your Itzamná, Petra. Seek his spirit within you. Maybe
   down the road you'll find your Ixchel as well.

"What is certain," Nonno concluded his story, "is that Itzamná is a very important figure in ancient Mayan culture. The figurine I found would undoubtedly be worth a lot of money. But its spirit must be protected, and respected, or we risk disturbing an ancient equilibrium between nature and the divine presence."

"Petra! Look! A hummingbird by the red hibiscus there," Nonno said, pointing in front of them across the yard. "It is so beautiful. The Mayans say that the hummingbird served as a messenger for Itzamná."

The hummingbird furiously and beautifully flapped its wings, its long beak pulling nectar from the hibiscus. In search of more, it sped from one plant to another, then unexpectedly crossed over the yard to hasten past Petra and Nonno. Air stirred by the hummingbird touched

Petra's cheek. She held it there on her cheek for a moment. They watched it flutter off into the distance.

Petra had a craving to hold tightly to Alocinia under her pillow that night.

As it turned out, Carlos played only a secondary role in their immediate plans. His disappointment trickled with a quiet drip, but he steadied himself for a later role.

Petra and Carlos absorbed a new arrangement between themselves as they sat together on the bench in comfortable silence for a few minutes before resting for the night.

"Carlos, do you miss our mother?"

"Petra." He twisted his feet together under the bench. Perhaps he wouldn't talk now either. "Words cannot express how I feel about our mamá. I wanted so badly to protect her. I feel happy that she is safe from our father."

"What do you remember of her? What did she look like?"

"It's easy to remember, Petita." Carlos almost never used her name in its diminutive. "I just have to look at you."

Petra's cheeks turned crimson. Her hand grasped her brother's shoulder, and she pulled him toward her.

CHAPTER TWENTY-ONE

The sweet whispers of night surrounded Petra—Nonno snoring, and the aging tethers of Carlos's hammock complaining as it rocked ever so slightly. Darkness muffled the chattering of the chickens as they climbed to their perches in the trees outside. Mice scurried to grab crumbs from the floor, and the pigeons settled into the eaves above her. The last of the family to pull down her bed, she was exhausted.

Petra wrapped the light blanket around her in a reassuring embrace. Her hand rested on the clay hummingbird under her pillow. The stark day faded into nocturnal dreams and sleep quickly crept over her.

Monkeys with fiendish grimaces pretended to be clowns. One, the color of buckskin, stood on its hind legs to dance, and laughed at her as it stumbled. The dun-colored monkey landed on her shoulder, twisted its lithe body to face her, and grinned to show its white teeth, then protested when she failed to respond.

A wailing falcon lunged toward them but diverted off to the side. Buckskin scowled at her, blaming her for the attack, while Dun snuck up behind her. She struggled to understand what she was to do. Dun offered a light tap to her shoulder.

Another light tap, and another. Her eyes fluttered open, and she saw a figure in the shadow, long and thin like the spider monkey, sitting next to her on the bed, staring down at her. A lean finger moved to his lips, then touched hers. She shook her head to try to separate imagination from reality. She stared at the figure but didn't quite fathom the meaning.

"Petra, come outside with me." Without thinking it, she had expected him to come. "Quiet, really quiet. I'll wait outside." She wrapped the white blanket around her, her feet bare on the cool ground, strands of her long black hair wrapped around her neck, streaming gently down her back. No one else stirred.

"Emilio." It was a simple statement. She still knew his face like the back door of her childhood. Gone—but so very familiar. Comforting somehow. She resisted the urge to tenderness.

"I had to see you before I leave, Petra. I may never see you again." Petra reluctantly allowed him to stand near her, so they would not wake anyone. They whispered through the moonlight.

Heat pulsed in a shroud around his skin, and his eyes smoldered toward her. He held himself taut, as if afraid a body part might escape from his control. Smells of the earthy forest wafted around them.

The Siguanaba breathed and exhaled deeply.

"Gusano wants to kill you," Petra said. She sent a barb through the lust he was circulating around them.

Emilio's eyes swooped back from the inside of a fantasy, and he pulled himself away from her a few steps. "And my father, too. So many times I thought my father would kill me, but he only beat me. But now —"

Petra interrupted with a gasp. "Your father?" Suddenly an image she'd put away for years resurfaced—Emilio's black eye at the market shortly after his mother's death.

"He tried to mold me by terrorizing me. He made me do things—so many things," Emilio hesitated and forced himself to breathe, "by crushing me. But.... Now, he *will* kill me. I can't go home." In his eyes, she saw a new determination emerging.

"Emilio." She loaded his name with pity. Never had she cared about him so much as she did at this moment. Quickly, she pulled her emotions up short. Only days ago, he had drugged her and hauled her off to great peril. Why did she waste her heart pitying someone like this?

"I wanted to warn you. The MS-13 will arrive in two days. Gusano and Mago will meet. Gusano has promised him a valuable Mayan artifact in exchange for a piece of his business. None of this is chump change, Petra. It's big. And his business is vicious. You and your family are in danger until Gusano gets his prize."

"He came yesterday. Gusano beat up my grandmother. He left a note. We're to go with him tomorrow morning to get the artifact."

Emilio winced; his jaw clenched tight. He spoke deliberately, holding on to calm. "He is moving very quickly, Petra. Gusano has never done anything so fast before. You need to leave this place, go where he cannot find you."

"What, and leave my grandparents to their mercy? I cannot leave my family, Emilio!"

"It is you they will hurt. And me. I have broken with the oath of loyalty and you have challenged their authority. At any cost, they will prove that they can control the women they choose. If you are not here, they won't touch your grandparents. They are too old." Emilio hung his head low. Petra lifted it with two fingers under his chin. "I am so sorry, Petra. My life is a hellhole, and I've dug it myself. And I may have dug it for the person I care most about. Petra, you have no idea what you mean to me."

"Well, apparently you think I belong to you, and you can take me however you please."

His brows knit together in pain. Petra closed her eyes and sighed. Her posture softened. Emilio said, "Can you ever forgive me?"

"What do you know about forgiveness, Emilio? Besides thinking of your own selfish heart?"

As she said it, she heard the Minister's sermon: "And if he trespass against thee seven times in a day, and seven times in a day turn again to thee, saying, I repent; thou shalt forgive him." She steeled her heart against the pity that pulled her. Did she have to forgive him? Trust was still deep in the distance.

"Petra, could you answer a question before I go? I need to know. A few weeks ago, when I hit Carlos and you ran away from me, you said you were sorry, that you didn't mean to. I don't understand. What could *you* possibly have done to *me* to be sorry for?"

"Just—I can't talk about it, Emilio." Petra wiped her damp eyes and turned her back to Emilio. She couldn't admit that she felt he had abandoned their friendship because she had failed to get help for his mother in time. She knew it wasn't really all her fault, and yet, the doubt tormented her. "We all do things we regret. That's all."

Emilio touched her on the shoulder, and she turned to face him again. He explored her eyes, as if the answer could be found there. He said, "All I know is you're an angel."

Petra shook her head and crossed her arms in front of her. She rocked on her heels.

"*Fíjate*, Petra. Please, look at me. I am trying to tell you the truth. You are the best person I have ever known. These past years, I've managed to keep a few sparks of you alive in my heart. I will earn your respect one day." He spoke earnestly.

"Emilio, you saved me from Potoo and Gorto the other day"

Emilio interrupted, "You have no idea how many times you have saved me…. What you don't realize is that you actually saved me that day. I'm finally free from it. The huge cloud that's buried me since I was ten is lifting." He reached for her hand, but she kept her arms tight against herself. "It's hard to start over, Petra." He spoke with such kindness. Where was that kindness when he carried her off and left her to the caprices of those delinquents?

"Before you found me the other day, I spit on Potoo, Emilio. I think I offended his dignity. I would have spit on you if you'd been there." She tried to swallow the bitterness, but the bile kept returning to her mouth.

"Petra, you have a way of saying things that keep popping up in my mind. The other day at the cabin, you reminded me of that time with Justina at the swimming hole. Times like those—I do remember, but they seem like distant movies, not real. Like little sparks of light."

"It was real, Emilio. But too much has changed since then. Justina, for instance, is gone."

He flinched but took a steadying breath. "That kid I was then is still in me, Petra. I'm going to search him out."

She eyed him skeptically.

"*En serio*. Maybe you'll see me again someday, and you'll see a better version of that kid, all grown up. I'm going to make sure those sparks don't burn out. I never want to see this life here again."

Petra said, "I won't see you again." She looked away. Emotions choked in her throat.

Emilio started to reach his hand out to stroke her hair, then stopped himself. "Petra, *no lo cree*. Somehow you are part of my destiny."

She squirmed at the cliché and moved to go back inside.

Pressured now, he added, "But Petra, I have to make you understand. Potoo won't stop until he takes his revenge on you. You are right. To him, it is as if you—and then I—smacked him in the face and stole his pride. He must get it back, and Gusano will make sure he does. It suits Gusano's own purposes for the pride of the X-14's name, and for your artifact and his business proposition. You need to get out of here quickly."

"*Véte*, Emilio. Find your life. I will worry about protecting my family, and myself."

"I couldn't forgive myself if something happened to you. *Por favor*, Petra."

Petra stepped stiffly away from Emilio. Emilio grabbed her hand, held it to his cheek. He gazed into her eyes. A lonely tear slid down his cheek and fell onto her hand.

After a moment, she pulled her hand back and said, "*Que vaya con Dios*, Emilio." She went back inside. She put her hand, wet with Emilio's tear, to her lips before she lay down her head.

CHAPTER TWENTY-TWO

A sharp banging on the door awoke the family. Petra bolted upright in her bed. The sun had not yet crested the horizon. Nonna whimpered. Nonno shouted out, "Martín! We are coming. Sit yourself down a few minutes."

Petra and Nonno soon climbed into the front seat next to Gusano. Potoo and Fernando rode in the back bed of the pick-up. Petra took one look at "*Rosita, mi vida*" carved onto Gusano's arm, shivered, and pushed Nonno in first. She held tightly onto the door handle, ready to fling it open if necessary. She sank into a deep silence.

Nonno began a steady patter with Gusano about their time at Juyú. Nonno drew a panoply of images—Mayan hieroglyphic texts, figurines, tools, bones used in sacrifice or buried in glory, and sections of a sophisticated water system—all the artifacts of the civilization he and Gusano had worked to discover when they worked there.

Gusano grunted. "*Viejito*," he said, "you talk too much." Gusano's machete lay by his side, pressed awkwardly between his leg and the dashboard. Knives clattered in the back of the truck with every bump.

"Martín, you were nine years old then. How did you come to work with those men?"

Gusano scratched his head. Nonno had touched a soft spot. The white knuckles gripping the steering wheel relaxed. "My mamá came home just before I turned nine, for a whole year. She brought home yet another man, Alfredo. But this one was better than the others. Despite everything I did to provoke him, he never punished me. No kneeling on kernels of corn, no switch from that damned tamarind tree." Gusano unwound a little as he talked about himself.

Nonno laughed. "*Sí, sí,* all of us went through that as kids."

Gusano glared at Nonno. "One time I came home with a busted head. The last time, by the way, I let a kid get the best of me. Alfredo came up to me, and I was all ready to run away if he tried to grab me. Instead, he asked me what happened and helped me clean up. He actually paid attention to what I said. No one had ever done that before."

"And Rosita?" Nonno pointed to the tattoo.

"Rosita," Gusano smirked, "kissed my cheeks, told me how much she loved her sweet boy, fondled me a little too much, then smacked me with a broom across my face for no reason. I would have laid my life down for her. In fact, I did, a couple times. There were a couple of vile men she brought home." Gusano rolled his shirt sleeve down over the tattoo. "But Alfredo—he wanted to get me out of her way, give me another experience. He was a just a lousy janitor at the museum, but somehow he wangled me a job as the all-purpose boy at the dig."

Once they passed through San Luis Hunahpu, Petra raised her eyes to take in a village she had never seen. Houses clumped together, a tableau of white-washed walls and red-tiled rooves, began under clusters of trees and dissipated as they climbed up the side of Sibalq'aq. Above the town, the volcano was darker, more rugged than the view from Las Leches. A haze of smoke hung over the crater, fading from pink to white, then to wisps of gray as it flowed away from the rising sun.

Nonno pointed out the Juyú Museum to her. He said it held many of the archeological artifacts found when he and little Martín worked at the site. People were still digging, he said. Petra looked at him questioningly. He answered with a subtle nod. She stared out the window at the long, nearly windowless museum building.

And then the five of them walked. Gusano held his men a few paces behind, so Petra and Nonno led. At least she didn't have to see the slithering tattoos at every step. Any moment now, Petra might collapse with fear. She sheltered herself in her grandfather's wisdom and under the protection of the ancient society which revered the sun, water, birth, and death. With all of her might, she held close the powerful myths that had raised and supported her. And she prayed to Jesus with each step.

The volcano loomed above them, as their path continued to weave around it and through the valley below. She had stepped into a land of wonder. Petra had only dreamed of seeing Sibalq'aq so close.

They crossed a mostly submerged causeway, a long passageway of stone, which had connected Juyú with a nearby acropolis. The day was heating up, the sun rising in the sky. They moved from open grassland to forest to tropical jungle. They tried to ignore the three men with their weapons following them.

A civilization lived here, under the shadow of Sibalq'aq, hidden under the ground but still breathing. The ancient world pulsed beneath her feet. While Petra pressed near to her grandfather, she dreamed of ancient people and of their own ancestors. The stories whispered within her.

Behind that tree, a warrior hunted the spider monkey, while watching his back for the lethal jaguar. Snakes dangled from the trees. Women wearing hand woven *huipils* planted and harvested. They gazed upward in awe of the great breadth of sky as they worshiped the moon and Ixchel in her mortal and godly forms.

A group of women sat, some near, some farther back, around a fire. Smoke rose in a straight path to the tufts of clouds above. Some ground corn and prepared food, others spun or wove skirts and *huipils* embroidered with geometrical blue and yellow patterns around the waist. One young woman was carving out a gourd from the hard shell of the fruit of calabash trees, which grew in impenetrable clusters behind them. Each of them kept an eye fastened on the movements of Ixchel, who gathered wood and searched the heavens. The clouds parted, and the sun reflected a bit more brightly onto the half moon in the dewy morning light.

Ixchel's hair rose in a turban on her head, her glistening black hair intertwined with cloth colored green, red, and yellow. A band of fabric covered her breasts, and her arms emerged from the loose-fitting *huipil*, her skin glowing in a resplendent gold. Around her neck lay a thick metallic necklace, a jade stone at its center. Large, hooped earrings swung with her movements above her bare shoulders. A luminous skirt, a rainbow of colors, hung below her knees, and her feet were draped with *xajabes*. The riot of carefully arranged color and adornment covering her indicated her high status. As they worked, Ixchel chanted, her gaze traveling between the fire below and the sky above.

Behind Petra and Nonno, the men's voices rose in anger. Petra glanced at them in alarm, but they were talking to each other. Crusted lava and hardened ash held their feet as they trudged along silently.

Nonno's voice arose as if from the earth, as if someone was speaking through him.

"Ixchel spoke to her husband, Itzamná. 'Have you noticed that the people, created by your father, are always sad and quiet?'

"'It is true, I have noticed,' he responded. 'But in truth I cannot discover the cause of the sadness, since the earth is so beautiful.'

"Ixchel said, '*Señor*, people are still imperfect. They have not been able to extract from the splendor of the natural world the sacred essence which leads to happiness. People need this.'

"'But how shall I give it to them?' Itzamná asked.

"'You must teach them to capture the happiness of the world which surrounds them.'

"So Itzamná called a conference of all the gods, including Chaac, god of water, Kukulcan, god of wind, Yumil Kax, lady of the forest, and A Kah Puccikal, heart of the night, among others. Gathered around Itzamná under the sacred ceiba tree, he asked for their help to shake off the sadness and silence of humans. And, according to the role of each god, each agreed to capture an essence.

"Kukulcan grazed its wind upon the water currents of the rivers to obtain its babbling. The gods bottled the song from the rain, kissed the corn to imprison the melodic essence of its leaves, and extracted the soul from the sea's waves. They acquired the echoes and sounds of the foliage which was in love with the shadows, the moans of the night, and the happy splash of the rain. The birds helped by collecting their trills and songs to produce a scale of sweet and sensual notes.

"Itzamná put all these essences and more in a large vessel and shook them, then slowly released the mysterious mixture. At the same time, he used his divine throat to emit the winged notes of the first song. This first melody began to give the residents of the earth the tools to unearth happiness. That is how song and music were born. Since then, people have made instruments and practiced their voices, multiplying the splendor of life."

Petra nodded deeply and smiled. At that moment, she felt so blessed that it was hard to concentrate on their mission, and even more difficult to appreciate the dangerous circumstances. She gazed upward at Nonno, who walked on as if he had said nothing. Birdsweet settled on the ground.

Boots clomped behind them. Dried branches snapped. Petra swung around, but it was only that Fernando had tripped. The jungle, a mass of moving, crackling life, panted. Ixchel's chanting followed them.

A bird screeched. A line of fire ants carried their supplies along a trail which led to a shadowy space beneath a fallen oak, their nest presumably under it. A scorpion crushed a caught spider. Two young deer escaped behind the trees.

A mass of trees hovered over them throughout—tripping roots, hanging vines, sprawling branches, massive trunks, spindly stems, fragile saplings competing for the sun—cuajilote, calabash, maple, chicle, box-elder, oak, fir. Round and oblong seeds drooped. An oak threw its nuts, trying to hit them on the head. Ahead the trees opened up into a glade, where a gumbo tree spread its wings, exerting itself to master its spot in the sun. The silver-saw palmetto shrub, splendid but sharply dangerous, fringed the edges of the wooded areas.

Two hours along, Gusano came forward. "*Viejito*, if you're playing games with us, you'll regret it."

"It is true that I am uncertain. Martín, it has been 35 years. The jungle evolves over such a long time. I think it is in that direction." Satisfied for the moment, Gusano dropped back with his cohorts again.

Petra looked questioningly at her grandfather. He said, "We have strayed miles from the cave now." A drop of sweat hung from his earlobe.

Wild grasses hid an outcropping of rocks. Nonno pulled aside the hanging vines, swatted at the flying insects, and stumbled through the thickets toward it. He gestured for Gusano to follow him. "I think the opening is near here," he said to him. Nonno and the three men spread out and began searching for the entrance to a cave.

The sound of lightly shuffling feet startled Petra, and she pivoted toward the noise. On a shelf of boulders above them, a jaguar paced slowly. It stared toward Petra, then to Nonno, while also concentrating on something of great importance beyond them. She considered that this was the animal that killed with one leap.

Petra could not divert her eyes from the jaguar's. Muscles rippled along its compact body. Despite the absence of any glint of light in this lush and tangled patch of jungle, its eyes glowed orange—suns of the night.

Slowly, steadily, Petra braced herself against an unexpected rush of alarm sweeping through her. Her head felt light, and her pulse raced. Potoo hovered over her. Justina bled and bled, soaking her dress in redness, bleeding into the river that had run dry. She collapsed in a sundrenched field of sugar cane. A shot rang out, and Emilio fell. Snapping branches and crunching leaves left footprints which tracked Nonno's steps. A machete cut through the sultry air.

Her heart heaving, Petra looked to the jaguar. Its massive torso and explosive strength drew her close. Its eyes lulled her. A celestial fire surged through her. The wild cat accompanied her through the onrush of terrors and laid a path leading away from them. She shoved Potoo away. She reclaimed her transcendent river in all its glory. The field of sun released her. Emilio lifted himself and bolted away, evading threat. Nature rustled and gnashed as it bore new fruit and passed into earth.

Nonno nodded silently to Petra. Petra gave thanks to the jaguar.

Nonno looked toward Gusano with a look of frustration, shaking his head. He pulled the bottle of water from the burlap bag suspended over his shoulder, took several swallows, and offered it to Petra. The wrinkles of his neck rearranged themselves around the strap when he replaced the bag. They moved back into the open glade.

The sky was darkening when they emerged. Thunder cracked, and the sky yielded the first rain of the season. Drops fell lightly, spattering peacefully onto thirsty leaves. Ixchel's singing stopped, and Petra thought she heard a woman's lament descend from the slopes of the volcano.

Petra shuddered. Nonno tilted his head to the side, stumbled, then winked at her.

The three men approached, their ire rising. Potoo and Fernando hung back, letting Gusano take the lead. He said, "Old man, you're running out of time. Where is it?"

Nonno wrung his hands. "We can keep looking, Martín. I have all day free."

"Jokes are not a good idea about now," Gusano said. "Here's the deal, *viejito*. Either you find the bird, or I take the girl. Not quite an even exchange, but it avoids beating an old man, which just doesn't sit right with me." He smiled mirthlessly. Potoo leered at Petra.

"Let's follow the rocks along this way. It's got to be here," Nonno said. "Of course, it's also possible that the archeologists found it sometime after we were here."

"Keep dreaming, *viejito*, and try to focus your decaying old mind."

A falcon flew overhead, emitting human-like cries which rose sharply in pitch like maniacal laughter, then fell off in a woeful moan. It was the call of the laughing falcon, the *guaco*.

Nonno led the way again. A pit viper curled in the grass near Petra's feet made her hop to the side. Bewitchingly brown and white, with black spots, its head lifted slightly from the inner reaches of its coiled body. Petra greeted it with serene reverence while passing by. She took note of its location.

The jaguar was trailing them back through the woods.

The pace slowed and Nonno stopped to scratch his head. Quietly, he said to Petra, "Hopefully Martín will give up this crazy quest. It might be time to work on Plan B." He smiled at Petra.

Under her breath, she said, "I'll leave Fernando for you, Nonno. I will do my best with the other two."

"This is crazy, *m'hija*. Tromping through sacred jungle with three gangsters."

"Who is crazy? The old man wrapped in tired old myths, or the one who lives in this world here and works to make his future a little brighter?"

Nonno challenged, "The world is nothing without stories, Martín. There is no life without imagination. Why else would you follow your nine-year-old self back to this place if you didn't believe that?"

Silently, with only a subtle movement, Nonno handed the bag with the water bottle to Petra, who slipped it over her shoulder. The sight of the tattoos oozing down Gusano's neck seized her and her body began to shiver desperately. Her thoughts grew wild and frenetic. With an explosion of willpower, she forced her mind to work and her body to still. He had handed her the bag for a reason.

"Martín. It is dangerous to abuse this figurine. It belongs to the ancient Mayans. The heavens have responded to your intentions with this rain." He swept his hands over the vault of sky. "God help you if you take it from its ancestral home."

The men guffawed. Potoo chimed in, his tone snide. "I plan to take this little girl from her ancestral home, old man. The statue, however, has nothing to say about our plans for it. Nothing at all. Nor does the girl, for that matter."

Petra knelt on the scrub grass, her hands wrapped around the bag before her. Without a word, she brought to mind a short prayer. She laid the bag gently on the ground and pushed it forcefully. It rolled away from her along the undergrowth, down the gentle incline, stopping some distance away. Potoo's eyes narrowed. He looked toward Gusano, one eyebrow arched. She walked back to stand with her grandfather.

Gusano said, "That's a fun game, Petra. Cute. What do you have in that bag? Now go pick it up and bring it here." He pulled the machete from his belt to bring home his point. Nonno smiled. "What makes you smile, old man? Eh?"

"You cannot win over the gods with a knife, Gusano," said Nonno. "Do you remember nothing from your time working here?"

"I remember all those archeologists thinking this stuff was valuable. Value that can be cashed in without the help of archeologists."

While they bantered back and forth, Petra followed the action with her eyes—evaluating, calculating, furiously holding herself together. On the side opposite Sibalq'aq, a lush swamp reeked.

"Do you remember when the jaguar sauntered into the camp, Martín? A wave of awe spread among all the people there when they realized. One after another, they stood to observe. It was like an apparition. Do you remember? You were pushing a wheelbarrow load at the time."

Gusano's eyes constricted as he remembered the scene. Nonno continued, "When you noticed the jaguar, you lost control, and the load fell over. Meanwhile, the jaguar made the rounds, walking in and amongst everyone, smelling the diggings, swaying its neck in grand fashion, holding itself aloof in high dignity. Everyone became utterly silent. Time stopped."

"Then the jaguar left, and everything returned to normal. Nothing happened, *viejito*," said Gusano.

"So it may have seemed to you. You were too young to grasp the significance. But the jaguar appeared just as one of the archeologists had found a jaguar god sculpted in stone. The jaguar is a god of the underworld. I remember clearly, the jaguar on the stone had square eyes with spiral pupils, and symbols of the sun were carved into it. That is because the jaguar crossed between the underworld and the heavens, directing the sun at night as it passed through the underworld. The jaguar we saw had been released from the spirit realm with the archeologists' find."

"That's a great story," Gusano said. "But how could anyone, let alone a dumb animal, cross between heaven and hell? The priest I remember never said anything about the two sharing much of anything."

"Ah, you are gravely mistaken, Martín. Good can be found in evil. The two are inextricably linked. You of all people should be grateful for that. The Mayan stories allowed people to sort through human nature —"

Potoo interrupted, "Enough of this!" He flashed his knife in a show of bravura. "Little girl, bring me that bag, right now! You are hiding the treasure there, *sí*?" He swerved suddenly toward Petra and grabbed hold of her, pulling her away from Nonno's arm. Hadn't she seen this situation before? Petra lifted a knee and smashed it with as much force as she had into that space between Potoo's legs.

Potoo yelped like a wounded puppy. He immediately dropped the knife and folded to the ground. He glowered up at her. "*Pinche puta!* Don't think you can get away with this again." He groaned.

Fernando pushed Potoo aside and reached down to retrieve the knife. Fernando said, "You will pay for that, little Petita. I will bury you in the same spot as my son Emilio." Imagination crossed back and forth over reality. Fernando's hands were bloody, or perhaps it was a reflection. His steely blue eyes tore through her. His squared jaw was so geometrically shaped as to seem inhuman.

While Fernando was stooping over, Nonno snatched the opportunity and kicked him hard in the face. Nonno fell backward with the effort and, for a moment, he looked as stunned as Fernando. But he quickly picked himself up.

Fernando lay dazed, holding his bleeding nose. His right eye remained closed.

Gusano stood his ground, still as a rock. He glared at Petra and Nonno and looked contemptuously at his fallen comrades. He spoke in a low, menacing tone. "*Now*, little girl, bring me the bag *now*." He lifted a corner of his shirt and pulled out a gun.

Petra walked slowly, dawdling. She hunched over low to the ground, her eyes searching. She stopped at the bag, stood slowly, gathered it to her abdomen, and walked toward Gusano, letting each foot fall with care before her.

Suddenly she flung the bag at Gusano, who dropped it and screamed, "It's a pit viper! *Chingado!*"

The viper spread out to its full length, flying in the air before Gusano. It flipped its tail in anger, trying to latch on to the outstretched arm. Gusano flung out his arms to swipe at it, staring in terror at its head. Petra watched the viper's menacing glory, its swollen triangular head angling toward Gusano, its penetrating eyes bulging forward in their rapt concentration on his face.

Gusano clawed at the snake and dropped the bag and his gun. In the blink of an eye, the snake, now frightened, opened its fangs and bit into Gusano's arm. Gusano screamed and fell to the ground writhing. Petra picked the gun off the ground and hurled it deep into the fetid swamp.

The snake slithered away. Potoo and Fernando watched the scene from their own spots on the ground, frozen in panic, and pain.

Petra picked up the bag, and she and Nonno ran toward the town.

The jaguar, unnoticed by anyone, continued to follow them as far as the edge of the town. Nonno said, "The jaguar has protected us. Itzamná is at peace. We can go home."

With his penknife, Nonno ripped holes in the two back tires of Gusano's truck. They watched the vehicle skew and sink. A young man gave them a ride to San Luis Hunahpu, where they soon caught the bus to Las Leches.

Once firmly settled into the bus, Petra said, "They will come quickly to find us."

"Yes, Petra. You must go now."

"Where will I go, Nonno?"

"It's time, Petra. You must go to your mother. Carlos will go with you as far as the border with the United States."

"But Nonno, you and Nonna must leave also! They will come and retaliate against you if they don't find me! And they will not give up on stealing Itzamná from the jungle as sure as the sun rises."

"We are getting old, Petita. I will stay and see what fate has in store. As for Itzamná, he is a very powerful god, and an old man's memory only gets more frail. They will leave us alone, I think."

Petra blinked in astonishment. "What are you saying, Nonnino?" Gravity sank Petra down into her seat. Her life was turning, and it twisted her insides. "How can I leave you?" Petra turned watery eyes to Nonno.

A world unknown stood before her. Her mind raced with possibility. She could continue to high school, learn about DNA, speak English, read books. Her mother and she would finally get to know each other. More than anything, she'd like to rest in her mother's arms. Maybe someday qualify for medical school! Dreams of an alien life.

But beside her sat her grandfather, a man of wisdom, love, and mysterious thoughts. He represented everything that was most important to her about life. She tried to picture herself setting off, carrying her knapsack on her back, leaving their home behind, abandoning her grandparents to face angry gang members intent on seeking revenge. No, she could never forgive herself if Gusano's group attacked Nonna again. Her heart ached.

Nonno watched the creases in her forehead deepen. He took her soft hand, and held it between his rugged, chiseled hands. "Petra, you will be my inspiration. And you will help so many others if you are free, if you get an education and succeed in your ambitions. As I get older, I may require your medical skills. But not now. Your grandmother and I—we need you to go. You must take the next step."

Her own voice telling Novina about the high school she wanted to attend echoed in her mind. She heard Eduardo's voice telling her to take steps to realize her dreams. True freedom could be found only when her will was healed by the grace of God. Would such steps take her toward that sort of freedom? That sounded rather selfish. And she didn't need healing!

Look at what had happened to her in these past weeks. She felt formidable—even indestructible! Right now, Itzamná felt stronger than

God. *Ay Dios*, no, Itzamná would not negate God. She would cherish both, protect them as they shielded her from harm.

Stories, myths. The grace of God. Where to look for it? Could she find it in the United States? She felt strong, and yet, if she closed her eyes for too long, she knew the exhaustion would come. How tired she had felt at Novina's apartment when she was given just a few hours free from worries. She worried she would become inert with despair. More than anything, there was no question now that Gusano would hunt her down, do everything in his power to bend her to his will.

God and Siguanaba, Vicenta and Emilio, they had come together, in a strange and wondrous way within her, to help her wend through a slew of perilous events. Two weeks ago, so far in the past, had begun in a state of abstract anxiety, with roiling fears about ashes and attacks on women in the village. Humility wrapped itself around her, and she knew she was not indestructible, would never be. She would have to keep struggling, keep moving forward, one small step at a time.

Confusion addled her mind. She closed her eyes.

Somewhere a hummingbird released its drop of water to put out the fire; it hovered, dove, flitted, in a blur of power.

At home, Nonno wasted no time. He found an ancient, grayed knapsack which had carried kernels of maize the week before. He shook out the dust and laid it down for her. She could only take what would fit in the knapsack. She put on two layers of long pants, packed a dress and a light sweater. Bits of tortilla, cheese, a bagful of beans. Her mother's address and phone number on a slip of paper slipped into a pocket. Alocinia hugged her leg in the other pocket.

From above, from a corner of the rafter, Nonna pulled out a packet of quetzals. "There are 500 quetzals here, Petita. Put some in your shoes, some in your bra, some in your pack. Never all in the same place. If you have time to stitch them into your shirt or the hem of your pants, even better. Keep the money for emergencies. It may seem like a lot, but 500 quetzals will not buy much."

"But, how —" Petra began.

"Your mother, Petita. We've been able to set aside a little from what she sends. We expected this day would come." Her grandparents continued to mete out their secrets.

The night before, she and Nonno had hatched their plan for the day, but no one had told her of the contingency plan they were acting out now.

She would go north at first only a couple hundred yards, as far as the field where Carlos was working. He had taken with him a shoulder bag with a few necessary items, knowing he could be called on at any moment. They would avoid main roads until Guatemala City—taking no chances of encountering Gusano or one of his cohorts. There they could find a bus to take them toward the Mexican border. Carlos had some notion of the route to the U.S. It was his last responsibility as bodyguard. He would return home once they laid eyes on the U.S. border.

Suddenly the sound of feet running up the hill startled them, shoes smacking the earth, headed for their house. Petra ducked out back. Nonno went forward to the yard to greet Potoo and Fernando, once again.

Petra faced her grandparents with a forlorn look. "You must go now, Petita. Keep our love inside you. We will speak when you are safe with your mother." There wasn't time to kiss Nonno or say a proper farewell to Nonna. When would she again hug Vicenta?

Petra hid herself behind a tree, fears for her grandparents gluing her to the bark. She heard Potoo and Fernando speak to Nonno, then Fernando yelled, "You will be sorry. We will find her and take her apart piece by piece."

But they were hot on a trail and departed quickly, back the way they had come. Torn between loyalty and obedience, love and hope, she trundled slowly into the woods to find Carlos.

PART II

You can live as if nothing is a miracle,
or you can live as if everything is a miracle.
—Albert Einstein

CHAPTER TWENTY-THREE

Over a couple of weeks, Carlos and she crossed Mexico, traveling alongside all the others who had no money for trains and buses. Their eyes glued to their destination, they spent interminable hours walking through cold, hunger, and fear, waiting in station yards for the cargo trains, riding the roofs of *La Bestia,* then walking some more. At night they shared caves with bats and curled up against logs in the forest with mice and snakes. Like a deer, she slept with an eye open, still weary when she woke.

Voices of the days merged with the whimpers of darkness. Dogs howled, crows screeched, the wounded moaned. The massacred, raped, and beaten, the orphaned children cried out. Wind creaked, and bird songs like hymns rippled across her chest. The wind sighed through trees, imploring her to help the innocent. She was never quite sure if she was awake or asleep.

They trekked over mountains, looking for the next village, the next train yard, and never had enough food or water. From time to time a kind woman would hand them a chunk of bread. Other times, a Mexican officer would demand pesos to let them be.

Hundreds of people scrambled for space on *La Bestia*. Children shared stories from the roofs and crannies of boxcars, or from a dark corner mid-tunnel. Families held close to each other when the wind rushed over a bridge. From their perch on a train, Petra and Carlos traversed an eternity of desert landscape, and village after decrepit village, where a few tired and dusty boys approached to sell them worthless trinkets or a few pieces of nopal fruit. Lonely shelters made from tin and scraps or crumbling adobe teetered on sandy ground.

Carlos and Petra leaned in close to each other. The unfamiliar terrain loosened their old patterns with each other. Now that he was not distracted by the harvest and his friends, Carlos focused on his sister's needs.

Petra allowed herself to trust him, and he responded by finding her food, giving her a hand up to the train, and reassuring her when the animals murmured at midnight. When she woke in the morning, she noticed that her head had fallen to his lap during the night, then wondered if his muscles felt as sore as hers did. When her energy flagged climbing the third desert mountain of the day, he put an arm around her for support and suggested they rest. When he wheezed from thirst, she forced him to sit in the shade of a tree and used the gourd in her knapsack to carry him water. They had never so closely attended to each other's needs.

They landed at Matamoros because that's where the last train they rode stopped. It also happened to be the shortest route to the U.S. Carlos advised her to stride through the city with confidence, like she knew where she was going, because the Zetas gang picked immigrants who looked vulnerable as their prey.

They headed directly for the international bridge. They didn't plan to hang around and encounter trouble. People in the border town told them that minors traveling alone could still get across. Immigration let kids apply for a special visa if their mother or father had abandoned them.

"Why don't you come with me?" Petra already knew the answer, but she had to ask once more.

"You need to do this. I don't."

"What will you do?" Petra noticed freckles under his eyes for the first time. She felt pity for him.

"Don't look at me like that. Maybe someday you'll become a doctor and send back enough money for me to build that fancy house in Las Leches. But I'm bound to my life in our village, Petra. I don't have dreams for this United States. I want to go home."

"Ay, Carlos." Feelings surged through her, for which she found few words. "Thanks for taking care of me. For so long. I always thought I was taking care of myself, but you were there behind me. I never realized. Now that I finally know, and I have learned I can depend on my big brother, you walk out of my life." She cocked her head and squinted one eye. "Well, I guess I'm doing the walking away."

Carlos looked down, but she saw his ears turn red. "Petra, honestly," he said to the ground, "sisters don't get much better." He coughed. "Besides, this way you don't have to worry about Nonno and Nonna. I will watch over them."

Carlos left her at the bridge to Brownsville. Her brother, the fragile thread that tied her to the familiar, turned back.

Alone, the toughness grown up through her childhood bubbled up to her chest. She marched directly up to the U.S. immigration office, and told an officer she wanted to join her mother in the U.S. She told them she had fled from men who wanted to kill her. An officer inspected her backpack. He fingered her underwear and took a long look at her dress. But when he took hold of Alocinia in his big hairy hands, she objected vehemently. "Aren't you a little old for dolls?" The man smiled contemptuously while he waited for a response. Mutely, she pressed her lips together and shook her head. They put her in a cold cell with a bunch of teenage girls overnight.

In the morning a man with kind eyes in a green uniform escorted her to a bus, where she sat for hours and days, through wide open expanses of boundless farmland, until she was suddenly in the middle of a big city they said was Chicago. Cars rushed by the bus; the kids stared out the bus windows with blank faces. Buildings blocked out the sun, and people in gray coats endlessly hurried along the sidewalks.

Petra spent a month in a juvenile immigration group home while she waited to be released to her mother. She fretted about Carlos, about her grandparents, and about the little clay hummingbird, the jewel she kept in her backpack all day, curling her arm around it on her cot at night. No one else would lay a hand on Alocinia. She paid more attention to English instruction than ever. Nurses there stuck her innumerable times with vaccines.

She kept to herself, raising a familiar shield against the barrage of fears presented by the outside world. The insults and indignities hurled at her during this period piled on top of each other until she thought she couldn't last another day. Why did the staff dislike her, as apparently they disliked all the girls they were charged with? Day after day passed, and she bore them all until the shield became part of her. Emilio never crossed her mind.

CHAPTER TWENTY-FOUR

Late May 2017
Providence, Rhode Island

Then, finally, her first plane ride, Chicago to Providence. Which probably would have been more exciting if two very large, morose, gray-haired women in the window and middle seats hadn't blocked any view out the window. Or if her stomach hadn't been churning, maybe partly because of the airplane, but more because she was about to see her mother for the first time in ten years.

While Petra was at the group home, her mother and she had talked on the phone several times a week. The faraway, silky voice had become more familiar, but there was a gulf between a voice and a full person. Now they would find out if the gulf had a bridge.

Perhaps her mother and her new elderly husband would have a baby together. Wyman might resent the presence of this child of his wife's former husband. For now, her mother thought she'd be happy to see Petra, but they didn't know each other. Petra was bound to upset the order of things at their home. Would she ever find a place that felt like home?

The plane bounced on the runway and, for a minute, she was pretty sure they weren't going to slow down in time to avoid running onto the highway beyond the airport. Luggage fell from the bins above into the waiting arms of too many people crowded into the tiny aisle between seats. One of the morose women bumped and scraped by Petra as she squeezed out to the aisle without so much as a glance. Passengers burst out of the plane's door and up the enclosed ramp. Shoulders jostled against her, little wheels carrying black bags squeaked, the pumped-in air pressed on her lungs. Blindly, she followed the crowd.

How would they even recognize each other? Carlos said she looked just like her mother, but he hadn't seen her for ten years either. Maybe she was turning prematurely gray or had developed lots of wrinkles around her mouth and eyes.

In the past month's phone calls, Petra hadn't given up the defensive distance she had always fallen back on with her mother over the years. But her mother had spoken of one thought that Petra couldn't get out of her mind. Her mother said she longed for someone who could understand her as only family can. Despite a marriage with a good man, she said, he couldn't possibly share the feeling their family had for Itzamná's laughter, or the fleshy heft of a banana leaf wrapped around tamales or the sheer sensual joy of a Guatemalan bus. Nor could they share the ties of blood, like the knowingness behind a smile or the way some silences communicated elation, others dread.

Unlike her mother, Petra had, until now, been surrounded by her family, albeit missing one important member, and by her own culture, for better or for worse. Nonno had always told her that Petra and her mother shared the bond of blood. Was it possible that she was bringing a gift to her mother, something her mother had desperately missed?

When she passed through the last set of doors, crowds of people were suddenly everywhere—kids running behind parents, adults hurrying to get somewhere other than where they were, everyone crisscrossing each other in every direction. What would she say to her mother? She wanted to tell her everything that had happened to her in the last ten years. She wanted to tell her nothing at all. She closed her mind against the confusion, sealing everyone else out of the picture.

Long black hair very much like her own came running in her direction. In less than an instant, her mother stood before her. A nervous smile, which looked very much the way Petra felt, radiated through the tension. And then arms folded around her, a cheek nestled against hers, a quiet vibration like a voice greeted her. But no sound came through to Petra. Only muted sensations. She did remember her little girl's ear against her mother's stomach. It was her left ear. Now they were cheek to cheek. She regretted missing all the hugs that came in the years between the stomach and the cheek.

Her mother didn't let go. It was the same suffocation of the phone calls. Her mother's desperate need to hold on to her. Petra wanted to push back, to run away. Her bones stuck out, her clothes were awkwardly drab, she couldn't find the right place for her elbow. From over her mother's shoulder, she looked at her long shiny hair—or was that her own hair? She couldn't tell which strands belonged to her, and which to her mother. How strange. For just a moment, she relaxed into her mother's arms. The silky voice had a strong and soothing body, arranged quietly against her own. Finally, her mother eased away. Cool air slipped between Petra's shirt and her skin.

Deep brown eyes peered into Petra's. In the corner of one of those brown eyes, a tear hovered, unsure whether to let go or retreat. Her mother's mouth was moving, but Petra's ears were blocked. Blockaded. No entry, no exit. The shield had not lowered, not yet. Was there still time for her mother to know her?

She followed her mother out of the airport. Petra had little concept of what North Americans looked like, but there was no doubt her mother was no longer fully of Guatemala, despite the high Mayan cheekbones she had inherited from Nonna. Her mother sparkled with an Americanness expressed in the bright blue shirt that fit tightly across her breasts, the silver glittering on her ears, the way her arms swung casually by her sides. Petra looked down at her own tired Guatemalan clothes which had now traveled across a continent. Assuredly, there was a ten-year gulf between them.

At least her mother didn't hide behind a lot of make-up. A scar followed her eyebrow across a broad forehead. A twinge of sympathetic pain raced across Petra's forehead. Troubling things had happened to her mother, as well.

Outside it was drizzling, but the air felt good, and her chest expanded. Then they were in a car, and they were alone, and she began to see and hear more, though her mother's voice still sounded far away. She was as beautiful as Petra had dreamed. Petra laid her palm down on the seat between them. Then her mother's palm touched the back of her hand.

Amazingly warm and soft. So this was what a mother felt like.

Her mother smiled at Petra, a smile her heart recognized, a smile that swept her in. Nonno's smiles were wondrous and inviting, but not quite so close. She looked at her mother's face and saw something. Something familiar.

Eyes fastened to the road, her mother nevertheless gazed at Petra. Quietly, gently, her mother's eyes asked, comforted, connected. Petra felt the blood flow more freely through her. She said, "Mamá. Is it really you?"

"My sweet lost child. *Sí*, Petita, it is me."

CHAPTER TWENTY-FIVE

As sprightly as an old man in a wheelchair could be, Wyman wheeled himself around the kitchen, preparing eggs and plantains, while the tail of his white shirt trailed out behind his wheelchair, and his collar rode haphazardly up the blotchy skin of his neck. The way the lines around his eyes and mouth curved and curled—they must have been etched by years of laughter and kindness.

In English, Wyman said, "Petra? Eggs scrambled or fried?"

She laughed nervously. In Spanish, "What does this 'scrambled' mean, mami?" The juvenile detention home had given her English classes for all of three weeks, approximately doubling what she had learned in school in Guatemala, but now, just days after being released to her mother's custody, Wyman asked complicated questions in English. After explanation, she picked fried.

Wyman added, "Is your mind scrambled or fried, Petra, with this new world?"

Her mother explained that one, and they all laughed. Maybe she could get to like this new husband.

A coffee perched before her. It was the third morning Petra had taken part in her mother's daily routine. Her hands rested on a small kitchen table covered by a tablecloth of Mayan fabric. Standing to look out the raised window, Petra gazed at the backyard from their second-floor apartment. There was no porch, no bench to sit on, no hummingbirds or banana trees. Not even a volcano to orient her.

Wyman got breakfast ready so her mother could concentrate on getting herself ready for work. The arrangement would take some getting used to. So far, Petra contributed by washing dishes. Clean water spilled out of the faucet on command, making it so easy to wash the few dishes in the sink. For now, she didn't miss the stream down the dirt path. She thanked God for the family she found herself living with—with a full half of her heart.

The chain link fence marking the end of their property framed beautiful purple phlox and bright yellow and orange tulips. The two plantings had run together since her mother had planted the tulips, the neighbor the phlox. And lush green grass—a lot of grass, everywhere!— and cement, and papers, smashed bottles, old bags, and cups blowing about in the wind. Hardly any dust and ashes. She smiled to herself. She wouldn't get to see snow for months.

A thin but muscular arm embraced Petra's shoulders. Her mother pulled aside her dress and gently sat down next to Petra. Petra smiled noncommittally. She imagined her mother in her job as a certified nurse's assistant, lifting elderly women from their wheelchairs into their baths, helping them onto the toilet.

How elegantly arresting her mother was. Her beautifully satin skin, the color of leaves laying on a forest floor, tempted Petra to nestle in her mother's arms. Instead, she sipped her coffee and took it all in from a safe distance. Even sitting there at the table, her mother sat tall and straight, her head lifted like nobility, Mayan nobility.

Petra wiped coffee from her lips with the back of her hand. Fear lurked behind her wide-open eyes.

Her mother watched her intently, as if she could see inside her, as if she knew the sweep of emotions passing through Petra since her arrival. "We have so much to talk about, my love. So much to catch up on. It is not easy to start your life over in a new world." Her mother's brown eyes met hers, saying so much more.

Petra remembered what Tonyo said about her mother's "big, sweet eyes, dripping with benevolence." Now those eyes were for her! She checked the thrill that ran through her. But—how could she trust any of it?

"My head is spinning a little." Her mother nodded warmly and translated for Wyman.

Wyman put one hand up in the air, and with the other, twirled his wheelchair in circles, the spin recasting itself into a dance. The airborne hand fluttered and turned until Petra broke into involuntary laughter. "*Olé*," said her mother. Her mother wandered out of the kitchen, then returned with a handbag retrieved from their bedroom.

"Sorelly, come to me," he said with playful coyness. He wagged a hand, beckoning her mother. She flung the handbag over her shoulder, and took long, deep tango steps toward him. When she was within reach, he brashly snared her hand and drew it to his mouth, tendering a loud smack on her curved fingers with his lips. "Thank you, my twirling beloved. You have fulfilled your mission. My mission for you, just for now, that is."

Her mother backed away, shaking her head. "Chances are, you'll get used to this man, Petra." She put the sandwich Wyman had already fixed for her into her bag.

Petra cocked an eyebrow. This wheelchair-bound old man was intriguing.

Her mother coughed, and each of them sat more firmly in their seats again. She said, "My boss is giving me the day off tomorrow, Petrita, so I can take you to get registered for school. Hopefully you can start school soon."

A smile broke out across her face. "*De verdad*? I can't believe it's happening so quickly! Is it far away, this school?"

"Not at all, only five minutes in the car."

How easy it was to get around with a car. "Have you had that car for a long time?" Petra asked.

"Just since a few months ago when I finally got steady work. It's hard to get around by bus in Providence if you need to go a lot of places, like I do for work. But I have to be super-careful, because I can't get a license."

"Why not?"

"No immigration papers, no license. There are some difficulties about life here."

"They gave me lots of papers at the border. They told me I have to go to Immigration Court."

"Yes, they told me. We have lots of papers, too. We had to send so many forms and documents so you could come to us. We'll talk to a lawyer about all that soon."

"Mamá, where did that ring on your finger come from?" She had been wanting to ask since the car ride back from the airport.

"Wyman." She smiled at him. "It's my wedding ring. It makes me a little nervous to wear such an expensive piece of jewelry. I asked for emerald. The green keeps me grounded."

"And the necklace?" Petra asked.

Her mother lifted it in her fingers so Petra could see. "Do you know who it is?"

"She has a snake emerging from her headdress, and her hands are clasping the moon. It has to be Ixchel."

Her mother beamed at her. "You must have been talking to my father."

Petra's heart stirred. "Where do you think I should go today? I want to explore the neighborhood." Petra was ready to conquer the entirety of Providence.

Her mother's eyes suddenly avoided Petra's. "Maybe start off to the right from our house, toward Broad Street." She paused. "I'll be home late tonight. I couldn't cancel this meeting when I found out you were arriving. It's a church event."

"Church? Can I go with you?" asked Petra.

Her mother hesitated. "I think… not this time, Petra. You might want to attend the church service before jumping into this group. We'll go together on Sunday."

Petra rolled her eyes and pushed back from the table, abruptly heading to her room.

Her mother stopped her. "I should explain." Again, she glanced away. She took a big swallow of coffee. "I, well… I participate in a group that supports former gang members. Many of them are from Guatemala." She looked up with false brightness at Petra. "You might know one of them from Las Leches—Lucas?"

"Lucas, the son of Don José, the overseer at the cane fields?"

"That's the one."

"Lucas, who was also in the X-14 gang with Emilio? Who quit the gang and went into hiding?"

"And then fled to the U.S. when the gang found him and tried to hang him from a tree. Yes, Petra."

"But why? Why would you help a bunch of thugs?"

"Actually, I feel drawn to the work, Petra. I feel a personal responsibility to do what I can with the mess our country has made of so many young men's lives—and women's. Petra," her mother hesitated. "I should tell you the whole story, now that we've begun." Her mother laid her chin in her hand, her fingers curling up her cheek, and looked to Wyman. Wyman couldn't follow the Spanish flying by him, as hard as he tried, but he squeezed his lips between his thumb and forefinger and looked at Sorelly sympathetically. Her mother continued. "Emilio is not part of the group yet, though we want him to participate. He's living with Lucas. Lucas has made a lot of progress since he's been part of our group."

"Emilio is here?" Petra's voice was shrill, accusatory. Her mind flipped back to that night in Guatemala, just before she had to run away. *Híjole*, he'd lied to her! "What do you mean Emilio's here?! You talked to him?!"

"Calm down, Petra. Listen. Emilio showed up at the front door one day, a couple weeks ago, looking lost and bedraggled. He told me he finally found someone who knew me at a church where he had gone to get food. He'd been slogging about the city to all different churches trying to find someone who knew me. He needed a connection with someone, to get started. He'd been living on the streets."

"He was in a gang in Las Leches! He had disgusting friends! Do you have any idea what they did to people there?"

The scar on her mother's forehead turned a dark purple. "He was also your friend, Petra, don't forget. His mother and I were also friends, since our school days. We both married very difficult men around the same time. It's because of our friendship that you and Emilio became friends as little kids. Helping Emilio a bit is the least I can do in memory of Liana. I can only imagine what Emilio lived through in that household."

"Can you imagine what *I* went through, mami, in all those years after you left us?" Long bottled-up feelings rose, arrived at her throat, boiled in her head, and turned her cheeks bright red. "Emilio is not my friend anymore! He hasn't been since he joined the X-14 gang years ago! I thought coming to the U.S. I would leave behind that mess. I didn't think my own mother would invite it back in!" Turning her back to her mother, she stalked out. The door to her bedroom slammed hard behind her.

She stood just inside the door. But instead of the roiling anger, relief flooded through her. And—even—satisfaction. The ability to close a door and be alone! To shut out her mother when she needed to. This wasn't the first time she'd needed to, but it's the first time she did it. Out of sight, accountable to no one, she could recover herself, process her thoughts. Privacy—she had barely considered the concept until now. And there in her room, recently converted from a living room into her bedroom, a computer. Wyman was teaching her to use it. Along with a bunch of books, and notebooks, a soft bed—all for her use!

For almost two months, Emilio had barely crossed her mind.

Now, her hands pressed against her head, the conversation flooded back over her. She flopped down on her bed and tried to contain the rage that rose again to pulse against her temples. Her mouth quivered; hot tears burned her cheeks on their way to her pillow.

Her mother knew nothing! How could she disappear from her life for ten years, then return just to bring her worst nightmare back into her life?

She thought about that night when Emilio visited her as he was fleeing from the X-14. He must have already known he was going to the U.S. and would look up her mother. He'd been so full of sorrowful words— he'd never see her again, could she ever forgive him—she'd almost felt close to him. He'd failed to mention that little detail.

After so many years away from Petra, her mother now expected her to accept that she was going to watch over Emilio, over her own daughter's needs? Shudders of outrage swept through her body. Clearly, her mother didn't really care about her. She hadn't waited to get to know Petra, to find out what her life had been about, what she had accomplished and suffered, what she had hoped and dreaded, before inviting Emilio into their lives. This was not a mother who held her close to her heart.

For so many years, mention of her mother always filled Petra with a confusion that ripped at her heart. Only in those last days in Guatemala had she begun to open her heart to her mother. Such a fragile daughterly peace, held together by the thread of Nonno's advice, Tonyo's love, and that last phone conversation from San Luis Hunahpu. But it could all snap with the tense realities of actually meeting face to face again. Now, her mother had to prove herself to Petra, convince her of her love, show her that they actually had something in common.

The tears suddenly stopped. Had she ever experienced such fury before? It felt horrible. She had to hold onto self-control. That's what had gotten her through all these years. She'd have to hold these other feelings tight when she interacted with her mother.

Something new and mysterious was happening to her. She tamped down the uproar inside her down into her chest, where it lay heavy but quieter. Numbness took over as her thoughts shut down. Her eyelids sagged over her eyes. Her head sank into the very soft pillow.

A light knocking on the door. "Petra? Are you okay? Can we talk?"

Petra ignored her mother. Another set of taps on the door, followed by waiting, breathing. Then her mother's footsteps retreated. From a corner of her consciousness, she heard soft voices of conversation between Wyman and her mother.

"Don't give me that look." Her mother sounded annoyed with Wyman.

"She needs some time, Sorelly. It's too soon, too close."

"She's angry with me, Wyman. There's a wall there—so many years have gone by since I left."

The voices faded. The hinges of the back door creaked, then it clicked shut. Her mother had left for work. The pillow was deep and comfortable. Like Novina's snug couch that had dragged her into daytime sleep, too. Petra's pillow enveloped her, and she fell deeply away from consciousness.

A dark space, large and wide, fleeting snatches of dimness. Pure desolation veiled her view. Rises like cliffs ranged out toward the obscure horizon. The landscape before her climbed up in stages. Crooked branches swung down in the wind. Skeletal shadows hurried through the blackness. Each step made a squish-sucking noise in the mud at her feet. Lots of people, or rather human-like creatures, wandered aimlessly around her. With horror, she discerned faces screwed sideways, noses and ears missing, eyes like huge cavities, wire-like hair vaguely attached to heads. Bodies were wasted away, showing more bones than skin. Everyone was on the move, uphill. Most hopelessly strained to clamber up to the next level but collapsed below.

People guarded the heights, hauling a few gaunt figures up a rise, refusing to take the hands of others. They chose who could rise. Petra looked ahead, picked out a young woman with a cloth the color of lead covering waist to thighs, and raised her hand to her. The woman took it and pulled her up.

Another expanse of mud appeared. Wind and rain pelted her. A sense of urgency gripped her, as if time was slipping away. She must get to the next rise before it caught up to her.

Something—she refused to acknowledge it—was following her from behind, moving quickly. Where was Alocinia? Her eyes beseeched, desperately searching for Alocinia, hurrying to escape it.

Memories floated in the dark mist, bad memories, forgotten memories. She tried to run. Bodies turned toward her, inspecting her. Her skin crawled. Mud splashed up to her thighs, then oozed down the backs of her legs. Fear slithered all over her.

Xibalba. This was Xibalba. Anger held her here, time shoved her, and guilt pressed on her. Alocinia guided her hope. That meant she had to climb nine levels to return to the light. Eight to go.

Black bats tore through the wind just above her. She slogged through the mud. A man with a mutilated arm and tattooed head looked upward at a bird perched on a pole. The bird was awkward, slouched over, its beak flattened out. The man shot at it with a gun held in his one good arm. The blasts startled. She fought with the foreboding that tried to strangle her.

The next hill was covered with roots. Human-like figures ahead slipped on the roots, their feet jockeying for steady position on roots that moved and slithered like snakes. Emaciated feet caught in the roots and separated from bodies. Petra grabbed the roots with her hands and pulled herself up to the next level. Mud-splashed hands grabbed at her, trying to hold her back. Night became deeper. Time stalled, pursuing her from behind. Twigs thrashed at the air. Shifting roots followed her.

A shadow lay ahead, beyond the next cliffs. Was it Alocinia? She ran now, but the mud held her feet with each step. Dust and ashes covered the trees, but under her feet, the overflowing water turned them to more mud, endless mud, which gripped her feet. There was so little time. She had to hurry. The mud encasing her ankles turned white, like glue, and spread onto her clothes. Frantically, she tried to clean it off, but it stuck to her.

A bloody figure bleated out a call to her. She could not look. Mud caught her in the eye. Encumbered by vines encircling her limbs, pressure weighed her down. Bawling, howling, then a whimper. She turned away from the tattooed man and dragged on, refusing the eyes. His gaze stung her from behind.

Bats swirled around her head. She managed a couple more rises, ascending toward the light, her strength flagging. A softer shadow appeared far above. It could be Alocinia. She shouted, trying to make herself heard through the din of sloshing feet, moaning souls, and skeletons slipping backward.

The falcon appeared—*guaco*! A loud, heroic call, blurring the line between laughter and sorrow. It flew far away into the light, then returned to the dark, breaking through the underworld with messages from earth and the heavens.

The bats turned into hummingbirds. Too many. Long beaks jabbed into her arms like needles, and wings fluttered around her cheeks like sandpaper. They forced her to wade through whipping branches, deeper mud. Her legs sank in down to the knees, but she made a heroic effort to move forward. Buried anguish was still following her, pressuring her to get out fast. Dark shadowy reminders of the evils below. "Alocinia!"

- I'm here. Come join me. Just above.
- I can't see you. The mud is holding me down. I don't know if I can make it.
- Get to the next rise. I'll pull you up.
- I can't see it. So many whipping branches. The hummingbirds have turned on me!"
- Let go of the fury. Face up to the mud and tattoos.
- They're a part of me. I don't know how to live without them. No, they're chasing me, pushing me forward. I'm trying to outrun them.
- Stop running. Don't fight. Accept the evil but find the rise. Evolve out from it.
- Alocinia! You're fading!
- I am right here. Feel me here.

She reached her arm out, reaching higher, farther, upward. Her heart weighed heavily in her chest, but she went within, touched it, and it breathed again. A tree appeared, ready to pull her up, but the branch was loaded with spiny fruits that stabbed at her hand. She let go of it.

The hummingbirds floated away, and the *guaco* swooped by her side. Itzamná! Suddenly the distance to the light disappeared. The light merged into the dark, the evils slipped into place amidst the day.

- Alocinia! I'm here, but where are you?
- I'm here.
- But the voice was distant.
- I can't find you. I've made it to the middle world, but I can't see you.
- The fear is chasing you. You have to look at it in the eyes. It is trying to pull you under the mud.
- I can't face it. I'm not strong enough.
- The underworld will hold you until you acknowledge your demons.
- *My* demons? I'm terrified they might recognize me.
- Look back in order to move ahead. Don't give up. I'll be here.

Petra choked on her longing for Alocinia. The fight to get air into her lungs roused her. She pulled the clay hummingbird from under her pillow and glared at her, trying to pierce her meaning. The rageful demons of the underworld remained locked in her dreams.

She reached for the glass of water next to her bed to bring the material world back to her body. Then she arose to meet the now late morning.

That evening, when her mother returned home, Petra ventured out of her room. She said, "Just tell me one thing before we go to bed. What places do I need to avoid so I don't see Emilio?"

"Well…. He could be anywhere, of course. He's been finding his way around here a little longer than you. But he's living on this street, three houses down toward Elmwood Avenue, sharing an apartment with Lucas and a couple of other young men."

"So, are you telling me that the entire X-14 has followed me to my mother's house, to Providence, Rhode Island? Three houses away?"

"Just the exiles, my love. The ones I know about, anyway. These are the ones who have repented and are trying to make over their lives. I'd like to support the effort. People at my church want to help, as well."

"*Ay Dios mío*," sighed Petra. This *was* a new world. And yet it seemed those problems of forgiveness and flawed humans had followed her here. Her yearning to find God's grace was still with her as well. Was it too much to ask for some space between her and the gangs before she was asked to forgive? Surely forgiveness didn't happen when one was backed into a corner.

CHAPTER TWENTY-SIX

Humming to herself, Petra set off to school the following Monday down Elmwood Avenue. To avoid Emilio's house, she took the long route around and then over to the main street. She peeked around the trees and corners of buildings in case something unexpected lurked. She half-expected to look up and see Don Fabio's house or run into a careening bicycle.

The hospital on the left side of the main avenue was a thousand times the size of the clinic in San Luis Hunahpu. It dwarfed the little stores selling Dominican and Southeast Asian foods, with towers rocketing upward on each end of the massive building, wisps of smoke floating into the sky from one end of the roof. A police officer hovered around an ambulance parked at the side entrance, his hand gesturing emphatically. He carried on a conversation with a woman dressed from head to foot in green. That green uniform—back in Guatemala, Itzamná had given her that image of herself in those clothes. Doctor's clothes.

As hard as Petra strained to know what was happening, all she could hear were static and mechanical voices coming from the box waving in the officer's hand. A portable bed emerged from the back of the ambulance with a body-sized wrap of sheeting strapped to it. She couldn't see an actual person on the bed. Some people rushed in and out of the various entrances, others meandered around the bustle to just make their way down the street. Such constant movement! So many people incessantly hustling about their urgent tasks.

Across the street lay acres of gravestones, the cemetery dreary and covered with litter. A man with a stubbly gray face was gathering up a sleeping bag, stuffing it into a cart with wheels. He snuffled and looked around him as if searching for a friend. Another person lay unmoving on a decrepit bench. A few trees barely held on to life. As many dead branches littered the walkways as trunks stood vertically, but there was no lack of cement.

Petra stopped and turned around in a full circle. An immensity of cement covered all the surfaces, in every direction. Not a ceiba tree in sight. On the block, one thin tree rose out of a small patch of dirt maybe three square feet, surrounded by a cracked sidewalk, heaving above a root. Clearly, nature was stronger than cement.

If all this activity took place on one street, what universes might she still discover in the city and beyond it?

Pods of kids were planted in front of the entrance to the school. From a big yellow school bus parked in front, teenagers streamed out the doors and toward her. The bus looked much like the buses in Guatemala, but without all the vibrant colors and exhilarating music.

Slowly, hesitantly, she pushed open the door to the school, but before she could get through, a group of jostling, bustling students pushed past her, swinging the door wide open. Security guards ushered her through mystifying metal detectors.

In the front office, a kindly woman with hair towering over her head gave her a schedule of classes, which meant she had to find a different classroom every 45 minutes. After waiting in the office for a half-hour, a third-year student who was to be her mentor and guide introduced herself. Clara spoke to her in stilted Spanish, then started mixing in a lot of English words in her conversation. It turned out her parents were born in the U.S., in Puerto Rico, but she'd been raised in Rhode Island. Her parents always tried to talk to her in Spanish, but she answered them in English. She was friendly enough, but she did tend to get distracted from showing Petra how to find places.

By the end of the first day, Petra's back hurt from all the books she was lugging around in a knapsack—one each for world history, biology, math, learning English as a second language—and folders of papers kept sliding onto the floor. Clara finally remembered to tell Petra she had been assigned a locker where she could leave the books. While she fiddled with the lock, metal doors clanged shut. The pandemonium of kids made her uneasy. A couple of times she found herself ducking at what turned out to be phantom perils coming at her.

Petra got lost at least seven times among the many halls and floors of the school, as she wandered between classes. In her wanderings, though, she found a gym full of echoing voices and pounding balls and an auditorium whose empty seats looked lonely. There was a room filled with musical instruments. A gleaming set of drums dominated the back corner of the room. The library made her jaw drop. It was just like the school library she'd described to Novina.

Clara explained that she should call black kids "African-American," although some of the Latino kids called them "*Negros*." The kids she took to be Chinese at first were called "Asian-American," and from so many other countries besides China she'd never heard of. But the most confusing were the Latino kids. The first girl she talked to didn't understand when she spoke in Spanish, even though she was pretty sure she was Hispanic. It turned out she was half white and half Philippina. This could get complicated.

The lunchroom was the noisiest place she'd ever been in. She sat in a corner, her head buried in her biology book. Before getting to her assignment, she flipped through the book and finally learned what DNA stood for. She found a whole section on photosynthesis. She wouldn't give up this book until she could read through the English and understand it all.

A girl with glasses and a cute, slightly turned-up nose sat down opposite her. Petra didn't look up, except for a short glance accomplished without actually moving her head. But the girl stuck out her hand at Petra. She spoke to Petra in Spanish. "You're new here," she announced. "Where'd you come from?"

Petra took the proffered hand. It was very soft. "Guatemala," she said cautiously, and turned to the next page of the biology book.

"No, not where are you from. Where'd you *come* from? Like, how is it you're just appearing now when there's only a few weeks of school left?"

Petra considered the question. "*Sí*, from Guatemala. I just got here two weeks ago. From Guatemala."

The girl raised her right eyebrow and winked. "I'm Yasmin. Nice to meet you. From Honduras. Ten years ago." She pulled a container of food out of her backpack and began to eat. "Biology, eh?" Yasmin turned her head as if to acknowledge two girls walking by and calling out her name, but she didn't release eye contact with Petra. Yasmin shooed them away with a sweep of her hand and a faint smile. Fine black strands of hair draped themselves around her glasses and onto her fleshy cheeks, while a thick braid disappeared behind her back.

"Yeah, check out all the topics in this book. Cell structure, genetics, the endocrine system, circulatory, digestive..." To herself, Petra read over the list at the head of the chapter again. "Oh, you probably have the same book."

"Reproductive. Don't forget the best one." The corner of Yasmin's mouth lifted in a half-smile. "Do you know you have incredible eyes? I saw them from way across the cafeteria. You looked at me for a second, but I don't think you saw me."

Petra laughed. For a few minutes, she was self-conscious every time she blinked.

Yasmin bent over to look at Petra under the table. "You look like a soccer player. Strong legs." She raised her eyebrows to indicate it was a question.

"Are you kidding? I played at home ever since I could walk."

"*Bélico*. I'm on the team here. Well, the season is in the fall, so it's over now. Plus the freshmen mostly just sit on the sidelines. Tryouts for the next year's team are a week from today. Sophomores can break out, if you're good, and get some real playing time. I'll take you over to sign up if you want."

"Thanks, Yasmin. That'd be great."

"I play with computers in my spare time. I like to build new apps for my phone. You got one of these yet?" She pulled out her smartphone.

Petra reached into her back pocket and laid hers on the table. "I don't understand it too well yet." Wyman had taken her to a store full of shiny objects and buttons to get it after she got registered for school.

"Can I see it?" Yasmin asked. Petra pushed it over to her. Yasmin tapped and slid her fingers across the screen. "Have you used this calendar yet?"

"Not yet. The counselor was showing me about putting the class schedule in there…"

"Here. Look! You have a date on Friday night! My house— pizza, a couple of kids you might like. Will you come?"

CHAPTER TWENTY-SEVEN

The last thing she knew she had been sitting on the floor of Yasmin's living room, the boxes of empty pizza scattered amongst the six of them, quietly taking in the conversation between Yasmin and her friends.

Then, suddenly, she was outside in the night air with Benji, completely disoriented.

"Hey, *guapa*, where did you come from?" asked the tall Dominican girl moments after Petra walked in Yasmin's door.

"I'm from Guatemala," Petra said, proud that she easily understood and answered in English.

"Cool. But I meant more like how did you get here, to this lit gathering. How did you find *us*? *Como llegaste aquí entre nosotros en esta casa tan calidá?*"

"*Chilero!*" Benji said, showing off his knowledge not just of Spanish but cool, Guatemalan slang. "Awesome friends you collect, Yasmin, if I do say so myself."

Petra's eyes crinkled at Benji, amused at his tall and elegant demeanor and the entirety of his outfit. Blue eyeliner with glitter shone from under his eyes. He held his head high in an almost regal bearing. The colorful West African scarf around his neck dramatically contrasted with the army pants.

"*Janguiando* with the classy crowd—*buen trabajo*, Petra. You found the best of the best pretty quick, eh?" Petra couldn't remember the name of the Puerto Rican woman who spoke.

Travis said, "Hey, *brokis*. Hand the pizza over here, Petra. *Por favor*." Even the white guy spoke a Spanish she didn't understand. She'd seen Travis before, from a distance, across the room in her math class.

Yasmin pitched in to help her. "*Brokis*: Puerto Rican for li'l bro', buddy. *Janguiando*: Puerto Rican for *paseando un rato*." Guys, let's go easy on the girl, and give her a chance, eh?" Yasmin looked encouragingly at Petra to let her respond. She passed over a box of pizza.

"*Un pajarito me invitó*," Petra said. "I can say in English, too. A little bird invited me." She grinned at Yasmin.

Yasmin responded, "I found her in the lunchroom at school one day, huddled in a corner between biology and math. She needed good company in a big way."

"Speaking of math," she said, "*que pasa con ese maestro de matemática?* Travis, you have Mr. Flanken for math, too, right?" Petra remembered holing up with her math book that day, trying to make sense out of the teacher's assignment. Mr. Flanken rarely talked in class at all. He spent the class writing numbers on the board and pointing at students to come work on them.

Travis said, "I think he's been teaching for about a hundred years, so his voice has all burned out." He frowned seriously and chuckled at the same time.

Benji said, "Watch out for those corners in the lunchroom, though. That's where some of the sketchy *boricuas* hang."

Petra looked to Yasmin questioningly. "*Boricuas* are Puerto Ricans. Sketchy is for someone who looks like maybe you shouldn't trust them."

Petra's head kept descending underwater with all the newness. Yasmin stayed close to her. Yasmin's tongue ran over her lips when her back arched toward Petra to explain what someone had said.

There was American English and English with West African and Puerto Rican accents, and the flip between Spanish and English three times in one sentence. Words twisted around in her mind—"*boricua*" and "*brokis*" had easy Spanish sounds, but "awesome," "burned out," and "huddled" were all new. Her mind played with the sounds. The flat "r," the "th" that didn't flow off her Spanish tongue, consonants chopping off the end of words.

Through the fog, she heard her name again. "Petra, what's your sport? You going to sign up in the fall?" the Puerto Rican girl asked.

The question animated Petra again. "I'd love to play soccer. I was goalie in Guatemala." At least she played when no one was holding a knife to her throat and ending games prematurely. "I heard maybe I can play in the fall?"

"Definitely. I just sit in the bleachers, but I'm a big fan."

"Do you play sports?" asked Petra.

"My biggest sport thing is avoiding the snow. My roots are deep in the beaches of Puerto Rico, you know? I go back every summer and go surfing and skateboarding. You haven't seen the fun of the cold and the snow yet, just wait." She looked so confident and relaxed.

Petra laughed. "No *fútbol* in the snow, right?"

Benji said, "American football, *sí*." His eyes blinked, showing off the long eyelashes.

"What's your sport, Benji?" asked Petra.

"No no, you got me all wrong. No sport." He wagged his head. "I do art and politics. Travis here is my politics buddy, though it's hard to keep up with him. Anything you need to know about the history of the world, anywhere in the world, literally, he's the one."

Travis took it as a complement. "*Imperialismo* in Africa. Fascinating stuff in class right now. Beats Nebuchadnezzar and Babylonia and all those old stone ruins. *Anti-imperialismo* gets less attention in our school, but that's what we learned about in Liberia. Or anyway, what I personally studied in Liberia." Travis's eyes were glued to Benji. "Tell her about your art, Benji."

"Better to see than talk about. My thing is painting. Inspired in Nigeria. I have a flair for color." He fingered his light blue and red patterned scarf. It was colorful, and gorgeous, but not the way Guatemalans put colors together at all.

Benji had a sweet dignity, a noble aspect. What a completely different kind of young man, but so—stunning. She thought about her niece Julina and her creativity in making her own colors.

There were other languages, too. "*Eka ta minto le?*" Travis said. "Or, as some of you plebeians say, 'Where are you going?' That's Mandinka to you." He flirtatiously pushed Benji's shoulder. Under his breath, but loud enough for Petra to hear, he said to Benji, "Damn, why are you so enticing?"

"*Se iwo maa ba mi jo?*" Benji answered with a cock of his head. "Will you dance with me? That's Yoruba to you, mister master of languages." He grabbed Travis's hand and pulled it to his lips, kissing his fingers before he let go. Yasmin turned up the volume of the music. Benji gently pulled Travis into a slow dance. The vein in Travis's neck pulsed. His teeth tugged on his bottom lip. Benji elevated his chin and a smile reached up to his eyes.

Yasmin stood before Petra, blinking her long lashes at her, smiling, and narrowing her eyes. Petra swallowed and took her hand, and all at once everyone was dancing. While Petra tried to emulate the others, she thought about the dances in Las Leches, where only "bad" girls went. Where Señor Menendez's daughter was picked out and almost killed.

Somehow none of that seemed to apply here.

Yasmin leaned into Petra and explained, "Travis learned Mandinka because he lived in Liberia for a couple of years. And in Paraguay, and Vietnam. He's an embassy brat—his mom works for the U.S. Embassy, so he moved around a lot. Yoruba is Benji's tribal language, but he learned Spanish here in Providence, in middle school. Not perfect Spanish, but pretty good for an African."

Yasmin's lithe movements fascinated Petra. Her limbs and the braid down her back both swung loosely. Her glasses perched on her nose. Petra got lost in the pools of emerald behind the glasses.

Petra tried to keep up with the haphazard dancing, shifting partners, eyes batting, parted lavish lips, doing her best to imitate the others. The Dominican girl—Petra couldn't keep everyone's names in her head—led the less graceful Travis in a salsa of short quick steps, her hips and upper body swinging with her feet, her long thick eyelashes beating slowly against her cheeks.

Then a familiar song came on. She recognized this singer. It was like the song she had heard at Vicenta's store. Yes, it was that same singer she heard at Vicenta's store that night! The gravelly voice, the references to indigenous cultures.

Soy centroamericana,

tengo la sangre de Hunahpu, la vision de Xbalanque,
lleno mi bolsa con la luna de Ixkik,
entrelazo la cesta del mimbre con la luz de Ixchel,
amarro la cosecha a mi espalda con el lazo de la selva,
la que el jaguar me protege en el Aq'ab'al.[2]

Benji noticed her double take. "What's up?" His soft voice fit right into the fragile hollow of her mood.

"This singer! I heard her before in Guatemala."

"You like? She's pretty unusual. For us offbeat kids."

"Sorry, but everyone seems pretty unusual to me right now. How do you mean 'offbeat'?"

"Some people think we're weird. I'd say extraordinary. I think you fit right in. I'm happy you came tonight." Half in Spanish, half in English. His face opened up in a wide smile.

Embarrassment that she only half understood Benji made her face turn red. Benji's glittery eyes flashed sweetly at her, inviting her to relax with him. "Don't worry," he said. "It's all good."

The music quieted, and everyone spread out on the floor. Yasmin said to the Dominican, "Girl, you need to teach me how to do those moves."

"Anytime, Yasmin. I'll dance with you anytime." Her cheeks folded into a dimple, and she extended an arm to show how short Yasmin was compared to her. "You know our Club has a dance coming up at school soon. All kinds of sweet music. Merengue, salsa, bachata, cumbia, even some American music—hip-hop and stuff."

"I'll go if Petra will go with me," Yasmin said coyly. Their eyes locked, and Yasmin slipped a sweaty hand into Petra's. Behind her, she heard Benji draw his breath in a low whistle.

"I'd love to go anywhere with you all, but what's your club?" Petra said.

Benji answered, "The Club, with a capital C, *señorita*, is where it's

2. I am Central American,
   I have the blood of Hunahpu, the sight of Xbalanque,
   I fill my bag with the moon of Ixkik,
   I weave the willow basket with the light of Ixchel,
   I tie the crop to my back with the rope of the jungle,
   From which the jaguar protects me on Aq'ab'al.

at. That's where all the cool and extraordinary people I was talking about hang out." He winked at Yasmin and Petra. "I might just attend that dance."

Yasmin said, "The Club puts on dances where anybody dances with everybody. Lots of times it's two girls together, or two guys, or girls who dress like guys, or guys who are almost but not quite as charming as Benji here." Her eyes flickered with delight toward Benji.

Benji cocked his head and smiled proudly, batting his eyes. "Travis, you going?" There was an edge of hopefulness in his voice.

"I'm not sure, man. My mom wants to travel to D.C. that weekend. Hard to say. Hey, I thought your dad doesn't like you to go out to the dances."

"There's a lot of things my father doesn't want me to do. I have to decorate my face," he said, delicately touching the corner of his eye, "out in the street, after I leave home. Can you believe he doesn't like the way I dress?" He laughed.

Travis said, "You know you look a lot like your dad, though, right? I can see you as a chieftain like him in Nigeria. You have that same proud bearing."

Benji answered, "Ah, the struggles of being the son of one's father…. Being so alike despite all the differences."

Travis said, "As I say, *Eka ta minto le*. The teenage struggle. Just a thought to keep in mind."

As she sat there, Yasmin whispering into her ear, Travis handed her a glass of punch, scooped out of a big pot. Petra didn't want to advertise her ignorance by asking what was in it, and the enchanting drink found its way to her lips. The sweetness rolled smoothly down her throat. Fruit drinks had never felt so warm before, but then everything was different here. It definitely wasn't pineapple or guava. It was light pink, with a slightly pungent smell, and so silky in her throat.

Petra wondered what Yasmin would look like if she unbraided the hair that hung half-way down her back. Her close-fitting jeans accentuated her nicely muscular thighs, highlighting the curves of her body. Yasmin pursed her lips and pulled her fingers back to her wrists. She looked directly at Petra, out of the corners of her eyes. Sweat began to bead on the skin behind Petra's neck.

Well, she wasn't the only one, at least, who didn't understand Mandinka and Yoruba. Conversation ensued in Spanish and English, back and forth, in and out of languages, ordinary words fashioned into kaleidoscopes of ever-changing shapes. The five of them participated with an almost unconscious amusement as the words spilled out playfully.

Yasmin seemed to know without Petra telling her when she didn't understand what someone said. Yasmin's breath was warm on her neck when she inclined to whisper to her.

Petra sipped on her drink over the next hour or so. She felt warm and relaxed, safe with these people, and descended into the floor a little. She tried to keep her eyes from rolling back into her head. Bright yellow wall to wall carpet was soft under her thighs. A velvety image of Jesus hung on the wall. Sprightly shadows of the kids leapt around the room in the flickering candlelight.

Petra sat on the floor, practicing words that floated through her mind. "*Eka ta minto le.*" "I think you fit right in." "Some people think we're weird, I'd say extraordinary." "Embassy brat." Enthralling words, enthralling people.

Then they passed around a sweet incense, wrapped in a thin paper. Yasmin sucked on it, and the smoke rose around her. She held up the cigarette to Petra's mouth. Petra had never smoked before, but this was more like an herb than a cigarette. It smelled light and earthy. It looked homemade, not like the nasty Marlboros her uncle smoked in Guatemala. Petra puffed graciously.

The television from the back room droned in and out of her consciousness. Petra wondered why Yasmin's parents didn't come join them. Her upbringing kept tugging at her to go in and make polite conversation with them, but Yasmin and everyone else ignored them, so she stayed put.

Then came brownies for dessert. Even the chocolate here in the U.S. tasted different. In Guatemala, she'd never tasted chocolate in cakes like this. Everyone was having such a great time—giggling, laughing, dancing, hugging.

A few bites later, Petra sank down on her side on the floor, her hand propping up her head. The music swirled around her. Her new friends moved around and over each other. Words unraveled in conversation

Petra no longer tried to follow.

Petra laughed and laughed. Her voice bubbled out of her. She wasn't sure why, but she loved these people utterly. Benji's head rested on Yasmin's stomach, then Yasmin rolled over to lean against Petra. The warmth rose from her feet up to her head and settled in her mind. A hand massaged the back of her neck, and Petra no longer knew up from down.

That's when the cool night hit her, and Benji stood next to her. She didn't remember how she'd gotten outside from the living room floor, but he seemed to think they were in the middle of a normal conversation. He stood next to her, with his arm wrapped around her, supporting her. Blurred good-byes passed by her as Travis disappeared through a car door, and others walked off into the night.

Benji said, "Nice kickback, right?"

"Kickback?".

"Like a nice party, fun get together with our squad," Benji explained.

"Ay, Benji, maybe stick to Spanish. Squad?"

"Sorry, I use a lot of slang. Means our group of friends."

"Where is Yasmin?" Petra wanted to say good night and thank her for the evening.

"Well, I did see her stagger off to her bedroom after you gave her that farewell hug. You guys seem to have a nice thing going."

Struggling to remember any hug, Petra bundled up close to herself. "OK, I guess I'll thank her when I see her at school on Monday. Benji," Petra looked at his glittered eyes tenderly and directly, "I've never known anyone like you all. Like you. What makes it all so different?" She wasn't feeling at her most articulate, but, somehow, she felt Benji had the answers she was looking for.

Benji stood erect with his hands clasped behind his back, proud and proper, while his face emanated a disarmingly carefree warmth. "Difference is what makes life interesting. Don't you think?"

"You are not like anyone I've known before is." Petra was surprised at the way these words came together. She was also surprised to find herself on the street talking to her new friend Benji.

"Don't take it too seriously, Petra. You can get fooled by what's on the outside." He wrapped the wonderful scarf around his neck. "You'll be all right walking home?"

"Sure, Benji. I'm fine. It's only a couple of blocks." She was surprised to hear her voice coming from someone else's body. "I never met an African chieftain before. Do they all wear blue eyeshadow?"

Benji's shoulders shook with laughter. Petra giggled. Then they couldn't stop laughing. They parted on Elmwood Avenue at her block, and Petra continued down toward her house.

Through the blur that enveloped Petra's brain, impressions of Yasmin merged with images of Vicenta and Novina. Matronly dress, unruly gray hair, weathered hands gently cupping a coyly curved neck. Smooth, luscious skin of honey, succulent lips, eyes as penetrating as a falcon's, emerald pools for wading. Novina touching Vicenta, startled into jumping off the stool, ample breasts unbound on her chest. Yasmin lithely scooping Petra's body within her own. A quiver of anticipation rose into her chest.

Then it kept rising, less pleasantly, into her throat. Nausea roiled her stomach. Her head was swimming. She leaned over, almost falling, then threw up into the bushes next to the sidewalk. Her throat felt dry and suffocating. Petra sat down, just for a moment, in the night under the streetlight that hid nothing. Almost immediately, she began to feel better.

"*Hola, muchacha!*" It was a familiar voice. She turned her head up and tried to focus.

"*Ay Dios.* Tell me it's a mirage," Petra said. Emilio stood over her. Now of all times. The gods were playing with her. Or was he following her?

"Petra. I've been hoping to see you. Not necessarily in this way." He glanced toward the bushes and sat down next to her. His eyes searched her, reviewing his knowledge of her, repositioning her in new surroundings.

Petra moved to get up. Emilio offered a hand. She ignored it and stood on her own. "I'm okay now. See you later." And she started to walk off.

"Hold up, *muchacha.* Talk to me." Emilio pulled her up from behind with a hand on her shoulder.

Petra flung herself around and flipped his hand off her. "You think anything's changed, Emilio? It hasn't. You're still the same gang monkey you became years ago. Try to convince me you've changed! I'll give you ten seconds."

Emilio's forehead furrowed into a disturbed frown.

"Sorry, time's up. I gotta go home now." Petra was in no mood to sympathize with Emilio. But the scenario was all too familiar. She had to draw a line right away. She'd go back to Guatemala rather than put up with him following her around and menacing her again. "What are you doing out at midnight, anyway? Hanging with the Providence hoods now?" As soon as she said it, she realized he could easily ask why *she* was out at midnight.

"Actually, I just left the auto body shop where I'm working."

"You seriously want me to believe that? You're working in the middle of the night?" Of course he was trailing her again.

Emilio twisted his mouth and sighed. "Look at the car grease all over my hands, Petra."

Begrudgingly, she looked. He did look pretty dirty.

"Your mom helped me find this job. My boss is an immigrant, too—Dominican. We're lucky to have a lot of work. I've actually been coming home about this time pretty often. Give me a break, Petra."

"Why should I?" Fiery indignation rose up and turned her cheeks red. Her hand reached out to the fence to make everything stop spinning, though her mind felt icy sharp.

Emilio deflated, and his shoulders sagged visibly. "Maybe you shouldn't. I don't deserve it, really."

"In that last talk we had in Guatemala, you neglected to tell me you were going to the U.S. to look up my mother, didn't you? You think I'm going to forget about everything that happened now that we're here, and make friendly like my mother's doing? My mother has no idea about you." But the darkness on the street tamped down her words. The dust hid itself under the grass. The bitterness seeped out into the night.

Redness flooded through Emilio's face and neck. The veins in his neck throbbed. "Petra, you know what I've been doing here? I slept on a bench or under the bushes in the park over here for weeks, hoping to run into your mother or Lucas—the only people I knew in this entire country. I was eating grass, Petra, pushing the duck feathers out of the way to drink from the lake."

More slowly this time, Petra turned and began to walk toward her house. *Ay caramba*, only a few houses beyond Emilio's. Maybe he would walk behind her and make sure she got home. She wasn't about to ask for his help, but her stomach wasn't feeling so good.

She didn't slough him off this time when he steadied her by putting his hand under her elbow. "Petra, you're sick. Let's get you home now, and we'll talk tomorrow. We need to talk, really." Thankfully, he didn't ask why she was out so late.

When they showed up together at Petra's door, her mother hurried over to greet her. She was wide awake, worry written across her face. Shock overlaid the worry when she realized her daughter *and* Emilio were coming through the door, apparently voluntarily together.

Petra separated herself and headed for the bathroom. She left the door ajar so she could hear.

Her mother said, "Your friend Lucas left a few minutes ago. He came by to show me some messages on Facebook. Can we talk tomorrow?"

"I'll come over in the morning if it's okay. I'd like to talk to Petra again, if she'll let me."

When her mother said nothing, Petra poked her head out the door. Her mother put a hand to his shoulder. His dark eyes lingered a moment, then he turned and headed down the stairs.

CHAPTER TWENTY-EIGHT

The next day, Petra woke early but stayed in bed with her math textbook. She was methodically working her way through the book. She started with the problems assigned to her class near the end of the book, but then returned to the beginning to ingest the background. She worked three times as many problems as the teacher had gone over in class. Math was a little easier because there were more numbers and less English involved. The book weighed in her hands, and her head throbbed with a headache like she'd never experienced before. How sick she had gotten last night, and a major headache today—as if she was a drunk!

After math she tackled English. New vocabulary swirled in her head, along with past participles, irregular verbs, strange spelling rules. For three hours, nobody disturbed her behind her closed bedroom door.

The work was grueling and time-consuming. Her pen flew across pages, practicing, copying, working through problems without regard to how many pages she used up. She had only a few weeks before school let out for the summer. She planned to watch some television later in the day to work on her comprehension in English. She needed more English to tackle that intimidating biology text.

Mid-morning, her mother knocked on her door. Petra was beginning to recognize her mother's style. Gentle taps to respect her privacy, caressing eyes to probe what Petra was about at any given moment, and a lightness of step to keep everything from getting too serious. Her mother sat down on the bed next to Petra.

The events of the night before came spilling out of Petra. She told her mom all about the gathering—about the herbal cigarette she'd tried, about the flirtation between Benji and Travis, about the music and the words that enthralled her. She left out a few details about the dynamic between her and Yasmin.

"*M'hija*, I can see you will be teaching me about things I have not yet experienced in this country." Her mother was peering at her intently, searching out who her daughter was in all this.

"Everything is so new, mami. I don't know how to fit myself in."

"There's time, Petra. Go slow." Her mother glanced around Petra's bed, taking in all the books, pencils, and papers covered with scratchings. "On the other hand, with all this work around you, maybe you're adjusting just fine."

"But my head hurts. Maybe it's too much." Petra propped up her head with her hand and rubbed her forehead. After so many years of not knowing her mother, how could she feel like such a familiar presence? Her mother perched next to her on a new, soft bed, surrounded by her schoolwork—it was uncanny how natural it all felt. Her heart opened to her mother's words of gentle guidance.

In Guatemala, her mother said, people sat and mulled things over, and change came slowly. Look at the violence—Nonno had grown up in the violence of war, her mother had fled domestic violence, and Petra had to cope with gang violence. It did change, but it also stayed the same. In the U.S., people worked hard, moved fast, and things changed constantly.

Her mother stared vaguely out the window. "But when a person has just arrived in this country…" Her eyes embraced her daughter, and her hand pushed a lock of hair back from Petra's face. "You need to take it slowly. You can't do everything at once. Give yourself time to get accustomed, to understand things."

"I miss home in Guatemala, and I don't miss it. Everything going on here—it feels exhilarating. There are so many possibilities."

Her mother leaned back against the wall. "Clearly your experience here will be different than mine has been. A couple of things I can share with you, though," her mother said. She pointed out that Petra had not consumed mere brownies last night, but rather pot brownies, with marijuana in them. The herb in the cigarette was also marijuana. And the drinks were certainly laced with alcohol. "So you got sloshed last night." And now Petra was feeling the effects. "But Petita, you must have had some idea what they were offering you."

Petra had been so busy trying to understand the kids. She was paying such close attention, trying to understand the English, and the other languages. She'd never met people like them.

Her mother nodded. "It was easier just to take what they offered."

"*Sí*," Petra admitted.

Then her mother filled her in on some background. She explained that, a couple of years ago, the highest court in the U.S. said that gay men and women had the right to get married. Two men, or two women. "Do you understand, Petra? Something practically unheard of in Guatemala is the law of the land here."

Petra was amazed, though she considered that it was not completely unheard of in Guatemala. Her mother's education on this subject had begun when she caught the tail end of a march in downtown Providence the previous summer. At the head of the parade, big hulking women dressed in leather rode motorcycles, followed by wisps of men in purple dresses dancing in the streets. And so much more she'd never imagined. But the real surprise, she said, were the crowds of people cheering for them, throngs at the park festival after the march. "It's a new world here," her mother said, "and the kids at your school are growing up with so many new possibilities. I know the kids are playing with culture and language. I guess now they're playing with gender, too.

"Your friends are playing with gender as much as they play with culture and language. It's the kids who are creating new definitions."

"When will my head stop spinning?"

Her mother laughed. "You do get used to it. But it'll take some time."

Petra wanted to learn everything. She planned to study all weekend and looked forward to taking a break to watch television with Wyman. She asked her mother, "Do you think I can learn English by the time school is over?"

"Petra, it will come. You don't have to force it. They'll probably ask you to go to summer school, so you have some extra time."

She could keep learning all summer long!

"One more thing: The choices here are endless and can overwhelm someone new to it all. Choices of everything—from apples in the supermarket, to music, clothes—and sexuality. Just remember who you are. Think deeply and consider where you want to go."

Petra leaned her head against her mother's shoulder, her head tilted up toward her face. "That's what Travis said last night. That the teenage struggle is all about finding out where we're going."

"The only problem is that it's a lifelong struggle. It never ends." For a minute, her mother stared off out the window again. "But if you forget to think about it, you can end up in a dilemma like Emilio has been struggling with."

Petra sat up, and her teeth clenched at the mention of Emilio's name, but she ignored it for now. The choices were inspiring. She was out of practice with friendships, but it felt different in the U.S. She could search out the places between the rules here, challenging and exciting places. Her mind was turning upside down, but that seemed like a good thing.

Her mother's face turned ponderous, as a frown swept across her forehead. "Petra, before you came in last night, Lucas came over."

"What'd he want?" she grumbled.

"Play nice, Petra," said her mother.

"Ay, I'm not ready to deal with gangs again, mami."

"You and I, we're going to talk soon about forgiveness and moving on in one's life. But for now, I need to tell you about what Lucas said."

Her mother would have to hear about what came before forgiveness first—all the evils carried out by Emilio's gang. Petra held her head, so she could bear what her mother wanted to tell her.

Lucas had shown her mother a threatening message he received on Facebook. Apparently, he hadn't realized he was still connected with some of the X-14 gang members from Guatemala. Petra sat up. Gusano had not given up. He was demanding that Lucas turn Petra and Emilio over to some gang in Providence.

"Gang in Providence?! But there can't be any X-14 gang in Providence!"

"He didn't say, but the MS-13 is here. These people know each other."

"But—here there are police, aren't there? Why didn't he call the police?"

"He did. Actually, I did, for him. He was too scared. I called them last night when you went to bed. They said they would come to his house to talk with Lucas this morning."

A banging on the door made Petra jump. Emilio let himself in.

Before Petra could adjust to the idea of Emilio in her home, he was already sitting at the kitchen table sipping on some coffee. Her mother was just like Nonna, always wanting to bring Emilio under her wing. Nonno had given Petra the impression that her mother took after him, with all his charm and mystery, but so far, Nonna's naïve regard for wayward men appeared to be the strongest influence. And yet—her mother seemed to know her. No one had known her quite that way before.

Emilio was saying, "Do you know that the cop spoke Spanish? I think he's Puerto Rican maybe." That darting glance returned to Emilio's eyes as he talked to Petra and her mother. Petra got that he was nervous.

Emilio said he was trying to understand the right way to handle this situation. Emilio and Lucas were astonished by the detective's respectful attitude toward them. But apparently he couldn't do much, because Lucas didn't know who the gang connection was here.

Worse, though, Gusano and Emilio's father were also contacting Emilio. He'd gotten a message through Facebook that scared him, so he got rid of the message. The next day he decided to delete the whole account. Then they wrote to him on WhatsApp. He changed his phone number, and they found the new number. Now he'd gotten yet another message, and he was getting desperate.

He held out his iPhone for her mother and Petra to read. His hand was shaking.

Petra read, "'This is your final warning, piece of s—. Delivery of the girl is overdue. We'll tell you where to make delivery. As for you, don't think you can walk away from us.'" Petra's headache was getting worse.

Emilio claimed he didn't know who had sent the message but was pretty sure it was either Gusano or one of his minions.

Petra buried her head in her hands. Her head was on the verge of exploding. Her mother looked between Emilio and Petra, searching for the next step. Petra threw back her chair and stood up, ready to bolt from the room.

Emilio stood and held up a hand to her. "Wait, Petra, we have to talk.

Come outside with me for a few minutes. Please?"

Petra's mother nodded to her. "I'll be right here, Petita."

Two heads hanging low, they walked like a couple stewing over a huge fight. Surely Emilio didn't think they were going to be friends or anything, not after he had treated her like a piece of meat! One he could chew on at his pleasure, pump up with drugs, drag off to wherever he felt like, and leave to the mercy of his slit-eyed friend! To Emilio she said, "Pardon me if I don't hand over all my trust, Emilio."

Repulsed by the vision of him standing guard as they took Justina away, she lagged behind Emilio. On the other hand, he did seem different here, walking along a sidewalk under the maple trees. He looked pretty good in American blue jeans. His face had softened. Black grease still stained his hands.

"Talk to me, Petra. It's the only way we'll ever get past it." He glanced at her briefly, but his gaze lacked conviction, and it kept sliding down to his feet. That same discomfort with himself had drawn her to him as a child, and it made her lower her defenses against him now. By being uncomfortable in his skin, he somehow let in different ideas, like accepting Petra even when she broke the rules for how girls should behave.

Petra's eyebrows came together in a moment of puzzlement. She shifted into higher gear. She kept her voice down, but a fierce anger fueled her whispers. He'd thrown away their friendship, and instead gone down some god-awful path to perdition. "You left, Emilio! I didn't even recognize you anymore! You could have turned to me, Emilio. My grandparents and I would have stuck with you."

Why did it feel like his gang life was in the long ago past, when it was only far away in distance, not time? Space was making time stretch. She fought off any softening toward him.

Emilio slowly raised his hand to her face, wiping off a tear that had accumulated in the corner of her eye. She flinched inside but stood stock still. He seemed to take it as a sign of encouragement. "We were too young, Petra," he said solemnly. "I wanted to keep you as far away from the viciousness as possible."

"Well, I guess I was too young to lose my best friend!" Petra walked off several paces ahead.

"Dammit, Petra, listen to me. Look at me! I have to get this off my chest, and you have to listen! Please, Petra."

Reluctantly, Petra nodded.

He paused, visibly gathering strength to put the words forward. "I didn't want to steal or hurt people, but he beat me, Petra, if I didn't do what he said. He started to treat me the way he'd always treated my mother. And my mother couldn't get in the way and take it for me anymore."

For once, Emilio looked directly into her eyes, as if he were begging her to understand. He had never talked to her this way before. She stared at him, dumbfounded.

"He told me I was worthless, and forced me to take cocaine, the way he'd done to my mamá. Until my father succeeded, and I started wanting the stuff on my own." With sudden force, he sniffed air into his nose as if the rush would fortify him. "Dammit, I was only ten or eleven then."

Petra moved toward him to interrupt, but his face begged her to listen. "I can't keep hiding what happened. For the sake of our childhood, please." They had circled the block and were standing on the sidewalk close to Petra's house. He sat down on a ragged stone wall, shifting side to side to find a comfortable spot. Petra stood to his side, arms folded across her chest, staring off across the street. Occasionally she glanced back at Emilio as he spoke.

"Remember when I stole that meat from the butcher at the market, and you ran after me? When I showed my papá what I'd stolen, I thought he'd finally be happy with me. I felt ashamed to have betrayed the old butcher in his ancient leather sandals. I knew him—he'd been at the market every month since I was a little *patojo*, traveling hours from his home in the mountains to make a few sales, shuffling in carrying that fold-out table with sacks of meat on his bent back, desperately smiling at all the people because he never learned to speak Spanish."

As far back as her memory took her, Petra, too, had known the old man Emilio was talking about. She remembered the look of dismayed resignation spread across his face when Emilio ran off with his slab of meat. And she remembered her own disillusionment as her childhood friend and his gang continued to cause pain to so many people.

"My conscience hurt so much. I knew it because it pounded at my head every time they ordered me to do something bad, and I started to get terrible headaches. But I had to do it to get my father's approval.

"When I showed my father the meat, he slapped me across the face, told me I was a piece of garbage, that any five year old could steal a little item like that." He ordered Emilio to demand money from that butcher every week to get a stream of income going. "I did it because I wanted the beatings to end." Emilio lowered his eyes.

Petra gulped the air. She thought about that moment when Emilio's mother was dying and he shoved her away. She had felt betrayed, rejected, but his circumstances were so much more complicated.

"When my father decided his beatings weren't enough, he brought in Gusano to intensify the punishment." Emilio was trembling, holding back. He swallowed hard. "So I tried not to feel bad for people anymore. Do that for a while, Petra, and you forget how you used to think. You forget who you are."

Quietly, Petra said, "Did you ever think about our friendship, Emilio?"

He shook his head. "There was no place for friendship. Whenever I cared about something, my father crushed it. It was better not to care about anything."

Petra sighed.

Emilio continued. He tried to crawl his way up in the X-14 so he could take charge of his own life. At the next month's market, he threatened that old butcher and anyone else who looked like they were selling a few things and making a little money. He stole it all from them. And if they didn't give it to him, her sent his father or Gusano to make good on the threats. Finally, Gusano stopped whipping him. Soon, his father made him bodyguard to the young guys trying to recruit more members. "Working my way up, right?" His mouth contorted into a pained smile.

Petra felt her heart melting, just a little. She sat down next to Emilio on the uncomfortable stone wall. But the biggest question plagued her. She had to know. "Why Justina, Emilio? Why?" Now her tears came running out. Petra tried to hold her breath to keep herself under control. They sat on the wall in front of her house.

Emilio sucked in his breath. His head turned away from her. "Not yet, Petra. I can't talk about that. Not yet." He shook his head as if shaking off the poison.

They climbed back up the stairs to Petra's apartment.

Her mother was still sitting at the table when they came back in. Emilio sat across from her, but Petra was too agitated to sit. Quietly, Petra said, "How did Gusano find you here, Emilio?"

Emilio said, "I don't know. I never thought they'd follow me here."

Standing behind her mother, Petra's hands curled into tense fists. "You called them, didn't you?" she asked accusingly.

Petra watched Emilio's knuckles go white where his fingers sat on the table, tightly laced together. His head rocked slowly back and forth. Her righteous anger dropped a notch. "Goddamn Potoo has a son who's something like twelve years old. He goes back and forth between his mother—I don't know where, near New York, I think—and his father in Guatemala. He was born in the U.S., so he's valuable to them because he can travel back and forth. Both of them are raising him in the gangs the way my father raised me. It's another link between the X-14 and the MS-13. But if our gang is hooked up with the MS-13 now, they can find anyone. Those guys have computers and tracking devices and networks of *orejas*. They have more money than they know what to do with. The spies—they'll do anything for them."

If Emilio was really trying to leave gang life behind—which she still doubted—his lifetime of experience could help them. Petra hesitated, but she couldn't just hide behind ignorance. "Do you think they know where I am, too?"

Her mother closed her eyes. "*Ay Dios.*" Petra's heart was doing somersaults.

Emilio looked not just somber but grim, his mouth taut, his eyes leaden. "I think they would have contacted you already if they did. They're thinking I know where you are though. Me they found because they started off with my phone number and information through Facebook. Are you on Facebook or Twitter or anything yet?"

Petra sat down between her mother and Emilio. "Nah. I was hoping to figure it out this week with some kids at school." She pulled the new phone out of her pocket and stared at the screen as if it contained the answer.

Her mother said to Emilio, "What did the police tell you?"

"The detective gave me his number. He said to call if anything happens." Her mother wrote down the detective's contact information.

The atmosphere in the room sagged as if the air had completely deflated. None of them knew what to do. Emilio went home.

A black cloud enveloped Petra. She slid to the edge of her chair. She wanted to scream. The tension created rigid cords down her neck and tightened the muscles around her heart. The intensity of the anger boiling up in her surprised her again. Before she had found this island of relative peace, she had been afraid sometimes, but not so utterly incensed. She had never wanted to confront her elders. Here she thought she'd found a bit of tranquility with her mother and Wyman. Where was all this anger coming from?

"How could you do this to me, mamá? You brought me all the way here, but you invited the gangs to our doorstep right behind me!"

Her mother took a deep breath. "I trust that we can keep you safe, Petita. Emilio and Lucas deserve a chance to have secure lives as well. As long as they are on an upward path, I want to help them."

"Do you even care what I went through in Guatemala?" Petra felt the burning behind her eyes.

"I do care, Petra. You know I do. But you don't move on by burying your fears and never facing up to them."

Petra's face turned red. Tears began to form in her eyes. Her mother thought she knew what she'd been through, but she didn't. "Emilio has haunted me since he killed Justina."

"He didn't actually kill her, did he?"

Smoke blew out her ears. Hearing this from her mother was ten times worse than when Nonna had said it. Why did her own mother pay more attention to Emilio's needs than hers? When she had gotten frustrated with Nonna, she had always thought at least her mother would understand. "Do you think it matters? He was there! He was protecting the gang members that took her!"

"That happened so long ago, Petra. People do terrible things, but they can still —"

Petra interrupted. "But he never stopped! He harassed me all the time. He would stop me when I was going to church or school and flirt with me in a nasty, sick way. He threatened to hurt me if I didn't become his girlfriend! He punched on Carlos to get to me."

She hesitated to tell her mother more, but if she didn't do it now, she never would. Her palms were wet with sweat. "And then just two months ago he kidnapped me, mami. He took me to a horrible place with his gang buddies, where nobody could hear me or find me, and they wanted to feed me drugs and rape me. They wanted to force me into the gang." Petra's chin trembled. She drummed her feet on the floor so her legs wouldn't shake.

Her mother was quiet. She folded her hands over her mouth and sighed. "Petita. This I didn't know." Her mother stood with her hands in her pockets and shuffled into the living room and back to the kitchen. Awkwardly, she squatted down next to Petra and tried to hug her. Petra pushed her away and gave her a fierce glare.

Her mother sat down, holding her head in her hands. "Maybe I have pushed you too fast, Petra."

Petra scoffed. "I can't deal with all this, mamí." The blood had drained out of her face, leaving a closed mask to stare at her mother.

"Petra, there's something else going on here. It's mixed up in this problem around Emilio. Let's talk about it."

Petra opened the refrigerator, quickly glanced inside for something she could chew on, and closed it again. She opened the cabinet, took out a cup and filled it with water from the faucet, then put the full cup down next to the sink. Empty-handed, she went into the living room and flopped on the armchair there. She had no doubt what her mother was referring to.

Just a few steps behind, her mother followed her, as Petra knew she would. Her mother asked Wyman for a few moments alone with Petra, so Wyman disappeared into their bedroom. They sat together, Petra aloof, her mother looking uneasily at her own hands.

Loaded silence hung between them, until Petra's resolve to say nothing cracked. "I waited so long, mami. I still remember when you left, you said you would send for me and Carlos soon. It's been *ten* years."

"Ten *long* years, Petra. Every single day of those years I tried to figure out how to get you here with me. It hasn't been easy for me, either, Petra." Her mother shifted to sit on her legs and tucked her dress under her legs. "There're also a few things about me you don't know."

Petra said nothing, but her eyes challenged her mother to make it good.

"There's something that happened that I haven't told anyone about, Petra, not even your Nonno." Her mother twisted and folded her hands in her lap and popped her knuckles. Petra winced. "For the longest time after I came here, no one heard from your father. This was a great relief to me, and I assumed he just went on with his life. But one day, after I'd been in Providence a couple of years, someone knocked on my apartment door shortly after I got home from work. I was shocked to see Xavier's face on the other side."

Her mother's voice quivered. She had all but memorized this story for Petra. She must have been imagining this conversation for some time.

Her mother continued. "I had been so lonely, Petra, you can't imagine. I missed you and Carlos every day, and I was always trying to find a decent job so I could send you all a few dollars. Honestly, I was hungry a lot. Your sweet five-year-old face was suddenly there, right before me, in his cheeks, in his nose. Your angelic eyes are from me, though. He doesn't get credit for those." She smiled, her eyes distant. "Apparently I have a weak spot for men who apologize and say they want another chance."

Petra interrupted. "You and Nonna both. Hello, Emilio?"

Her mother nodded. "If it wasn't for Nonna, I wouldn't have married Xavier so young, *seguro que no.*"

"And she would've had me marry Emilio, despite everything."

"*De verdad?*" Her mother's eyes reviewed her own memories in the back of her head. "*Pues sí*, I can imagine that. I'm glad you didn't, Peta. And won't."

"So you invited my father in?"

"*Sí*. He'd been in Los Angeles for a few months. He checked with friends in Las Leches and got hold of my address here." Her mother rubbed her forehead. "We lived together for three years."

"What? You never told me you were living with my father! For three years?"

She had been too ashamed to tell anyone, her mother said. And she didn't want to give Petra any more bad news about her parents. For a little while, she remembered why she loved her father when they married. But soon enough, the bad Xavier came out again, and she couldn't believe she had let him back into her life. "He got crazy jealous. He flew into a rage if another man looked at me on the street, or if I was five minutes late coming home from work. Soon he wouldn't let me go out at all, except to work—he did want my money. I couldn't even talk to you and Nonno unless he went out for a few minutes. I was afraid to call the police because they might have sent me to Immigration. I was desperate to find a way out. But then… I got pregnant again."

"What? You had another baby?"

"No, no, I didn't. When I got pregnant, Xavier started beating me again." Her mother's fingers probed the scar on her forehead. How many other scars did her mother have, hidden from view? She thought he was going to kill her, she said; she was terrified all the time. All her energy went into keeping him calm, trying not to upset him. "I lost the baby, Peta, when I was six months pregnant. She would be five years old next month if she had lived."

"*Ay dios*, mami. I would have liked a little sister."

"I've made some bad choices, Petra."

"But—is he gone now? What happened to him?"

When she lost the baby, she continued, the nurses found out that he'd beaten her. He was arrested and went to jail for around six months. It turned out there were people at court to help victims through the process, and they didn't call Immigration. She got a restraining order so he'd go back to jail if he came near her. "I think he went back to Los Angeles. I haven't heard from him again."

"In case you're wondering, I have no desire to see him." Would she see herself in her father? Maybe someday, after she established herself here…

"I was pretty sure," her mother nodded. She didn't really get back on her feet again until she started studying for her CNA license. "Then I met Wyman."

"And I came."

"Which proves the people at church were right. Never give up. The church group has helped me a lot, *m'hijita*. I've learned some things about moving on after suffering abuse. But you know? I have learned this about myself. Once a man says he's sorry, I bend over backward to help him." So now she was trying to orient her volunteer work so other people were involved, to help her see the bigger picture. She just wanted, she said, to do what she could to help Guatemalans not repeat the cycle of violence and trauma over and over again. This was a big topic of conversation at her church meetings.

Her mother said she hoped Emilio would agree to join the community group working with ex-gang members. "But in the meantime, I feel that I owe this to Emilio, Petra. Try to understand. The way his mother died…. He never had a chance." She scratched her neck and brooded a moment. "Tell me what happened that day, Petita. I want to help."

Petra slouched down in her chair. Abruptly, she shot up and headed for the back door. She said, "I need to go out, Mami. My head is on fire." She didn't wait for a response.

As she bounded down the stairs, she heard her mother's voice trailing behind. "Use that phone if you're going to stay out long! Call me!"

CHAPTER TWENTY-NINE

Petra turned toward Broad Street so she wouldn't have to go by Emilio's house. She wandered in and out of the neighborhood blocks before she headed to the main street.

Her hand bumped along the top of a chain-link fence. Branches of a big pink magnolia tree drooped over it, and shoots of new grass lined the small yard. Blades of grass and weeds broke up the long rows of cement bordering each side of the street. Cement sidewalks bordered the paved streets. It struck her again—so little dust, so few ashes.

A tree grew here and there, butting into and around the electric wires strung between long wooden poles, high above every block. But it was early June—the trees were in bloom. Every now and then she spotted an iris or a cherry tree, or the sweet aroma of a lilac bush would waft in her direction. She watched her feet kicking little stones into the street and thought about Carlos kicking rocks on the road to Las Leches. Not a one jacaranda tree.

A sharp edge of the fence cut her finger. She swore at it. What was this new feeling of irritation? She'd never even been tempted to swear before.

Shards of a shattered car window covered the weeds that clogged a sewer and crunched under her feet. She was so tired of thinking.

She started jogging, then faster, running through the streets. A stray dog turned its head to watch her go by. A squirrel disappeared up the back side of a tree. A group of teenagers hanging on the front steps of a house yelled out, "Go, baby!" She flung herself forward, the wind rushing across her ears. She shut off the faucet of thoughts.

- Can I come with you?

Petra didn't see anyone, but she shook her head wildly back and forth.

- Go away!

- Petra. It's me.

The voice was so calm, piercing the distress. She listened.

- Oh. Alocinia. Where have you been?

- Your mind has been so full. I couldn't find a crack to get through.

- I thought maybe you stayed behind in Guatemala.

- Everything is right here, you know. Nothing stayed behind in Las Leches. It all came with you.

- You're wrong. The Siguanaba, the coyote and the hen, the spider monkeys—they all stayed.

- Even Itzamná is here. We are all your creations.

- I can't feel Itzamná. The spirits are all diminished.

- The sun still follows a path from light to darkness. The dew still shrouds the morning growth. Part the seas, Petra. Without water, you will drown. The sea can bring you back.

- Water—the stream—means death. Justina.

- No, Petra, it can't. It doesn't. Water transforms. The Creators destroyed the imperfect humans they created in a flood. But then Ixchel prepared the way for the final creation, the Fourth Sun, by pouring waters from her jar. The dew from heaven lies on the ground every morning, transforming us, laying the path of renewal.

- Noah's ark and Ixchel. I did also love the stream.

- Ixchel's moon is here. In her weaving, her whirling spindle was at the center of the motion of the universe. The jaguar melds your inner instincts with the spiritual forces. Don't forget that he helped reveal your subconscious fears and allowed you to transform them. The jaguar, too, is here. The process continues.

- Xibalba. It was in my dream.

- You see, you have brought it with you.

- It screamed out at me, pressured me. It taunted me with my fears.

- You must know your fears to transform them.
- There is something in me that's holding me back. What is it? I can't find it.
- What have you failed to look at?
- In the dream, there was something. I turned my head away.

Petra stumbled on a section of driveway that had bubbled up over a tree's roots. Now she had a skinned knee and a cut finger. An overflowing metal garbage bin shoved behind a Latino grocery store sheltered her while she gathered her wits.

Half expecting to hear Potoo's voice emanating from inside the store, instead she heard a Spanish voice straggling down the street, telling her companion that her son preferred to drink with his buddies than go to church with the family. A window glinted in the sun. The sharp edge of Potoo's knife flashed in the open field, then stung against her neck. She started, then swung her arm out as if fending off someone. The screen door at the back of the store rattled in the wind.

Inside the store, Petra strode down the aisles. The San Luis Hunahpu market was here, too, in this cramped and dank place. Had it really *all* come with her? The yuca, batata, jícama, malanga, plantains. An assortment of chili peppers, three kinds of bananas.

And oh! The rolls of *Galletas Marías* cookies, from Vicenta's store! She pulled some bills from her pocket, and the cookies found their way into her ownership.

As she pushed the door out to the street, she eagerly ripped open the wrapping. A dark-skinned youth stepped aside to let her out, and she looked up to excuse herself.

"Benji! What are you doing here?"

"I live a block down. Hey, watch where you're going there, eh? Here, I'll take one of those." He snatched several cookies.

They walked together for awhile down Broad Street, munching, relieved to have each other for company but absorbed in their own thoughts.

The wide, flat avenue offered Petra a vast open view of South Providence. She imagined MS-13 spies planted on corners with orders to search for her. Up the expansive avenue the morning sun reflected off the plate glass window of a Spanish clothing boutique and a check cashing store. Raucous Guatemalan male voices riffled through the air from the auto body shop sheltered behind wire fencing. Perhaps they allied themselves with gangs as a second job, and they were arguing amongst themselves about their next target.

When they passed a popular Latin dance club, shuttered for the daylight hours, she wondered if gang members tried to flatter and recruit young women there. The ever-present litter strewn all over the sidewalks intimated its own stories. Crushed cans and broken bottles succeeded drunken fights. Kids in flight from threatening phantoms abandoned the now torn pages of homework.

To the north, the avenue led downtown and to their school. A haven of diversity, the street radiated activity ranging from festive to sinful to downtrodden. An elderly African-American man clattered past them pushing a shopping cart and mumbled, "Got change for the bus?" A group of young men gathered around the Dominican food truck, apparently more interested in socializing than buying.

Petra's eyes dashed about, vainly searching out menaces. A worker at the self-service gas station yelled at a customer who refused to pay cash up front. Flowers shielded by their plastic wraps concealed a frail young woman who sat quiescently on her stool waiting for buyers. A sprightly man with a long ponytail hurried up the path of an imposing historic building to its front door, which was adorned with a symbolic Native American headdress. A car's horn pierced the din of traffic as it tried to cross two busy lanes to make a U-turn.

Petra tried to keep her anxiety under wraps, but when the horn made her flinch, Benji turned to her with concern and put an arm over her shoulder.

The brakes of a bus squealed, and it puffed to a stop in front of them. Impulsively, Benji grabbed Petra's hand and led her on board. In the seat in front of them, a burly woman held a bag tightly to her side, a toddler flopped over her shoulder. Dried mucus framed the girl's nose, and her big black eyes fastened on them. Petra smiled and reached a hand to touch the tips of the girl's fingers, which brought forth an eager grin.

After a few moments, Benji unpacked his backpack and began to apply blue eyeliner to his eyelids, flares of yellow in the corners. Raptly concentrating on Benji's movements, the girl playfully covered her mouth with her fingers. Dark mascara lengthened his eyelashes, which he swatted coquettishly at Petra. The girl's stubby fingers tugged on her eyebrows. He added a bit of glitter for emphasis around the eyes. The yellow eyeliner delightfully accented the lightened ends of his short afro. Black honey lipstick balanced the dark red, blue, and yellow patterns of a West African scarf.

Little girl lips smacked together in amused imitation. Benji's hand glided to his neck to smooth the scarf around his shoulder. With the army fatigues on his lower half, his style was complete. Sufficiently embellished, he nodded with satisfaction, sat back, and looked to Petra. The girl's head bounced up and down, and Benji laughed.

The bus crawled through downtown, its buildings hovering over them. Petra's relative smallness somehow gave her comfort. Out the window, men and women, almost all of them walking alone, were dressed in dark suits. Hunched over and preoccupied, they traversed the slow-moving river that cut along the edge of downtown. The bus slowed to let two students pass. On their heads, they balanced long strips of sheet metal. They headed up to North Main Street.

Benji said, "Sorry to be so distracted for a few minutes, sweets, but now I feel presentable."

Petra smiled. "Personally, I can't take my eyes off you."

"You're very gracious." Demure but ever coy, Benji cocked his head to the side.

Soon they were only a couple blocks from Travis's house. Benji steered them out of the bus and up the hill. As they climbed, he texted Travis.

"He's waiting for us on his porch," Benji said.

By the time the three of them entered Swan Point Cemetery, the cookies were gone. The boulevard leading to the cemetery contrasted distinctly with the sights of Broad Street. Solemn, sturdy homes bordered the splendid avenue. A middle aisle lined with green flowering trees streamed with runners and strollers and dogs of all sizes and shapes on leashes. Bicycles flowed along the sides like droplets of water down a shallow arroyo. Recently fallen cherry blossoms blanketed the ground beneath the leafy trees which stood guard at the cemetery's front entrance.

The three teenagers sauntered through the stone gate and continued down a lane of magnificent oak trees, noble giants which protected neat rows of military gravestones.

"Gosh, this isn't a cemetery, it's a grand park! Look at all these trees!" Petra exclaimed.

Travis began to spew out some of the facts that filled his brain. He told them that the cemetery had been here since the 1840's, before the Civil War. Before any of the houses and roads to the west. The owners of the land had the whole boulevard constructed, as well as a stone shelter and a trolley that took people along the East Side and down the hill to the center of town. "Check out these gravestones, and the statues and mausoleums all around. Veterans from the Civil War up to the recent wars in Iraq and Afghanistan usually get the smaller plots. Rich and famous people in Providence's history get the really big markers."

Benji said, "How do you know this stuff? I know you have a thing for history, but really, sometimes it's just… impressive."

Travis said he liked to spend a Saturday at the Providence library, where he had found fascinating archives about how Providence developed. He told them that a century before the cemetery grew up, in 1739, the first business—Hoyle Tavern—opened in the West End behind their school. Since King Philip's War it had been farmland, with Long Pond right in the middle. Then…" Petra was lost in the unfamiliar English and local history.

Benji interrupted, "Whoa, man, sometimes your photographic memory gets away with you." He looked toward Petra and switched to Spanish. "Sometimes this guy talks too much. We have to keep him under control," he said, smiling at Travis. "He remembers everything he reads, Petra. Photographic memory. This is something you need to know if you're going to hang with Travis."

"I guess I know who to go to if I have trouble with schoolwork," Petra said.

"Anytime. But don't ask me anything about math," Travis said.

At the eastern edge of the cemetery, they began to descend the curving hill to the Seekonk River below. Alocinia silently mouthed the words, "Part the seas… The water can bring you back." If the water parted, perhaps she could escape to freedom.

Petra sprinted down the hill, drawn to the river as if it were her own meager river in Las Leches. But this one was wider—much wider.

Boulders lined the edge, and she scrambled up to reach the water. The water was too far to reach and, worse, smelly muck rode up the sides of the boulders. The stink of dead fish forced her to back away.

Benji came up behind her and saw her disappointment. "Yeah, it's kind of dirty." His eyes scanned the river. "Look at the swans out there!"

Petra was enthralled. "*Ay! Qué bello*! I've never seen this kind of bird before. There's two of them, swimming together."

"They find a mate and stay with them for life. There's a pair in Boston that've been together for like fifteen years or more. They call them Romeo and Juliet, but it turns out they're both female—Juliet and Julieta. They try to keep the lesbian relationship part quiet, but word has gotten out, I think." Benji laughed.

Travis yelled from down the road, "Come on, guys, let's go down to the boathouse. It's not so smelly down there."

By the time Benji and Petra got to the boathouse, Travis had untied a rowboat and pushed it off the dock into the water. He said, "People come here to go sculling in really long skinny boats. They're in those long sheds. But no one's around today. Fortunately, they also have this rowboat, 'cause those sculling boats are tough." Indeed, the place was deserted.

They piled in. Placing himself in charge, Travis took the oars. Benji lay in the middle, facing backward, in Travis's direction.

Travis's face lifted toward the sun, his legs extended out on the floor of the boat. His muscles rippled as he pulled the oars. Benji followed his every movement, and Travis basked in the attention while pretending he didn't notice. Benji glanced at his own thighs at the spot where Travis's now bare feet leaned up against them.

Petra sat in the front, looking out at the water ahead, sitting very delicately, afraid to rock the boat, but fascinated by the view. As they glided upstream, Alocinia pointed at the bow of the boat parting the waters. Furrows of water glanced off the sides. In the windless day, their boat dispersed the water into shallow waves which glinted and crinkled in the sun.

Petra ruminated. Her mind continued to race, trying to keep up with herself. Perhaps these were new friends, the first friends she'd made for so long. Did she really want to allow them in? But how could they understand where she came from?

If Benji's father was a tribal leader in Nigeria, perhaps myths helped form him, too. Travis covered himself up with facts and history, but she sensed complex undercurrents. She was amused at the idea of Emilio meeting Benji. Now that would be interesting. Macho former gang member meets gender-ambiguous, delicate African immigrant.

Somehow she would need to open herself to new people if she was to find her place in the world. The path must entail finding that grace of God, and the hearth of the Mayan gods, inside herself. Faith implied trust and sprang from making progress against everyday mortal struggles. Like reconciling herself to the multiple roles Emilio played in her life.

If God is most apparent when we feel that we are mortally insufficient to the world, or that the world is mortally insufficient to us—then when we are wrestling with earthly challenges, that's when we're working out the meaning of things, the God behind everything.

It was too easy to shield herself from others, when she might really be struggling against her rescuer. The priest in Las Leches had given a sermon some time ago when he talked about how the members of God's community have many roles. As a community, the many are one body in Christ, and individually, we are members one of another. For the Mayans, community was everything. People had to rely on each other not only to survive, but also to create joy. Each person was made stronger by drawing on the talents of the members of the community.

Perhaps Benji and Travis had come to her life for a reason. Could Emilio be her rescuer in some unexpected way?

When she put her hand in the water, the water divided again, swirling past on either side of her palm, just as it rushed past the boat's bow. So the sea was parting—how was she to go through? All she felt was resistance against her palm, where the escape route should lie.

Her brain sank deep into her skull, leaving a throbbing vacant space. Her thoughts thudded against her cranium, tired of grappling and skirmishing. Her headache, she realized, had dissipated.

Benji interrupted her reverie with a pat on the shoulder. He inhaled from what looked like a pen, then handed it to her. She started to refuse but changed her mind. She breathed it in, more deeply this time. It had a pleasant, sweet taste. She inhaled again and reached behind her to return it to Benji.

Petra considered the waters parting before her, and Alocinia, her hummingbird. Messages from her heart to her soul, from the underworld to Itzamná.

When she was very young, Nonno had told her a Mayan legend of the hummingbird. It came back to her now. The pen inhaler continued to make the rounds.

Her mind was lighter, drifting around like a butterfly in the breeze. In a voice as softly musical as the lapping waters, she said "This is so beautiful. Do you see all the colors in the ripples? The green, blue, red, yellow, playing in the sunlight?" The air had become luminous, weightless. Without that sensation, she wouldn't have the gall to talk about her world of myth. "It reminds me of the most beautiful bird in Guatemala, my favorite. It would visit me and the hibiscus flowers in our front yard. The hummingbird has been like my guide. Travis, you know a lot of history. Do you know the history of the hummingbird?"

"Um, no, I don't think so. History of the bird?"

"The real history. How she was created. Do you want to hear the Mayan story?"

Travis nodded. Benji put his hand out dramatically toward her as if presenting a famous movie star. She handed back the smoking pen and turned to sit on the front seat. She hoped they would understand the tale in Spanish.

"When the gods created *el colibrí*, she was so small and delicate but could move her wings at lightning speed. No other bird could fly backward and hover in one spot. The hummingbird's feathers were dull, but she took pride in her flying skills. When it came time to get married, she was sad that she had no bright jewelry or gown to wear. Her friends decided to help." As she found the rhythm of the story, she became a silver-tongued spinner of yarns.

"The flycatcher gave the crimson ring of feathers he wore around his throat. It became the hummingbird's necklace. The bluebird donated blue feathers for her wedding dress. The motmot offered turquoise blue and emerald green. The cardinal gave red feathers. The oriole, who was an excellent tailor and engineer, sewed it all together into an exquisite wedding gown. The spider wove threads together for her veil. Honeybees got together and brought honey, nectar, and blossoms to the reception. The *plumería* tree dropped a carpet of yellow and white petals on the ground of the ceremony. The apple tree, and the guava and papaya bushes provided fresh fruit and wine. Butterflies danced gaily at the wedding. She was so happy and thankful that the gods admired her humility and allowed her to wear her new gown for the rest of her life.

"The many are one, and individually, we are members one of another. Actually, that's from the Bible." Petra turned her watery eyes down, unexpectedly self-conscious.

When she raised her eyes, Benji was grinning from ear to ear, and leaning back against Travis's legs. Travis had stopped rowing, and the boat was drifting quietly in the water.

Benji said, "Your Spanish is so beautiful. It is mellow like the gentle plains of West Africa." He looked up pensively. "Our Yoruba people have rich mythology also. When I was a child in Nigeria, my Yoruba aunts and great-aunt told me many tales. I spent a lot of time outside my aunt's thatch-roofed, mud hut in the family compound of ten or twelve similar homes. She's the best story-teller for miles, so there was always a bunch of us kids sitting on the ground listening." Benji's eyes were peering backward into his memories. "While my aunt narrated, my great-aunt would fry up the *garri* from cassava—*gbágudá* in Yoruba—that had been ground and fermented. I will share the story of the parrot, *el loro*, called Odidere, or Ayekooto. This is one I remember best.

"Ayekooto means 'the world rejects truth.' In ancient times, animals and birds spoke and understood the same language as people. The parrot has special mystical powers that it still retains today.

"One ominous day, a man was visiting a farmer. While the farmer was out, he killed the farmer's buffalo, eating part of it and smoking some to store for later. When the farmer returned, the man denied knowing anything about the missing buffalo.

"The parrot told the farmer the truth. The farmer summoned the man to an audience with the king. Overnight, the man covered the parrot's cage, dropped water into it, and banged on the metal bars. The next day, the parrot was the main witness against the man.

"In his defense, the man claimed the bird could not be trusted, and he asked the bird what kind of night we had last night. The bird said that rain fell, and thunder kept him awake. At this, the king set the man free and banished the parrot from living among people.

"Hence the parrot was given the name Ayekooto, because it learned that telling the truth to humans would only create trouble. Now, it merely repeats what others say.

"Odidere can still master any word spoken and can remember to repeat whatever has been said in the past. Its special abilities give Odidere a home in royal palaces, but it is very difficult to find in the wild. One must travel deep into the thick forest to find it. It lives in the hole of a huge tree. The eggs of the Odidere are sacred and cannot be seen by mortals. As a symbol of the elite, it combines beauty and mystical attributes.

"I think..." Benji looked at the floor of the boat. "A man like me must always seek his beauty and his own truth, even if the world rejects it." Travis screwed up his lips, then his eyes twinkled down at Benji. Benji said, "I only go home to visit my aunt at Christmas-time now." He rubbed his temple with two fingers.

Travis stood suddenly, his feet spread apart to keep the boat in balance. Benji's head dropped back. Hastily, Travis reached down to catch Benji before his head hit the seat. He said, "I will remember these histories! And I also —"

Benji grabbed the side of the boat, and Petra pitched forward. The boat rocked to the side, and water dipped into the boat.

Benji used his shirt to dab splashed water from his face without mussing the makeup, but his pants were soaked. He scooted over to get his feet out of the water, and the boat tipped dangerously to the side. Petra hung on to the gunwale, but her weight lurched the boat over further. Her right side was drenched in water before Travis was able to right the boat by leaning over to the opposite side.

"Still, everyone!" Travis shouted. Order was restored. Petra laughed. Travis's shoulders shook with laughter. Benji held his sides and couldn't stop until he was doubled over. A small island of roaring laughter floated on the river.

Travis pointed to Benji. "You don't need to pee in your pants, man!"

Benji threw up his hands, forcing his breath in and out to get himself under control. "Yeah, so how did you manage to stay so dry, huh?" Benji pushed Travis in fun, and Travis slipped backward, his legs hanging over the front of the seat. Benji grabbed his hand to pull him up again.

After a moment of calm, Travis said, "Seriously, now that I understand your meaning, Petra, I do know bird history. The phoenix appears
in Greek, Egyptian, Native American, and Chinese and other east Asian
cultures, so this is an international myth. I actually heard it from a
Vietnamese diplomat friend of my father's when I was living in Paraguay."

His voice rose like a strong wind but finished like melting honey. "A
young man named Huy decided to sell his greatest possession, a golden
pheasant. As he walked toward the city, he dreamed of a magnificent
future. He always imagined that the world was filled with color, light
and music.

"Minh saw the young man and couldn't help but notice his bemused
smile. He asked Huy why he was smiling. Huy said he had been dreaming of Phuong Hoang, the exotic phoenix, known for its virtue and grace.
Phuong Hoang combined yin and yang, male and female energy. Minh
asked if the bird in the cage was his Phuong Hoang.

"Huy looked at his prize bird and said, why yes, this was his Phuong
Hoang. Minh decided to buy the Phuong Hoang so he could give it to
the king and the king would reward him, because Phuong Hoang only
appeared in peaceful and prosperous times and so belonged in a royal
setting. He agreed to pay a small fortune for the creature.

"As Minh continued along, carrying the golden pheasant in the cage,
he told many people about his Phuong Hoang, and news reached the
king that he was to receive a wonderful gift. Sadly, when Minh woke
up after a night's sleep, he found the bird dead in its cage. He was very
upset, not at the financial loss but because he had wished to present it to
the king.

"Some days later, the king summoned him. Minh was very nervous,
because he had no gift to present the king. However, when he appeared,
the king bowed to him. He asked Minh to allow him to reward him for
the gift he wished to give, saying that his generous plan to give his king
such a wondrous gift was in itself a gift. He paid Minh twenty times what
he had paid for the golden pheasant.

"The eastern phoenix, Phuong Hoang, reigns over all the other
birds. The phoenix has the neck of a snake, the beak of a rooster, the
face of a swallow, the breast of a goose, the back of a tortoise, and the tail

of a fish. Its body corresponds with the celestial bodies—its head is the sky, its eyes represent the sun, its back the moon, its feet the Earth, and its tail the planets. Its feathers have five colors—white, black, red, green, and yellow. It sings with the five notes of the pentatonic musical scale.

"The phoenix is a link between our world and the heavens. Originally, there were two, a male and female who faced each other, but they were blurred into one feminine entity.

"The magical phoenix, radiant and shimmering, is born out of the sun and lives for five hundred years or more. When it is close to death, it ignites its own nest with a single clap of its wings, and it disintegrates to ash. Within a few days, the phoenix is reborn from the ashes. It symbolizes rebirth, regeneration, immortality and second chances. It hides itself when there are wars or troubles and appears only in places that are blessed with peace and prosperity, so it also symbolizes peace and beauty."

Travis ran his fingers through Benji's hair. "We had a peacock on the grounds of our house in Asunción. In my mind, it was the phoenix. While I was there, it disappeared. I asked my father where it was, and he said it was very old and had probably gone off to die. For weeks, I looked all over for a pile of ash so I could see it being reborn. One day I did find a pile of ash behind a restaurant nearby. The ash was muddy, because it had just rained, but there was a dip in the middle like a nest. So that's always the image in my mind when I'm looking for a second chance." He blinked at Benji.

A silence fell over the three of them. Slowly, Benji raised his head.

"Oh my but we have a lot to live up to," said Petra.

A thrill ran through Petra as she realized that these people could relate to her myths. She wanted to ask them what the stories meant to them, whether they were part of their lives. She wanted to hear their thoughts about what Itzamná and Phuong Hoang had in common, and what it all meant about forgiving people for doing terrible things and finding a divine spirit in their lives. But there would be time for that.

Travis said, "Thankfully we don't have to start from scratch. And the birds shall lead the way."

"Where's that smoke?" said Benji. "Hand it over, Travis. I say the fume and a little bit of merriment, *alegría y alborozo*, will help us find beauty and light."

By the time Travis could maneuver the boat back to the dock, Petra's chest hurt from laughing so much, and her mind wasn't sunken and throbbing anymore. Her thoughts swam pleasantly in the juices of her skull. The sun was starting down the other end of the sky now, drying their clothes and still warming their skins.

Travis locked his arm playfully around Benji's neck on the dock, pulling him down to his chest. When Benji looked up again, his eyes gazed longingly at Travis for a moment.

"Heave ho, my little hummingbird," said Travis. Together the three of them hauled the boat back onto the dock and tied it up.

Petra looked up first. There at the head of the dock stood a man, arms crossed over his chest, silently staring at them. Petra recoiled. She nudged Benji, who blinked several times, then scowled.

Inhaling noisily through the phlegm in his nostrils, the man said, "Who the heck are you taking this rowboat out? You got permission for that?"

Travis said, "It… it… it was my idea, man. Um, the water was calling to me?"

"Did the water call out the need to get permission to use a boat that's not yours, young man?" The man's cheeks were red with indignation. His beer belly swayed slightly as he paced the dock, and he held a cheap beer in his hand.

"I'm sorry, sir. I can pay you for the rental fee," said Travis. He kept running his hand through his hair.

"How about I call your parents, then, and we'll leave it at that?"

"It's my fault. You can call my parents," Travis tried again.

"And who are these angels with you? I do believe I saw three people in the boat." He peered more closely at Benji and Petra. "A white kid, a black fairy, and a Spanish girl, eh? I'm trying to keep my imagination in check." He leered at Petra, his eyes examining her from top to bottom.

Travis moved to put his body between the man and his two friends. "Cool it, man. The boat's not harmed. Here's my number."

The three dangled their legs into the water as the man called all the parents, and they waited and worried about what awaited. Above, a crackling in the woods that separated the cemetery from the steep hill down to the river drew Petra's attention. A not-quite-adolescent boy clad in white pants and white jacket stood, legs spread wide, at the top of the hill, looking for all the world like master of his kingdom. Her breath caught in her throat so she couldn't swallow. He stared down at her, smiling.

Faster than Petra could have imagined possible, Travis's mother appeared at the front of the dock in a sleek, sporty red car. Branches fluttered back into place where the boy had stood, his figure disappearing back toward the cemetery.

CHAPTER THIRTY

"*Ay mi Petita, qué has hecho?*" her mother asked as she wrapped her arms around her, cradling her head, leaning her forehead against Petra's. "*Pero qué?* What's that smell on you?"

The living room felt surprisingly comfortable, almost—like home. Nevertheless, Petra turned away from her mother with downcast eyes. "You know, right?"

Her mother nodded. "I do, yes. Petra, you get sloshed last night, and now again today?"

Petra said, "I'm not drunk." She actually felt a lot better than the night before.

"But why, Petra? You never so much as touched alcohol in Guatemala. We're not the kind of people to use drugs." Her mother looked as bewildered as she felt herself.

"I don't know, mami. But when I left here earlier, my head wanted to explode. And now I have two real friends, and I feel calm."

Her mother said, "Marijuana doesn't do that for you, you know. Nor does stealing a boat, by the way." Her voice turned stern.

Petra said, "I never thought it would feel so nice. But—it does scare me a little, too. It was so nice to be on the water, mami." She'd never seen so much water in one place before. And to float on top in a boat, it was amazing. "When I looked down, I couldn't even see the bottom!"

Her mother closed her eyes for a pensive moment. Petra knew her mother didn't want to disparage her experience when it had obviously made her feel so much better. "Listen, *chica*, if you're serious about working hard in school and learning English so fast, you're not going to have time for your brain to float around on marijuana. Sliding through the water is something else. Maybe you can learn to swim at the community center this summer."

"Where's Wyman?"

Her mother said, "He's in bed, Petra. He wasn't feeling well this morning. The social worker from the Veterans Hospital came over to help him out."

"*De verdad*? Is he okay?"

"Don't mention it to him, or you'll embarrass him. He uses a catheter, and a bag collects his urine, Petra. It's related to his spinal injury from the war. The catheter got clogged up. The social worker knew what to do to help. And she referred him to get some help for depression."

"Oh, mamá, I don't mean to give you more to worry about."

"You wouldn't say that if you knew how glad I am that you are finally here with me. You could give me any number of problems and I would just thank the Lord that you are here with me."

"I'm scared, mami. I'm afraid the gangs are looking for me." She told her mother about the boy watching her. She was ninety percent sure it was Potoo's son.

Her mother's eyes widened. "It's not the same as Guatemala, *mi cariño*, but you're making me worried that they really are looking for you. Don't forget, though, this is not Guatemala. There are all kinds of people to help here. The police, the church—different organizations that care about people like you and Emilio and Lucas, and they want to help. I think we need to have you talk to this detective." Her mother pulled the slip of paper with the information Emilio had given her from her pocket.

Slowly, Petra framed the words. "I might like it here, mami. Maybe. So many changes are coming at me. I miss things, but .... I think I have some friends who might understand me. I want to learn how to trust people again."

"Petra, I've been thinking. Life is asking a lot of you right now. To transition to a new country. To leave behind the life of warrior and protector and become a mere teenager in an imperfect but mostly peaceful community. To grow up and become a woman. I have regretted that I could not celebrate your *quinceañera* with you. But now I'd like to plan some kind of gathering, like a rite of passage, to help guide you in these transitions. We can invite a couple of your friends, whoever you want, and make it up as we go along. But I have some interesting Mayan ideas for it."

Images of jaguars and Itzamná, Xibalba and the ceiba tree, the Siguanaba and Ixchel poured through her mind. Yes, she wanted. How she longed for the home of the myths, for the forests, for her Nonno.

They agreed to hold it in June, as soon as she finished school.

CHAPTER THIRTY-ONE

Hushed mutterings roused Petra out of a book. Her head was popping from two hours of inscrutable biology and almost as obscure math. She sat in the big cushy living room chair, her legs folded up under her, her lap and the arms of the chair covered with school books. It was Sunday, the last day of the weekend to devote herself to her schoolwork.

The cheerful sound of her mother's hands slapping the *masa* dough and the soothing aroma of onions, garlic, and tomatoes cooking in a pot of beans drifted from the kitchen, where her mother was preparing beans and tortillas for the coming week. Wyman was resting in their bedroom.

"What's that noise?" Petra asked.

Her mother held onto the door frame and leaned into the living room. "I don't hear it."

"Like a chattering. Are there mice here?"

"Never saw any. Not even a cockroach."

Petra jumped up, scattering her books, and wandered around, poking in a niche behind the television. "What is this, mamá?" Five tiny people made by hand from clay stood there, like little goblins dressed in traditional Mayan clothes. "The *aluxob*! I didn't know they were here, too! It's like they're talking in little, tiny squirrel voices." Several nuggets of corn tortilla lay in their niche.

"Oof! I didn't realize you hadn't met yet." Her mother came over and cradled two of the group in her hand before introducing them to Petra.

Swelling her colorful traditional Mayan dress, a tiny woman's breasts sat atop a rolling tummy. Her hands held tightly to her thighs, and her eyes turned up toward Petra from under a pointed cap. The little man wore a long, furry beard that draped over her mother's hand. Crouching in bare feet in her palm, two bony hands held the sides of his head, which wore an expression of offended consternation. Their movements were subtle, but they were not inanimate, not to Petra's eyes.

Her mother did after all have Nonno's Mayan spark in her.

"I leave a piece of tortilla or honey for them every morning, so they don't become disgruntled or create mischief. We especially need them right now, I think, to keep the household from harm."

Petra said, "At home in Guatemala, they were on the shelf in the kitchen, not hidden like this."

"Ah, but the *aluxob* are rarely seen. We must ensure their privacy."

Petra held out her hand, and the offended *alux* crept onto her hand. She said to her mother, "You realize they are talking to us, right? But look at the expression on this little man!"

"I don't hear anything, Petra," said her mother. She looked carefully at Petra. Petra felt her mother's eyes as if they were passing through her skin to share Petra's sensations. "Wait. I do. I hear a tiny murmuring. Oh my Lord, I have never heard that before."

"Something is not right. They're trying to warn us." Petra glanced sharply around the room and quickly replaced the *alux* in its home behind the television.

She bolted over to the window to check for strange men. "I think the gang is close! It's Potoo's son leading them here, mami. They know where I am!"

Wyman rolled out of his room to see what the commotion was about. Her mother sank down on folded legs to the kitchen floor in front of the bean pot, her forehead in her hands, concentrating, thinking. "There's no one out there, *mi amor*," she said. "Peta, we're going to see the detective tomorrow. There's no need—"

Petra said, "Really, it's obvious, isn't it? Emilio has been in here a couple of times in the last two days. His old buddies in Guatemala are demanding that he deliver me to them, so he's saving his skin and giving them what they want! One way or another, he plans to lead them here!"

Anger draped itself around her head and squeezed out other thoughts.

Petra tore out the back door, bounded down the stairs and down the street. She banged on Emilio's door. Her mother followed close behind her, leaving Wyman in the middle of the living room to puzzle out the meaning of the uproar and to finish cooking.

Lucas opened the door. Petra screamed, "Lucas, I have to see Emilio, right now!" She was breathing hard, gasping out the words.

"He's gone, Petra. They took him this morning—"

Running up from behind, her mother said, "Who, Lucas? Where is he?"

"Some guys from a gang here. I already called the detective."

Blinded by fury, Petra interrupted. "You mean he went off to arrange to give them what they want!"

"Petra, *tranquila*." Her mother pivoted away from Petra. "Lucas. No!" she exclaimed.

Petra looked at Lucas. His deep-set eyes were sunken with a dark purple circle around the right eye. The skin of his forehead was torn, and dried blood ran up toward his temple. The area around his right cheekbone was swollen. He dabbed at his eye with a wet washcloth.

Lucas gave Sorelly and Petra chairs, and he recounted the events of his Sunday morning.

It all happened while Petra was safely ensconced in church, attending to a homily about Jesus on the cross who, with his last breaths, pleaded, "Father, forgive them; they know not what they are doing." While Jesus suffered, the crowd mocked, cheered, jeered, hurled insults at him. The leaders hated him with a fierce passion and were happy to see him die. Talk about difficult circumstances in which to offer forgiveness.

Lucas said that three guys had barged through the door when Emilio peered out to see who was pummeling it. The edge of the door clipped him on the side of the face, throwing him backward. Two of the men rushed toward him, waving around a knife and a gun.

Lucas threw himself on top of the bigger guy, and the gun whipped across his face, cutting his cheek near the eye. The guy froze Emilio in an armlock, and two of them pulled him through the door and pushed him into their car at the curb. One lingered long enough to tell Lucas not to call the police or tell anyone, or he'd be the next one to die.

"They didn't take me because they knew I'd answered the WhatsApp message. I told them I'd go meet with them. Here's the address they gave me. Emilio was trying to talk me out of it."

Petra had one thing in her mind. "Did he tell them about me?"

Lucas said, "What about you?"

"They want Emilio to take me to them!"

"I don't know Petra. They didn't say anything about you this morning."

Her mother tried to intervene. "Petra, calm down. We don't know—"

Petra interrupted. "Emilio would so easily use me to save himself!" Petra didn't wait for the answer. She fled out the door.

A creaky blood red bicycle was leaning on the wall of the basement. Petra had noticed it when she carried some boxes down there for her mother. But then she had immediately turned away, because bicycles made her feel dizzy. For a moment, she was nine again, gazing at the dusty, rusty red bike with its colored streamers hanging from the handlebars, how Emilio's thumb twisted to the side to ring its bell. How he tore down the road like Chac, reborn as a conquering warrior.

Now she raced for the bike, hauled it up the stairs, and straddled the seat. She closed her eyes to settle the sick feeling that spread over her, said a short prayer, and wobbled forward. By the end of the block, the wobbling straightened itself out.

Remembering that her phone had an app for maps, she squeezed the brakes hard, so hard that the back wheel lifted off the ground, so she had to steady herself again. Impatiently, she fumbled with the phone and poked at the screen, which wouldn't cooperate. She took a deep breath and forced herself to stand still, until she finally got the directions out of Google maps. Then she hurtled onward to the West End and the address on the message Lucas had shown her.

The one-block road was tucked between a short highway and a busy street in a run-down neighborhood. The three houses on the block were surrounded by trash-filled abandoned lots, a set of squat garages, and a Dominican auto mechanic at the corner.

Petra spotted the house number on a small rusty mailbox at a four-story apartment building. The building listed noticeably to the side on a crumbling foundation. An old white Toyota pick-up was parked in front.

Around back, the door was ajar. She steadied herself and climbed up the dark passageway, alert for sharp noises. Without the sound of a crashing chair, a thrown body, or a gunshot, she hadn't a clue which door to open. She picked the third floor because she could see through the crack in the door. Just as she quietly pushed the door open, she realized she had no plan, no idea what would happen next.

As she crept over the threshold, there seemed to be no one home. Then she heard the rumble of men's voices from the far end.

The apartment's layout was similar to her own—the kitchen just inside the back door, behind it a living room, then the room fronting the street, where the men were talking. In her apartment, that was now her bedroom. Off to the right, a recessed hallway with a bathroom and another bedroom.

Petra crept soundlessly into the hallway, out of the line of sight of the men, and scanned the space, closing the bedroom door soundlessly behind her. Emilio was lying face up on a filthy mattress on the floor, his arms tied to the radiator behind him.

With a wry smile, Petra whispered, "In trouble again, eh, Emilio?"

He tried to smirk at her, but dried blood cracking around his mouth froze the expression on his face.

"Did you already tell your buddies where to find me?" She almost spit the words out in rage.

"What? Petra…. No!" Emilio looked confused.

"Funny boy. I know they're looking for me, Emilio."

"While they were hauling me off and beating me, they didn't mention you, Petra. They seem to have a gripe with people who try to ditch their gang loyalty." Emilio grimaced. "Does it look like I'm with buddies, Petra? What are you doing here? You shouldn't be involved in this. These guys have a stack of guns and knives, and lots of friends. They're just taking a rest from playing with me to take in some beers. Or something stronger. They'll be back soon."

Petra leaned over Emilio to loosen the ropes binding his wrists. She felt him stiffen with her closeness and inhale deeply. She whipped her hair behind her shoulder and glared at him. Behind the radiator, she spotted a heavy wrench. She pulled it out and let it swing from her hand near the floor.

Emilio asked, "How do you know they're looking for you, Petra?"

"I saw Potoo's son yesterday, Emilio. He had followed me clear across town."

Emilio raised his head in alarm. "He's here, Petra, in this apartment. I think he's gotten in thick with the gang here. I wouldn't be surprised if Providence is the training ground for the big stuff in New York."

Sweat lined her armpits and the back of her neck. She said, "Maybe we can sneak out of here the way I snuck in."

As soon as the words were out, they heard the clicking of a pair of boots on the wooden floor. She held out her hand to tell Emilio to stay still on the bed, though his arms were now liberated. She stood, legs apart, shoulders firm, her hands holding the wrench menacingly before her. A shadow appeared at the door. She readied to swing, arms raised, her palms sweaty around her weapon.

A pointed, stylish cowboy boot appeared first around the bend of the doorway. In a split second, she recognized it. The white pants and a white suit followed, attached finally to the face of a twelve-year-old boy—the same boy that had accompanied Potoo in San Luis Hunahpu. The same one she had seen from the boathouse. He still strode with confidence, as if he'd just dismounted from a rich man's steed. She wouldn't use the wrench against a boy, despicable as he may be. It clattered to the ground.

The boy gaped at her in surprise as she swiped her foot around his legs like she was kicking a soccer ball around the opposing team's forward. His hands caught himself in the fall, but he yelled out.

Emilio leapt over and grabbed him, putting a hand over his mouth, but the boy kept up a muffled shriek. Clacking and thudding footsteps approached the room, too many to count.

They slammed the door shut. Neither of them knew what to do next.

Through clenched teeth, Emilio hissed, "Shut up and listen to me, Luciano—"

A thud hit the door like a body thrown against it, interrupting whatever Emilio had in mind. Thumping, crunching, scraping, so many feet pounding the floors. Groaning, clicking of metal, pounding on flesh, tearing clothes. Shouting, screaming, then more authoritative orders. Emilio and Petra looked at each other. The boy had quieted down, as attentive as they were. Emilio let go of Luciano and placed his body in front of Petra. He was trying to protect her!

"Open the door! Police!" The door flung open to the sight of two cops pointing their guns, first at both of them, then just at Emilio. "You okay in here?" The female cop spoke abrasively to Petra. #2244 was pinned to her chest pocket.

How could the police have known to go to this apartment? Were they following her, too? The two police looked far more intimidating than any police she'd seen in Guatemala. Their manner brooked no doubts nor allowed any room for maneuver. They knew exactly what they were doing and intimidated with their absolute self-assurance. They wore thick leather belts laden with heavy weapons of various kinds and a phone that carried on speaking in scratchy tones. The male cop, tall and burly, shuffled over with his gun aimed at Emilio.

"Wait! He's the victim here! They kidnapped him. He's my friend!" Petra blurted out, sitting down now next to Emilio.

The word "friend" to describe Emilio had slipped out of her mouth without thinking. She put it in the back of her mind to consider later. This could have some significance. That old feeling she had when they were kids had come rushing back. She wanted to protect Emilio. His bottom lip was curling under.

"This one," she pointed to the twelve year old. "He's working with the gang. I saw him with a gang in Guatemala, too."

Guns lowered, the male cop took Emilio aside and began to question him.

Number 2244 raised her eyebrows and turned to the boy. "Yes, we know each other well, right, Luciano? Well, you've been traveling?"

Luciano answered testily, like they were disturbing his day. "I went to visit my dad, okay?"

Suddenly it was as obvious as the stars on a moonless summer night. Potoo had seemed too young to be his father, but of course Potoo had probably impregnated some girl as a teenager. A girl he was able to successfully conscript into the gang, apparently. Luciano had been learning the gang trade from his father, just as Emilio's father had indoctrinated him, but with an added asset, as Emilio said. Because he was born in the U.S., he could cross the border without a problem—undoubtedly very useful to the gang. And so it passed, from one generation to the next.

"Your dad helping you learn the international ropes in gang banging?"

number 2244 asked.

He grunted in haughty, pre-teen fashion.

Number 2244 said to Petra and Emilio, "We'll need you both to come to the station to give a report. You can each have a parent there with you if you want." 2244 and her partner walked Luciano and Emilio outside.

Left alone, Petra wandered to the front room. Below the window there, a swarm of red and blue flashing lights sent warning signals around the neighborhood. She looked around. Cops outside, cops inside. They busily filled little plastic bags with white powder and green leaves, knives and guns. On the street, there were so many police that some were milling around eating donuts, drinking coffee, making jokes. Five separate police cars each held one of the men, and Luciano, in their back seats.

Petra spied her mother talking to Number 2244, who was keeping a close eye on Emilio standing next to her. Of course—her mother! When Petra fled from the house, her mother would have called the police and given the address Lucas had given both of them.

Stepping lightly around the detectives, Petra ran down the stairs. How did she ever live without her mother's hugs? She melted into her mother's breasts as they stood in embrace in the middle of the road. Number 2244 smiled sympathetically. Emilio looked uneasily at his feet.

Neighbors from the nearby blocks, gathered in a circle behind yellow tape that had appeared around the house, stared at them. When Petra lifted her head and laid it on her mother's shoulder, she saw a woman with tears in her eyes, nodding to her. Her mother wrapped her arm around the back of her head.

Emilio refused a trip to the hospital once they let him clean up a bit in the bathroom of the third-floor apartment. Number 2244 took Petra, her mother, and Emilio to the police station. The officer informed them they would likely spend the afternoon there.

CHAPTER THIRTY-TWO

Petra's eyes swung around the cavernous entry to the police station. She was amazed at the size and somberness of the place. The policeman at the entry desk managed to smile and be completely stern at the same time.

Hallways and locked rooms jutted off in all directions. The clang of heavy doors echoed throughout the open chamber.

A Latina woman inquired in halting English where she could get an accident report. The officer answered in halting Spanish, incongruously friendly. Everyone scurried around looking busy—people still greasy in their work clothes, police in various shades of uniforms, little kids trailing their parents, people in suits and dour dresses. Heels clicked on the hard floor.

For hours, they answered questions. Because she was a juvenile, Petra's mother sat with her the whole time. The detectives interrogated Emilio separately and, with no adult in charge of him, on his own.

They talked to Number 2244, also known as Officer Quiroa, then to detectives, sometimes in Spanish, sometimes with translators, conversing with five or six officers of various ranks and duties before they were done.

Officer Quiroa pressed Petra on why the gangs were pursuing her and Emilio, even here in the U.S. Petra didn't hesitate. "They have a bottomless need to control women, for one, but it's worse because they were trying to impress the MS-13. I'm thinking they still are." She explained about her connection with the Itzamná artifact, and how the X-14 wanted to use it to buy their way into the MS-13. I don't know if they've given up on finding Itzamná yet." Her mother sat back and watched Petra take charge over the story.

"Then, too, Emilio created a reputation problem for Gusano. They need to show the MS-13, and everybody else, that they can keep their people in line, especially since Emilio's father was second in charge after Gusano. Punishing the two of us, even killing us, would send a strong message to anyone else who might try to escape from their demands."

Petra trembled when she described Gusano's tattoos. The officers and her mother encouraged her to take a break anytime she needed, but she wanted to tell it all.

She described her own abduction by Emilio, Potoo, and Gorto. At that time, she had convinced herself that she had escaped through her own ingenuity. She admitted to the police, and for the first time to herself, that she wouldn't have escaped without Emilio's assistance. Not only had the situation required more than her own wits and courage, but Emilio would have been her last choice if she'd had to pick someone to help her. But now she conceded. If it hadn't been for him, she would have been sexually assaulted, perhaps worse. The biggest surprise was the sense of relief that flooded through her as this realization came to her.

Her mother pulled her close, leaning against Petra's arm, and she felt her mother's heart beat next to hers. It was the first time her mother had heard the details of her kidnapping. The presence of the police broke up the intensity of telling her mother the story directly. But she was glad her mother knew it all now.

It was also the first time Petra had acknowledged Emilio's change of heart when he rescued her. Suddenly, the emotional agonies she had witnessed in Emilio that day at the cabin seemed significant. Perhaps that episode *had* marked the start of a major transformation in him.

Something about the gravity of the police presence encouraged her to delve beyond her emotions and dig out the truth. She persevered with her initial instinct to protect Emilio.

Late in the afternoon, a federal agent joined them. Inside, Petra panicked that they would be suspicious about the immigration status of her mother and her, and Emilio. For reasons Petra couldn't imagine, they never mentioned immigration.

The questions continued to roll out. They inquired about the gangs in Guatemala and their connections to the U.S.; about Luciano's father

Potoo, and Gusano, and Emilio's father, Fernando; about the planned meeting between Gusano of the X-14 and Mago from the MS-13; about Emilio's role in the gangs; and about the threats and messages in the U.S. The officers listened carefully when she told them about what Fernando and Gusano said when Emilio's mother died. They wanted to understand the relationships between the different characters involved.

The officers were so intent on gathering information about the gang world through her experience that she began to feel pride in her past experiences. She really did know a few things about the gangs. All those years of fear had led to this. When her mother beamed at her with pride, Petra glowed.

Nonno's advice about her mother reverberated in her mind: "You must bring her closer, Petrita. She is in your heart, much closer than you think. Reconcile your beginnings with your future. In order to accomplish your dreams, you must retrieve the seeds of your soul. And you will need a full soul to experience Itzamná." Itzamná pulsed in her soul.

Petra wept when she told them about finding Justina's body. She wasn't sure the killing was relevant to their investigation. But Officer Quiroa handed her a clean handkerchief from her own pocket, and they all listened carefully. The officer's hand was rugged, the fingernails painted lilac. She spoke to Petra as an equal. She trusted the federal agent, and especially Officer Quiroa.

The officer sat up straight and scribbled quickly on his yellow notepad when Petra described Potoo putting a knife to her throat, telling her Emilio was a dead man, and how she wondered about the boy with the boots and white clothes who was shadowing Potoo. She told them that Emilio had fled right after that to the United States because he had betrayed the gang by helping her. Now he seemed to genuinely want to leave that life behind.

"Why are you intent on protecting Emilio when he helped kill your best friend and put you in fear for so many years?" Officer Quiroa wanted to know.

Petra spoke carefully, considering every word. "I'm not sure myself. I've spent so many years despising him, I think the feeling is spent. I know he's here because he risked his life for me. He deserves a chance to set himself right."

Her mother squeezed her hand under the table. There was a new lightness in the air.

"Well, he doesn't seem to have committed any new crimes in the U.S.," said Officer Quiroa. "We'll give him support, but we'll also keep an eye on him. For many reasons, former gang members often go back to the criminal life."

Somehow all of these events spilled out of her, while she had told Nonno and her mother only bits and pieces. The officers took the gangs' threats against her seriously. Something had changed, and the recounting was changing her. A tangible self-respect was seeping in. All the trials with Emilio and gangs had left her with a certain kind of strength.

If she could help the authorities tamp down the power the gangs wielded over their victims, she was willing. Proud to play a small role in providing valuable information to the police, she also, for the first time in years, felt safe—not the false bravado kind of safe when she told everyone how confident she was, but the real security of having some perspective on the whole thing, knowing that she was more than all those fears.

Petra got the feeling that these police were not controlled by gang payoffs. The gangs' power over her, she understood now, was diminished in the U.S., where the authorities actually had some control.

She kept imagining Emilio sitting in the next room, talking about his experience with the gangs. She found herself wanting to speak up for him, so they wouldn't judge him too harshly. They had both been traumatized by the X-14 gang in Guatemala. A new bond with Emilio grew in her mind, as they shared the struggle to recover and start new lives in this new country.

Before they left, an officer called the Nonviolence Institute and gave Petra and Emilio contact information. They could both get further support there, both psychological and practical aid, especially for Emilio, in separating from the gangs and creating a new pattern of daily existence.

Petra left with the name and number of the detective in charge of the Providence Police gang unit. He told her to call him if anyone from the gangs, in Providence or Guatemala, sent her a message.

As they were leaving, Officer Quiroa whispered to her that she should call immediately if Emilio ever threatened to harm her again. "No one will call Immigration. They need your help too much, the help of other immigrants like you, to tackle the gang problem here." Her eyes moist, Petra looked directly into the officer's eyes and held out her hand. They shook hands.

CHAPTER THIRTY-THREE

Wyman had two of the *aluxob* in his lap when he wheeled his chair into the kitchen upon the arrival of Petra, her mother, and Emilio. "They have been thoroughly reprimanded," he said.

Petra squirmed. Anger had blinded her completely. "The *aluxob were* chattering, though," she said, humility knitting her eyebrows, blood rushing to her cheeks.

Her mother summarized the high points of the afternoon's adventures for Wyman's benefit. "All's well that ends well." She laughed. "It's a new expression in English that Wyman taught me. *Bien está lo que bien acaba.* But it sounds good in English."

Wyman put the *aluxob* in her mother's hand. She said, "They're a playful lot. Maybe they were upset that I hadn't introduced you properly. Remember I said they create mischief and scare children when they are perturbed? Guess they scared you, Petra. They have good hearts, though."

Wyman looked fondly at her mother and reached out for her hand. She stood next to him with a hand on his shoulder. The few wisps of hair on his head shifted with his movements, and the folds of his neck twisted as he turned to Petra.

He said, "You, *ma petite*, are made in your mother's image. You hear what others can't, and your heart runs very deep. My dears, I'm glad you're both home and safe."

Her mother said to Wyman, "Are you sure you're willing to put up with the two of us, creating trails of havoc wherever we go?"

Wyman said, "If you'll have me, I am humbled to have both of you in my life. But," he stopped himself, "I do have an important program to watch on television now. It's the new season of *All the King's Secrets*. The King had his wife's head chopped off at the end of the last season. Must to see if the bishops and his people will forgive him."

In their absence, Wyman had finished cooking up the rice and beans, so the three of them sat down to dinner, while Wyman turned to the problems of the king. Her mother and Emilio chatted, her mother making a valiant effort to calm the spasms of the day. Petra remained silent through the meal, until her mother tenderly elbowed her. "*Qué hubo, m'hija?*"

Petra looked up, her watery eyes betraying the toil within. "There must be a better way to express how I feel. I'm sorry, Emilio. I've been arrogant and closed-minded. And I leapt to judgment today."

Emilio's eyebrows shot up; his brown eyes widened. "Do you realize you've been saving me since we were kids? You're still doing it."

Petra spoke carefully but decisively. "Now. We need to finish the story now. I've got to know—tell me about the two days with Justina." Her heart pounded against her chest. She received her mother's look of concern and nodded back, closing her eyes to keep her heart in place.

Emilio held his breath, then released it slowly through his mouth. "It was the last stage of graduation into the gang. The point, I hoped, where I'd move from being beaten up all the time to being the one on top. If I wasn't promoted along the path set out by the gang leaders, I would never be safe. My father had made me a bodyguard when I was about fourteen, and I had to start recruiting new people for the gang—boys and girls, about twelve years old and up.

"But finally, Gusano directed me to target somebody personal to me, somebody that mattered. I had to prove I had a heart of steel, that I'd do whatever it takes, and I was prepared to obey no matter the cost. It had to be you, or Justina."

Her mother gasped. Petra said, "Me or Justina what? What did you have to do?"

Emilio said, "Are you sure you want to hear this?"

Petra said, "*De veras*, no. I'm not sure. But it's hanging over me, Emilio. I can't face it until I know what it is. Maybe it's the same for you?"

"Yeah. Maybe. I don't know how to live with myself anyway." Emilio hesitated, visibly searching for the strength. "Sorelly, do you have any beer?"

Her mother said, "Sorry, Emilio. Nobody here drinks. Some tea?"

Emilio nodded. "So, I was bodyguard to Chato and Pinza, a couple of short-tempered guys. The two guys who were with me when we found you and Justina at the river. The plan was to take Justina back to Gusano's place, and convince her, one way or another, to join the X-14. They wanted the prettiest girls to service the guys, to look sweet and innocent when they haul drugs, and lure in more men to the gang. In the meantime, they cook, have sex, satisfy the guys, and we keep them happy with the coke."

Petra tried to keep comments to herself. She felt like vomiting.

"She was pretty compliant to start off, didn't complain. Probably because she was in shock. But then she got more and more aggressive. She slapped Chato, insulted Pinza, and screamed at me. We couldn't make her calm down, so Pinza brought out his knife."

Petra said, "Is this standard operating procedure among you guys?"

"He just cut her a little at first, on her thigh. Chato was holding her down, and they told me to put a rag in her mouth. Pinza got carried away. He kept cutting her. He lifted up her dress so it covered her eyes, and lines of blood moved up her thigh, till they got to the soft parts between her legs." Emilio hung his head. His words blurred, so Petra had to pay close attention.

Petra stopped him. "If this is a repeat of what Potoo and Gorto did to me, I don't need to hear it."

"Right. Except nobody rescued Justina. When it was happening to you, I was overpowered by memories of what we did to Justina. I couldn't let that happen again. Not to you, especially."

"*Híjole.* What a compliment. God help us." Petra said.

Sucking on strands of her long, thick hair, her mother's eyes shifted mutely between Emilio and Petra.

"Look, I don't want to tell this, you don't want to hear it. Let's just say things went from bad to worse. She didn't cooperate. She kicked Chato in the teeth. Pinza never put away his knife. There was a lot of bleeding. They held her down and took turns with her.

"I tried to intervene, Petra, but they just laughed at me. I didn't try hard enough. My insides were a wreck. I couldn't take what Gusano and them were doing to me anymore."

Emilio ran his tongue over his lips, then his teeth clamped down on the inside of his cheek. His forehead contorted into a crooked frown. "I stayed there because I was afraid what would happen to me if I left, but my mind went somewhere else. I remember feeling like I was watching a horror movie on television. When she wouldn't stop bleeding, they dumped her back at the river.

"Those two, their hearts were frozen already. They'd already killed people, tortured others. You can't do that and still be human. My heart was half frozen from what they'd done to me already, but the other half tortured me. I let them do those things to me. It's my fault, I know."

Emilio didn't cry, but his face turned red, his mouth awry. Her mother touched his hand, but he pulled it back. A tremor had hold of Emilio's hand. He locked one hand inside the other, but it wouldn't stop shaking.

"What did they do to you, Emilio?" Petra's mother asked gently. The care in her eyes penetrated deeply. "What would've happened if you'd run from that place?"

Emilio took a deep breath, trying to steady himself. His head rocked back and forth like he couldn't carry the weight of it. He shoved his chair back and began pacing around the kitchen.

Wyman shouted from the living room, "Everything okay in there?"

Her mother went to talk to him for a moment, then returned to the kitchen. She pulled her chair close next to Petra. Under the table, her mother laid her hand over Petra's, quieting her bouncing leg. "What happened to you, Emilio?" she repeated.

"I might as well complete the confession." His hands fled deep into his pockets. "Sometimes, starting when my mom died till I was about fourteen, I would confess to my father how bad I felt for somebody who was suffering because of our gang. Right after, Gusano would show up to put me in my place. You saw a little of Gusano, Petra, but you have no idea." Emilio stopped.

Her mother said, "Did Gusano punish you, Emilio?"

Emilio wet his lips. He shuddered. "He has a thing for young boys who are on the lower rungs of the X-14. He thinks of it as initiation into the gang, but it's sick, Petra, it's really sick. He forced himself on me, so many times. I was still so little…" Emilio's voice broke into sobs, then quickly swallowed hard and froze all emotion in his face. "After I got through that 'graduation' ritual with Justina, he left me alone, and turned to boys younger than me." Emilio's voice had lost all expression and rhythm.

Petra said quietly, "You mean…. When you were just ten or eleven, Emilio?"

Emilio sucked in his lower lip and knitted his brows. "I still pass blood sometimes. The memories come all the time and mess me up. The other day, when I was changing tires at work, I couldn't stand it. I lashed out at my boss and had to leave the shop." Emilio looked spent. His head hung low on his neck.

"*Qué barbaridad!*" said Petra's mother. Casting her hair behind her shoulder, she grasped Emilio in a full body hug. Tears began to fall onto her shoulder. He pulled away, ashamed and self-conscious. His arms folded across his body. He rocked back and forth.

Petra's head dropped; her eyes closed. Concentrating as hard as she could, she tried to unearth a memory. Emilio's disclosure was prodding her, stabbing at her brain. Nausea rose in her gut.

- This is it, little Petita. This is the moment.
- I'm trying to find it. It's all covered up.
- Memories. How they hide behind hot air. Red ribbons and bicycle wheels.
- This is what I turned away from in Xibalba, isn't it? The foreboding I ran away from.
- Remember the red ribbons? You were so cold.
- I'm cold now, Alocinia. I don't feel well.
- The mud was sticky in Xibalba, you remember?
- It was everywhere. I couldn't wade through it. It was all over me.
- The bicycle wheels were spinning. The jacaranda flowers dying.
- *Ay sí*. The day Emilio's mother died. You came to me again that day, Alocinia.
- The day you met Gusano. All those tattoos.

Petra convulsed as the memory poured through her. Suddenly, the words blurted from her mouth. "He had a thing for little boys." She hesitated, swallowed hard. "And for little girls. *Ay Dios*, I never remembered."

"What is it, Petita?" said her mother. Beads of sweat lined her mother's forehead.

"I was nine when your mother died," Petra said.

"When my father killed her, you mean," Emilio intoned. "He smashed two beer bottles across her head. He forced her to take cocaine, and when she couldn't make his breakfast, he killed her." He recited the information as if it had nothing to do with him.

Her mother covered her mouth with her hands, gently clasped together in prayer, her eyes fastened upon the two of them. "Go on, Peta," she said in a hushed voice.

"I was nine. I ran to get help. Your mother was bleeding so bad.

"There was a car. I looked to see if the driver was nearby. Maybe they would drive me so I could get help faster. A frightful man, a phantom—his head covered with horrible tattoos, was at the turn onto the road. He offered to give me a ride, so I got into his car. He talked to me about his mother, I remember. Then he pulled off the main road and drove into the woods.

"He took off his shirt and bared his chest to intimidate me. The tattoos kept going, all the way down his back and chest. He came around and pulled me out of the car. He grabbed my hair so tight and pulled my head back and forced me to the ground." Petra's voice cracked, and she continued to talk through sobs. "Mamá, he was all over me! I squirmed and tried to slide away, but he glued me to the earth. I felt the elastic on my panties pull tight, and he put something inside me, mamá. It hurt.

"Then there was white gooey glue on my stomach, all over my dress, and he was gone. I grabbed a handful of leaves to wipe it off, and it turned into a dirty sticky mess. I couldn't get it clean. I was so cold, and the red ribbons were flying above me.

"Then I ran and ran until I got home, and I made my mind concentrate on Emilio's mother, getting help. When we got back, she died, mamá, and it was because I was so slow. Because I took so long.

"I didn't remember about Gusano, I just knew it was my fault she died. My fault Emilio wouldn't be friends with me anymore. How could he be friends with me if I took so long and couldn't help save his mother?"

Petra moaned, then wept and wailed. She stared at some point on the wall beyond her mother. Her mother remained rooted to the table. Her hands covered her head, which had sunk down so her forehead was on the table. Abruptly, her mother jumped up and ran into the bathroom. Sounds of retching carried to the kitchen.

Emilio crossed to Petra's side of the table, lifted Petra out of her chair, and embraced her. They held onto each other as if their lives depended on it.

CHAPTER THIRTY-FOUR

From that day, Petra never failed to give offerings to the *aluxob*. She left pieces of tortillas, a bean or two, or a spot of honey. They reached a truce. Sometimes as she was sitting in the big armchair doing homework, she heard one or the other giggle at her, or scurry about. When she looked over, they went quiet. She never mentioned them by name.

Together, Petra and Wyman researched Mayan history and mythology. Sitting next to her by the computer in her room, he guided her as she continued to discover what it could do. With a few clicks, they looked at museums in Boston and Rhode Island. An archeological museum in Boston collected Mayan and Mesoamerican artifacts and sculptures. Soon they would visit.

Petra scratched her head and tried to put her reaction into words to Wyman, "I keep thinking about the cave where Itzamná lives. Where the jaguar protects it. Where my grandfather decided to leave it so many years ago, because it belonged to the memories buried in the land there. The museum—it's sterile. The gods' echoes are missing in this country."

Wyman said, "Let's search for Guatemalan Mayan groups in the area."

And so they found one in New Bedford, a short jaunt from Providence. The internet told them that the area was full of indigenous people from Guatemala. Many of them worked in the seafood industry around the old whaling port. They found articles about the new white American director of the group, who spoke neither Spanish nor Quiché.

He had taken over when the former director was fired. A court later sentenced him to jail for sexually assaulting a female client of the group.

Petra said, with irony in her voice, "Great. I guess the sexual violence and craziness of Guatemala is bound to end up in the groups we create in the U.S. I don't see finding a connection to the Mayan culture with these people."

At a dead end, they switched to images of Mayan artifacts, of gods and hummingbirds and jaguars. Petra said, "The whole world is in this computer, Wyman."

"Just don't forget the world waits to be discovered out there, too." His hand swept toward the window. He touched her lightly on the shoulder. "I can't believe how quickly you are learning English, Petra. You're using the English learning program online, aren't you? Maybe I should try a Spanish program so I can keep up with you and your mom."

Petra laughed. "I'm glad you don't speak Spanish, Wyman."

"Really?" His eyes opened wide with surprise.

"I don't know if I'd trust you with my mother if you were Hispanic."

Wyman chortled, his laugh coming from deep in his throat, breathlessly finding humor in himself.

"Wyman, will the internet tell me what I need to do to become a doctor? What happens after high school?"

Tests, applications, courses of study, colleges, medical school—it was all there to research and prepare herself. Wyman told her that the local hospitals were always looking for volunteers to help care for patients. He would take her there one day after school. During the summer, she would have more time to get some experience around real doctors.

The month of June tempted Petra to Roger Williams Park over and over. Yasmin and Petra raced down Yasmin's street into the park. Petra stopped to smell the rose bushes lining the history museum. Ducks quacked; Canada geese flew overhead. The green of the trees' leaves brimmed with summer energy. The zoo's sloth sent her friendly vibes. The howler monkey screamed at her. The cheetah telegraphed greetings to its cousin the jaguar.

Petra watched Yasmin out of the corner of her eye as her fingers lingered over the roses and a ring of lush salmon-colored peonies. Magnificent blossoms and lush summer greens flourished everywhere. They rounded the lake to the far end, where people were more scarce.

Yasmin trudged along in silence. Her arms didn't swing so loosely this day. Petra laced her fingers around Yasmin's.

"*Qué hay*, Yasmin?" asked Petra.

"You ever worry about the future, Petra? Worry that maybe something will happen, and everything you hoped for will be pulled out from under you?" She looked up at the trees, not meeting Petra's eyes.

"Are you kidding? I spent my life worrying that I'd never even have a chance, that life was pulled out from under me every single day."

"So many things can go wrong, though. Here, too. It's no utopia here in the U.S., you know?" Petra had never heard such a defeated tone from Yasmin.

They sat down on a log nestled between some bushes and the lake. Petra said, "Talk to me."

Yasmin sighed. "You have enough to worry about."

"Well, now I'm worried about you. C'mon, *dígame*."

"It's my dad, Petra. The cops stopped him for nothing, for a broken brake light. But he didn't have a driver's license."

Petra put a hand over her mouth. "Yasmin, he doesn't have immigration papers?"

"You didn't know?"

Immigration had never come up in conversation. Petra said, "You've been here since you were five years old, right? I assumed you all had green cards already."

"Bad assumption. One year goes by after another, and nothing changes. They gave me a work permit, I guess because I came when I was just a kid, but my parents got nothing. Sometimes I don't even want that work permit. My dad has been working his butt off landscaping rich white people's gardens for ten years, but it's like he's always hiding. My parents almost never go out, they're so nervous about what might happen. But he does have to drive to get to the houses he works on." An edge of bitterness crept into Yasmin's voice.

Yasmin's right arm hung by her side, her eyes downcast. Then her voice lifted. "Oh! What's this?" She leaned over the log to her right, murmuring softly, "It's OK, come on out. You're so beautiful."

She stood up with a snake wrapped around her hand. Green, with a long black stripe, it looked small and innocent. Yasmin laid it gently on Petra's lap, but its beaded black eyes never left Yasmin's face. It raised its head to get a closer look at Yasmin. The jaws of its mouth parted slightly, its lips curled up in a smile.

Petra laughed. "Yasmin! I think love is in the air." She laughed and remembered another time, years back, when a tarantula had bitten Emilio because he handled it roughly. She wouldn't have to step in to help Yasmin this way.

"I do love snakes. They're all so innocent around here. But I'll leave her alone. Here you go, *culebrita*." Yasmin set it back down by the end of the log, and they kept walking.

Petra brought them back. "What happened with your father, Yasmin?"

"The policeman knocked him around, treated him like dirt. Called him a dirty spic. Then arrested him. He's got a court date next week. We're afraid Immigration will pick him up when he goes to court. Or before." Yasmin turned to face Petra, wincing with both eyes, her forehead crumpled.

The police didn't always behave as well as they had with her, then. "*Híjole*, Yasmin. *Qué susto*! No wonder you're scared."

"They didn't have to treat him that way. My dad—he already doesn't stick up for himself. He's thinking about going back to Honduras before court. He says if the Americans don't want him here, he won't stay."

Petra groaned. "It's hard in Honduras, especially if you used to live in the U.S. The gangs threaten anyone who they think might have a few *centavos*. I've heard it's even worse than Guatemala."

"He doesn't have anything to go back to. His dad was killed by the gangs. That's why we came when we did. His brothers went to Los Angeles. We don't have a house in Honduras or anything. There's no way he'll find a job. He's too old for any employer to bother with him there. And there's not such a demand for landscapers there, you know?"

"Would you and your mother go back with him?" Petra was afraid of the answer.

"I don't know!" There was a desperate edge in her voice. "I don't know how we can live here, but I can't live in Honduras! My mom doesn't even work. My dad has always taken care of us. But at least we have a chance if we stay here. My mom can find a job here, I can work part-time. Maybe I'd have to leave school to help support my dad, too. See what I mean about how everything might be pulled out from under me?"

"*Huy*, Yasmin. I'm really sorry this is happening."

Then in a hushed voice, "Not to speak of you." She cocked her head and lifted one cheek. "I'm kind of hoping you feel the same way."

Petra rubbed an eyebrow with consternation. "I guess I'd be pretty devastated if you left. I didn't want to put myself into it."

"And me. If this is who I am, I mean, I can't be this way in Honduras."

They sat down on the grass between two pine trees. Petra pushed a wisp of hair that had escaped from Yasmin's braid behind her ear. Yasmin took off her glasses and laid back.

Petra felt the invitation in her pores. Yasmin's eyes reached up to Petra and pulled her down next to her. Petra lay on her side, propped up by an elbow, and returned Yasmin's visual embrace. Her hand reached out and met Yasmin's. Their hands folded together just below Yasmin's breasts. The hairs on Petra's arms stood on end. She swallowed hard. She refused to acknowledge the lump of memory in her throat, the way Justina's breasts had felt against hers, the ultimate annihilation of their intimacy.

Yasmin said, "I'm falling for you. All over you." Her cheeks wore slight dimples.

Petra giggled quietly. A bird warbled up in the branches somewhere. Petra closed her eyes to contain the electricity shooting through her, from her throat through her torso, like butterflies in her belly.

Yasmin turned toward her, and their breasts slipped together. Warm breath, then the softest lips glancing against her own. A hand on her cheek, and the lips melted into supple heat. Her eyes slitted to absorb the soft pleasure of Yasmin, Petra gave herself over to the long kiss. Exploring, seeking, probing.

Petra wanted this, had wanted it. Heat rose and lodged in her throat. A calm settled over her mind in a way she hadn't experienced since she and Justina had promised each other everlasting friendship. She was still getting to know Yasmin, but—those eyes! Through half-closed eyes,

Petra never lost sight of the emerald green.

Petra's hands craved to touch the warmth, the gracious arcs and bends of her breasts. Yasmin's thighs, so pleasantly plump and round, drew Petra's touch like a hummingbird to honey. Fingers explored skin so silky smooth.

Her breasts swelled, while flesh breathed. The bare flesh of Yasmin's stomach brushed against the swelling. An ache rose to her mouth and passed through her lips to Yasmin. Petra felt a moist pulse throbbing between her legs. She ached for more.

They parted and gasped at the unexpected pleasure that pulled them under, but it was too new, they were in an open park. Petra pulled back. Surprise mixed with tenderness. She pushed back the same lock of Yasmin's hair and caressed both sides of her glasses to steady them on Yasmin's head.

Petra blinked, gathered her feet under her, and reached for Yasmin's hand to pull her up. "Hey, let's go have fun in the park."

CHAPTER THIRTY-FIVE

The mixture of law and family relationships is fraught with flimsy twists and turns. It is not easy for a stranger—for example, an immigration officer—bound by forms and formalities, to decipher a thing as complex as a marriage in the confines of an uncomfortable interview. Worse than uncomfortable—more like hopelessly unworkable and painful for all concerned. The applicants are often not well educated, arrive replete with a different set of cultural norms, and have every reason to fear the authorities. Furthermore, all words pass through the filter of dubiously qualified interpreters, and the family is naturally overwrought in its awareness that the rest of their lives depend on giving the right answers and producing the right papers.

Ignorant of immigration law, Petra, Sorelly, and Wyman handed over all their trust to their lawyer to wade into the mire of the immigration system and pull them out the other end. They did decide to keep Sorelly and Petra's cases together as beneficiaries of Wyman's petitions, though it might have been easier for Petra to make an application based on her father's abandonment of her. The lawyer said if all went well with the petition, Petra might not need to go to her hearing at Immigration Court. All of them, even the lawyer, were fearful that anything about immigration could change at any moment. The soil under immigrants' feet was shifting even faster than usual.

With that in mind, one fine day in mid-June, Petra's heel tapped the linoleum floor of the Citizenship and Immigration Services office.

Dressed in a miniature black tie and suit, the young child of an African couple ran back and forth across the room. Two Colombian women chatted vociferously between themselves. A husky man in lawyer costume paced by the window as he repeatedly jabbed his fingers into his cell phone.

The world was full of strangers who desperately needed to be welcomed, Petra thought. Novina's words came to her: "Perhaps by offering a safe place to you I open a safe place within myself." Novina had welcomed her, a stranger to Novina then, by offering her safe haven. Petra remembered how overwhelmed she felt by the generosity Novina and Deacon Eduardo had shown her, but she couldn't deny the grace in their good will. She hoped the Immigration Service took this point of view.

Petra's mother desperately sorted through papers—arranging photos, making one pile for birth certificates and passports, another pile for their lease, bank records, all the documents of their life together—while gaping anxiously toward the elevator to sight *la Doctora* Lucía, their attorney. The Spanish translator they had hired for the interview sat behind her mother, her demeanor calm and aloof. A chime, then the clatter of elevator doors yanked Petra back to the present. Lucía hurried around the corner, her eyes focused on her cell phone, swinging a briefcase at her side. Her mother spilled the pile from her lap. Petra scurried to pick it up.

A male voice floated vaguely into the waiting room through a crack in the door to the offices. No face was visible. "Wyman and Sorelly Sibley, Petra?" Silence. *La Doctora* waved at them hurriedly to usher them through the door. The officer widened the door, and said, "Only Wyman for now." The lawyer disappeared through the door with Wyman and his wheelchair.

The minutes on the clock clicked forward one at a time. Apprehension laced with anticipation filled the waiting room. A few long moments passed, and Wyman burst out through the door, briskly informing Sorelly he needed the documents. Arms now loaded with paperwork, he rolled back to the now closed and locked door, waiting for it to open again. A minute, two, five minutes. Lucía pushed the door open from inside, and Wyman re-entered the vault.

"Mamá, don't worry," Petra said. "The lawyer said we'll be fine." Petra wished she'd gone with her mother and Wyman to the meeting with the attorney a few days before. But she had to believe the officer would see the that their marriage was genuine, not just for immigration.

Her mother's head bounced up and down a few times, and she went back to organizing papers. "It's not fine. Wyman is thirty years older than me. We don't speak the same language. They're going to think we married for the papers."

The translator rolled her eyes and ignored them.

The door to the secured area opened again. Petra jumped. The disembodied voice called, "Mr. Django?" Someone else. She breathed again. Time crawled. Five minutes, ten, then twenty.

Petra swung her legs back and forth under the chair. We humans are all strangers to God. The Mayan gods tried over and over again to create the quality of humans they wanted. She envisioned the humans collapsing into a pile of mud, then walking stiffly in their wooden form, but without the dignity of the gods that created them.

Mr. Django's kid stood in front of Petra, sniffling and wiping his nose with the back of his hand. Petra raised her eyebrows, and her eyes flickered. His mother yelled to him, and he ran off down the aisle of chairs.

Similarly, the Christian God sent Jesus to try to raise His imperfect humans to more closely align with God's image. Jesus became a stranger in our midst. The savior was a stranger. Gods all tried to relate to their creations, but they remained strangers to each other. The immigrant was a strange savior. She would have to think further about that.

The voice returned: "Ms. Sibley and Petra please?"

They leapt from their chairs, and the translator followed.

Petra raised her hand and swore to tell the truth. Chairs caught on the rug as they tried to fit everyone in. Wyman's chair blocked the office door, and Petra tried to reassure herself she was not really trapped in the small room. The translator sat behind the computer monitor, passing words between Spanish and English but blind to the officer. Her mother squeezed between Wyman and the translator. *La Doctora's* head bobbed back and forth from behind the translator, trying to catch the officer's eye. Petra sat behind her mother. They shuffled papers and documents, ID's and birth certificates.

Despite the officer's smile, Petra felt a distinct lack of warmth or friendliness from him. His eyes remained glued to his computer screen and the paperwork on his desk when he spoke. His hand held a pencil upside down so that the eraser pushed each sheet of paper along, one at a time but continuously. His questions snapped brusquely, often throwing them off balance in an unexpected change of direction.

The questions launched at her mother. "What is your husband's date of birth?" "What date did you get married?" "What date did you arrive in the U.S.?" "What date did you move from your address three years ago?" "What dates did you work for that company five years ago?" The months and years swirled in Petra's head. Her mother leaned forward in a stance of utter concentration, unaware that she seemed too eager to please, but she plodded through the answers.

"Have you ever been arrested, cited, charged, or detained for any reason by any law enforcement official, including but not limited to any U.S. immigration official or any official of the U.S. armed forces or U.S. Coast Guard?"

"No," said her mother. Why didn't the officer just ask what he wanted to know? So many complicated words to mix up the question.

"Excuse me, officer," Lucía injected. "These are questions for the application for permanent residence. We're just reviewing the visa petition now."

The officer didn't look up. "We have the right to ask these questions now."

He continued. "Are you the spouse, son, or daughter of a foreign national who illicitly trafficked or aided, or otherwise abetted, assisted, conspired, or colluded, in the illicit trafficking of a controlled substance, such as…" Petra lost track of the point. So did the translator, apparently, because the translation was a fraction the length of the officer's question.

"No," repeated her mother. Petra wondered if her mother could possibly understand the questions.

"Do you intend to engage in any activity that violates or evades any law relating to espionage, including spying, or sabotage in the United States?"

"Are you the spouse or child of an individual who ever committed, threatened to commit, attempted to commit, conspired to commit, incited, endorsed, advocated, planned, or prepared any of the following: hijacking, sabotage, kidnapping, political assassination, or use of a weapon or explosive to harm another individual or cause substantial damage to property?" Petra thought that if the questions were that detailed, they would probably never end.

"No," her mother said again, her voice so toneless that Petra couldn't tell if she registered any meaning. The officer didn't seem to care whether she understood.

The questions droned on. Then, "How did you meet your husband?"

"Wyman?" Her mother tried to adjust to the sharp turn in the questioning.

The officer said sarcastically, "Is this your husband next to you, Ms. Sibley?"

Her mother fumbled into English in an uneasy attempt to relate to the officer. "Sorry, I'm feeling a bit nervous."

The officer: "There's no reason to feel nervous, ma'am." No reason for him to feel nervous, of course. Surely he didn't imagine that they had no reason. "I would remind you, even if you speak some English, you have brought an interpreter, so please use her and keep your answers in Spanish. That is your best language, is that right?"

"Yes, sir."

The officer waited in silence.

Her mother's elbow knocked a passport onto the floor. "What was the question?" The officer repeated, now impatiently, "How did you meet your husband, Ms. Sibley?"

"I work as a CNA. I mean, a certified nursing assistant —"

The officer interrupted, "I didn't ask what your work is, Ms. Sibley. Could you please pay attention to the question I am asking? If you don't understand, just ask me to repeat the question."

"Thank you, no, I do understand." Her mother's eyes flashed in anger, but she held back and tried to regroup. "I met him at his house. The CNA agency sent me there to help him with some of his daily activities. He had just had surgery and was going through a difficult time."

"I see. What were these daily activities you helped with?"

"I helped him bathe, get dressed, cleaned his bed, things like that."

The officer said, "Tell me about how the relationship developed."

Sorelly's eyes looked back in memory. "Wyman was very kind. He talked to me about his service in Vietnam, and he asked me a lot about where I was from, about my life. Over the next months, we became very friendly."

"I see." Petra squirmed at the demeaning tone of the officer. "Do you speak English, Ms. Sibley? I see you have an interpreter here with you today." He had just told her not to speak English. Did he really think using an interpreter here meant her mother spoke no English?

Her mother said, in Spanish, "I do speak some English, sir. I have found that communication happens, despite language differences, where there is an openness, and affection, between two people. That has certainly been the case between Wyman and myself."

"I see." The officer paused for effect. "Did you and your husband, and your daughter Petra, eat dinner together last night?"

"Yes, of course."

"Please tell me what you ate and who prepared the food."

"Wyman had dinner ready when I arrived home from work. Petra ate with us, of course."

"What did you eat, ma'am?" The officer's voice was tense as he repeated the question. Did the officer really need to go into such trivial details of their lives to decide if her mother's marriage was authentic?

"We had macaroni and cheese, with a salad."

"Did you use dressing on your salad?"

"Yes, I believe so."

"What kind of dressing did you use?"

"I think it was the orange kind. I don't know the name."

The officer nodded solemnly, as if that was very significant. "And what did you drink with your meal, if anything?"

"I usually have tea."

"Did you have tea last night, ma'am?"

"Yes, sir."

"What kind of tea?"

Sorelly lowered her head, thinking. The officer said, "I remind you that if you don't know the answer to a question, you should say so."

"I'm not sure."

"You can't remember what you drank just last night?" Didn't he just encourage her mother to say she didn't know if she was unsure?

"I think it was an herbal tea, a greenish color. I'm not sure."

Questions continued for at least an hour. Her mother began to hold her head in her hands and look confused, but the officer persisted. Finally, he turned to Petra. "Can you tell me your address?" He spoke condescendingly, as if she were eight, not fifteen years old, and might not know her own address.

She gave it to him.

"When did you enter the U.S., Petra?"

She thought for a moment. "Let's see. I presented myself to officers at the border over the bridge. They sent me to a group home in Chicago, and I was there about a month. Then I came to live with my mother, and I started school here in May."

The officer looked confused. "Well, thank you for all that information, Petra, but I still don't know what date you entered the U.S. Can you tell me?"

Her mother said, "I don't think she knows the exact —"

The officer interrupted. "Mom, let's please let Petra speak now. Please don't answer for her."

Petra said, "I don't know the date. I think it was near the beginning of April."

"Of what year, please?"

This man didn't seem to be fully human. "This year, sir. Just a couple of months ago."

"Are there any parties or celebrations planned at your house, Petra?"

Petra looked to her mother but knew her mother had better not help her. Uncertain as to whether she should mention the ceremony they had discussed, she hesitated. Lucía caught her eye and nodded. "Well, not exactly a celebration."

"Can you explain, miss?"

"We will hold a kind of ceremony."

"What do you mean by 'ceremony'?"

"Well, it is instead of a *quinceañera*. Like to help me adjust to all the changes and think about the future." She didn't really want to tell this man about such a profoundly personal experience.

"Petra, have you ever been arrested, cited, charged, or detained for any reason by any law enforcement official?"

She waited for the translation. "No."

"Have you ever met with police at the police station?" Petra looked at her mother. "Again, I'm speaking with you, not your mother, right now."

"Um… yes, I met with several officers there a couple weeks ago."

"Why were you there?"

"They asked me to tell them what I know about gangs here in Providence and in my town in Guatemala."

"Are you, or have you been, involved in gangs, either here or in any other country, young lady?" For the first time, the officer looked directly at her eyes.

"How do you mean "involved?""

"Young lady, please answer the question."

Her mother reached a hand behind her and touched Petra's knee. Petra licked her lips and pulled her upper lip between her teeth. "The gang in my hometown tried to "involve" me, but I refused. That's why I came to the U.S." Talking to this officer was nothing like her discussions at the Providence Police Station. This man didn't seem to care to understand anything at all.

"Okay. That's fine, then. We will complete the procedures from our end, and you will hear from us."

Petra wondered what he thought was fine but said nothing more. Lucía and the officer exchanged words in English. Petra was too tired to try to make out the conversation. They all shuffled out of the office and into the parking lot.

The lawyer told them they had done well. She said the officer asked specific questions about their lives in order to compare Wyman's answers with her mother's and be sure they really lived together. Apparently, Wyman and her mother had met with Lucía before the interview, so they had some advance idea of what would happen there, though her mother told Lucía the tone of the officer's questions was difficult.

Lucía nodded grimly. "It happens every day. I know. They're getting tougher every day under this President. Every day they find new areas to probe, trying to find a problem they can hang a denial on." She said they could expect a decision on whether Immigration believed the marriage was bona fide within a month or so. If they approved the marriage, Sorelly and Petra would apply for residence, and have a final interview at the U.S. Embassy in Guatemala City before they could return to the U.S. as permanent residents.

CHAPTER THIRTY-SIX

The deep, sonorous drumbeat throbbed in Petra's gut. His face flushed with intensity, Wyman clutched the drum tightly to his stomach. It was a wooden drum wrapped with a membrane made from the hide of an animal. Wyman claimed it was the hide of a jaguar. Yasmin blew into a simple bone flute, rendering an airy, poetic melody. Emilio crouched under branches that sank limply as they spread out, partially hiding him. Textile printed with the yellow and black spotted skin of a jaguar covered his body from the shoulders down. Balanced upon his thighs, his fabric-draped arms held a simple marimba—really just a wooden xylophone with two mallets to hit the notes. Petra's cheeks glowed bronze. Her nostrils flared with intent. She stared directly in front of her, lost within suddenly amorphous time.

Their homemade ceremony began at Lincoln Woods Park on a cloudless morning during Petra's two-week vacation between the end of ninth grade and the beginning of summer school. Her mother said the woods there were the closest thing she could think of to the forests around Las Leches. They rented a picnic area that bordered the lake.

Sitting on a thick bed of pine needles near the water, their backs were each propped up against a tree for support and for connection to the earth—except Wyman, who nested comfortably in his wheelchair, its back propped against a withered beech tree. Petra's tree rose higher than all of the others.

Her mother braided a piece of cloth, patterned purple, white and yellow, through Petra's hair, tied back in a thick ponytail. A small fire burned in the pit by the picnic table, which was covered with her mother's Mayan tablecloth. A shallow bowl of water lay upon a bed of pine needles. Yasmin said it was morning dew she had collected.

Once everyone settled under the trees, Petra's mother began quietly, her voice gaining intensity as she spoke. The ethereal sound of the flute resonated against Petra's skin. "We join together today in a gathering which will honor the role of ritual and myth in healing and thriving. We have borrowed a few elements from Mayan traditions which have meant something to my family. Having missed her big chance for a celebration of her *quinceañera*, Petra now wishes to experience a different kind of ceremony with all of us. This is a day to engage with the magic of life and to aid Petra in reconciling her past and finding her future. I fully reclaim the role of mother today and, as such, I will lead the proceedings." She grinned proudly.

Petra's mother invoked the four cardinal directions for the Bacabob, four of Itzamná's children, the first four humans created by the gods. One by one, she hung red ribbons from the lower branches of Petra's tree. "The Bacobob had the ability to see through space and time. When the Mayan gods gave humans senses, they lost the ability to see through time and to see the consequences of their actions. The concept of forgiveness arose. The tree that Petra leans against represents the ceiba tree, connecting the past and the underworld with the earthly present, the future, and the heavens above. We are aware of the presence of Itzamná. We will continue to honor Itzamná, and we invoke his spirit today as the great creator. With consistently good humor, Itzamná ruled day and night. Itzamná's flight represents the unfolding of time, the passage between past and future, between the underworld and the heavens."

"Petra," her mother stated. Petra blinked out of her inner gaze. "You wanted to begin."

Yasmin and Emilio gently laid down their instruments.

"We begin with the past," her mother continued, "a healing of old wounds, a cleansing of the soul. Forgiveness is both offered and accepted. The vulture feeds on the dead, clearing away the past. As such, it is a source of great wisdom."

Yasmin handed Petra a wooden vulture figure. Its closed wings resembled slumped shoulders, its red neck and head leaned pensively forward, its black eyes and beak shone. "If you have forgiveness to give, it is time to share it." The drumbeat came faster.

The throbbing of the drum reverberated in Petra's pulsing blood and gave rhythm to her speech. "I hope that this forgiveness will ease a bitter barrier from inside myself. Mamá, first to you. For many years, I have held on to resentment against you. I knew it was wrong, and yet it lay untouched within me. You left me and my brother Carlos when I was five years old. You expected me to share myself with you when you called, but you were never present for me—when I fell down, when I needed a hug, when my teacher named me the best student of the year—and when I couldn't cope with the loss of my best friends." Petra sniffled as the back of her hand swiped at her nose.

"By leaving me and coming to the U.S., you also provided me with food, money to go to school, and a safe, loving family with Nonno and Nonna. You saved both of us from my abusive father. You were presented with a terrible problem with no good solutions. I now see what I missed all these years. *Te quiero mucho, mamí.*" Petra stood and looked into her mother's eyes, and said, "I forgive you, mamá." She handed the vulture to her mother.

Her mother's eyes sparkled with wetness as she stroked the vulture's wings. "Thank you, *m'hijita*. Your words will lighten my load of guilt. I so regret the turmoil to which I contributed. I will always carry sorrow for those years which tore at my soul every day I could not see you." For a moment, she hung her head. Then she looked back into her daughter's eyes, and said, "I accept your forgiveness, *mi hija. Gracias.*" She returned the vulture to Petra.

Petra said, "Emilio." She exhaled slowly, searching her mother's face for the right words. She turned to Emilio and saw fright in his eyes and smiled at him to tell him to relax. "Forgiveness won't change the past or deny the pain which you have contributed to. I have blamed you for turning away from our friendship at a time of crisis in your family, for killing my closest friend Justina and threatening me, for participating in the despicable life of a gang. You have made mistakes, just as we all make mistakes. You, too, were presented with impossible choices.

"It is possible that these events, as awful as they were, do not have to define my life—*our* lives. I am releasing my bitterness toward you and letting go of the past. You are human. You, too, have suffered and made difficult choices. I will leave judgment to you and your God or gods."

Petra stood and approached Emilio. He rose to face her. His lower lip quivered. She smiled and touched his mouth with a finger. "Emilio, I forgive you. I wish for you the freedom to go forward." She put the vulture in his arms and blushed. "By giving you the vulture, I am asking God to bless you."

Emilio pushed back the cloak to free his hand and pushed the hair off his forehead. His teary eyes glinted in the candlelight, and he pursed his lips together, then smiled nervously and said, "Petra, I never thought I would hear you say those words. Only in my dreams." He cradled the vulture in one arm, but he kept lifting his other hand to run the fingers through his hair. "It's so hard to say I accept your forgiveness. I will keep working to deserve it, I promise."

Her mother said, "Try, Emilio. Say the words."

Emilio's lips pressed together, and he blinked slowly. "I accept your forgiveness, Petra. Thank you, *mi amiga*." He handed the vulture back to Petra. Tears ran down her cheeks as she sat down.

Her mother said, "Emilio, would you forgive Petra?"

Emilio and Petra exchanged glances, confused. He said, "Me? Forgive Petra?"

Her mother said, "Think, Emilio."

Emilio's shoulders slumped as he sat silently. Then he nodded, and his full black eyebrows arched. He took the vulture back from Petra. "When you were nine years old, Petra, you were guilty for nothing, nothing at all. But especially not for my mother's death. You were not guilty for delaying in getting help, and you were not guilty for not understanding what was going on. My father killed her, and my father put Gusano in your way. He and Gusano were responsible for the assault on you and for defeating our friendship. I can only forgive you for a responsibility you felt, not one I ever blamed you for, not in my most wretched moments. Please accept my forgiveness and take the vulture baby."

The light flickered on Petra's lips as they slowly curved to a smile. The two wounded warriors, Petra and Emilio, clasped each other in an embrace. The drumbeat vibrated delicately in Petra's bones. A moment of silence hung over the room.

Yasmin began to hang red ribbons on the branches of the "ceiba" tree. She threw a cloak over her head. Her eyes peered out from the costume like a slit-eyed bird, with a comically round head plastered with feathers, and a broad but short bill. She stood absolutely still and began a low mournful moan, growing alternately louder and quiet. Over his head and down his neck, Emilio laid the jaguar cloth on the ground and donned a head mask which was covered with the likeness of tattoos.

Petra shrunk back behind her tree. The drumbeats grew louder and faster, thundering in rhythm. The potoo and "Gusano" joined hands and danced around the ceiba tree, as the ribbons fluttered about. Petra threw a bewildered look toward her mother, who closed her eyes and lowered her chin. Petra's secure family gathering seeped away through the pine needles covering the ground.

The dancing figures drifted toward Petra. The wings and arms lifted high over their heads and flung back to their sides, slithering like despicable worms to Petra's side. On one side, they poked her. On the other, they pushed. A wing veiled her face. Hands covered each of her ears, so that she was deaf and blind. She folded her arms across her chest to keep out the cold.

Petra pushed away the hands and stuffed her fingers in her ears to block out the harsh noise. She felt herself transported to another time and place, now looking out from a hole beneath a decaying log. Carlos's feet danced about but refused to come to her. She craned her head upward to the top of the Ayacahuite pine tree that guarded the path up the Sibalq'aq volcano. Grasping the top edge of the log, her fingers slipped on a clump of pine needles. Slowly, she pulled herself up, until her legs steadied herself on the ground.

The potoo stared down at her. She strained to keep it in sight because its gray-brown feathers melded with the tree's branches, making it invisible. Its eyes were deeply slitted. It was preparing to plunge down to attack its prey.

Without further warning, a chaos of wings scraped at her bare arms and legs. The sharp beak broke the skin on her neck. She felt the blood rise from the gashes to her flesh. The potoo pulled on her shirt, stretching it so tightly that she couldn't breathe. As the wings circled her, its eyes remained fastened to hers. No longer slitted, they were now unworldly spherical yellow balls with black beady pupils which wanted to jump out at her. She wanted to cry out, but her mouth would not open.

She thrust her arm out to knock away the pandemonium attacking her, but instead lost her balance and fell to the ground. At once, feet, covered with tattoos down to their soles, pushed on her chest, holding her down. Tattooed hands tore at her pants. A tattooed face mocked her. She flailed helplessly. The bird swooped down again. Her hair flew up with the movement of air and became entangled with the bird's claws. She tried desperately to free herself from the potoo and the tattoos. Her feet found the ground again.

"Don't hold it in," she heard her mother say. Her voice drifted down to Petra from far away.

"Mamá, what should I do?" Petra spoke into the haze surrounding her.

"What do you want to do?"

"I want to scream."

"Well, then…. Scream."

Suddenly it felt possible. Petra let out a blood-curdling scream. She wailed for help, while her body shook with cold. Red ribbons danced from the ayacahuite tree, taunting her. The tattoos pranced and threatened her. Her muscles deserted her, and she dropped to the floor.

Then she felt bits of the morning drop like beads of sweat onto her arms. Beautiful brown fingers released warm dew from heaven. Yasmin said, "God's dew. It lies on the ground every morning, transforming us, laying the path for renewal."

Her mother's words traveled to Petra from far away and long ago. "Remember Ixchel, Petra. The half-light of the moon guides the water— the tides, the dew. Her whirling spindle of feminine energy is at the center of the motion of the universe."

The wings dropped away, and the tattoos became cartoons. The commotion subsided. Through the mist trapped by Sibalq'aq, Petra saw Ixchel at her loom by the campfire, her spindle turning threads of wool. The beauty and force of nature enveloped her. Other women formed a wide circle around Ixchel, whose spindle twisted the fibers. The whirling spindle became the center, and its wool grew and receded with a touch of Ixchel's fingers.

The women stopped their activity and their thoughts united, the spindle at their center. The center rotated with the movement of the universe, and as they watched, the universe spun in sync with Ixchel's spindle. The women's own hands followed until they too turned. The wool settled and became the earth. The drafts of air released by Ixchel's work rose up to become the wind, the skies, and the clouds. The spindle radiated light and began to burn her hands as it turned so rapidly that even she could no longer grasp it. It soared up to the new sky and became the fourth sun. The glow which remained in Ixchel became the moon in the sky. The final creation and a new world had begun.

A warm hand and an inviting shoulder nuzzled Petra's chest. Her mother stood before her, arms open to receive her. Emilio and Yasmin reappeared in normal human form. As she fell into her mother's embrace, Petra looked over her shoulder and settled on Emilio's dark gaze and curled lower lip. A wafting, silvery tune arose from the flute. Petra approached the tree, and began to untie the red ribbons, transferring them to her belt loops, looping them onto her wrists and ankles.

The jaguar's spots sparkled fleetingly in the light of the fire. Emilio, enveloped again in the jaguar skin, reached for her hand. The power in his hands surprised her. Strong fingers folded around hers, and he led her stealthily through the darkness of the trees.

Bones rattled, the air itself creaked. Bats grazed her face, and she scratched at the bugs crawling on her legs. Then her feet caught in mud. Only with effort could she raise her legs and continue moving forward with the jaguar.

The ceiba tree grew branches that became a dense forest full of shadows and reeking of decaying leaves. The mud dried to dirt, and Petra gave herself over to the energy of the earth. As dusk fell upon the trees on the slopes of Sibalq'aq, the spider monkeys descended from the trees and slinked away. The jaguar roared through the deep fog, and she heard "w-ah w-hah gwa co haw gwa co ha ha hahaha har harrar." The sounds repeated, dominating the background sounds of the forest. Joyful, even maniacal, then mourning. The beating wings of a falcon passed overhead, and Petra made out the finely sculpted head, the black mask which stretched from its face down to its neck in a narrow collar, and its stately white chest. The jaguar responded again with a friendly mewing.

Through the impending dark, Petra saw a speck of light, which grew as she glimpsed the crest of the volcano. She tossed aside the vines hanging over her. Pushing on, her energy intensified, and a new vitality spread through her. The light ahead became a glow, spreading down along the hillside. Her own hands felt so warm. She raised them and saw that they glowed through the darkening landscape, lighting her way. It was as if candles had been placed along her path to welcome her.

At the summit, though enshrouded in darkness now, the dim light began to define the shape of the old, wizened woman whom she had found there with Alocinia. But this time Petra was alone. Petra knelt before the woman, who seemed to exist within the shouts of the *guaco*, within the throbbing drum and the cadence of the marimba. The woman laid a hand on her head, and a restorative calm coursed through Petra.

The falcon—Itzamná—flew above, then sank lower and lower, finally laughing from a perch on the branch of a nearby tree. The jaguar roared again. Its massive paw swept along the line of the horizon, and the atmosphere radiated with light. Petra's glow and the old woman's light further brightened the night sky.

The sound of the drum throbbed in her veins and down into her heart. Dim light returned, as her mother lit a set of candles. Candlelight glimmered and winked at her. Emilio stood next to her, his strong hand gently clasped around hers. He looked questioningly into her eyes. The jaguar responded with a friendly mewing. Firelight glimmered and winked at her.

In a voice resonating with the slow lilt of the flute, her mother said, "The jaguar has accompanied you from the dark to the light, revealing your subconscious fears from the underworld, allowing them to be transformed into strength and wisdom." The Siguanaba rose up within Petra.

Her mother continued: "There is a joining of opposites which has taken place. Light and dark are so mixed up together as to be inseparable. Good and evil are hopelessly intertwined. To find yourself, you must lose yourself. And in order to release the old and make way for new ideas, you must surrender something, offer a sacrifice. We will begin with the easiest sacrifice, as you yourself have wished to surrender it. Wyman, you have the scissors?"

Wyman reached into his back pocket and handed them to her mother. "Come, my daughter," she said.

"Really?" Petra asked. Her heart skipped a beat. Her mother pointed to the space before her. Petra sat down cross-legged, her back to her mother, who began to unwrap the vivid cloth from Petra's hair, until her thick black hair flowed down the length of her back. As the scissors chopped away her hair, Petra heard Emilio gasp. Yasmin laughed. "We'll fix it up a bit later," her mother said. Petra ran her fingers through her short hair and shook her head to exult in the freedom. Her mother tied the cloth around Petra's head.

Her mother continued, "*La sangre* is a powerful symbol of the life force, as well as a sign of sickness and death. Blood flows in a relationship between mortals and the gods and ancestors. You will give of your blood, as so many Mayans gave in sacrifice, thereby losing a part of yourself. In so doing, a new, powerful tool of transformation may emerge. Wyman, the needles?"

From his pocket came several sharply pointed needles, which he doused with alcohol and handed to Yasmin. Petra raised her shirt to uncover her left breast, laying her right hand on the upper part of the breast to indicate where Yasmin should draw the tattoo. Her mother said, "The hummingbird will silently accompany you on your journey from now on. It will remind you of the magic, keep alive the connection between your heart and your soul, and guide you to face your fears while you pursue a path to renewal."

The drum reverberated in the background, spreading a wash of energy through Petra. A chanting arose as if from the drum, voices singing quietly with the percussive din. The tempo increased, and a community of hands rhythmically struck legs.

Petra looked up at Yasmin, who stood before her. "You've done this before, right?"

"Hope I still remember." Her mouth spread into a broad smile, her eyes flashing. "My cousin works in a tattoo parlor. Although this method uses more traditional techniques." Yasmin paused, looking skyward. "I must bless the spot first. Could I have the alcohol, please?"

Yasmin squatted, put one hand on Petra's shoulder, then stroked her neck. She leaned slowly toward Petra and kissed the top of her breast, lingering there a moment. Petra shuddered. Goosebumps appeared on her arms. Warmth spread through her, and she relaxed. Yasmin worked meticulously, sterilizing, stenciling the design, carving the small slits, then applying the yellow, white and black inks. The others chanted and watched, mesmerized. Wyman's head fell to the side as he napped briefly. Hours ticked by into the early afternoon.

Petra peeked at the drops of blood forming on her breast and thought of the lines of blood on Justina's inner thigh. The blood pulled the warmth out of Justina's body. Drops of blood fell on the river stones, cooled, dried, and solidified beneath her. Petra's lips brushed against Justina's lips. Her tongue sought an immortal intimacy. Petra's throat rose up in a sobbing lament.

Yasmin jumped up and staggered back in fright. "Did I hurt you?"

Petra brought herself back to her friend's side. "Yasmin." She took a moment to reorient herself to her mother and friends. "The blood reminded me of someone else." She breathed deeply. "It's okay. Don't stop."

Her mother said, "You are sure, Petra?"

Petra said, "I feel better now." With the blood, a warmth lay on her breast.

Yasmin peered at Petra. Reassured, she smiled and continued her work.

A Mayan image of the hummingbird took shape. Alongside a sharp, confident eye framed by an expectant eyebrow, its long slender beak pointed the way forward. Black feathers held its delicate body aloft as it sought its path and spread its inspiration. Yasmin gathered the seeping blood and directed it into a bowl, which she placed beneath Petra's ceiba tree.

"But that barely hurt at all," Petra said. Finishing up, Yasmin grinned, and passed a tube of ointment to Petra to apply until it healed. Yasmin covered the new wounds with a bandage, and Petra let her shirt fall back in place.

Petra leaned forward on her knees, her arm encircling Yasmin's head, and she kissed Yasmin's cheek before letting her up. Her mother glanced sharply at Petra. With a wry smile, Petra remarked, "Well, I need to offer and receive gratitude. *Pues*, I am grateful, Yasmin."

Petra's mother closed her eyes and regained her composure. "Now we move to the third sacrifice, perhaps the most difficult, Petra. You remember that the ancient Mayans greatly honored those selected for sacrifice. The rulers deemed them worthy as messengers to the gods, and therefore exempt from the perilous journey through Xibalba, instead rising directly to the heavens. The hummingbird served as Itzamná's messenger to the gods —"

Petra interrupted. "No, mamá! Not Alocinia! She's part of me. My guide, my link with…" She floundered for words.

"With the gods? With your higher self? said her mother. "How long has Alocinia been with you, Petita?"

"Since…. I was five. You gave her to me when you decided to leave me." Petra began to sob. Her mother sat on the ground facing Petra. Petra cried, "Alocinia supported me when you weren't there, *mamí*. She accompanied me when I searched for Mayan wisdom, when Emilio's mom died, and when Gusano forced himself on me. You want to take my closest friend! *Ay*, I wish I had not told you that she is still with me."

Her mother put her hands on Petra's shoulders, and looked intently at her daughter. She said simply, "I know a lot about Alocinia, Petra. Don't you realize that Alocinia was my friend, too? When I gave her to you, I gave over a part of myself for you to keep while I was gone. Along with her story, which has become a part of you."

"And now you're back," said Petra.

"If you will be so kind as to let me in," said her mother. "Remember why the hummingbird had access to the honey of the gods? It was because only she had never lost faith in the Mother. When the other people understood this, they too thrived. The hummingbird opened people's hearts. When the hurt that caused them to close their hearts got a chance to heal, their hearts were free to open again. To find yourself, you must lose yourself." Petra gazed silently into her mother's eyes, staring and sobbing.

Yasmin started to come forward, but her mother held her back with an outstretched hand. Petra disappeared into the blue and yellow sparkling irises behind her mother's brown eyes. For a moment, Petra became a part of her mother, blended with her spirit, shared her blood and, finally, prepared to be reborn.

"Give me a minute," Petra sniffled.

- Alocinia? Are you there?
- You're fading, Petra. You're leaving me, aren't you?
- Alocinia, I love you. You're everything to me.
- Remember when you let go of my hand to go through the hole to the other side? I didn't want you to go, but you said you had to take risks to get anywhere.
- But I came back!
- You weren't ready. But you saw the shimmering mountaintop. You glimpsed the breadth of the universe.
- I was afraid. I came back for the cookies. And for you.
- Now, you are ready. The space to crawl through is bigger. You're almost there, on the other side.
- Where will you go?
- I will climb high up the branches of this ceiba tree, and disappear into the timeless, glowing colors. I see them now, reflecting in the embers of your fire. It is my destiny as messenger.
- Who will carry messages from my heart to my soul?
- When your heart is free, your soul will soar, Petra.
- I can barely hear you. You're so far away, Alocinia!
- I am here. I am you.
- Goodbye, my little hummingbird.

"Okay," Petra said quietly.

"Sure?" said her mother.

Petra just nodded. The tears had stopped. She was ready. "How do I let her go?"

Wyman set down the drum and rolled his chair over to Petra's side, cradling the small clay hummingbird in both hands. Petra admired his fine-boned fingers nestling the hummingbird. Its green and yellow wings spread wide, the fine red head perched on a glistening blue body, its broken beak leading the way.

"You'll still have the story, Petra—all the stories," her mother said.

Wyman waved his arm with great flourish and presented the hummingbird to Petra as if it were a crown of jewels.

In a low voice, her mother said, "Smash it to pieces, Petra. Use the hammer." She pushed over to Petra a cardboard box, with a hammer and plastic eyeglasses inside.

Petra's eyebrows shot up, her eyes dewy with tears again. "My beautiful hummingbird. I send you on your way to the gods. *Que te vaya bien.*" She put on the glasses and took hold of the hammer, gently placing the hummingbird inside the box. Her arm came crashing down. A smash and the shattering of hardened clay echoed through the forest. The hummingbird on her breast roared its acceptance. Alocinia, her sweet hummingbird, was dead.

Itzamná screeched from the heavens above. Petra rocked back on her heels and stared up at the sky.

A few moments later, Wyman appeared with plates for everyone and serving bowls full of corn, beans, rice, and tortillas. "A veritable Mayan feast!" he said as he laid it all on the gorgeous Mayan colors covering the picnic table.

Wyman sat in his chair, forever dignified, a plate balanced atop his wooden drum. Once everyone had gotten food, her mother carried a chair to Wyman's side, so she could sit level with her husband. She passed him a glass of water with his evening medications. He placed a hand over hers and appraised her fondly.

Emilio grabbed a plate of food and huddled in a corner of the forest. Petra placed her food in front of him and lowered herself to the ground at his side. In silence, Petra peered at him out of the corner of an eye. He waved his head in acknowledgment but didn't meet her eyes. Legs folded before them, their knees touched as they ate.

Yasmin peered over at Petra and winked. She grinned back at her. Red ribbons fluttered innocently from her wrists as she spooned rice into her mouth.

Her mother said, "With this bounty of nourishment, we now go to the final stage, the transformation. Petra, you wanted to share your visions for the future, especially for prosperity as a community."

Petra's eyes focused on the fire, the calming scents of the forest and the fire that permeated the air. She inhaled attentively. Yasmin stood to collect the empty dishes.

Petra returned to her place at the ceiba tree. She said, "I am thankful that the magical and mystical escort me in life. Thank you all for coming into my life. I look forward to a wild and strong future. I once thought my past wouldn't go away, and my future probably wouldn't happen. First I came to my mother, then I came to know her a little, and now I hope to find trust in her. As well as in the Mother. Oh, and I still want to become a doctor and help people in the poor villages of Guatemala."

Emilio tentatively raised a hand halfway and took his turn. "I am grateful that you, Sorelly, and my mother formed a friendship before I came into this world. Without that friendship, I would never have known Petra, the shining star in my life, or been the recipient of your generosity to me here in Providence. I look forward to a future which I never imagined could be mine, and I am only beginning to glimpse. May the jaguar lead me forward."

Yasmin giggled. Petra took one look at Yasmin and began to laugh. Uncertain, Emilio broke into a smile as fragile as butterfly wings. The solemnity broke into manageable pieces.

Petra's mother said, in her accented English, "Wyman, you have said little here. Would you like to go next?"

Wyman said, "Despite my limited understanding of the Spanish language in this ceremony, I am fortunate to absorb many of the evening's lessons through the skin of this drum and the vibrant synergy. A world of sensation and joy has infiltrated my home through this family, for whom I am exceptionally grateful. My future seems to hold endless refills of love and kindness."

Yasmin sat with legs folded beneath her, gripping her bone flute tightly in both hands. Her eyes squinted with concentration behind her glasses. When she began to speak, the flute dropped into her lap and her right hand gestured in curves and swoops. "It so happens that I was born in La Ceiba, Honduras. Or so I am told. I remember almost nothing about it, since my parents brought me to the U.S. when I was only five. They tell me it is a gorgeous city on the Caribbean coast.

"The only image I have retained is of a large plaza, the ceiba tree rising from its midst." She gestured toward the ceiba tree behind Petra. "The trunk was massive. I remember wanting to stretch my arms around it in a hug, but I was afraid to touch it because of the huge thorns covering its bark. As much as I craned my neck upward, I couldn't find the top of the tree, which extended so high it seemed to vanish into the sky. At its base, the ponderous roots flowed far out into the plaza, disappearing finally under the cobblestones.

"As a five year old, I revered that tree. It left me with a life-long impression of sanctuary and grandeur. That tree connects me with life itself, and now," her fingers brushed the limbs in front of her, "with Petra and this extended family. The ceiba informs my vision of the future I will strive toward—of inner strength, wisdom, and beauty. And I will work hard and love the people around me on my journey." Yasmin's eyes flickered at Petra as she stopped speaking and her hands settled. Once again, she clenched the flute firmly.

Petra's mother drew a deep breath. "It remains to me. I am moved by everyone's thoughts. It is difficult to follow such heartfelt reflections. But I have no doubt as to the appreciation I must express. For some years, no matter what I did, my life felt incomplete. A hole had grown inside me, plaguing me, longing to be filled. I now know what was missing. It was my daughter, Petra, the person who was born from my very own body, whom I loved and nourished for five years. Then she was torn away from me when I came to the U.S. and left her behind. Sometimes life requires us to make awful decisions, and I will never know if I made the right choice at that time.

"I do know, now that Petra is here with me, that I feel whole again. I am so grateful for your intuitive certainties, Petra, your enigmatic depths, which have recalled to me the essence of a life. I envision a future of family and community, which we will build together and separately, and share in our hearts."

The drum beat resumed, forging a sense of unity within the group. All eyes focused on the embers of the fire, until they became ash. Finally, all the dust and ashes settled, and the gods slept.

CHAPTER THIRTY-SEVEN

Carlos picked up the phone on the first ring. "*Hermanita, qué hay, comó estás, chica?*"

Now that Petra's mother had a steady job and a responsible husband, a little more money flowed to the family in Guatemala, and they'd made two life-changing purchases. The first was a cell phone. No more treacherous hour-long bus rides to San Luis Hunahpu in order to stay in touch with Petra and their mother.

"Carlos, how is Nonna? Did she get the results from the doctor?" The second important purchase was a visit to the clinic in San Luis Hunahpu to get medical treatment for Nonna.

On the positive side, Carlos said, it probably wasn't cancer. On the downside, the pain attacks were coming more often now, and Nonna often had to lie down for hours before the pain subsided. The clinic told her to go to the hospital in Guatemala City to get more tests. The doctor guessed that it might be a digestion disease, or a diseased organ they could take out in surgery. He gave Carlos the medical names, but he didn't remember them. Anyway, Carlos would have to take her to the hospital a couple of times before they would know for sure. "She trotted right off to the *curandero* as soon as we got back from the clinic."

Petra made a mental note to look through medical sites on the internet to try to figure out what it might be. "Oh, Carlos, what if she decides to stay with her Mayan healer? Do you think she'll be willing to follow up at the hospital?"

"Don't worry. She came back from the *curandero* more relaxed. That's a good thing. She says she'll go to the hospital with me."

"*Gracias a Dios*. At least something's in progress finally. Just say the word, and I'll come back to help, Carlos."

"Not necessary, Petra. You come back when you can come and go legally on a plane, okay? I don't want to take that trip across Mexico again."

"Well, I'm pretty sure we'll be going back soon, anyway." She wasn't about to so easily give up hopes of going back to visit. In the meantime, Petra would be praying for Nonna every day.

"Vicenta left her post at the store for a few minutes yesterday to come spread good cheer. She brought up cans of peach nectar and a pack of *Galletas Marías* cookies. Don't tell Nonna, but she also snuck me a can of beer." Carlos audibly breathed out in satisfaction.

Petra laughed. "Well, at least you didn't waste any money on it."

"Vicenta sends you her greetings. She sent a message she said you'd understand. She said she hopes you have found some books up there that are as stimulating as Novina's books, and to enjoy your freedom. Then something about becoming the woman you were meant to be. Not sure what she meant by all that. Oh, and she says if you ever come back, Novina wants you to play on her soccer team."

Petra smiled broadly. "Please please tell her I love her. And please watch out for her, Carlos."

Carlos said, "But Petra, there's big news here. Maybe you heard through Emilio?"

"I haven't seen him this week. What happened?" Worry seeped into her voice.

"It's a story, *muchacha*. You ready for the sordid tale?" Carlos asked.

She prepared herself for a tale. Carlos did like to embellish with a few of his own details. "Of course. Is everybody OK, though?"

"*Pues sí y no*. This is the story as it comes down through my sources in town. You remember the meeting Gusano and Fernando, Emilio's father, planned with Mago and the big men from the MS-13, right?"

"So I heard," Petra drawled.

"Well, Mago never showed for the meeting. The X-14 bosses got uptight, thinking maybe they'd fallen out of favor. They figured word about losing the Mayan artifact had gotten out, so maybe Mago thought they couldn't be trusted. They decided to take a trip to Guatemala City to find Mago and persuade him to give them a piece of the drug trade.

"But Gusano and Fernando are really *campesinos*. In their experience, San Luis Hunahpu is the big city. They might have visited Guatemala City a couple of times, but they don't know their way around."

"They got themselves to Mago's neighborhood, with armed thugs on every corner, drug dealers counting their money behind doors two feet from the street, girls dragging around in bare feet and big bellies, *chamaquitos* with vacant eyes sniffing glue and sorting through the garbage piled up in empty lots. I can imagine they were already feeling unsuited to the task just walking up the street there."

"It turns out the 18th Street gang and the MS-13 have been engaged in battle over the turf in that area, so Gusano and Fernando got caught in the middle of a gun battle, in broad daylight. A shot whizzed by from behind a house, then another. Fernando was probably scared out of his wits, not thinking straight. They were way out of their element. Rumor says they didn't make it ten minutes into the neighborhood before Fernando opened his big mouth and got gunned down for disrespecting the wrong crowd. *Pendejo*."

"When the smoke settled, Fernando was lying dead on the street, and Gusano had fled the scene. I bet the dogs were moving in on the flesh before the police showed up that night to take the body."

Petra absorbed the information. "*Bendito sea Dios. Qué horror!*"

"Gusano is back in Las Leches and already back at work organizing the underlings to pick off vulnerable young people from your old school and make them gangbangers."

"Carlos," Petra considered. "I don't think Emilio knows. His father…"

"*Jesucristo*! I hadn't thought about that. Oh, Petra, you might have to tell him. Sorry that falls on you."

"Carlos, what about you? Aren't you worried they might target you? They know that you have family here in the U.S., and that we send money home."

"I'm thinking they've had enough of our family for now. Gusano doesn't want his pride bruised anymore."

Petra was skeptical, but she didn't know what to do with the worry.

There wasn't much they could do but pray.

"It's looking good for mamá and me getting approved by Immigration. That means in a few months we'll go to the U.S. Embassy in Guatemala to become U.S. residents."

Petra continued, "Wyman can petition for you, too. You could come to the U.S. with a green card." She knew what Carlos's answer would be before she asked.

"Yeah, thanks anyway. I'll take my chances on the life I know here. But, Petra, I almost forgot. Little Julina is going. Jacinto is finally breaking free from the clutches of Leila. He says he's going to travel there with Dolores and Julina. *Tío* Arnoldo wants to stay here and run the *chaparro* business. The X-14 *muchachos* are demanding money from Dolores's store all the time, and they're messing with Julina whenever she's around. Julina is afraid to go to school."

"Julina is coming here? To Rhode Island?"

"Sure, that's where you are, right? Our American family gets bigger all the time."

"*Vaya*! I have a friend here she'll love! He's an artist like her." She'd take Julinita to the zoo and the merry-go-round at the park as soon as she arrived. Her heart raced with excitement at the thought of connecting Benji and Julina. "But—Immigration is changing a lot here. They don't like Central Americans anymore. They're making it tougher to get across the border all the time. I was lucky to come when I did." Maybe Julina would make it to the U.S., maybe not.

When Petra hung up, she leapt up from her chair and called out to her mother. Abruptly, she stilled herself, listening to the air breathe. "Mamá, do you hear the whimpering?"

Her mother put a hand to her ear and concentrated. She blinked several times and appraised her daughter. "Wait, give me a second." Wyman smiled as he contemplated mother and daughter. Her mother's eyes fastened onto Petra's, then closed. "Yes, a tinkling—like the whining of a small animal. What is it, *m'hija*?"

"The *alux*. He's crying. It's the little bearded man who always looks offended."

Her mother said, "He overheard you say we are going back to Guatemala. Maybe he's worried we plan to leave him altogether."

Wyman shook his head as if rearranging his reality inside. "The two of you. Your hearts beat as one." His adoring gaze embraced mother and daughter.

In Petra's mind, Nonno had a broad grin on his face and was shaking his head, watching his daughter and granddaughter reunited in the spirit of the ancient Mayans. Her feet caught her excitement, and she scurried about the living room, "Oh, I can't wait to see Nonno again!"

"But, Petita, don't count on it being so soon. The lawyer says there are a few steps to go."

Petra looked at her mother. "She said we did well at the interview, though. Don't we go as soon as they approve the petition?"

"Well... You know Wyman and I met with la *doctora* Lucía again after the interview. She wanted us to know that every step with Immigration is slow and painful. It could be months until we hear from Immigration, and a lot of times they send a notice requesting more documents and declarations from us before they'll approve the marriage petition. Sometimes they ask for the same documents we've already sent, but it takes months for them to review it again."

"What?" Petra felt her hopes sinking.

"Lucía says their question about your involvement with gangs might not go away. They could ask for proof that you haven't been arrested or working somehow with gangs. If they do, we'll have to go to juvenile court to get a paper saying you've never been arrested."

"Ay, I'll never escape the gangs! Really?"

"And *then*, after all that, I'll have to ask for a waiver because I've been in the U.S. illegally so long. You don't need that because you're a child. We'll have to get Wyman's health records and write declarations to explain how Wyman will suffer if I can't come back to live with him as his wife. And then file that application and wait again."

"So... Not a couple of months."

"No. It could be a couple of years." Her mother raised her eyebrows sympathetically.

Her burst of energy deflated, Petra arranged herself in the big fluffy living room chair, leaning her head into the sun spreading across her face.

She'd hold on to the idea of seeing her Guatemala family again soon for a little while longer. Her heart constricted with longing for her Nonno.

"Mamí, can I go with you to your church group next weekend? I want to tell them a thing or two about the gangs in Guatemala."

"Oh, really?"

"Yup." Petra liked the way that word sounded in English, like a burp. "I think they need an advisor, somebody with some recent experience." Petra tilted her chin up playfully.

"There's some tough guys there, Petita. Are you sure you're ready to deal with them?"

"No, definitely not sure. Can you help me?"

"Petra, it would be my pleasure. *No es por nada* that they call me mamá."

Petra's mind drifted toward the future. The sun melted her consciousness, and she slipped into a dream.

The clunky old American school bus, repainted in the glorious colors of the quetzal, stopped near the museum of Juyú. Petra, her mother, and Nonno climbed down to the dusty road below. Petra looked forward to finally laying eyes on Itzamná. It was only fair, since Nonno had taken her mother to see it years before.

Petra's old friend Sibalq'aq smoldered before them. It was still the most beautiful sight Petra had ever laid eyes on. Her mother raised her hand to block out the sun as she admired the perfectly sloped volcano, its crater rising above a swath of mist around its middle. Standing back, Petra studied her mother. The volcano, the jungle, the spirit of the land— they lived in her.

Her mother lifted her arms over her head, reaching out to the horizons, and nodded to Petra. "They live in you, also."

They set off across the grassland, skirting the edge of the forest, keeping to the shadow of the volcano. The winter season was full upon the land, when the sun still shone about half the day, but clouds would gather and suddenly burst into torrents of rain. The vegetation beneath their feet sparkled as the sun glanced off the wet grasses from the morning's shower.

Petra said, "This is the final trip, mamí. A part of me feels like we really did find the artifact the last time we came, Nonno, and that Itzamná has lived with me ever since. Now I can let him rest in peace. Itzamná will remain forever in the ancient Mayan lands with the gods and their creations."

Nonno said, "Petita, I do believe you will carry Itzamná in your heart the rest of your life. The real Itzamná will stay with you."

"If we can't find Itzamná, I can look to the hummingbird to guide me in the trip from my thoughts to a corner of the spirit world." Petra grinned and placed her hand over her upper breast.

"Don't underestimate the jaguar," Nonno said. "The hummingbird may be there," he gestured to the place of her tattoo, "but the jaguar is also there." His hands swept out to the forest and the rise of the volcano. "The jaguar patrols its lands, always."

Petra stepped carefully, skirting pit vipers and other natives. As they passed by the campfire in the open glade, she silently gave thanks to Ixchel for the melodic sounds of nature and the splendors of life.

Sorelly took Nonno's hand and said, "Papá, I have missed you these long years." They walked a ways off, and Petra turned her gaze to the volcano. A faint echo of Alocinia called to her from the trees, but Petra didn't reach out to her. The volcano simmered, and the clouds drifted by, caressing its sides. Deep from within, it spoke to her in the heartbeat of drums and the pulsing of blood. The throbbing started in the earth, shaking the trees, radiating into the sky to push the clouds aside, blowing the grasses, vibrating in her skull. Petra closed her eyes. The earth became utterly silent.

A vague mewing sound rose off to her side, amidst the jungle vines. Then a deep, chesty grumble, not human. Birds fled, and mice scattered. Branches crunched amidst the vines. From the far side of the practically impenetrable trees, she heard the slow slog of footsteps, nearing the clearing where she had greeted Ixchel. There followed a swiping at branches, falling limbs, and the sound of a machete clearing a path. Then an immense roar, and the full breadth of a jaguar leapt from a tree, crossing next to her in broad stride until it found its mark. Utter grace wrapped in opulence, yellow and black spotted elegance led by perfectly focused green eyes.

In a massive show of strength, the weight of its body tackled the tattooed torso of Gusano.

The sun disappeared behind a cloud, and Petra jolted out of the dream. She left the jaguar to keep watch over Gusano. It wasn't real. Gusano wouldn't even know when they arrived. He lived too far from Las Leches, and Emilio's father wasn't around anymore to report on their movements.

Itzamná would always live amidst the jungle where the jaguar would offer protection. And the ancient equilibrium would be maintained.

CHAPTER THIRTY-EIGHT

Summer had officially begun, and the late June afternoon brought rain tumbling down. Metallic pings played percussive rhythms on house gutters, while the birds' chirping subsided as they holed up in bushes and trees. Petra leapt across the puddles as a lone woman trundled down the street, pushing her umbrella up against the wind. The rain accumulated in the collapsed sidewalk, and she ran to Emilio's house.

After knocking lightly, then banging on the door several times, Lucas cracked the door and peeked out. Petra said, "Lucas, is Emilio home? I was hoping to talk to him."

"Mmmm. Yeah, he's home." Lucas hesitated.

"Can I come in?"

"Just a second." He closed the door and left her waiting in the hallway.

Footsteps shuffled along the linoleum kitchen floor, and the door opened wide. "Hi, Petra. Come on in." Emilio's voice was raw.

The stovetop, the sink, and the table were cluttered with empty beer cans. The smell brought back the stench of the cabin in the woods when she'd regained consciousness, and she recoiled. Emilio's eyelids hung down thickly over his eyes. The shadow of a mustache was emerging on his upper lip. "Is this a bad time?"

But this wasn't that cabin. Nothing about it was the same.

The Nonviolence Institute had paired Emilio with a man who had scraped his way out of the gangs in New York City, then moved up to Providence to make a new start on his life. The two men had gotten together a couple of times since their visit with the police to talk about flashbacks, emotional crises, outbursts of anger, and how to build a normal, crime-free life.

"It's OK. I'm not feeling too well, but the problem is all up here." His fingers bounced off his head. He flung himself into their threadbare armchair. Dirty clothes hung from the rafters and from random hooks on the walls. Petra sat on a wood box in front of him.

"Emilio." She reached out to take his hands. "I keep thinking about you and me, how we're both warriors finding a home in a more peaceful world."

"Sure. You're right. Except you're home with your mother, and I'm alone with my nightmares."

"You were lonely last weekend at the ceremony." Petra knew it was true, so she stated the fact.

"I guess," Emilio intoned, expressionless.

"It wouldn't have been the same without you. You know that, don't you? Emilio," Petra searched for the right words, "I hope you're back in my life for good now. You've been a part of me for so long—a tortured part, but a part, nonetheless. I'm hoping we can be friends again, for real."

Emilio looked to the side. "Petra, I don't think you get it." He leaned forward until he was inches from her face. In a muted voice, he said, "I've been in love with you for years. In my own twisted way, that's why I pursued you in Guatemala. Things are different now—but I'm still in love." His lower lip curled under, and his chin began to quiver.

"I know." Petra narrowed her eyes, scrutinizing Emilio. His eyes switched about like a horse's tail. "Emilio, I know. That's why I came over here."

Emilio smirked. "And that's why my head hurts." He plastered himself against the back of his chair, as far from Petra as he could shift without getting up. "And you—you're falling for a girl—that Yasmin." He paused. "She's cute." He was floundering. The words drifted into the air.

"I think girls have been on my mind for a while, Emilio." She stood up and walked aimlessly around the room. "I didn't quite know it myself." She spoke slowly, conscious of every word. "There's one thing you never understood about me. I was in love with Justina, Emilio. You all stole her from me right after I kissed her for the first time." Now Petra turned red, and her eyes became moist. Her stomach churned.

Emilio's eyebrows spiked, his voice animated in astonishment. "*En serio?* You guys kissed? But *I* was in love with her. *And* with you!"

"Well, I always knew we were all close. Confusing, isn't it." It was not a question.

"Confusing isn't the word." Emilio put his head between his hands.

"*Pues sí.* I wanted to tell you out loud about this relationship between me and Yasmin. We're definitely getting to know each other. But, Emilio, it doesn't change how I feel about you and me. I'm here for you." She sat down again on the box facing Emilio.

Emilio glanced at her briefly and looked down. Then his eyes rose slowly up to hers. "Your long black hair—it's gone. I loved to see it flow down your back, blow around in the breeze."

"La Siguanaba. I know."

"Eh?"

"La Siguanaba. It's a long story. It's a tale my grandfather used to tell me about a woman who outsmarted a man when he tried to abduct her. Sound familiar?"

Emilio's laugh came from deep in his belly this time. Petra thought about it, then began to laugh. She threw her head back with pleasure, and her hair did not fall into her face.

Emilio closed his eyes firmly, his expression determined. With trembling chin, his eyes flashed at Petra, and he pulled the box forward so Petra was trapped between his legs. He clasped his hands behind her neck and drew her head toward him. "We would be good together, Tita. We both know it. How long have we wanted to be together?"

Petra pushed against his chest. "Emilio, no! This means too much, don't!"

The pupils of his eyes dilated, and his lip curled under and trembled. He held her inches from his face. She smelled old beer. Under his breath, he said, "You don't need that girl. I've got everything you need." His grip tightened against her back so she couldn't move.

Petra's heart struggled, but her brain was firm. She blew out her breath and yelled, "Emilio, no! Let go of me!"

Then she heard Lucas, his voice sharp. "Hey man! Leave her alone!

Emilio! *Ave María*, what are you doing?"

Emilio sputtered and backed off. His shoulders began to shake uncontrollably. His nostrils flared wide, and his eyes blinked wildly, flashing left and right. His hands flew to his face, and he ran out of the room.

Lucas came close to Petra, searching her face with concerned eyes. Delicately, he said, "Petra, he wouldn't really do it. He's struggling too much. You have no idea."

Petra frantically brushed off her clothes and ran to the kitchen sink, where she filled a cup with water and gulped it down. "I thought he'd changed!" She tossed water onto her face and neck.

Lucas said, quietly, "He *has* changed. He's dealing with a lot, though, Petra. He wakes up screaming with nightmares every night. He has flashbacks about stuff that happened in the gang that make him crazy. Sometimes he gets angry when I look at him the wrong way. The last couple days, he started drinking because I guess he can't handle it. He's trying really hard, but seriously, I'm worried about him. He feels really alone, and he thinks about you way too much. He needs help, Petra."

Composing herself a bit, pity tugged at Petra. If she was really there for him, as she'd just promised, she had to deal with the Emilio before her, the damaged and tormented young man, not the version she dreamed up. "There's more news from Guatemala, Lucas. I don't know if I should tell him. The 18th Street gang killed his father. I just talked to my brother."

"Holy shit!" Emilio flooded back into the living room. "He's dead! For real?"

Lucas said, "Easy, 'mano."

Petra said, gently, "Emilio, that's not how I wanted to tell you. I'm so sorry."

Emilio guffawed. "You're apologizing to me again? Quite the thing, isn't it?"

"I'm sorry for your father's death. Not sorry you grabbed me—again. I mean, I am sorry you grabbed me, but that was your fault, not mine." She shook her head. "You know what I mean."

Lucas laughed. Emilio's eyes crinkled with exhausted pleasure. Emilio said, "Petra, one thing at a time. I *am* sorry, really sorry. And I'm quite aware that sorry doesn't work too well at this point. My head is exploding, and I can't quite figure out what I'm doing here." He hung his head and peeked up at Petra with a wry expression. "As for my father, he was a first-class bastard, and I'm glad he's gone."

Petra said, "Yeah, he was pretty awful. But anyway, he was your father." In her head, she acknowledged to herself that she couldn't care less about her own father.

"It's too much. I can't ever go back. Gusano would kill me for sure. My father might have restrained him a little bit, but even that is gone now. But I'm hopelessly illegal in this country."

"We have a lawyer, Emilio. My mother and I can take you to meet her. She seems pretty smart. Or else the Nonviolence Institute could hook you up with some legal help. Maybe you can apply for asylum here."

Emilio flopped down in the armchair again, while Lucas went to look out the window. Petra stood in the middle of the floor, keeping her distance from Emilio. "Maybe you should stay away from me for awhile, Petra. It's like there's a fire burning in my skull, and sometimes it blows up. I'm embarrassed for myself all the time."

But forgiveness wasn't about deciding that what Emilio did was okay. It wasn't okay in Guatemala, and it wasn't this afternoon. The important thing was she no longer found anger and bitterness inside. "I have a vulture for you," she said to Emilio, and smiled at him.

For awhile, she would see him only together with her mother or in safe places. Her mother would know how to get him more help.

Lucas skewed his head in confusion. Emilio said, "You know you're way too good for me, Petra. But—I could use a friend."

Petra said, "My mother and Wyman want you to come over for dinner tonight. Can you come?"

He turned his head to indicate the empty beer cans and the mess of his life. For a moment, he was quiet. His chin wobbled, his eyebrows folded in on themselves, and he glanced at the ceiling. "I'll think about it."

Lucas got up to let her out. "Thanks, Petra. Thanks for coming over."

Discussion Questions

1. What does the hummingbird represent to Petra, and how does it change throughout the story?

2. Forgiveness and redemption play major roles in the story. When is it appropriate to forgive someone for atrocities they committed? Does it make a difference to your opinion when you consider the childhood traumas that the perpetrator—Emilio, for example--suffered himself? What does forgiveness actually mean between Petra and Emilio? How is it different between Petra and her mother?

3. Talk about the role of imagination and magic in Hummingbird. How does Petra draw on her culture and connection with the spiritual/mythical world? How does she balance ancient mystical culture with Catholicism and more Western values?

4. Not long after Petra's arrival in the U.S., Petra's mother pushes her to forgive Emilio. What do you think about this? How did Petra ultimately respond to her mother's perspective on forgiveness and reintegrating gang members into society?

5. How does this story affect your feelings about immigrants or immigration? What do you think might have happened if she had not had the option of fleeing to the U.S.?

6. What do you think will happen to Emilio? What do you hope happens to him? Do you feel sympathetic with him, despite all of his bad acts? Do you feel optimistic for him? What do you think will happen with Yasmin, given her family's immigration problems?

7. Do you think that Petra benefitted from a supportive family, despite grandparents who could not take the place of parents, an abusive father, and an absent mother? Her healing process was also aided by community, and a special ceremony, akin to a ceremony for returning warriors. How much do you think such a ceremony could help in healing from trauma?

Acknowledgments

In the journey from writing legal documents as an immigration lawyer to producing a work of fiction, I am indebted to a number of people:

Kevin Atticks and the students of Apprentice House, for for their hard work on my book, especially to Lark Thompson for her dedication and creativity in design, to Lara Pagendarm-Winter and Tyler Born for their editing, to Claire Marino for her work on promotion, to Elle White on managing the project, and to Kevin Atticks for overseeing the whole project.

My freelance editor, Sarah Cypher, of The Threepenny Editor, for pointing the way forward and believing in the story and for teaching me a lot about writing fiction in the process.

Barbara Morrison, coincidentally also an Apprentice House author, for mentoring and guiding me in the initial stages of understanding fiction writing and along each step thereafter.

Sandy Judd, whose clever mind, innovative writing, and incisive editing were both inspirational and instructional. Thank you, Sandy, for leading the peer editing group in southern Vermont. It has been an organizing principle for my writing and that of many others.

The rest of the peer editing group, which has provided step by step advice and encouragement since the early days of this novel, especially: Gail Grycel, Eric Strickland, Dave Wilbur, Roger Brown, Susan Chamberlin, Mia Gannon, Mary Collins and Nick.

Many friends and family slogged through one or more drafts and provided insightful suggestions, and for this I am deeply thankful to: Jessica Frye, Stephen Born, Alan Mills, Deborah DeBare, Carla Zubiría, Carol Cohen, Teresa Born, Lynn Leighton, and Margot Born.

I particularly acknowledge with gratitude my partner Jessica for standing by me, for her constant love and support, and for putting up with my moods and inattentiveness when my life sometimes became swallowed up by Petra's.

I will forever be grateful to the people in my law firm who dedicated so much of themselves to help recently-arrived residents of this country gain the right to a new chance at life, especially: Stephen Born, Mark Morrison, Amanda Biaison, Mihaela, Taisha, Cindy, Rosa, Ondine, Amber, Juan, Kimberly, Connie, Melissa, Stephanie, Brenda, Faustino, Tiago, and many more.

Foremost, I want to thank the thousands of Central American immigrants, especially the teenagers and youngsters, who allowed me to touch their lives and in turn opened my heart to so many all over the world who emigrate from their beloved homelands because they simply want to live without fear.

About the Author

As a Spanish-speaking immigration attorney for twenty years, Susan Mills prepared asylum cases for thousands of immigrants from Central America, with a focus on unaccompanied minors. Some of her family members journeyed from the war-torn countryside of El Salvador to the U.S.. This is her first novel. She now divides her time between the green mountains of Vermont and the wonderfully diverse city of Providence.

Apprentice
House Press
Loyola University Maryland

Apprentice House is the country's only campus-based, student-staffed book publishing company. Directed by professors and industry professionals, it is a nonprofit activity of the Communication Department at Loyola University Maryland.

Using state-of-the-art technology and an experiential learning model of education, Apprentice House publishes books in untraditional ways. This dual responsibility as publishers and educators creates an unprecedented collaborative environment among faculty and students, while teaching tomorrow's editors, designers, and marketers.

Outside of class, progress on book projects is carried forth by the AH Book Publishing Club, a co-curricular campus organization supported by Loyola University Maryland's Office of Student Activities.

Eclectic and provocative, Apprentice House titles intend to entertain as well as spark dialogue on a variety of topics. Financial contributions to sustain the press's work are welcomed. Contributions are tax deductible to the fullest extent allowed by the IRS.

To learn more about Apprentice House books or to obtain submission guidelines, please visit www.apprenticehouse.com.

Apprentice House
Communication Department
Loyola University Maryland
4501 N. Charles Street
Baltimore, MD 21210
410-617-5265
info@apprenticehouse.com
www.apprenticehouse.com

CPSIA information can be obtained
at www.ICGtesting.com
Printed in the USA
LVHW040242060123
736553LV00002B/79

9 781627 203739